GIRL FROM NOWHERE

GIRL FROM NOWHERE

TIFFANY ROSENHAN

BLOOMSBURY
NEW YORK LONDON OXFORD NEW DELHI SYDNEY

BLOOMSBURY YA
Bloomsbury Publishing Inc., part of Bloomsbury Publishing Plc
1385 Broadway, New York, NY 10018

BLOOMSBURY and the Diana logo are trademarks of Bloomsbury Publishing Plc

First published in the United States of America in July 2020 by Bloomsbury YA

Bloomsbury books may be purchased for business or promotional use.
For information on bulk purchases please contact Macmillan Corporate and Premium Sales Department at specialmarkets@macmillan.com

Library of Congress Cataloging-in-Publication Data
Names: Rosenhan, Tiffany, author.
Title: Girl from nowhere / by Tiffany Rosenhan.
Description: New York: Bloomsbury Children's Books, 2020.
Summary: For Sophia Hepworth, the terrors of living in dangerous places with her diplomat parents are nothing compared to facing American high school, but friendships and romance bloom just before her past catches up with her.
Identifiers: LCCN 2020002040 (print) | LCCN 2020002041 (e-book)
ISBN 978-1-5476-0303-9 (hardcover) • ISBN 978-1-5476-0304-6 (e-book)
Subjects: CYAC: Fear—Fiction. | High schools—Fiction. | Schools—Fiction. | Love—Fiction. | Family life—Montana—Fiction. | Montana—Fiction.
Classification: LCC PZ7.1.R67245 Gir 2020 (print) | LCC PZ7.1.R67245 (e-book) | DDC [Fic]—dc23
LC record available at https://lccn.loc.gov/2020002040

Book design by Jeanette Levy
Typeset by Westchester Publishing Services
Printed and bound in the U.S.A. by Berryville Graphics Inc., Berryville, Virginia
2 4 6 8 10 9 7 5 3 1

All papers used by Bloomsbury Publishing Plc are natural, recyclable products made from wood grown in well-managed forests. The manufacturing processes conform to the environmental regulations of the country of origin.

To find out more about our authors and books
visit www.bloomsbury.com and sign up for our newsletters.

To my four daughters:
You each inspired the best in Sophia,
may she always inspire the best in you

Sont en sommeil

Pearl of the sky, long stays high
Persephone, sunken earth
Seeds lie fallow in her realm,
Awaiting amber, arise

CHAPTER 1

Another knock at the door—I seal my grip tighter around the pistol.

I haven't slept all night, haven't closed my eyes. Through the window I've watched darkness fade into a cold gray morning. I've listened to the quiet stillness surrounding me and felt the softness of the sheets beneath me, constantly repeating to myself *it's over.* I don't have to be afraid anymore.

Because I am here now, finally. I am safe.

Safe.

The word echoes inside my skull, ringing until I shake my head to make it stop. I remove the gun's magazine, check the rounds, and then snap it back in.

There is another knock, two sequential taps, then the knob turns and she steps inside. I sit with my legs off the bed and wipe damp hair from my face.

My head is pounding. Lack of sleep and many hours of flying make it feel like a hammer is banging inside my forehead. It takes all my concentration to look at her, pretending I've just woken.

Walking toward me, she frowns. I wish she would stop staring at me this way, like I am a fragile glass object about to break at any moment. Because I'm not. Anything weaker than me would have already shattered.

It's the same apprehensive way that colonel looked at me when he arrived fifty-two minutes after it happened, surrounded by four marines carrying M16s—locked, loaded, and aimed at me.

She sits down. "I see you're not quite ready." My mother starts to straighten the blanket, then, deciding otherwise, leaves it in a heap at the foot of the bed. "Your father will take you."

I look down at the gun in my hand, acutely aware of the cold metal against my clammy skin. I know I'm no longer supposed to need it, yet my hand is clamped so tightly around the pistol grip my knuckles are white.

For the fifth time, I check to make sure a round is chambered and the magazine is full.

When I finish, my mother rests her warm hand on the back of mine.

Gently, she takes the pistol from me, checks the safety, and places it back under my pillow. "Leave it, Sophia." She brushes my hair behind my shoulder. "You won't need it here."

CHAPTER 2

My mother cooks pancakes and bacon. "It's what everyone eats for breakfast here," she explains.

I'm not hungry; I can barely swallow the orange juice she sets in front of me. After shoving a piece of bacon in my mouth to satisfy her, I gather my things and follow my father out the front door.

A shiny SUV is in the driveway.

"From Andrews," the man told us at the West Glacier Airport last night when he gave my father the keys.

I've never met Andrews. I only know he's important—important enough to send my father all over the world. And to give us a silver all-terrain Denali.

Dropping my Swedish backpack at my feet in the passenger seat, I force my breathing to steady. *Four minutes*. Four minutes until this feels real, right?

I look out over the high-altitude valley. Perched deep in the mountains against a backdrop of wilderness and cedar-hemlock forest, this new town is quaint, charming even. Apart from the pickup trucks in every driveway, Waterford looks more like a Tyrolean village than how I'd imagined an American town in Montana would look.

My parents described it on the Black Hawk last night. *You can enjoy your new life now, Sophia*, they said, promising that Waterford would finally be home.

But as they said this, the soldiers on board watched me—stealing glances with their heads leaned back against the fuselage wall, their Kevlar helmets lodged between their boots. Even if they wanted to, they couldn't speak to us, couldn't strike up a conversation to ease the boredom of the eleven-hour trip. We were cargo.

Now, I watch my father's face while he drives—the soft lines around his hooded eyes, his permanently crooked nose, sun-damaged to a burnt-orange color. I lower my eyes to the Heckler & Koch holstered at his waist, to his left ankle where he straps a spare magazine, and then to his right ankle, where he keeps the Kabar he taught me to use when I was ten.

His eyes dart from the road to the mountainside to me and back again. He isn't nervous, it's simply how he drives—constantly assessing the vicinity as if we might need an escape route at any moment.

After two decades in the navy, his diplomatic duties have taken us around the world too many times to count. Of the last six weeks alone, we've spent two in Tashkent, one in Doha, two in Sarajevo, and then the past seven days in Tunis.

Shivering, I let go of my necklace, a delicate gold chain with a pendant that rests at my collarbone, and fold my arms across my chest.

Tunis.

I glance down at my shins. I'm wearing a pleated wool skirt and black opaque tights, but that doesn't stop me from seeing it—the way my bare skin looked with his blood spattered all over. Like someone dipped a brush into a can of crimson paint and flicked it at me.

It wasn't until we arrived in Waterford last night that I scrubbed it off completely. I used a toothbrush, scouring the pores of my skin until the bristles went limp.

The drive is short. Moments later, we enter a circular driveway in front of a symmetrical brick building, two stories high. Stone-engraved words arch over the front entrance amid neatly trimmed ivy: *Waterford High School, est. 1954.*

My father stops at the curb. "Bearings?" he asks.

I wave my hand flat in the direction of the sharp granite peaks. "North," I answer. We both stare ahead at the majestic range.

"Mountains make it too easy." He smiles. "Now, go straight through the main doors." He hands me a schedule with a map stapled behind it. "We'll see you this afternoon. Unless . . ."

"I don't want to wait until Monday," I insist.

"Sophia, a few more days won't make a difference. Who starts school on a Friday?"

I open my door. "I do." Slinging my backpack onto my shoulder, I get out of the car.

"We're good?" my father asks.

I study the map and pass it back to him. "We're good," I say.

As soon as I close the door, he drives away. This is his way of encouraging me. Expressing confidence in me.

It doesn't work.

As he turns the corner, my thoughts spiral.

It's all happening too fast. It's been eighteen months since I last attended school. Now I'm supposed to step beneath an ivy-covered plaque and be a student again—an American one—just another teenager in high school.

But how do I pretend that forty-two hours ago I wasn't alone inside that sweltering safe house? Pretend I hadn't heard his footsteps? Hadn't wondered why they left me alone if they knew he would come?

Listening to the empty street, I stand in front of this enormous brick building and check that my ironed, white-collared shirt is tucked in.

A crisp autumn wind whistles past my ear and chills the backs of my legs.

This is just school. School.

I've done this dozens of times. There is no reason to be nervous. No reason to be afraid.

Except there is.

Because this new American life I'm expected to live? It terrifies me. Now, I'm expected to belong. To fit in. To accept that for the first time in my life, we plan to stay.

I can't do this.

CHAPTER 3

I can do this—all I have to do is blend in.

Class has started by the time I check in at the office and reach my second-period classroom. I pause at the doorway. The students look like the American kids at my international school in Brussels—except rather than Chanel and cashmere, they are wearing Patagonia and denim.

". . . just the questions on the board," the teacher says from his perch on an oak desk in the front. He is dressed as casually as his students—a frumpy shirt tucked into tan trousers.

In the front row, a petite girl stands. "*Bonjour. Je m'appelle Lydia . . .*"

When she finishes, the teacher looks over at me. "May I help you?" he asks politely.

I straighten my blazer and step inside. He glances at his clipboard. "You're new?" he asks, squinting at me through his eyeglasses.

"Yes, sir."

He corrects me. "*Oui, monsieur.*"

"*Oui, monsieur,*" I repeat.

"Welcome." He inclines his head, switching back to English. "I'm Monsieur Steen. Why don't you sit over there?" He motions to an empty seat in the corner. "I assume you took the requisite courses at your last school?"

"I believe so, sir." I walk across the classroom, sit down, and put my backpack beneath my desk.

The girl beside me is wearing skinny jeans, a cream sweater, and red sneakers. I can't help feeling self-conscious in my pleated skirt and tights. Doesn't my mother know how casual they dress here?

"We're practicing introductions. You can listen and then have a turn," Monsieur Steen tells me.

A brawny boy named Cole Richards stands next. He was born in Waterford, has two brothers, and wants to be a cake farmer—or so he says in French.

Sighing, Monsieur Steen removes his eyeglasses and cleans them with the hem of his shirt. Putting his glasses back on, he nods to me. "Time for our newest student to introduce herself."

Wiping my palms on my skirt, I stand. Everyone murmurs, craning their necks to see me. I keep my eyes on Monsieur Steen.

"Shoot," he says pleasantly, tapping his kneecap with a pencil.

I eye him, confused, before interpreting that *shoot* means start. Glancing at the questions on the chalkboard, I answer rapidly in French:

"*My name is Sophia Hepworth. I was born in Finland. My parents are diplomats. No siblings. I'm not sure what I want to be when I grow up; I don't think about it anymore I suppose. But when I was little, I dreamed I would grow up to become a ballerina.*"

The murmurs hush. I've done something wrong.

"*We haven't gotten to those yet,*" Monsieur Steen says in French.

"*To what, sir?*" I respond.

"Past subjunctive, future conditional. You're French?"

"Not exactly, monsieur," I answer.

Monsieur Steen turns up his palm and sighs, *"Let me see your schedule."*

I take the white sheet of paper from my binder. It is folded neatly in half, and I attempt to press out the crease before stepping forward to hand it to Monsieur Steen.

"If you're a native speaker, why did they place you in this class?" he asks.

"They said a language is required to—"

"Yes, but it won't count. You must transfer into a beginning foreign language course. We also offer Spanish, German, and even first-year Mandarin. I'll give you a hall pass and you can leave."

Monsieur Steen reaches across his desk. "Here," he says in English, handing me a fluorescent slip of paper. "Go to the main office, and a counselor will put you in the proper class. Would you like someone to walk you?"

Shaking my head, I take the note. It crinkles between my fingers. *"I am in the proper class, sir."*

Monsieur Steen opens his mouth to object, but I intercept him. *"They won't allow enrollment in a beginner course in a language you already speak. Since I'm required to take a language, I chose French."* I shrug. *"I like it best."*

He slides onto his feet. "You're fluent in Spanish, German, *and* Mandarin?"

Hearing the hushed whispers erupt around me, I nod. My ears go warm.

Monsieur Steen shakes his head. "I suppose I'm stuck with you."

I can't tell if he's upset.

He continues, "*Very well. For credit, you can write essays on French history and literature, okay?*"

"*Oui, monsieur,*" I whisper. "*Merci.*"

"*And Sophia?*" he says in French, barely looking up at me, "*don't tell Principal Thatcher how bad my accent is.*"

"*Never,*" I answer, smiling almost imperceptibly.

I turn around to see the entire class watching me.

So much for blending in.

CHAPTER 4

"Sophia!"

The girl wearing the red sneakers from French class saunters toward me. "Steen asked me to give you this," she says, reaching me. She pushes a sheet of paper into my hands. "But I was late to gym, and then Cole stopped by my locker and, anyway, here. I'm Charlotte by the way."

Charlotte says all this very fast. She's graceful, with a silky mane of chestnut hair, radiant dark skin, and her knit cream sweater shows her stomach when she switches her books from her left arm to her right.

"Thank you." I unfold the paper: *Write a three-page essay on a seventeenth-century French poem. Your choice.*

I slip the paper into my French composition book.

"Do you know where the cafeteria is?" Charlotte asks.

"At the end of the hall, take a left. It's twenty meters ahead on your right."

"*I* know where it is!" Charlotte laughs, "I was making sure *you* know! Come on"—she gestures down the hall—"I'll walk with you."

"You must be the new girl." A Caucasian boy with sandy shoulder-length hair and vivid white teeth steps up beside us. "Charlotte said you're from China—"

"I did not, Mason!" Charlotte hits his right tricep. "I said she speaks Mandarin!"

"—but she is obviously wrong because you're blond."

Charlotte rolls her eyes as I glance down at Mason's bag—on it is a patch of the US Ski Team.

Although I'm not exactly hungry, I walk with Charlotte and Mason into the noisy cafeteria. Rows of tables and chairs clutter the room, the floors are sticky with dried soda, and it smells of fried food and greasy pizza—*this* is what I've been missing.

While Charlotte grabs a sandwich from the line, Mason walks me to a rowdy table beside a bank of windows that resemble a hand-painted mural; in the distance are the jagged granite peaks, dotted with emerald spruce and golden aspens.

"Take a seat." Mason points to an empty chair tucked in to a two-meter-long table crowded with students.

"Where are you from?" an athletic girl with plump pink cheeks and long auburn hair asks. "Abigail said Sweden, and Lydia said France—"

"Let her sit, Emma," Mason says, catching an empty soda can before it hits him in the chest. He sits down among a rambunctious group of boys—Liam, Henry, Ryan, and others I recognize from my morning classes. I stare between Emma and Mason: same sapphire eye color, same shape to their ears.

"You're siblings?" I ask.

"Twins." The girl with the auburn hair nods. "I'm Emma," she continues. "So where are you *really* from? Idaho?"

"Oh no, I've never been there."

"You haven't been to *Idaho*?" Charlotte sits down beside Emma.

I shake my head.

Emma dips a carrot stick into hummus. "Where did you move from?"

It's been so long since I've talked like this—carried on a conversation with girls my own age—that my voice clogs in my throat, making it hard to say anything at all. "I came here from North Africa," I finally say.

"Africa!" Charlotte and Emma say in unison.

"Did you go on a safari?" asks Charlotte, leaning toward me.

"No. I mean yes. I mean, I've been on safaris of course, but those are in southern and eastern Africa. I came from the north."

"Where? Egypt?"

"Did you see the pyramids?"

"Actually, I wasn't in—"

"Did you climb to the top? What's it like inside? I've always wanted to walk through them!"

"Does Egypt look like Arizona?" Charlotte asks.

"Possibly? I've never been there either," I answer.

"You haven't been to *Arizona*?" they say together.

"No, I—"

"Was Egypt dangerous? Did you wear a hijab and cover your face?" Emma asks.

"Do you mean a burka? A hijab only covers your hair and your ears; a burka covers the face too, including the eyes; a niqab covers the face but not the eyes, and you know, a chador doesn't cover the face at all, only the head and body. But Egypt is secular so women aren't forced to veil, unless they choose to, and actually . . ."

I trail off, realizing I'm talking as fast as Charlotte.

"So, what are you doing in Waterford?" Charlotte asks quizzically.

"My parents retired," I say, desperate to change the subject. "Are you both from here?"

Emma puts her hand over her heart. "I am," she laughs, "but Charlotte was the new girl. Until you showed up."

Charlotte opens a bag of cookies. "Except I'm from Seattle. Not, like, *Africa*."

"Oh, good," I say quietly, "I'm not the only one."

"No, you are. I moved here in seventh grade." Charlotte pushes a cookie to me. "What was it like growing up in Africa?"

"I didn't grow up in Africa," I clarify.

"Where did you grow up?"

Trying to be polite, I take the cookie. "Everywhere. Lebanon. Belgium. Uzbekistan."

"Uzbekistan?" Emma laughs, "I've never even heard of Uzbekistan."

Charlotte watches me, wide-eyed. "Why did you live in all those places?"

"We didn't live there permanently. Sometimes we'd only travel for a few weeks, or days, at a time." Their mouths open, but I press on, hoping to steer the conversation away from where I know it's headed.

"My father works for the State Department," I say, reciting the line I've shared since I was seven. "He facilitates NGOs in developing countries, sometimes in active war zones—hot spots. He travels a lot. He never stops moving. *We* never stopped moving."

Charlotte sighs. "I'm jealous. My mom's Korean, my dad's Dominican, and I've never left America. I wish I spent my life vacationing all over the world and—"

"No!" I say hastily. "I mean . . . it wasn't . . . vacation." I've dropped my cookie and hurriedly scoop the crumbs from the table onto a white napkin. "We traveled because we had to. I would have much rather stayed in one place like Nairobi or Beirut or Waterford and never have gone to Kabul . . . Grozny . . . Crimea . . ."

. . . *Tunis* . . .

I feel it coming on. I close my eyes to make it stop.

I have to get out of here. Abruptly, I stand. My chair topples over, clattering to the floor. I scramble to set it upright. "I—I'm sorry," I stammer, "I have to get to class."

Charlotte opens her mouth, but I dart from the cafeteria and sprint down the hallway, through the east wing and up the main staircase until I reach the landing. I collapse against the railing.

My fingers curl around the bar, steeling my body.

Count, I tell myself. *Count to ten in Russian, Mandarin . . . Count backward in Arabic from one hundred.*

When this strategy doesn't work, I plot the fastest route back to the house—down the stairs, past the office, out the front doors, 30 degrees northeast across the front lawn, cut west across Fourth Avenue, and turn left onto Edgewood Drive.

Distraction works.

Seconds later, the tension in my chest releases.

My mother says I should allow the flashbacks to come, that the more I recall them, the more I can control them. But the truth is, they control me. When they come, my limbs stiffen, my body immobilizes—like I'm trapped in a nightmare and my legs won't move.

Leaning my forehead against the window, I breathe slowly, how I learned in Varanasi—*in for three, hold for three, out for three.*

How did I think today would go? That I would suddenly be able to turn it off like a switch? That I could simply prevent being triggered?

Everything is supposed to be different in Waterford, but I don't feel any different. I don't want it to take time. I've had time. I want it to be different *now*. I want to be normal *now*.

I stand on the landing, midway between the first and second floors, where the windows overlook the front lawn of the school. Focusing on the shadows cascading between the cloud cover, I concentrate on counting the ocher hemlock trees circling the perimeter of the front lawn.

Exhaling slowly, I release the railing. I tell myself to return to the cafeteria. Finish lunch. Finish out the day.

The slightest pressure on my forearm causes me to spin.

"Sophia!" Emma gasps.

I look down. My hand is clutched around her wrist. Blood rushes to my cheeks. I uncoil my fingers instantly. "I'm sorry—"

"Did we say something wrong?" Emma asks, nonchalantly shaking out her wrist. "You ran off so fast—"

"Not at all." I attempt a smile. Behind her, students hurry up the stairs. I glance at my watch—class starts in seventy seconds. "I didn't want to be late."

"What's your next class? I'll walk you." Emma seems genuinely concerned.

I retrieve my schedule, showing her I have Calculus II—second floor, fourth classroom west of the staircase.

Emma looks between me and the schedule. "Lucky girl, you're with all the seniors." As I follow Emma, passing students watch me with unfiltered curiosity.

Charlotte meets us at the top balcony. "Do you want to come over tonight, Sophia? We're going to make mudslides."

"Mudslides?" I ask, imagining the dry protein pies the Red Cross delivers to displaced people after natural disasters, months after the foreign aid stops.

Charlotte grins. "The most delicious food ever. Do you want to come?"

The warning bell rings.

"Tonight?" I ask. Is she being nice? Is this normal? Am I supposed to say yes?

"It's Friday," Charlotte says, applying a nude lip gloss. "Don't Egyptians have weekends?"

"Kind of, I mean, it's different in Egypt. Sunday is the beginning of the workweek, so technically the weekend starts on Thursday night and goes through Saturday night, so it's not exactly the same although . . ."

Emma and Charlotte both look at me like I'm speaking Finnish.

"Friday. Right, sure, thanks. I'll check with my parents first."

"Give me your phone, I'll put my number in." Charlotte holds out her hand.

"I don't have . . ." I look around at everyone else tucking away phones while scurrying into classrooms, ". . . an American number yet. Tell me your address."

The tardy bell rings. Charlotte squints at me like I'm pranking her.

"I'll remember," I tell her.

"Fine. 124 Woodland Star Circle—I'm at the mouth of Silver Canyon, okay?"

A lanky boy standing at the classroom entrance looks over at us. "Door's closing in five, four, three—"

"She's coming!" Emma says, pushing my back toward the door, laughing.

The calculus teacher, Mr. Krenshaw, is a musty old man wearing a tweed coat with suede patches on the elbows. "Who are you?" he barks at me.

"Sophia Hepworth." I pass him my schedule.

"You're late." He inspects the paper. "You're a junior. You shouldn't be in this class," he says gruffly.

"I took a test."

He peers at me from behind wire-rimmed glasses. His hair is long and gray and looks like wool. "When?"

Scanning the classroom, I notice everyone is either chatting or playing on their phones. I recognize many of them by now. Waterford High only has 403 students—404 including me.

"In August," I reply.

"Where?" Mr. Krenshaw persists. "The district office?"

"In Tunisia," I answer, feeling hot sweat burst onto my skin.

Mr. Krenshaw stares at me impatiently. "Tunisia?" He emphasizes the word, like I'm joking. A few kids in the front row look over.

"Yes, sir, in Tunis." I push my nails into my palms to stop the shaking. "I took a test at the embassy. I take it every year to ensure I'm keeping—"

"What were you doing in Tunis?" he interrupts.

"My father's job."

"What kind of job? Military, Peace Corps?"

"He's a diplomat."

Mr. Krenshaw stares at me skeptically.

"He monitors NGOs throughout the world," I add.

He clicks his tongue. "School started two months ago. Calc II is for seniors who've completed my Calc I." He points at a wall of textbooks. "The midterm is in a few weeks, and you've missed valuable time already."

Mr. Krenshaw removes his glasses and tosses them on the desk. "Keep up or I fail you."

CHAPTER 5

I barely recognize the brick two-story house I left this morning. During the six hours I was at school, my parents tackled the overgrown weeds, mowed the lawn, cleaned and scrubbed the porch, and repainted the front door a soft blue gray.

Your new home, my mother said last night.

Home? Not yet.

A damp wind stirs the trees, blowing rusty-orange leaves across the pavement. I find my father in an unattached garage behind the house. A single light bulb dangles above his head, lighting up the makeshift table—two sawhorses supporting a piece of plywood.

I sneak up behind him. Then, loudly I exclaim, "Shiny!"

His shoulders twitch. He looks over at me and grins. "Every time you see the tiger—"

"—the tiger has long been watching you," I finish. "And you didn't see me."

He chuckles, "I did not. You're not quite a tiger, but you're becoming a dangerous . . . bobcat."

"Thanks," I say sarcastically.

"How was it today?" he asks.

"Fine." I shrug.

I sit on an upended bucket beside the makeshift table. Placed horizontally on it are two Stöckli skis—sleek and silver with neon racing stripes.

"If you'd like, I'll get a pair for you too." He drizzles hot wax onto a ski, waits for it to harden, and then runs the scraper down the edge.

Looking away, I brush off the memories—the burning in my quads, dry wind chapping my lips, prickly mountain air on my bare cheeks, frozen toes.

I clear my throat. "Dad—"

"I know what you're going to say, Sophia," he interrupts, "and I respect that. But when you are ready, so am I."

I fiddle with a clasp on one of the ski boots. "Um, thanks. But that wasn't what I was going to say."

My father squints at me. "Oh?"

"Two girls I met today, Emma and Charlotte, invited me over to watch a movie and eat mudslides—it's an American thing—and I wanted to see if—"

"Of course, you may go."

"Really? Because I don't have to—"

"Sophia, I trust—"

"I know you trust *me*, but maybe I should bring my—"

"I trust it *here*, Sophia, in Waterford." My father bends down to clean the scraper. "But I need to ask you a question." His voice lowers; it grates the inside of my ears, warning me, ". . . about Tunis. I need to be certain you saw his face." He stops his movement with the hot wax drizzling over the top of the ski.

My heart starts thumping. My airway is constricting, stealing my voice, so I nod.

He persists, "So you know—"

"Yes," I interject, wanting to end this conversation as quickly as possible. "I knew from the moment he entered the house. From the moment he breathed, like his lungs didn't work properly, and the uneven sound of his boots . . ."

Like a swift-moving current, the memories of the past few days flood toward me. Gripping the edge of the bucket, there is nothing I can do to stop them.

I was alone in the safe house when I heard the knob turn. By the time I ducked behind the fridge in the windowless kitchen, the door creaked open. I heard his footsteps—his boots thudding unevenly along the mosaic-tile floor. Clutching my pistol, I listened to him draw closer—unable to rack because of the sound. Even loaded, I'd only have a split second between the time he saw me and the time it would take to aim and fire.

First, he went to the side of the flat where two mattresses were wedged into the corner. Could I make a break for it? There was only one door to the apartment, and two windows. Even if I reached a window, we were on the fifth floor—the fire escape was down the hall.

He kicked over the mattresses, before turning back toward the kitchen. I had seconds before he would see me. I slunk farther into the shadows. Then, right before he stepped into the kitchen—*pop*!

He slumped to the ground, dead the instant my father's bullet penetrated the back of his head.

Just like that it was over.

Eighteen months of running, hiding, chasing, fearing—over.

Now I am returning to "normalcy" like it never happened. Like it's easy to make friends. Easy to forget how I lived every minute of the past eighteen months in fear that they would find us.

That *he* would find *me*.

Panting, I catch my father's gaze. He stands motionless, watching me, waiting for it to pass.

I grit my teeth to block the rest from coming.

Because the thing is, I'm not afraid of remembering Tunis.

It isn't hiding in that safe house, barely forty-eight hours ago, that chills my bones and fills me with panic—it is remembering what happened before Tunis.

It is fear that if I remember *any* of it, I will relive *all* of it.

Catching the wind, the light bulb sways and flickers off. Then it rocks back into place and lights up again, illuminating my father's face. He's always been so good at concealing his emotions. I fluctuate between despising him for it and envying him.

He resumes skimming the hard wax off the ski edges, but his eyes remain on mine.

"Yes, Dad, I saw his face," I say quietly.

"Your mother asked me to check with you, make sure you understand he's gone. That you understand what this means."

Nodding, I stand and set the glossy ski boot upright. "It means I can go out for mudslides."

CHAPTER 6

In the late afternoon light, beneath an awning of evergreen needles, the trail is awash in a silky mist.

I find the entrance marked by a wooden post adjacent to a tan clapboard house where pockets of brambles and quaking aspens merge into spindly pines and wild birch trees.

According to the map my father spread out on the kitchen counter, this indiscernible path of dirt dividing dense foliage is a shortcut to Charlotte's.

Although I'm running three hundred meters parallel to the road, a vast wilderness seems to separate me from civilization.

Out of habit, I look behind me as I run deeper into the forest. No one is there, but I'm not used to being alone, to having this freedom. I inhale deeply. Waterford smells of autumn—pine needles, burning leaves, and damp forest.

Storm clouds hover above the thick canopy of intertwining pine branches. It starts to drizzle—I gather my hair under the hood of my new windbreaker.

Quickening my pace, I curve around a bend in the trail, jump over a gnarly tree root, and skid to a halt.

Stifling a cry, I grasp a pine bough to keep my balance. *Seriously*?

My father didn't *warn* me? Wolves in the Carpathians. Lions in the Serengeti. He forgot grizzlies in Montana.

Instinctively, I run my hand over the waistband of my leggings—but I know my FN 5-7 is at home, tucked beneath my pillow where my parents insist I keep it.

The bear's backside is three feet wide; its head is the size of a boulder. Sniffing and grunting, it is so close I can see clumps of mud caked into its russet fur.

With an enormous paw, the bear whacks a tree limb, snapping it in half.

Although rain falls steadily, pattering onto the dirt in an acoustic rhythm, I hear something in the distance, getting closer.

I listen harder, gauging direction. I glance left, then right.

Heavy breathing. Fast. Too fast. Erratic. Multiple. Unsynchronized.

Beside me, a thicket of trees stirs. Two furry brown shapes tumble out of the dense forest undergrowth and scamper onto the path, loping toward the grizzly.

At this moment, three facts about North American grizzly bears come to mind: they are a subspecies of Siberian brown bear; they can run fifteen meters in one second; a grizzly with two cubs is as dangerous as a pack of hyenas.

I need to move. Immediately.

I start backing away. Spattering raindrops muffle the sound of my footsteps. Each step creates more distance between me and the grizzly. Two meters. Three.

Crack! I snap a branch.

The grizzly whips her head around. Her amber eyes meet mine. A plume of air rises from her nose.

I take another step back.

Wrong move.

She rears onto her hind legs. A low, threatening snarl tears from her mouth.

Thud! Landing on all four legs, she leaps forward.

Rapidly, she narrows the distance between us.

Bending my knees, I extend one arm toward the ground. My fingers fumble along the mud and pebbles until they clasp a jagged stone, barely the size of my palm. If I can somehow . . . hit her in the eye . . .

But she is charging me at full speed, ferocious growls ripping from her throat.

I try to recall my father teaching me how to fend off a grizzly attack, any method I can use to prevent her from killing me.

Frantically, I drop to the ground, fold my arms over the back of my head, and curl my knees into my chest. *Play dead.* That's what I'm supposed to do. *Don't run. Don't fight back.*

A guttural growl nearly ruptures my eardrum. She pins me down.

I cover my neck with my forearms.

Huffing and grunting, she swats my back, violently rolling me over.

My skull hits the dirt.

She strikes my thigh fiercely with her paw. I strangle the shriek in my throat.

She is going to maul me. Tear off my limbs. Rip me apart. I have to fight back.

Gnashing and baring her teeth, she arches her neck backward.

I secure the stone in my hand, preparing—

Suddenly a familiar sound punctures the rain, slicing open the forest like a firecracker.

In quick succession, it repeats. Six times total.

Instantly, the weight of the grizzly lifts from my chest. The growling stops.

Pattering thuds fade into the distance.

Like a thousand pinpricks, the hairs on my neck stand straight. The rain is falling harder now, splintering when it hits the ground. But only one sound echoes in my ears—*Pop*!

Dazed, I lift my head. The grizzly has vanished. In the distance, I hear breathing again. Low and steady this time. Human.

Footsteps are ten meters away. Five. I see a shadow moving, a blur in the rain.

Fear grips me. I scramble backward, but someone reaches me before I can stand.

CHAPTER 7

"Hey, don't move." He puts a hand gently on my arm.

I flinch, lodging my back against the tree root.

"Whoa," he says soothingly. "She's gone. Cubs too."

Since I was five, I have been instructed to assess people; someone is either a threat, or not.

I run my fingers along the mud until I retrieve the jagged, palm-size stone.

Even kneeling beside me, I can see he's tall—strong, young, with tousled light brown hair and smooth skin. Beneath his shirt is an outline of broad shoulders. A bolt-action rifle is slung across his back.

Where was he? How'd he reach me so quickly?

He scans my body quickly; his eyes descend from my head to my neck, over my chest, and down to my legs, then back up to my face.

Heat flushes my chest.

My hair has fallen over my face in a tangled mess of mud and leaves. I push it back under my hood.

"You're not cut," he murmurs in a deep, clinical voice, sounding both relieved and surprised.

I glance down at my leg. The bear must have struck me with

her forepaw—only fur and muscle—no claws. My leggings are ripped from the sharp rock edges on the ground; the material flaps open, exposing a swatch of my pale thigh, now turning a grim violet shade.

"Can you stand?" he asks.

"Yes." I rub the back of my head. "I'm fine, I think. Thanks."

With a taut grip, he pulls me to my feet.

Though I'm tall at 175 centimeters, standing I barely reach his shoulder. I look up at him. His face is cut hard and straight, with a square jaw, defined cheekbones, full lips, and piercing green eyes, staring intently at me.

"You're running out here by yourself?" he inquires sharply.

I nod.

Lightning strikes above us. Prying his eyes from mine, he looks over my shoulder.

Then he takes off his backpack and removes a scope. As he does, his shirt inches aside, revealing an oblong patch of black leather tucked against his hip.

Seeing this irritates me. I can defend myself.

He holds the telescopic lens to his eye, glancing around.

"Is she coming back?" I ask, swiveling my head to scan the trees. With the rain cascading in sheets, the forest blurs into a murky expanse of pine and evergreens. "Lions stalk their prey first," I explain, "then attack, then leave before returning—"

"You're not prey," he answers evenly. "She was just defending her cubs."

Another bolt of lightning flashes. Dropping the scope, he locks his vibrant eyes back on mine. Why is he looking at me so peculiarly?

My chest tingles beneath my jacket.

"Are you visiting?" he asks casually.

"I live here." I pause. "Technically, I moved here last night."

A flicker of familiarity passes his face—so quickly I can't be sure. He's attractive, and mature, but still youthful. Does he recognize me from school?

It doesn't seem possible to have *not* noticed him there.

He notices me noticing him. A wave of heat swells in my neck, collecting at my throat.

Flustered, I nod at his hip. "I hope you're better with your SIG than you are with a rifle."

He looks between the holster and me, amused. "You think a pistol could hurt a grizzly?"

My face goes hot. I avoid placing pressure on my left leg. The pain has to ease up soon. I can't go home with a limp. "It could if you had better aim."

He threads the scope onto the rifle. Pushing his lips together, he stares down at me. "*Better* aim?"

"You missed *six* times!" I snap angrily. "You nearly hit me."

He opens his mouth, then shuts it.

With a haughty look, he strides past me, stopping beside a narrow pine. He points at a glinting dark spot on the mossy trunk.

I follow, touching my fingertips to the shredded bark. Exactly three meters off the ground, in the center of the trunk, is a three-millimeter hole with a shiny copper bullet wedged inside.

To my left is another tree with another hole.

My heart rate speeds up with each bullet I spot.

Surrounding the patch of trail are six trees. Each now has a copper bullet lodged into its trunk, equidistant from the ground.

Six bullets. Six targets. Six perfect shots.

Beneath the hood of my jacket, the skin at the base of my neck prickles. *Impossible.*

When I look back at him he is watching me with an even, confident expression.

His muscles spread out across his shoulders and down his upper arms like they have been chiseled from stone. He is wearing only a long-sleeved shirt; his chest is sculpted to it, and he doesn't seem bothered by the rain and cold, or by me.

Which infuriates me, because I am bothered by *him*. And I can't articulate why.

His muscular left hand tightens around the rifle stock, grazing the edge of the scope.

"I didn't miss," he says assuredly. "I wouldn't have taken a shot if I thought I'd hit you."

I step backward. Wincing at the pain in my thigh, I stumble.

"Careful." He instinctively reaches forward to help, but I step farther back.

The grizzly is gone—my heart rate should be decelerating. Instead, it's accelerating.

I'm irritated that he stepped in to save me. I don't need to be saved, especially in Waterford.

If I'd been allowed my FN, I could have fired the shots myself. But mostly, I'm frustrated that I'm flustered. *Who is he?*

"Where were you?" I demand. "Were you watching me?"

His eyes flare indignantly. "I was coming down that ridge"—he indicates vaguely east with his right hand. "I heard the grizzly. Then I saw you."

Through the rain-smudged forest, a trail twists among the pine trees, converging with a steep ridgeline two hundred meters off.

I peer between his bolt-action and the ridge. "Those were some aggressive shots."

"She was an aggressive bear," he counters dismissively.

"I had it," I say. "You didn't need to interfere. I would have been fine."

"You had it?" he says, astutely. "Against a grizzly with two cubs?"

"Yes," I say defiantly, gripping the stone in my fist.

For several seconds we stare at each other in protracted silence. He is as intimidating as the grizzly. With his harsh, inquisitive look, I feel more scrutinized than I have all day.

Thunder crackles across the sky.

"Can I walk you home?" he asks. Glancing down, he seems to notice my ripped leggings. "Or to the clinic on Main Street?"

I'm in *Montana*. His story checks out. I don't have a valid reason *not* to trust him. I relax. Slightly.

"No, thanks. I'm headed to a friend's house," I explain. "Charlotte Cartwright. She's on Woodland Star Circle. Another half kilometer southeast . . ."

The corners of his lips turn upward in an exasperated smile. "You were just attacked by a grizzly and you want to go to your friend's house?"

"I'm not injured."

"You're not putting any weight on your left leg," he points out.

I put equal pressure on both legs. "It's only bruised."

He looks dubious. "Most people attacked by a grizzly are at least *shaken*—"

"*Most* people can't hit six separate targets in four seconds from two hundred meters with a bolt-action, let alone iron sights. And certainly not through trees in weather like this."

His voice cuts through the rain. "You really should get an X-ray to make sure you don't have a fracture in your leg. Something tells me you know the drill."

"I do," I declare. "So I know nothing's broken."

The angles of his face draw tight.

Standing with his rifle in his hand, shoulders back, chest out, he reminds me of the soldiers guarding the colonel in Tunis. Except he makes me uneasy in a different way—like my heart is bounding into my throat.

Around us, the sky is nearly dark, the air on the spectrum of a green-hued dusk.

"I'll walk you to Charlotte's," he finally says. "It's not far."

"I know where it is." I shake my head. "I'll walk myself."

He points at the muddy path. "This is a grizzly migration trail to the river. Locals stay off it in autumn, so you should too." Strapping the rifle across his chest, he nods his head southeast. "Let's go."

CHAPTER 8

Charlotte's door swings open before I've even knocked. "Sophia!"

"Hi—"

"What happened to you?!" Charlotte stares down at me.

Beneath the porch light, I notice that not only are my leggings ripped, but I am covered in mud, leaves, twigs, and possibly remnants of bear fur—*ugh*.

I wipe a chunk of mud off my knee and stomp my sneakers on the doormat. "I got caught in the storm."

"You *ran* here?" Charlotte asks, perplexed. She peers over my shoulder. "Alone?"

He had taken me on a trail that wasn't on my father's map, and we'd emerged from the forest near Charlotte's house, at the base of a narrow granite canyon marked by a sign—*Eagle Pass*.

Wondering if he waited for me to make it inside, I turn. Both the driveway and wet glistening road are empty.

"Yeah," I answer, realizing I still have the jagged stone in my palm. Discreetly, I toss it onto her lawn.

Charlotte drops back on her heels; her long hair cascades over her shoulders in waves. "Why didn't you drive?"

"I don't have a license."

She shuts the door, laughing, "Sophia, when you learn to drive—drive!"

Charlotte's bedroom resembles a tree house; two walls are plastered in a collage of Winter Olympics posters; the remaining walls are windows. After inspecting my throbbing thigh, mutating into various shades of violet and reddish-violet, I change into a pair of Charlotte's royal blue Waterford High sweats and return downstairs.

"Heard you got wet." Emma is removing bowls from a cupboard beside the fridge, wearing a plaid button-up shirt, with her auburn hair braided down her back.

Laughing, I detangle my damp hair with my fingers. "Slightly."

Emma sets down the bowls. "Too bad you missed cross-country. We needed you!"

"You run cross-country too?"

"Too?" Emma inquires.

"You're a swimmer, right?" I flush. "I saw the posters at school . . . and your hair . . . it was wet earlier . . . and smelled faintly like chlorine . . ."

Emma draws a strand of hair to her nose, laughing. "You're right, Sherlock. The season's about to start, so I've begun training in the mornings."

Charlotte pulls out a carton of vanilla ice cream from the freezer and hands me a spoon. "Have as much as you want. We have more."

They scoop ice cream into their bowls, then drown the ice cream in chocolate brownies, chocolate sprinkles, and chocolate shavings, before drizzling a thick chocolate syrup over the mound like a volcano. Our mudslides are so gigantic they drip over the sides of the bowls and I have to lick the rim before eating a spoonful.

As we settle into cozy velvet chairs by the fireplace, Charlotte turns to us intently. "Okay, let's play a game. *Never Have I Ever*"—she scrunches her nose—"been to Paris. You eat, Sophia, because you've done it and I haven't. Get it?"

My mouth already full of chocolate shavings, I eat another bite of ice cream.

Grinning, Charlotte points to Emma. "You're up."

Emma wipes her mouth. "Never Have I Ever . . . kissed Tate McCormick."

Charlotte rolls her eyes, distinctly not taking a bite. Emma motions to me. "Sophia?"

I wrinkle my nose, pondering. "Never Have I Ever . . . been to Idaho?"

Charlotte groans. "Weak. That was totally weak!"

Emma laughs. "Shouldn't even count."

"Okay, okay," Charlotte says. "Never Have I Ever . . . been alone with Aksel Fredricksen."

Emma's smile fades. She looks inquiringly at Charlotte, who points at my mudslide. "You're supposed to take a bite."

"Sorry?" I ask, confused.

"Sophia, you're a terrible liar!" Charlotte leans forward. "I *saw* him walk you here!"

"Who?" Emma's eyes flit between Charlotte and me.

"Yes, Sophia, who was it?" Charlotte asks innocently.

I twirl the ice cream around in my bowl. "I didn't learn his name."

"His name is Aksel, Sophia." Charlotte licks her spoon. "Aksel Fredricksen."

"Why?" Emma interrupts. "Was he heading home?"

Charlotte nods to the windows. "He lives a few miles up Eagle

Pass; it's at the base of Silver Canyon. He's the only one up there year-round of course; everyone else just comes to ski, so it's basically a private lane."

Staring into the darkness, I recall the steep ravine as we emerged from the forest—Eagle Pass is more a narrow chasm between granite rather than an independent canyon.

"Didn't you *just* move here?" Emma asks. "How do you know Aksel? Why did he—"

"I *don't* know him. It was an accident. I was running on this trail and there was a grizzly and she attacked me and—"

"A grizzly?" Charlotte nearly chokes on her ice cream. "And you're alive? Why didn't you say anything?!"

"I'm not hurt!" I exclaim defensively. "I only have a bruise, and some scratches—"

We are interrupted by the doorbell.

A crew of classmates enter Charlotte's house in a pack.

Nevertheless, for the rest of the evening, I try to keep Aksel Fredricksen out of my mind.

I fail.

CHAPTER 9

I wake at dawn. My forehead is damp, and the sheets are tangled around me. Extricating myself from the linens, I dash to the gabled window and unhook the latch. I inhale the crisp alpine air, trying to calm my nerves, to cool myself off.

Parched mouth . . . a smell of garlic and vinegar beneath the doorway . . . loud shouting on the other side of the wall . . . a blinding flash of light . . .

I cling to the window ledge. *That was the past.* I press my eyelids together until I see stars. It is over now. *Over.*

"Why did you leave so fast?" my mother asks as I hurry down the staircase a short while later, having returned home from my morning run with barely enough time to shower. "I would have joined you!" There is a reason I prefer running with my father over my mother—she can beat me, and he can't.

She nods at my outfit: a plaid button-up blouse tucked into high-waist jeans. "All part of blending in." She smiles ruefully.

"You're not leaving without breakfast!" my father orders from down the hall. I step into the small, modern kitchen—marble counters, a polished-nickel faucet, and French tile on the walls. My mother's favorite Stelton teapot is on the stove, and her Celine handbag is on the counter, but other than that—nothing. No photographs. No sticky notes with our handwriting. No handmade figurines. Nothing of *us*.

"They sell muesli in Waterford?" I ask, distracting myself from comparing my pristine, sterile kitchen to Charlotte's cozy, cluttered one.

The muesli package is open on the counter. My father has made three yogurt parfaits drizzled with honey. He gives me one.

"Found it at Alpine Market. It's actually not bad." My father eats so quickly he's emptied his dish and washed it before I take my first bite.

"Sit," my mother says sternly. "Some American habits I want you to learn. Others, I do not." She motions to me, standing in the middle of the kitchen, eating. I dutifully sit.

"Sophia," she says, casually glancing at my leg.

It's been a week since the grizzly attacked me. To explain my limp, I told her I tripped on the way to Charlotte's.

"Yes?" I say innocuously.

She taps her fingers on the tabletop, pursing her lips. "You can't run around Waterford with a 5-7," she eventually says, "but you can at least take your Ladybug."

I stare at her inquisitively; I lost my Ladybug at the Sport Club in Beirut.

She walks to her handbag and retrieves a delicate five-centimeter blade.

"You said I wouldn't need a weapon here," I say.

My mother walks behind me and pushes aside my hair. She reaches her hand into the back of my new blouse and lifts out the price tag. *Snip*.

Clicking the Ladybug closed, she leans over my shoulder and

puts it on the table beside my glass dish of muesli and yogurt. "Who said it's a weapon?"

Charlotte dumps her precalculus textbook onto the cafeteria table, "I loathe Krenshaw!"

I check my silver Skagen watch and groan. "I forgot Krenshaw's assignment in my locker." I stuff my thermos into my backpack. "See you guys later?"

"You better hurry!" Charlotte warns through a mouthful of pizza as I run out of the cafeteria and into the corridor.

Approaching the glass-walled vestibule connecting the cafeteria to the north hall, I notice something out of the corner of my eye—someone.

He is here?

Crossing the lawn with long, lithe steps, Aksel keeps his head bowed against the damp wind rushing in from the canyons.

One second, he is bounding up the stairs two at a time; the next, he is opening the door and stepping inside.

Aksel doesn't stop casually when he sees me. He comes to a deliberate halt a meter away from me—like I am either contagious or dangerous.

Aksel Fredricksen hasn't been at school all week. I'd know. Because harder than catching up on eighteen months of missed schoolwork has been trying to *not* constantly scan the halls, curious if I'd see Aksel at school—which is why it actually seems weird that I haven't seen him. Not once. Until now.

He's even more strapping and formidable than I remember.

Strikingly handsome, his features are angular, with broad cheekbones and full lips. He looks like he's been outdoors all morning. His light bronze skin is flushed and tan. In daytime, his deep-set eyes are even brighter—a pulsing, electrifying shade of green.

Why am I standing here—*staring*?

"So you do go to school here?" I blurt out.

I look down at the physics book in his hand. *Obviously*.

His face remains impassive. "Yeah. Of course."

"But you've been gone."

"Vacation," he answers easily.

"All week?" I prod. My cheeks redden. In Waterford, I'm supposed to stop noticing things—details—people don't like being inspected.

His piercing eyes don't leave my face. "How's your leg?" Aksel asks. His voice is deep, slightly hoarse; his lips are round and full and why do I keep looking at them?

Flushing, I bite my lip. How can *he* make me nervous?

"Healed mostly. It was only a small bruise." I wring my fingers together. "I'm Sophia, by the way," I chatter. "I didn't really thank you previously, so thank you. You're a good shot. My father would be impressed. He'd say only military snipers would have made those shots . . ."

As I speak, Aksel's entire demeanor subtly shifts. His posture stiffens, tensing, like I've startled him. Momentarily, his brow furrows.

He looks like he's inspecting me.

I'm hit by an unexpected sensation of familiarity.

". . . Where did you . . . learn?" I finish lamely.

Aksel watches me uneasily. A sharp tingle rolls up my spine.

Leaning fractionally away from me, Aksel arranges his mouth into a slight, forced smile. "Hunting," he answers reticently.

Brrrriiiiinnngggg!

The corridor crowds with students.

It's as though an invisible barrier has descended between us.

Easing his hands into his pockets, Aksel slips back into a composed posture and says, "See you later," before striding past me down the hall.

What was that about?

Ruffled, I dart to the north hall, collect my assignment, and reach Krenshaw's class as the tardy bell rings. At the whiteboard, Krenshaw clears his throat and presses out the sleeves of his tweed coat.

The door creaks open. It has a broken hinge, so it swings into the wall with a *thud*.

Krenshaw's eyes dart to the doorway, along with everyone else's.

Aksel strides into the classroom. Our eyes lock. My cheeks ignite.

Mortified, I spin back in my seat and inspect the calculator on my desk.

"Today is your midterm," Krenshaw declares.

Aksel sits down two seats over.

"No fair!" shrieks a girl to my left. "It's supposed to be next week!"

Krenshaw raises his arms, silencing the class, before distributing the exam. "Remember, midterms are a third of your grade."

I'm hyperaware of Aksel's presence, his movements; beside me, he is seated at an angle, drumming his pencil against his desk.

As the exam begins, I keep my head down, scribbling out factorials.

Yet, my pencil quakes in my hand.

There is something unsettling about the way he looked at me—for a second in the woods and that flicker just now—like he *knew* me, and I can't push it aside, explain it away.

I don't need to be on alert. Aksel isn't familiar. *He lives in Waterford.*

The shrill *whiz* of an electric pencil sharpener knocks me back into reality.

Forty minutes left and I haven't finished the first page.

However, I didn't study in bombed-out Crimean hotel rooms, without electricity, only to fail an American high school math exam. I desperately push aside my curiosity and focus.

With ten minutes left, Aksel stands, walks to the back of the classroom, and drops his exam onto Krenshaw's desk.

Surreptitiously, I watch Aksel beneath my lashes. He strides out of the classroom . . . without a look in my direction.

"Six o'clock good?" Charlotte asks, hauling open the heavy school door a few days later. "We'll get ready for the Stomp at my house."

My eyes have strayed behind Charlotte, watching Aksel stride down the main steps two at a time.

Since the exam, I've seen Aksel frequently at school, usually in Calculus and often leaving Physics alongside a ski racer named Henry. We say almost nothing to each other. He's not *mean*, he's just cordially indifferent.

Yet despite the impermeable distance between us, there remains a gnawing in my chest each day as I turn a corner or enter Krenshaw's classroom. I'm not sure whether I dread Aksel's presence or desire it.

It's nagging me that I can't figure him out, that I'm flustered around him, that if we make eye contact, my stomach inevitably churns like a baby goldfish is swimming around inside.

Like now. And he's barely out of view.

I snap my eyes back to Charlotte. "You mean a dance?"

"No, a *stomp*," Charlotte says, treading over brittle ocher and scarlet leaves piled at the curb as we skirt the crowd stampeding to the parking lot. "You do *not* go with a date, and if Ryan Rice asks you to see the hay rafters, say no!"

I scrunch my nose. "Hay rafters?"

"Hay rafters, Sophia! You know?" she laughs. "Never mind."

Opening my front door ten minutes later, I collide with stacks of cardboard boxes piled in the foyer, managing to catch the top box before it topples over.

"Movers left five minutes ago," my mother says, maneuvering toward me. Her flaxen hair is combed neatly, and she is wearing her typical pearl earrings and a cardigan, buttoned once, the second button down. She wipes her bare forearm against her brow. "It's nice to see everything again, isn't it?"

Careful not to bump my thigh, I kneel down. "How long has it been?"

My mother rips the tape off a box. "Four years, seven months, one day."

Curious, I watch her open it. Inside is her collection of Nordic folk art: wood carvings, embroidered tablecloths, and Dala horses painted red and blue.

I shuffle through several boxes before I spot a familiar piece of lace and velvet sticking out from beneath a mound of crumpled tissue paper.

Katarina looks as I remember her: blond ringlets, a cobalt-blue taffeta gown, and *Made in Russia* imprinted in Cyrillic letters on the bottom of her black satin shoe.

A Ukrainian diplomat, Consular Petrenko, gave her to me during a posting in Damascus when I was six. I hadn't known what to name her, so my mother suggested Katarina, a Russian ballerina she once knew.

For a very long time, I took Katarina with me everywhere. Every new place we moved I made a bed for Katarina beside my own. Together we would fall asleep as I imagined Katarina telling me stories of a simple life in the country where we would run barefoot in fields of wild berries and chase fireflies at dusk.

Then our last night in Bratislava, shortly after the movers left with our boxes, my mother flew into my bedroom—a small wallpapered room with a brass bed frame and a window overlooking the Danube River—and swept me into her arms. There was barely time to grab Katarina before I was whisked away—up the stairs and onto the tile rooftop. I watched the window of my bedroom erupt in flames as the helicopter ascended.

Not long afterward, we stopped unpacking altogether. I never saw our things again.

Carefully, I wrap Katarina back inside the tissue paper and tuck her into the box alongside the other dolls.

What is the point of having this unloaded? Here? Now?

Since we arrived, I've searched my parents' faces, trying to read between our reality and the facade they have established in Waterford. I can't find any reason *not* to trust them, *not* to believe that we are here permanently. So why don't I?

"What do you think?"

Startled, I turn. My father could have successfully snuck away from the grizzly.

"Stay alert, Sophia. Even a great predator like the tiger can become prey—"

"Why are we here?" I snap, wanting none of his instruction.

He drops his teasing lecture. "Your mother and I retired," he says carefully. His face is clean-shaven, and he keeps his silver-blond hair trimmed short. In his left hand, he holds a Prussian sword with a ten-inch hilt wrapped in disintegrating leather.

"Why not retire in Barcelona, or Hvar, or Positano? Why here?" I gesture around. Visible through the windows at the front of the house is a steep alpine summit. I can see golden quaking aspens and emerald pine trees, but no plaster apartment buildings with terra-cotta tiles; no dirty steps leading to underground metros; no art museums in elaborate old palaces.

I don't wait for his answer, instead broaching the unresolved questions still bothering me. "How did Farhad find us in Tunis?"

He points the sword tip down, looking steadily into my eyes. "I don't know, Sophia, but we're safe here."

"Except they keep finding us. No matter what we do, they are always one step ahead. What if they find us here?"

"They won't. He was the last one. You saw me kill him, Sophia."

"But if it's over, why move us *here* to the middle of nowhere?"

My father smiles. "I was born in Massachusetts, Sophia. Snow is in our bones."

"*Snow* is why we moved here?" I ask skeptically.

He shrugs. "Andrews said Waterford would be a good fit. It's quiet and mountainous. Soon we can ski—"

"So tomorrow we won't leave for Prague or Karachi or Nicosia—"

"No, Sophia."

"And you moved here to do what other *retired people* do. Not because we're waiting or hiding?"

My father runs the blade along his palm, examining it. Then he theatrically slashes left, slashes right, and—*swish*—slides the Prussian sword into its leather sheath.

"We moved here because it's time you finally experience *our* country."

CHAPTER 10

My country.

I've seen enough Halloween movies to get the idea. Nothing quite compares to the festivity permeating the air. My mother spends all day making caramel apples, and as I leave, a witch, an astronaut, and Spider-Man ring the doorbell.

We arrive to the Stomp an hour late—on time, if you ask Charlotte—and park in a field adjacent to the barn. Actually, we jolt to a stop; the car lurches forward as Emma mistimes the clutch. I have whiplash by the time she parks.

Charlotte unbuckles her seat belt and dramatically rubs her neck.

Emma scowls. "It's not my fault I'm stuck with this old Jeep."

Outside, the sky is a darkening slate. A breeze rustles the amber leaves lining the road; they drift around our ankles as we run through the plowed cornfield toward a gravel path lined with pumpkin lanterns.

"Why is the Stomp in a barn?" I ask, inspecting my costume as we approach the doors. Charlotte convinced us to wear fairy costumes, and to cover our bodies with a radiant, luminescent powder. We look like glowworms.

Charlotte laughs. "It always is—it's a *barn* stomp!"

"Your wings!" Emma squeals, pointing to my shoulders.

I reach for the straps—*darn*. "I'll catch up!" I say.

I run back down the path, scanning the darkening cornfield ahead. Quickly, I spot the shimmering wings. I pick them off the damp field and shake them out.

As I reach the gravel path, I hear a rustling in the distance. Swishing.

I look over my shoulder.

From out of the shadows, a dark figure emerges. He glides stealthily toward me—not slowing down or speeding up, but with a smooth stride—like a predator stalking prey.

Why did I come out here alone?

Backlit by headlights at the edge of the field, he's wearing a cloak with an upturned collar; a mask conceals his face.

His pace quickens.

Instinctively, I retrieve my Ladybug from my waistband.

Diverting around the lanterns, I turn the corner toward the entrance and—"BOO!"

Tate McCormick jumps in front of me, laughing.

Simultaneously, the shadowy figure steps out from behind me, snickering. Ryan Rice pushes off his mask and fist-bumps Tate, "Scared New Girl too."

Hot with embarrassment, I slip the knife back into my waistband. "*Surprised*," I say. "And my *name* is Sophia."

"You're safe with us, *Sophia*." Tate grins. He is dressed in an old military outfit, navy blue with yellow cording on the structured shoulders. His dark hair falls loose over his pale forehead. He takes off his cap and tucks it beneath his armpit, which is awkward considering Abigail Montgomery, dressed as a La Perla Cowgirl, is tucked in there too.

"Come on," Abigail squeals, urging us all indoors.

Strung from the rafters, thousands of glittering orange lights decorate the barn. The air is humid with body heat. I stay near the chilly entrance.

Mason walks over, offering me a plate loaded with cider doughnuts, toffee, and pumpkin bars. "Princess?" he asks.

"Fairy," I laugh, taking a toffee. "Obviously not a convincing one."

"You're a stunning fairy," he says, and his ears go pink.

Mason is wearing a vintage sweater with *Calgary 1988* embroidered above Olympic rings and a Union Jack pin on his chest.

"Olympian?" I guess.

"Eddie the Eagle." He unhooks a pair of oversize red glasses from his sweater and places them on his face. "Gutsiest ski jumper of all time." With his sun-streaked blond hair and tan skin glimmering in the lights, he looks more like a California surfer.

"Hey, do you want to check out the hay rafters?" a voice whispers in my ear. "It's supposed to be haunted up there."

I turn. "Aren't you here with Abigail?"

"No one has a date," Tate chuckles, snaking his arm around my neck. "Come on, Sophia," he continues. "You're probably the only person who hasn't been up there."

"Hey!" Charlotte intercedes, brushing aside Tate's hand. "Stop running off!" she scolds me, dragging me toward the swarm of sweaty bodies.

Mason snatches Charlotte's other hand, runs forward, and dashes into the crowd of people.

"Come on!" he yells. Carving into the solid mass like a surfboard through a wave, Mason tows us into the center of the dance floor under the dazzling orange lights.

All of a sudden, I am smashed among bodies. It is like being on the metro in Tokyo, or at a market in Delhi. Except these hot sweaty bodies are jumping and laughing and moving, in swirling unsynchronized steps.

Charlotte and Emma are ridiculously good dancers. Unfortunately, years of ballet did not equip me to dance at a Waterford High barn stomp.

Spunky country music vibrates in the air. Boys I've only seen sporadically in the halls push up near us. Charlotte seductively draws them close, then turns her back on them, regaining eye contact with us, her eyes wide with laughter. The only boy she dances with is Cole Richards, her on-off boyfriend for, like, ever, according to Emma.

Tate comes up behind me, places his hands on my hips, and sways with me along with the music. Imitating Charlotte, I playfully push his chest away. When this method backfires and he returns, even more tactile, I elbow him in the chest, right above his second rib. He puts a hand to his heart. "That hurt!" he laughs.

"It should!" I respond.

A bluegrass song begins. Suddenly everyone is shuffling into lines. Emma grabs my arm. "You stay behind me," she orders.

At first, it's impossible. Charlotte kicks right. I kick left. Emma turns sideways. I jump back. Each time I imitate their steps, I lag behind. *Kick. Spin. Forward. Cross.*

I'm terrible at this.

Charlotte links her hands into mine; in advance of each step, she prompts me. *Reverse. Spin. Kick. Repeat.* When I accidentally bump Abigail, she giggles, nudging me back in the right direction.

I feel completely out of place. While everyone dances deliberately,

I pinball between bodies, two steps behind. But soon the fervor, the energy of everyone moving in synchronization—*kick, slide, spin, turn, jump*—encompasses me.

In the row ahead, Cole, Mason, Oliver, Liam, and a bunch of other boys expertly rotate inversely, causing a spectacle—even more so because of their ridiculous costumes.

During a *double-skip-tap-spin* one of my wings tangles with Emma's. When Charlotte finally separates us, we can barely stand up straight from laughing so hard.

Somehow, by the final chorus, I catch on. The song ends in a fiddle crescendo—at the final note everyone jump-clicks their heels in the air, followed by boisterous applause.

Turns out, American line dances are really, actually, fun.

Several songs later, Charlotte hisses behind me, "Time to go!"

"Already?" I ask, looking back.

Because out of the corner of my eye—I see Aksel. He's standing at the periphery of the barn with some other seniors. And he's *laughing*.

I'm not sure why I feel so surprised to see him here wearing a cowboy hat and boots. Was he here the whole time?

"Isn't there another song?" I ask Charlotte as she tugs my hand.

"Sure!" she laughs. "But we never stay until the end!"

Outside, the temperature has dropped. Cold sleet falls from the pewter sky. Charlotte, Emma, and I run back through the misty cornfield, trampling leaves and stalks.

"Meet at the Creamery!" Mason hollers to us as we reach Emma's Jeep.

Turning out of the field, Emma approaches the intersection

perched atop a short hill, icy in the sleet. She stops. Yet, when she starts again, the Jeep stalls.

We roll back. Charlotte gasps. Emma brakes. Quickly, she restarts the ignition. Again, it stalls. "Come on," Emma moans, tossing her auburn hair off her face. "I hate this old Jeep."

Battered pickup trucks and SUVs queue behind us. At our bumper, Ryan Rice blares his horn. Tate is beside him, with Abigail Montgomery on his lap, chuckling.

"Put it in first. Let out the clutch slower, and give it a little more gas," I advise from the front seat. Emma tries, but stalls a third time. We slip back a meter before she brakes.

Tate yells out his window, "You almost hit us!"

"Hurry!" Charlotte urges frantically. Sleet slashes the windshield.

Emma goes so pale I worry she might pass out. It feels like half of Waterford High is now behind us, honking, waiting to exit the field.

"Is that car a little too much for you girls?" Tate taunts out the window.

His condescension irks me. Over my shoulder, I see him laughing.

"Switch places with me," I say to Emma.

"What?" Emma asks, turning the key a fifth time. Her hands are shaking. Charlotte covers her face with one of her fairy wings.

"Put the parking brake on and switch with me," I say.

Emma cranes her neck to see the cars behind us.

"Do it," I order.

Emma pulls the emergency brake and clambers across my lap. I wriggle under her into the driver's seat.

"You said you couldn't drive!" Charlotte says, terrified.

Putting in the clutch, I turn on the ignition and ease the stick into first. "Did I?"

With the parking brake on, I rev the engine, release both brakes, and accelerate past the stop sign.

Ahead, a row of cars snakes around the backside of the barn, blocking our route. In the rearview mirror, I check the distance between Ryan and us—150 meters. I slam on the brake, shift into reverse, and throttle up.

"Sophia, what are you doing?" Emma squeals.

We move backward at a clip. Up to speed, I yank the emergency brake and palm the steering wheel left, popping the stick from reverse into first. We rotate 180 degrees. I throttle again, getting traction as I shift into first. The slick road gives me too much angle, so I adjust the wheel, then pull down into second gear, accelerating. As we speed past Ryan and Tate, Charlotte blows them a kiss.

"*What* was that?" Emma shrills from the passenger seat.

"'Escape and evade.'" I shrug. "It's easier in a Lancia or a Fiat—"

"What exactly are we trying to *escape and evade*?" Emma grips her seat belt.

"Tate?" I suggest.

Charlotte throws her head back, laughing, "Did you see his face?"

Ten minutes later, we arrive at the Creamery on Main Street. I spot a parking place and make a tight U-turn.

"We won't fit," warns Emma.

Reversing, I palm the wheel right, then spin it left.

"It's too small! Sophia!"

I glide in centimeters from the curb. Unbuckling, I turn off the engine, take out the keys, and hand them to Emma.

"You don't have a license yet," she reprimands me.

Slipping my wings off my shoulders, I climb out of the car. Charlotte waits for me on the brick sidewalk, smirking. "Fast and furious."

Emma pockets the keys. "We are *not* going to tell my parents about this."

I lift an eyebrow. "About what?"

CHAPTER 11

By the following Monday, the excitement of the holiday is still buzzing on my skin. America is both weird and exhilarating and finally, I'm starting to acclimate.

Yet the general anxiety I feel walking into Calc II each afternoon is compounded today when Krenshaw divides us into groups and puts Aksel in mine.

We push our desks together. I sit beside a pretty girl named Priyanka, and Aksel sits down beside Cole—who does not stop talking—and somehow we make it through three assignments speaking only about derivatives.

However, with ten minutes remaining, Priyanka and Cole go to check our work with Krenshaw, leaving Aksel and me alone at the table.

Unable to explain the sudden queasiness in my stomach, I look down at my work like my vocal cords have been snipped.

Aksel drums the table. He bends over and makes a citation. He crosses, then uncrosses his ankles. Then he leans slightly forward.

"So how are you liking Waterford?" he asks in an even, polite tone.

I stare up at him. "I liked the dance," I say truthfully. "Did you?"

"Sure," he answers. His deep voice is both familiar and intimidating. "It's always fun."

"So are you from Waterford too?" I ask. He looks so *Montana*, yet there is this air of luxurious indifference—otherness—about Aksel I can't put my finger on.

Aksel wrinkles his forehead, watching me in a way that makes my heart leap into my throat. "I suppose so," he says casually. Carefully.

"Were you born here?" I prod, remembering Mr. Steen's French questions my first day of school.

Aksel doesn't answer right away, which is odd because it's a simple question.

"No," Aksel finally says, angling back in his chair.

"Where were you born?" I ask.

Over Aksel's shoulder, Priyanka gives me a thumbs-up from Krenshaw's desk.

When I look back at Aksel, his expression has shifted.

Why do I get the impression he is trying to read me?

His eyebrows knit together. "Germany, actually," he says coolly.

For several seconds we stare at each other in silence.

I *am* confused. He *looks* confused.

Which doesn't make any sense.

What did *I* do?

Cole and Priyanka sit back down. Priyanka drops a paper onto the center of our conjoined desks. "We got a perfect score so Krenshaw added another assignment," she says through gritted teeth.

For the rest of class, I resist looking at Aksel, though I'm certain I see him cast a furtive glance in my direction.

When the bell rings, we reach the door at the same time. Aksel steps left. I step right.

"Excuse me," I say, turning away down the hall, avoiding him altogether.

Considering my feelings about Aksel hinge on suspicion, I shouldn't care what he thinks about me. So why *do* I? Because he seems suspicious of me too?

I can't shake the feeling that there's more to it—more to *him*.

"Sophia!" Charlotte snaps her fingers. "Are you coming?!"

Her face is exuberant. We've been studying inside Waterford Bakery, which smells of warm bread and hazelnuts, for hours.

Fifty beds in eighteen months, and my first month in Waterford has exhausted me.

Autumn passed too quickly. By mid-November, snow replaced rain. Each morning, fresh snow dusts the town like powdered sugar, accumulating quickly along the roadsides.

Now, I pry my eyes away from the hypnotically falling snow.

Emma has divided art history flash cards into neat piles on the table in the center of our quaint window nook.

Charlotte is waving *Night Watch* in front of my face. "Didn't you hear? Mrs. Bernhardt is taking a group of art history students to Europe next summer!" Her voice rises until she's practically shouting. "Are you coming?"

Outside, wind churns the snow in swirling gusts across the windowpane.

Europe isn't touring art museums and architecture. Europe is reality—my reality.

. . . *Shouting* . . . *blinding flash of light* . . . *Yves Saint Laurent cologne* . . .

It comes on so fast.

Charlotte continues rapidly, "We need someone who speaks the language . . ."

. . . running . . . blood . . .

". . . to show us around . . . the shopping and cafés, the museums and châteaus!"

I've gone weeks without being triggered. I can hold it back.

. . . breathe in for three . . . out for three . . .

"You can be our translator!" Emma adds enthusiastically through a bite of apple tart.

"Interpreter," I correct her, distracting myself. "Translators handle documents."

"What's it like?" Charlotte asks wistfully, peeling off a golden layer of almond croissant. "Like, the Parthenon. In person."

Marble columns. Heat. The sea. A scent of olives in the breeze. I can do this. Easily.

"Sunny," I reply, swallowing the rest of my hot chocolate. "With the way the ruins are perched on the hill, you can stand among the fragmented columns and look out across the Saronic Gulf and see hundreds of rocky islands floating in turquoise—"

"Noooo!" Charlotte groans. "The one with the hole and Raphael is buried—"

"You mean the *Pantheon*, in Rome?"

"Yes!" Charlotte giggles, "That one."

I laugh. "Inside the Pantheon, when it rains, it comes blasting through the hole in the roof and hits the stone floor with a sound like an orchestra. The first time I visited, my father asked me to count the number of tourists who entered and exited the roped-in chapel within one minute. I was off by two, so he made me do it again."

Emma screws up her face. "Why would he tell you to do that?"

My cheeks redden. *I said that aloud?*

"Gelato," I improvise. "It was a game. He bribed me." I talk faster. "Listen. When you exit the Pantheon, cross the piazza northwest, take your fifth right, walk past the fountain, and turn left into a narrow cobblestone alley. Eighty meters down is a yellow door with glass panes. Behind it is Cremeria Monteforte, which has the most incredible flavors: chocolate-orange . . . lemon-fig . . . pistachio-hazelnut . . . lavender-honey—"

"*Lavender* ice cream?" Charlotte wrinkles her nose in distaste.

"You'd like it!" I laugh, "and you will *love* Europe."

Emma picks up her phone. "I'm going to be late for the meet!" she squeals. She crams her notes into her bag, shovels the last of her pastry into her mouth, and licks her fingers. "Wish me luck!"

Two hours later, Charlotte and I make our way to Fish Market—Waterford High's aptly named natatorium. The meet has started, and it's already crowded; the air is dense and muggy. At the top of the bleachers, I sit down beside Charlotte, who sits beside Mason.

Below us in the swimming pool, bodies skim across the water like Arctic seals.

"No swim team this year?" Charlotte asks Mason, who eats the remainder of her half-eaten croissant in one bite.

"Only one Jensen twin is getting a scholarship, and it won't be me." Mason grins.

Tate McCormick squishes down beside us.

"Why don't they swim in bikinis?" Tate snickers. "I'd come to watch that!"

"You *are* watching," Charlotte points out.

"Hydrodynamics," I say at the same time. "Loose fabric drags, causing friction, slowing the swimmer . . ."

Tate stares at me, open-mouthed.

Booooom! The starting horn blares. Everyone seated in the bleachers screams. My whole body tenses. *Noise. Shouting. People.*

Now is not the time. Now is not the place. Bodies press into me on either side, hot and sticky. The air gets heavier . . . *sweating . . . footsteps . . .*

Blurry images shift into focus, prompting a tidal wave of memories.

My fingertips grip the bleacher. I close my eyes.

. . . *Breathe . . . Count . . .*

I push my trembling lips tight, resisting.

But it is too loud. Too hot. Too muggy. Too crowded.

No matter how hard I resist, it still feels as though I am in a nightmare, unable to run, unable to move. My defenses are weak.

"Sophia?"

I open my eyes. Charlotte's hand is on my arm. She is watching me anxiously. Her eyes are wide with concern. Like I am fragile. Mysterious. Dangerous.

I am pale, sweating. It's obvious—something is wrong with me.

Weeks of progress are rapidly deteriorating.

. . . *It's coming on again . . . I have to make it stop . . .*

Cramped bodies are closing in around me. I feel like I can't breathe.

"I need water." Standing, I step backward, collide into a man's knees, and then hasten down the bleachers.

At the bottom of the stairs, I turn right. Students barricade the double doors. Throngs of sophomores linger in the lobby. *There's no way out.* I reach the water fountain and lean up against the brick wall. *Focus. Push it back.*

I squeeze my eyes and press my palms flat against the wall. I recite the elevations of South American capitals. The populations of African countries. When neither tactic works, I recite the series of numbers my father makes me memorize: *14-36-53 . . . 55-65-96—*

Booooom! Another horn blares. Fresh, cold air sweeps in through the open doors. The crowd thins. I watch the swimmers dive into the water and glide beneath the surface—one is far ahead of the others, only breaking the surface for air halfway across the pool.

I push my hands against the brick wall behind me. I trace my fingertips in the grooves, counting. I fight off the sensations: *oxygen burning in my lungs . . . heat searing my throat . . .* I wonder if I can hold my breath longer than the swimmer flip-turning at the wall of the pool and gaining another two body lengths on the swimmer in lane four.

Now I hear my mother's voice. *Remember, Sophia, so you control them—so the memories don't control you . . .*

I had been practicing with my father for months. After he spent the day at the embassy, he would come home and we'd walk to the swimming pool.

He instructed me how to do the simpler strokes first—Australian crawl and breaststroke—streamlining the technique to fit my narrow build, teaching me to float on my back, faceup, if I got tired and needed to rest. Then he taught me the harder strokes—butterfly and backstroke. Once I'd learned those, he taught me speed. *If there's a shark, you only have to swim faster than the person behind you,* he always said with a wink.

After I could tie him in a hundred-meter sprint, he taught me to hold my breath. Count rhythmically. Release my mind of fear and simply count to 120. One steady beat after the next. No bubbles. *Never bubbles.*

At first, I could only stay below for thirty seconds before I would inevitably claw toward the surface, gasping for air. My father never pushed too hard, and I enjoyed the thrill of being like him. One weekend, my parents chartered a ketch to sail off the coast of Djibouti for a few days. In the late afternoon of our second day, I was reading *Bonjour Tristesse* in the stern when I saw my father checking the radar constantly.

He picked up a pair of binoculars and scanned the horizon. He shouted something down to my mother.

Moments later, my mother emerged from the cabin, holding a Galil sniper rifle and spitting ammo wrapping from her teeth.

"Ninety seconds," he told her.

Hammering bullets into the Galil's chamber, she propped it next to the helm. Then she unclipped a Beretta from a thigh holster underneath her white linen skirt.

My father moved for me. Gripping my arm, we dashed from midship to bow. "Sophia, you need to go below," he said.

"Belowdecks?" I asked, frightened, glancing back at my mother.

"Below the surface, Sophia. Into the water. It's warm. Hold tight to the anchor chain and hold your breath. Count, honey. Count to one hundred. That's it. But don't break the surface—they can't see you, Sophia. Do you understand? *No bubbles.* You have to stay hidden, and that's the only place! Now go!"

While he said this, I heard a boat cruising toward us. Its engine idled a few seconds before bumping into the fiberglass hull on the starboard side. An anchor was thrown over—it landed on the deck, meters from where we crouched, concealed under a cover of the mainsail.

My father took my wrist. "Go now, Sophia! Do not break the surface until I come for you," he whispered, scrambling away.

Gunfire erupted. Raspy voices shouted. I wanted to return to the cabin and stay beside my parents. Instead, I crawled to the front of the boat and slid over the edge.

Huddling near the anchor at the bow, I hunched over and watched through a scupper—four armed men with bandannas covering their faces leaped onto our ketch.

Once they boarded, I followed orders. I slid into the ocean, took several deep breaths of air, then submerged, using the anchor chain to descend three meters underwater.

At first, I floated idly beneath the surface. After seventy seconds, I grew anxious. With every passing second, I gripped the chain tighter, swaying with the formidable current, trying to not let go. It was dark all around me and so deep I heard nothing from the surface. I felt only the pulsing of my heart and the aching burn of my lungs.

But my father had told me to wait.

So I held there, suspended between the black abyss beneath and the danger above. I pressed my lips together so they wouldn't open. I clung to the anchor chain because that was my link to survival.

The next thing I remember was an arm fastening around my waist. He pulled me to the surface. Choking out water, I gasped for air. My father swam us to the stern, grabbed hold of the ladder, and, in one motion, pulled me out of the water.

“Is she hurt, Kent?” my mother cried, dropping onto the deck.

My father placed both hands on my heaving shoulders and smiled at me. “No,” he said softly, “she did great.”

Then he hugged me so tightly I thought my lungs would collapse.

Over his shoulder I saw four bloodied bodies floating in the water.

Facedown.

CHAPTER 12

An outbreak of cheers, compounded by an earsplitting buzzer, brings me back to Waterford.

Catching my breath, I look up at the board. *Did I miss Emma's race?*

I walk forward through the lobby, squishing through the bodies toward the bleachers. I am scanning the crowd for Charlotte and Mason, when my gaze locks on somebody else instead.

Across the pool deck, Aksel stands out like a Vilebrequin ad on a Paris billboard. He's drying his wet hair with a towel. He has warmup pants on, but no shirt, exposing an enormous, muscular chest. I scan the scoreboard—was he racing?

When I look back at him, his eyes catch mine.

An embarrassed flush extends across my body.

Several thoughts cross my mind in rapid succession: Do I look away? Do I smile and wave? Do I walk over and congratulate him? Why is it always such a game between us?

With a vague nod of his head, Aksel turns away from me, tosses the towel into a bin near the bleachers, and ducks into the locker room. I can't decide which bothers me most: Aksel turning away from me, or the fact that I didn't turn away from him first.

While the flashback is gone, the sensations linger—my legs ache, my vision is foggy.

I still need air.

Maneuvering back through the crowd choking the entrance, I head outside.

It is a dark, clear night. Constellations of stars sparkle above.

I decide to walk toward Charlotte's Pathfinder at the periphery of the lot to wait.

Halfway there, I feel it.

My parents firmly believe in a "hex" sense—Greek for *sixth*.

If you don't want to be noticed, keep your head down, because if you look at someone long enough, they'll sense you looking at them and will look in your direction. *Wave-particle duality*, my father says.

This is what I sense now—quantum physics.

My eyes sweep the darkness.

At first, I see nothing. Then I notice a few rows back is a red truck with rust crusted around the wheel wells. Someone is alone inside it. Shadow obscures the man's face, yet a dim phone light casts a glow over the car's interior, illuminating his eyes—fixated on me.

The base of my neck tingles.

I have nothing to fear in Waterford.

I'm on edge because of the flashback, is all.

Nonetheless, the reflection of light in his eyes reveals he is still watching me.

Instinctively, I reverse. I back toward the nearest entrance—crowds, safety.

However, when I look back at the truck—it's empty.

I halt.

A bracing cold spreads down my spine and into my limbs.

Nearby, a car door opens, then slams shut.

My heart starts pounding.

Startled, my eyes skim the tranquil parking lot.

Out of the corner of my eye, I catch movement from the direction of the truck.

A shadowy figure moves between cars—in and out of my vision.

. . . *darkness* . . . *blinding flash of light* . . .

I whip my head side to side, listening. Straining my ears.

His gait is slow. Arrhythmic. Unfamiliar.

My fingertips slide to my waistband.

Ahead, I hear the footsteps approaching—heavy boots—accompanied by ragged breathing.

. . . *Wheezing* . . . *running* . . . *His voice* . . .

The footsteps near.

. . . *boots* . . . *sweating* . . .

I thumb open and lock my Ladybug.

Pivoting forward, I transition into a run—*Bam!*

I collide into something—someone—so firm I bounce backward.

Aksel catches me swiftly, steadying me. He immediately glances over my shoulder, before returning his confused gaze to mine.

Looking down at his chest, he frowns.

The tip of my Ladybug is up against his abdomen.

My left hand is coiled around his wrist in a steel grip.

Heat scorches my cheeks.

Rapidly, I retract my blade.

Hastily, I uncoil my hand from his wrist and drop it quickly at my side.

Aksel's face is flushed. He is holding a swim duffel in his left hand, glaring at me.

My heart pounds like it's going to leap into my throat. If he is expecting an explanation, I don't have one. In only one world is this normal—*mine.* With trembling fingers, I fold the knife back into my waistband. "I—I'm sorry," I stammer.

Aksel's eyes flick to my waistband. "Are you okay?" he asks. His tone is clipped. His eyes are still boring down on me. Stunned. Accusing.

Craning my neck, I look behind me. *No one is there.*

"Fine," I say. "There was . . . someone . . . I thought . . ."

Am I seeing things?

Aksel glances over my shoulder again. Behind him, the swim team is trailing out of the locker rooms. Farther down, a crowd is exiting Fish Market.

I've missed the whole meet.

I push my tongue against the back of my teeth to keep my lips from quivering.

Why has all my progress come crashing down—and why does Aksel have to see it?

Aksel doesn't lift his eyes from mine. His brow furrows, but the anger in his voice has subsided. He actually sounds concerned. "You're sure you're okay?"

"Sure," I answer casually. My hands remain clenched into fists.

We stare at each other in agitated silence. I notice that Aksel is as tense as I am, his posture rigid, defensive. He's like a mirror, reflecting my own fear and confusion. His gaze is both mesmerizing and terrifying. It's as though his eyes are drilling through me again, trying to read me, solve me.

Yet, though he seems affronted, even concerned, he does not seem all that surprised I just pulled a knife on him.

I should have recognized it earlier: The patterns, the tells. Controlled expression. Maintaining distance. Aksel is hiding something.

"Sophia!" Charlotte calls my name.

Deftly, Aksel returns to his composed mask of civility. "See you around," he says under his breath.

Beside me, he unlocks an olive-green '97 Land Rover Defender. A half meter of snow is piled on the roof, much more than is on the ground—how far up Eagle Pass does he *live*?

Aksel steps into the driver's seat, the line of his jaw clenched tight.

I bite my lip to prevent the tears. I'm not adjusting to life in Waterford. I am anxious—skeptical of nearly everything, and everyone.

Actually, I'm paranoid. I've been paranoid since we left Tunisia. I've been paranoid for eighteen months, and no amount of time living in Waterford can change that.

In the distance, I see the old red truck, rusty, with a broken taillight, turn out of the parking lot.

Reaching me, Charlotte's eyes flit between me and the Defender driving off. She whistles under her breath, "Never Have *I* Ever . . ."

When I arrive home, my parents are in the study. I pour myself a cup of rooibos tea and walk to the living room, still thinking about Aksel and what happened outside Fish Market.

It's exhausting: being suspicious, and experiencing a flashback, and trying to act *normal* . . .

I stop short when I see it. I stare, incredulous. They *kept* it?

It is an antique, nineteenth-century Érard; its black and white keys glisten in the moonlight streaking through the window behind it. Glossy in some parts, most of the color has been buffed away and its patina is now several shades of golden brown. However, its worn surface is deceiving; the inside is completely restored and plays beautifully. Or did.

Like a moon circling a planet, I feel a gravitational pull but keep my distance. After orbiting a moment, I move toward it. Memories, desires, fears all yank at one another in their own lunar tug-of-war.

My heartbeat quickens. My fingers twitch.

I trace my finger along a high F-sharp, careful not to press down.

Hesitantly, I sit. Despite my conflicted emotions, I feel the crescendo building, spreading throughout my limbs; I see the conductor in his black tuxedo, gold-leafed hall, gowns and tuxedos, the bright lights on the stage, my classmates huddled nearby. The melody resonates in my mind, vibrating down my spine into the tips of my fingers.

My hands reach forward. My fingers spread out like a peacock, poising carefully around middle C. I touch the smooth surface of the lacquered keys.

Sophia, you're going to play, my mother said. *I've ordered a gown for you to wear. We'll fly to Vienna for the weekend and be back in Istanbul for school on Monday.*

I stare at my hands—the pale color of my fingers against the black and ivory of the keys—tapping out a simple Chopin melody.

She had no way of knowing it would be the last time.

I hit a D instead of a C. The chord echoes egregiously in the room.

Like a snail curling up in its shell, my fingers roll beneath my palms. I stand, backing away from the piano like it's poison. I'm not ready. I'm not even close.

Upstairs in my bedroom, I ensure the window lock is secure. I crawl into the soft, lavender-smelling sheets and rest my head against the headboard. I lift my pillow to check my FN 5-7.

It's gone.

My fingers fumble along the empty sheet. Panic creeps up my arms. Scrambling to my knees, I push aside the quilt. I tear the sheet off the mattress. I shove my hand into the crack between the mattress and the headboard.

Lying flat on my stomach, I push my hand farther down, stretching my fingers.

My forefinger slides around the pistol. I secure my thumb around the grip. Roughly, I tug. Scraping the back of my hand against the headboard, I dislodge it.

Panting, I back up against the headboard. I unclip the magazine, check the rounds, and snap it back in. I stare at my scratched hand, holding the weapon I'm not supposed to need.

What am I doing here? I want to scream.

Why is this so hard? What is the point of trying to make Waterford feel like home? Trying to feel like I belong?

Can I ever be like Charlotte and Emma? Can I ever go to Europe for "fun"?

Why can't I brush aside my instinct that Aksel is hiding something from me?

I know it's irrational to hold him accountable for my convoluted emotions, so why can't I get him out of my mind? Because he thinks I don't belong in Waterford? And deep down I wonder if he is right?

Devastated, I tug my knees to my chest.

How has my fortitude to become *normal* in Waterford already collapsed?

Across the room, my eyes settle on Katarina—her porcelain lips are painted such that she looks cheerful one moment, melancholy the next.

My mother set her on the floral chair in the corner of my bedroom weeks ago. She must have thought I'd want her nearby.

I can't decide whether I do or don't.

CHAPTER 13

"Miss Hepworth!" Krenshaw barks as the bell rings the following day.

I stuff my textbook into my backpack and approach Krenshaw at his desk, "Yes, sir?"

"You failed," he says gruffly, returning my midterm exam.

One glance reveals that my efforts to catch up and prove I can fit in at an American high school have been eviscerated with four pages of paper.

"This is not good enough," Krenshaw scolds me. "I expect every student to put in effort and hard work—"

"I have been!" I fire back.

"I recommend dropping you to Calculus I," he tells me.

"I *know* that material, sir, and I'll do better on the final," I promise. "But how can I adequately prep for an exam you give a week early?"

His orange padded chair squeaks as he leans back. "I do the same thing every year, with every exam," he says dismissively.

"I didn't know that, sir," I say. "It's not fair—"

"Fair?" He sits upright. "Perhaps living in Waterford will teach you life isn't fair." He stretches his arm across his desk and clasps his fingers. The sleeves of his tweed jacket are too short for his arms; his wrists are covered in spindly gray hairs.

"You've had it easy," he drawls condescendingly. "This transition—leaving behind glamorous cities for a simple mountain life—must be hard . . ."

He leans across the desk. "However, mathematics is not subjective. You'll need to become less entitled and work much harder if you intend to pass."

Entitled?

He doesn't know me—*at all.* Nevertheless, fiery tears pool in the rims of my eyes.

"You have until the end of the semester or you fail *and* drop to Calc I."

On the brink of screaming at Krenshaw, I grab my backpack and head to Art History, but halfway down the hall I turn.

I descend the main staircase, push out the front doors, vector 30 degrees northeast across the front lawn, cut around the snowy field, and cross Fourth Avenue.

Ten minutes later, I reach home.

"Mom? Dad?" I call out. The house is empty.

A brass light on the piano illuminates Chopin sheet music, taunting me. Tearing the music in half, I throw it into the trash.

On the kitchen counter beside a bowl of apples is a note: *Fresh powder. Home at 16:40. Smørbrød in the fridge.*

Crumpling the note in my fist, I storm through the glass double doors into the den.

I observe the impeccably tidy room—folk art displays, antique swords, books seamlessly straight on the shelves.

There is a leather Eames chair in the corner, two pine tables used as desks, and dozens of silver frames scattered among the shelves—photographs of me in Petra, Abu Simbel, Dubrovnik, Samarkand, Ürgenç; standing atop a medieval rampart at Calatrava;

dressed in a shimmering, corseted ball gown for a diplomatic gala in Stockholm. I reach for the nearest photograph—the Serengeti. My favorite trip we ever took.

In the foreground, brittle, yellow savanna is visible, crumbling in the sun. I am seated between my parents in the back of a battered blue Toyota, wearing a school uniform, and laughing.

Slipping from my grip, the frame clatters onto my father's desk.

I *miss* my former life.

I definitely *don't* miss my former life.

But how can this new life be hard too?

Would I really rather leave than stay?

I have to get out of here.

Cold air pierces my lungs.

I head north, away from the center of town.

Waterford *is* idyllic and charming. For the first time in years, I have friends again—so why am I vexed? Afraid I might never "get over it"? Might never stop being triggered? Never stop fearing threats when none exist?

Has my past eroded my ability to move forward?

The steady rhythm of my feet comforts me. I rehearse the series of numbers—calmly this time—as both a pacesetter and a distraction.

I turn east toward Charlotte's, halting at the base of Silver Canyon. Her driveway is ahead, though she'll still be at school.

But somebody else lives this way. I shouldn't, but curiosity overpowers judgment.

Impulsively, I divert at the fork, veering straight into a steep, rock-walled canyon.

Fluffy snowflakes fall lightly, blowing horizontal in Eagle Pass.

On one side of the canyon, steep granite fissures are laced with miniature waterfalls, frozen solid. On the other side, the woods taper into a rushing, turquoise ravine that eventually estuaries into Waterford Lake.

Eagle Pass narrows until the road becomes one lane masquerading as two. Soon, I switch to the shoulder on the north side of the road, etched into the mountain. Here, the icy road is scattered with blue granules; salt residue provides traction to run safely.

Occasionally, I hear a quiet muffled sound behind me, like a radiator purring. Twice, I turn around. But it's only the rushing water. I am simply hearing things—every movement a trigger, every sound a threat.

Shaking off the oppressive paranoia, I run harder.

As I ascend, snowflakes fall thicker and heavier; I relish the ethereal sensation.

I'm not cold; I'm wearing a fleece jacket, shorts, sports bra, sneakers, and my favorite Dale of Norway headband-and-mitten set my mother found in a box yesterday.

Reaching a bend in the road, I slow to a jog. The wind is picking up.

Tucking my necklace beneath my jacket, I stop to get my bearings. Although the steep incline slowed my pace, I've still run far.

Down the canyon, I see Waterford. Straining my eyes, I calculate the distance home—about seven kilometers. I glance at my watch. Though barely four o'clock, it's November; the light is already sinking below the horizon.

One thing I have learned about Waterford—positioned in a high alpine valley—darkness falls quickly and with it, the bitter cold of night.

If I run double pace downhill, I'll return a few minutes after dark. My parents won't have to worry long—

Abruptly, a high-pitched sound reverberates between the canyon walls.

I go rigid.

Alarmed, I look over to see a car skidding around the bend.

Its horn blazes. The tires shred the ice. I see a blur of olive green.

Somewhere in my subconscious I register that this car is careening across the road—hurtling uncontrollably—at me.

I dive.

CHAPTER 14

Although the packed snowbank is cold, my body feels hot and afraid.

Ten meters away, in the center of the road, is an olive-green Land Rover Defender. The door swings open. A familiar, ruggedly handsome figure emerges.

Reckless. Stupid. What was I thinking?

Aksel is wearing a down sweater and boots. His face is tanned and beautiful, his emerald green eyes are wide and brilliant, and he is racing toward me.

I try to stand; instead, I keep sinking back into the snowdrift I impaled as I dove out of the way.

In seconds, he reaches me.

"I'm fine!" I snap, covering my embarrassment.

"Why were you standing in the middle of the road? Trying to get yourself killed?" Reaching for my right arm, he lifts me effortlessly out of the snowbank and sets me on my feet. "Are you lost?"

Lost? I shake off his hand. "No!"

His stoic demeanor is shattered. He seems agitated, flustered.

I stare up at him, trying to ignore the blistering heat rising on the back of my neck. My stomach twists. Seeing Aksel only exacerbates my conflicted feelings about Waterford.

"This time, I *did* nearly hit you," he seethes.

"So don't drive so fast," I fire back, unnecessarily combative.

His hostile eyes bore into mine. "I wasn't going too fast!"

Aksel circles the Defender and steps onto the running board to inspect the ski rack, which is screwed into the white aluminum top. The rack wouldn't have unbolted or shifted when the car braked, which means Aksel isn't actually inspecting it; he is looking for an alternative to talking to me.

Stepping off the board, he glances down the canyon toward Waterford before bringing his eyes back to mine.

My impulse to be afraid is overshadowed by the peculiar sensation occurring in my stomach when his eyes roam over me. I try to avoid his gaze, but with nowhere else to look, my eyes return to his brooding face.

"What are you doing up here?" Aksel asks.

"Running."

His eyes smolder with agitation and accusation. "Running—in the steepest canyon in Waterford—in the middle of a snowstorm?"

I gesture at the dusting of flakes. "This is hardly a snowstorm."

"It will be," Aksel corrects me. "No one can see you running in the daylight, let alone when it's snowing." His eyes narrow. "You *do* know where you are, right?"

"Eagle Pass," I say.

Aksel closes the distance between us. He is so close I can see flecks of turquoise in his otherwise green eyes. He looks both dismayed and bewildered.

"What are you doing here?" he repeats in a quiet, determined voice.

"*Running*," I restate slowly, as if he hadn't heard me.

"I mean, in Waterford."

"I live here now. And you won't have to keep trying so hard to avoid me because I doubt I'll be here long!"

Is it that obvious I don't belong in Waterford? Don't fit in?

Flustered, I bend down to tighten the frozen laces on my shoes, which have hardened into icy straws. When I stand, Aksel hasn't moved; his eyes remain trained on me.

His stony gaze is unreadable, yet that same familiarity ripples through me again.

I'm certain of it now. Aksel *is* hiding something.

Although I was warm while running, my jacket is damp from snow and sweat. Standing still, the cold creeps into my limbs.

Averting my eyes from his face, I look down the steep canyon. Thick snowfall has decreased visibility; I can barely see the shimmering lights of Waterford sparkling in the V between the mountains.

Aksel doesn't relax his stiff posture. If anything, he seems more tense, watching me uneasily, as if *I* somehow make *him* nervous.

My stomach remains knotted in a confused mess. *Why* did I run up Eagle Pass?

What exactly did I intend to do? See his house? See *him*?

Trying to stop the blush rising to my cheeks, I turn away from Aksel's antagonistic stare. "I should get home."

Wind gusts sweep through the canyon, chilling my bare legs.

"I'll drive you," he says abruptly, nodding toward the Defender. "It's cold and getting dark. This road becomes a sheet of ice in these storms."

The urgency in his voice unsettles me. With his feet planted firmly on the ground, Aksel resembles a bronze statue, towering above me.

Before I can respond, the quiet snowfall becomes a soft rumbling.

Aksel swivels his head toward the steep rock wall of granite, watching it quizzically. Then his face darkens.

The faint rumbling swells, echoing through the canyon in cracked groans.

I step closer to him. "What is—"

Suddenly, Aksel's hand fastens around mine. Shocked, I look at him.

"IN—NOW!" he commands.

Instinctively, I obey.

I run to the Defender. Apparently, I'm not fast enough because Aksel slips his arm around my waist and nearly throws me into the passenger seat.

"Cover your head," Aksel warns.

I wrap my forearms across my head. The rumble magnifies.

Aksel flips the ignition and shifts the Defender into first.

The jagged canyon wall hurls toward us as Aksel juts his arm before me like a protective steel pipe and rams the Defender into the mountainside.

CHAPTER 15

Stars erupt across my vision. My forehead pounds.

I can smell pine and leather. Someone is shaking me gently.

Disoriented, I open my eyes. I remember a *thud* . . . a deafening rumble . . . his arm across my chest . . . I lay my head back. *Aksel* is shaking me. "Are you—"

"I'm fine," I murmur. "You?"

"Yeah," he answers, sounding relieved.

I blink, adjusting my eyes. It is dark except for the piercing beam of a flashlight in Aksel's hand. In the artificial light, I observe the Defender's interior: leather seats and a grooved rubber floor are scattered with skis, boots, and miscellaneous alpine wilderness equipment.

To my right, the window is intact, but a hairline fracture bisects the glass; centimeters away is granite. To my left, snow is packed against Aksel's window. The windshield, the rear window—white.

I stare up through the sunroof, relieved to see it isn't covered in snow too.

Fuzzy noise fills the car. Aksel checks the stations on a small CB radio cradled in his palm. Nothing but static.

The right side of my forehead is tender. It stings when I touch it. Wincing under my breath, I look down at my wet fingertips. *Seriously?*

"You're bleeding," Aksel says sharply, looking over at me. "Let me see."

"It's a scrape," I object, wiping my fingertips on my shorts.

Aksel sets aside the radio, extends his forearm across my lap, and opens the glove compartment. With his right sleeve pushed up, I can see his arm, hard and strong. It hovers above my leg, inches from my bare thigh.

He takes out a metal case with a red cross on it and puts it in his lap. Leaning forward he snaps the glove compartment shut; his forearm brushes against my skin, and I suck in sharply.

"If you'll turn toward me, I can check it out." His voice is composed, courteous. Reluctantly, I face him. Up close, I can see every detail of his face: his chiseled bone structure, his clear skin, flushing in the cold.

Readjusting the flashlight, Aksel touches his finger gingerly to my forehead. His eyelashes flicker over his crystalline eyes as he inspects the cut.

"A nice gash to replace your bruise." He glances at my thigh where only a faded mustard residue remains. "I don't think you'll need stitches," he assures me in a deep voice.

"You can tell?"

"I can guess"—he pauses—"I watched my dad stitch up half my friends on our kitchen counter."

"What kind of doctor is he?"

"Neurosurgeon," he says softly.

I try to take normal breaths. However, with Aksel's hand on my skin, every nerve in my face is kindled.

My father has always taught me to control my heart rate—lower my beats per minute, breathe in slowly, hold, exhale—but lowering my heart rate while sitting alone in a car with Aksel Fredricksen is like trying to snorkel in a typhoon.

Aksel digs into the first aid kit and removes a cloth, bandage, alcohol swabs, and disinfectant cream. When he looks back at me, I blush all over again.

"If you keep still, I'll clean it. It might sting." His voice is sultry in the confined space.

Now, Aksel's hand is on my face again, checking the wound; the other is reaching onto the floor of the passenger seat to grab a water bottle. His arm brushes my leg again. My heart skips a beat. Was that intentional? No, of course not. Aksel is like a military medic in the field—all business.

"Will I have a scar?" I ask.

"Do you want a scar?"

"Undecided."

He eyes my blond braid draping over my shoulder. "If you end up with one, you'll resemble a Viking warrior."

"Shieldmaiden," I say.

"Next Halloween," he says with a slight smile. His teeth are even and straight; when the corners of his flawless lips turn upward, my stomach does a little flip. "But no," he murmurs, looking closely, "I don't think you'll have a scar."

He unscrews the lid to the water bottle and pours a few drops onto the cloth.

"So . . . how exactly are we wedged underneath Eagle Peak?" I ask, attempting to distract myself from the feeling of Aksel's fingers on my face.

He brushes hair off my temple, sending tingles down the side of my cheek.

"Avalanches are unpredictable," he says in a steady, restrained voice, as if he doesn't want to frighten me. He opens the cellophane around the bandage with a PenBlade.

"We didn't have time to drive away, because you can never tell how wide they are, and those woods descend into a sheer ravine two hundred feet down. I figured the best option was to get the Defender under Eagle Peak"—he points upward, toward a tapered shaft of grayish light—"and hope the avalanche would pass over us."

Wetting the cloth, he presses it against my face. His motion is smooth and gentle and only takes a second, then he wipes my skin with the alcohol swab.

I eye the avalanche surrounding us like we're a tiny village in a massive fjord.

"And this snowpack is stable?" I continue, keeping my breath steady.

"Precarious," he surmises, "but stable. Yes."

Tossing the swab into a small plastic bag, he takes the cream and squeezes a dollop onto his finger, spreading it on my temple. I find myself watching his lips more than his eyes.

"How long will we be here?" I ask. "Can we call someone—a tow truck? Your parents? My parents?"

Reaching into his pocket, Aksel pulls out an iPhone. "You can try, but there's no coverage in this section of the canyon."

I glance at it. Zero bars. Of course.

"The snowpack should hold as long as the wind doesn't shift," Aksel explains casually. "Our best option is to ride it out until the plow comes through in a few hours."

"*Hours?*" I exclaim. "Won't anyone else drive up here beforehand?"

Aksel averts his eyes, focusing on the medical kit.

"Unlikely," he says under his breath.

"Don't you live up here? It can't be more than a few kilometers. Can't we walk—"

"In a blizzard?" He looks at me incredulously.

I didn't leave a note—my parents have no idea where I am.

I reach my arms to the sunroof and slide it open; loose snow falls onto the console.

"What are you doing?" Aksel's emerald eyes spark.

"Leaving before the storm gets worse," I answer. "I can hear it coming. I have twenty minutes. I'll sprint—"

He pushes the sunroof closed with one hand. "You can't just leave."

"My parents don't know where I am!" I protest. "I have to get home!"

I can't do this to them . . .

They'll think . . .

Rising to my knees, I move to open the sunroof a second time; however, two strong hands grip my waist, pull me down, and swiftly maneuver me into my seat. Aksel's hand trails up my waist around my back—his touch sends an electric current up my spine.

He is leaning over the console with his arm in front of my stomach, blocking me.

Not threateningly—protectively.

"It's a blizzard, Sophia," he implores. "Frostbite. Disorientation—"

"I know!" I exhale angrily. "I know. But I can't be stuck here all night!"

My heart thumps wildly in my chest.

Aksel is smart and skilled—confident—out here in the wilderness. So am I.

We're in a precarious shelter, and *my* panic is concerning him. I have to calm down.

Aksel eyes me warily. "I know it may not seem like it, but we *are* safe here. We'll wait out the storm. Then the plow will arrive and you can go home."

Slumping into my seat, I cross my arms, irritated.

"Sophia, you're still bleeding," he says. "Can I finish?"

Embarrassed, I look over at him and nod.

Aksel tears off a piece of gauze, opens the bandage, and applies it to the wound. A few minutes later, he gathers the empty packages and soiled cloth and places them behind his seat.

I touch my forehead, clean and dry around the bandage.

Covered in snow on three sides, and with a rock wall on the fourth, I'm somehow not too cold. Despite the lack of heat, at least the frigid wind is blocked—*igloo physics*, my father would call it.

Aksel doesn't stop moving. Tucking the radio into his pocket, he now opens the sunroof.

I sit upright. "I'm coming with you—"

"I'll be right back," Aksel says calmly. "I'm just checking things out."

For a moment, his intense green eyes linger on mine, but then he looks away and hoists himself through the sunroof.

To my astonishment, he begins scaling the rock wall, using the tiny nooks and crevices in the stone to secure himself to the granite.

Within minutes, he's free soloed to a triangular declivity

halfway up Eagle Peak. Here he looks around, apparently trying to get a read on our predicament.

If someone drives up Eagle Pass how will they know we are here?

I step into the back seat. Rummaging around through the outdoor gear—a Pendleton blanket, a duffel bag with some clothes, swim fins—I spot a backcountry mountaineering probe and a hunting vest.

Reaching to the floor beneath the driver's seat, I grab the Pen-Blade from the medical kit. I slice the bottom off the vest, creating one long strip of fluorescent orange. I hook the strip onto the probe and knot it.

I go up through the sunroof in time to see Aksel descend the wall lithely.

Soon enough, he is back on the roof.

Shaking snow from his tousled hair, he pulls the collar of his sweater taut around his neck and blows into his hands. His breath, heavier now, causes his defined chest to heave in and out under his sweater.

"Are we going to climb out?" I ask.

"Let's hope we don't have to. That upper wall is ten meters of ice."

"But it's a climbing wall, right?" I point at the anchors drilled deep into the granite.

He looks at me, perplexed. "In *summer*."

"You *just* climbed it," I counter.

"The bottom half. And I've been climbing Eagle Peak since I was ten."

"I climb," I scoff. "If that's what you're worried about."

"It's a vicious storm; there isn't another shelter even if you *can* climb out. Actually, I'm more worried about the plow driving straight into us."

I switch the probe to my right hand and double-check the knot.

"Me too," I say. Then I launch the probe as high as I can—up and over the snowpack—like a javelin. I imagine that if it landed properly on the other side, it resembles a gravestone.

And if it didn't? At least I tried.

When I look back at Aksel, his mouth curls upward in a way that makes me feel slightly dizzy.

"Do you have any spare clothes?" I ask, knowing the answer. "I need to change."

Aksel looks startled. "Sorry?"

Standing on the roof, I am very aware of how cold I am. The snow clinging to my clothes has melted, and although my shorts are still dry, my jacket is not. My feet are numb inside my frozen shoes, and even with my mittens, my fingers resemble purple icicles.

"Hypothermia," I explain. "I need dry—"

"You're wet?" Aksel looks at my damp jacket, then scans my bare, goose-bump-covered legs from my thighs to my ankles. "Why didn't you ask earlier?"

We swing down through the roof and drop onto our seats.

Without waiting for an answer, Aksel climbs into the back seat and hands me the thick wool blanket. It is a red tartan pattern and smells of cedar and campfire smoke. After rifling through his duffel, he assembles a pile of clothes. Then he pulls off his sweater.

He is wearing a waffle knit Henley underneath it, and I see a T-shirt underneath that.

As he hands over the pile, his fingers graze mine, igniting flames across my skin.

"I'll wait up top," he says brusquely, avoiding eye contact.

Alone in the Defender I unzip my jacket with stiff fingers and shimmy out of it. I pull on the undershirt Aksel gave me, and his sweater. It is warm from his body heat and soothing to my skin. Plus, it smells like him: pine and leather and sandalwood.

Above me, Aksel paces the roof. I ease my numb feet out of my shoes, peel off my wet socks, and slide my feet into his thick wool ski socks.

I flip the rearview mirror down. Attempting to fix my hair, I run my fingers through my braid, but it's so tangled I simply brush it back from my face and readjust my headband over my ears.

Opening the sunroof, I say, "I'm done." My voice comes out squeaky and high-pitched. I sit back and wait for Aksel to hop down.

"Warmer now?" Aksel asks, checking out my new attire.

My skin burns under his gaze. "Much," I answer. "Thank you."

Aksel drums the steering wheel with his fingers, pausing intermittently to check the old radio. Still nothing but static. Scowling, he throws it back onto the dashboard.

A gauzy shaft of light filters down on us from above, suffusing a dim glow over this temporary cavern.

Trying to keep my eyes from darting back to Aksel every few seconds, I unfold my hands from behind my knees and stretch them out, pretending to be interested in the shape of my knuckles.

"In the forest . . . ," Aksel says abruptly, propping his knee against the wheel. He leans against the window. "With that grizzly, you seemed to"—he pauses, as if deliberating—"know quite a bit about guns. Why?"

I tug on the sleeves of the sweater. *His* sweater.

"I know a little." Focusing on his eyes, I shrug. "I have a Belgian FN 5-7. It saved my life."

"You've been attacked by a grizzly before?" Aksel's voice catches between caution and concern.

I drag my forefinger along the seam of my shorts. *Allow them to come*, I hear my mother's voice in my head. But I still fight it—*If you let one in, you let them all.*

"We were living in Kenya." I exhale. "On the border, near Sudan. A perk of school in East Africa—you go on game rides for field trips. This one time, we were pretty far into the reserve. I was watching an antelope herd through my binoculars when I saw an army truck rumbling toward us through the savanna. I told our guide, Katu, who looked through his own binoculars. Immediately, he ordered our driver off the road into the dry brush. Our driver skidded into a ditch. Nearly rolling, he drove back up the bank as the truck swerved ahead, blockading our route. We had to stop.

"Four army rebels, wearing old soldier fatigues, filed out of the truck's canvas doors. Firing their Kalashnikovs into the air, they ordered us off the Land Cruiser. Katu calmly told us to obey, so we climbed down and put our hands in the air.

"They searched us roughly. When one groped my friend Anika, her brother Peter shouted at him. The rebel hit Peter so hard with his rifle barrel, Peter staggered into the bumper, bleeding from his ear.

"After gathering our cash and valuables, the commander lifted his Kalashnikov and shot our driver. He crumpled onto the dirt, dead. Katu aimed his hunting rifle at the rebels, shouting, '*Let them go! They're children!*'

"Samuel, our spotter, had jumped into the driver's seat and

throttled into first . . . and suddenly, like that"—I snap my fingers—"the commander shot Samuel too."

"'Stay back!' Katu ordered, trying to stand in front of all seven of us at once. When the commander pointed his AK at Peter, Katu finally pulled the trigger . . . I'll never forget that sound . . . *click!*

"Katu's ammunition had jammed in the chamber. He looked over at me—like he *knew.* I reached into my boot, pulled out my 5-7, and fired twice. The commander dropped to the ground. A rebel shot Katu, so I shot him too, a double tap into his stomach . . .

"'Go! Go! Go!' Katu yelled. Bleeding, he knelt like a sentry in the back of the truck, firing to cover our escape . . . A kilometer out, I used my belt to tourniquet Katu's leg. Samuel was barely alive. I plugged the artery in his neck with my fingers. Peter drove, blood seeping from his ruptured eardrum the whole way.

"My parents met us at Kenyatta National Hospital. A few hours later I was in Johannesburg. I never saw Katu, Peter, or Samuel again . . ."

Aksel watches me intently.

I look down at my fists, clenched to prevent the shaking.

"Turns out, they weren't rebel Sudanese soldiers looking for quick cash . . . so that was the first time I saw them face-to-face." I keep my voice from shaking now too.

"Saw who?" Aksel asks tentatively.

Let the memories happen so they cannot control you.

Exhaling, I look at Aksel. "Terrorists."

CHAPTER 16

"Who *are* you?" Aksel says with a low whistle.

His hand hasn't moved from the gearshift, centimeters from my bare leg; no, less than centimeters, millimeters. Aksel's face has transformed—his shield of animosity or indifference, or whatever it was between us, has been stripped away.

"You saved them," he states.

"Not our driver," I say quietly.

Aksel shakes his head. "I'm sorry. I shouldn't have asked—"

"No, it's okay. I should talk about it. It's healthy possibly?"

Aksel's jaw is set firmly and his expression is stoic, but his vibrant eyes watch me earnestly. My heart turns inside my chest.

Aksel drops his knee from the steering wheel and angles his body toward mine.

I feel his presence like electricity—pulsating currents pass from Aksel's eyes into my skin, rippling through my nervous system and causing the hairs on my arms to stand on end.

"I haven't been *avoiding* you—not the way you think."

"It's fine." I shake my head, embarrassed I'd said it aloud earlier. "You don't have to explain why you don't like me, or whatever. I did pull a knife on you . . ."

An elusive smile passes his lips. "That's what you think?"

All of a sudden, the Defender, surrounded by snow and ice, feels incredibly hot, like I am starting to sweat when I should be freezing.

"It's the truth, isn't it?" I say defensively.

Aksel appraises me with a steady, unwavering gaze. His eyes feel like they are boring right through me, trying to connect something.

Apparently, our polite interlude is over.

His full lips part over straight white teeth. He looks perplexed. "Yeah, but this has nothing to do with whether or not I . . . like you."

"What other reason is there?"

Readjusting the flashlight, he drapes his left hand on the wheel as if he needs a place to put it. He watches me discerningly, carefully arranging his words. "I wondered why you came to Waterford. Not a lot of people from abroad move here."

"So because I'm new you think I don't belong here and expect me not to be confused, or wonder about whatever it is you're hiding—"

"Hiding?" he interjects. His hand rattles the gearshift, startling me.

But he releases his fingers, stretching them out.

He seems genuinely confused. "I thought that's why . . . I thought you knew . . ."

"Knew what?"

His brow is tight with frustration, like he expects me to admit something, say something. But *what*?

I inspect him from beneath my lashes, suddenly self-conscious of my wet, tangled hair and bandaged forehead.

All this time I've been wondering who *Aksel* is. Has he been wondering the same about me? Disjointed thoughts thread together, weaving into a recognition. Aksel's scrutinizing looks aren't because *he* is hiding something, but because he thinks *I* am? Forcing air into my lungs, I start talking rapidly, deliberately. "In the hallway, I saw it in your eyes, but I didn't realize . . ." I stare over at Aksel, deciphering my tangled thoughts.

"You recognized me," I conclude, "didn't you?"

Aksel's gaze is penetrating. I wish I could read his severe expression, but he breathes in through his nose, calming himself, concealing emotion.

I recall every place I've been recently: Tashkent, Vienna, Tunis . . . I push my memory to the brink: a night in Beirut, two days in Rabat, a weekend in Helsinki—I can't conjure a memory of Aksel.

"We met before I moved to Waterford?" I ask.

Aksel's vivid eyes don't leave mine. "Not exactly." He props his arm on the back of my headrest.

"So, we *haven't* met?"

Aksel's face smolders underneath an impassive expression, as if he's pleading with me to get it.

Aksel shakes his head. "You don't remember?"

"No," I say, "and I remember things—faces."

He eyes me guardedly. "So do I," he says quietly, "and I remember yours."

"From where?" I practically shout.

His eyes pierce mine. It seems like a battle is raging within him, like a part of him wants to answer and another part of him doesn't—I can't tell which will win out.

He seems to be constructing a response.

"I saw you a little over eighteen months ago," Aksel finally discloses, "at the US Embassy. In Berlin."

CHAPTER 17

Berlin.

Everything around me spins. My heart beats like a bass drum; blood throbs in my ears.

Anxiety and dread pulse inside me, radiating through my veins, from my heart to my fingertips.

Foggy images shift into focus.

Closing my eyes, I fight to block them: *Fluorescent light . . . people in suits . . . a microphone . . . a typewriter . . .*

I desperately want to recall seeing Aksel: where he was and what he was doing, but remembering that day will sweep me up in a tsunami of memories I won't survive.

"Wh-what were you doing there?" I stammer. "When did you see me? How?"

Earlier, curiosity eclipsed my intuition. Now, my instincts take over.

My world is simple: someone is either a threat, or not.

I must assess Aksel, immediately. He is left-handed. If I want to hurt him, I have to go for his right side. I examine the sunroof. Can I escape? I reach inside the tiny key pouch in the lining of my shorts and slide my forefinger around my Ladybug.

With my thumb, I discreetly unfold the blade from the handle and lock it into place.

Aksel notices my movements. He leans subtly away from me, distancing himself; is he assessing me too?

The crevasse between us is both widening and narrowing at once.

"Where did you see me?" I demand.

He eyes me hesitantly. "Outside the Bubble."

The Bubble.

Such an innocent name. Soundproofed in every way, a bubble is the only unmonitored location inside an embassy for a secure conversation. It often does resemble a bubble; the walls are made up of rippling waves of partially transparent glass; the room usually contains only a table, several chairs, and, occasionally, a typewriter.

"I . . . I don't understand," I falter. "What were *you* doing there?"

The muscles across Aksel's shoulders flex. "I was visiting relatives in Germany when I got an invitation to meet with an official at the embassy." He drags a hand through his hair. "So, I went."

I shake my head. "I didn't see you—I would have remembered . . ." *Somebody who looked like you*, I refrain from saying.

"Look, maybe you didn't see me," he finally says. "But I saw you, and I never forgot."

Now, I understand.

I didn't recognize Aksel—I recognized *Aksel recognizing me*.

Aksel sits forward, agitated. His high cheekbones and furrowed brow don't conceal his frustration.

"At first, you just looked familiar," he explains, "but you said you had just moved here, so I brushed it off. Then at school, it was something about your profile, the fluorescent lights, I *knew* I'd seen you before. When you asked me in class where I was born"—he shrugs—"I remembered instantly."

I know there is more—much more—but memories are thundering toward me and I have to focus. I can't be triggered. Not here. Not now. Not with Aksel.

I put my palms against my thighs, grinding my teeth. I have to block it. I have to make it stop.

Remembering Berlin is like remembering Tunisia; if I let that memory in, I let them all in.

I fold the knife blade back into its handle but keep holding it tight.

For several minutes we sit in heady silence.

Then, a deep rumbling sounds outside our cave, breaking it.

A fresh speckling of snowflakes dots the windshield.

Our eyes lock.

"*Now* we climb?" I ask.

For the first time, Aksel looks worried.

Aksel opens the sunroof and swiftly hoists himself through it. "Wait here," he mutters.

I don't wait.

Though my shoelaces are a frozen, tangled knot, I manage to slide my sneakers halfway on. Aksel has scaled the wall four meters before I scramble onto the roof.

As soon as I am out of the Defender, my teeth start to chatter.

Swirling gusts of wind pile snow onto our tomb.

"The w-w-winds changed?" I call up to him.

Aksel leaps backward and lands on the hood of the car.

He scowls. "If the drift blows through the snowbank it will collapse and—"

"Bury us," I finish.

Placing his hand on my back, he urges me inside.

I take my sneakers off and pound the shoes harshly on the dashboard to loosen the laces.

"Here." Aksel takes one shoe and unlaces it. With quick even movements, he guides my foot into it and ties the laces. He then does the same with the other.

When he finishes, he pulls the ski socks up over my calves as high as they can go; when his fingers touch my bare calves, a wave of heat passes from him to me.

Kneeling in front of me, with the flashlight propped on the dashboard, shining on his face, I can see how within the green of his eyes are flecks of gold, azure, and cerulean all blending together, pure and calming, like the Ionian Sea at sunrise.

Aksel takes my hands in his, forming a heated cocoon. His fingers are thick and muscular, calloused along the edges. He must rock climb—often. I should have noticed earlier.

"You're an icicle," he remarks, massaging my palms to keep the blood flowing.

"You're a furnace," I say.

Chuckling, Aksel releases my hands and crawls into the back of the Defender. Rummaging around the gear, he retrieves a rope and tucks it into his backcountry pack; he attaches the snowshoes to the pack and pulls the straps over his shoulders.

As we exit, I look over my shoulder, certain we missed something. Instinctively, I stretch between the seats, grab a solitary avalanche flare, and stuff it into my woolly sock.

Back on the roof, Aksel wraps the rope in a loose ring between his shoulder and hand; it slides smoothly along his palm.

"We'll go up through the middle," he tells me. "It's the easiest route—"

"But that's only because of the slope," I interrupt. "We'd have to climb to the top to get out, and you said that top half is all ice. If we take this route"—I point over Aksel's shoulder—"we'll reach that ledge sooner. It's flush with the top of the snowpack; we can traverse to the far side and then climb down, right?"

Aksel makes a smaller loop, runs the end through it, then makes a second loop and attaches it to the first.

He glances between me and Eagle Peak, a hint of a smile on his face. "Right."

"Though we'll have to stay—"

"Together," Aksel finishes.

He lowers the rope to my knees. I look down to see what he's been tying. A harness. Of course.

Uncertain, I step into it.

His strong hands slide the harness around my waist, tightening the rope. I can feel his broad chest hovering over my back as he checks the knot.

Goose bumps rise up my spine.

"How's that fit?" His breath tingles the skin on the back of my neck. His hand skims over the knot, checking it. My heart races.

"Good," I say in a dazed voice. "Where's your rope?"

"Here." Aksel points at the tail end of the rope.

"No way," I say furiously, struggling out of the harness. "You're not climbing attached to me—"

Aksel pulls the rope taut and knots it so tightly around my waist it nearly cuts off my circulation. "You're wearing the rope," he says in a low voice. His hand lingers on my arm, on the skin of my wrist between my shirt and the gloves.

Our breath rises up in a misty vapor from our mouths before vanishing into the air.

"Like you said, we have to stay connected. Besides, unattached, I have no way of lifting you."

"You're not," I struggle to say the words, "*lifting* me."

Aksel runs his fingers through the rope, catching the end. His eyes settle onto mine, bright and daring. "I'm also not letting you fall."

As he secures his own harness, the rope moves swiftly through his fingers like fishing line. His actions are cool. Natural. Confident.

Gathering my hair back into a loose bun, I follow him down onto the hood.

Aksel walks over to the granite wall. "Stay close enough to see my route—"

"I'll be fine," I say. "It's easier going up than coming down, right?"

Aksel tilts his head; the corner of his mouth twitches. Then his calloused fingers roam over the rock and slide into a fissure high above his head, and he begins to climb.

Aksel ascends the wall methodically. With the abrasive wind and snow, it's slow progress. When he reaches five meters, I tuck my mittens into my shorts and blow on my hands.

My *turn*. Reaching up, I slide my fingers into a jagged crevice, and follow.

After a few treacherous minutes, I look down—the Defender is blanketed in snow.

Funneled in the cavern, snow whistles around me like a whirlpool, making it difficult to secure my fingers around the protrusions and cracks in the icy wall.

Spiraling gusts lash my cheeks. Snow pelts my face. Temporarily blinded, I fumble for a split in the rock, using my feet to propel me upward, but I find nothing.

Keeping my toes taut in the crevices, I stretch my arm.

I reach for a crag, even a narrow cleft.

Desperately, I claw at the rock.

Slipping, my fingertips slide along the smooth granite surface—

Got it.

I exhale.

Sliding my thumb securely into a chink, I reposition and continue.

But as I pass the triangular declivity, I hear a shrill *screeeeeech*!

I'm hit by a sheet of sliding snowpack. My body is knocked off the wall.

I'm falling . . .

The harness fastens around me like a snare. I'm suspended in midair. The rope swings, propelling me toward the granite.

I regrip onto the rock.

Adrenaline courses through my veins and I continue my ascent. Seconds later, I near the ledge.

Through the blurry white mass of snow and wind, Aksel's silhouette emerges.

Keeping both feet propped against the rock, anchoring himself, Aksel hauls the rope adeptly toward him, one hand smoothly over the other. He's knotted the end around a protrusion of granite—leveraging it to stabilize the rope.

As I summit, Aksel lunges for me, pulling me onto the ledge. His chest heaves as he drags me even farther back.

Clamping his arm around my waist, Aksel holds me against his side in a steel grasp as we scramble off the ledge and onto the unstable ridge cresting the snowpack.

Suddenly, a gust of wind lashes our backs.

Aksel's arms lock behind my spine. Together we dive. We slide down the snowpack, landing in a tangled, rolling motion—then all of a sudden, I am lying on top of him, and then he is on top of me and then we are still.

Crack!

I whip my head to the right to see the ridge splinter loose.

In a rumbling wave, the entire snowpack collapses, burying the Defender.

When I look back at Aksel, his eyes are trained on me. Even in the opaque white of the storm, I can see every shade of green in his eyes. Flawless skin. Full lips. Arms so sculpted they look like they were carved from granite too.

In a low, husky voice in my ear, Aksel says, "Easy, right?"

CHAPTER 18

I am intently aware of Aksel's arms knotted behind me, blocking my back from the ice and snow; his upper body shielding me from the wind. Aksel's eyes move from my eyes to my lips.

An unfamiliar excitement ripples across my chest.

Abruptly, Aksel rolls off me. Sliding his hands from my back to my wrists, he lifts me to my feet.

"Keep moving," he warns. "We have to keep our heart rates up."

Bending down, he brushes the snow off my numb, quivering legs. "Who wears shorts running in twenty-degree weather?"

"It wasn't this cold when I left," I answer through chattering teeth.

He rubs my arms and shoulders as I burrow against his warm chest.

"There's this tool called a weather app," Aksel remarks in a raspy voice. "You should check it before you go out running."

I half shiver, half laugh. "Weather prediction is only fifty-seven percent accurate at this elevation."

"Eagle Pass motto: Be prepared."

"Hepworth motto: Preparation is one percent physical, ninety-nine percent mental."

"Fredricksen motto: There's no such thing as bad weather, just bad clothing."

"You stole that from the Danes," I say.

He grins. "But they stole it from the Germans."

We are standing on a sheet of snow and ice. Around us everything is being pounded by the blizzard. Aksel's eyes follow mine in the direction of the ravine. "You didn't think we'd make it, Sophia?"

Something about the way he says my name catches me off guard. I feel a flutter in my chest, right below my throat.

I shiver. "Who said we've made it?"

It's the first time I hear Aksel laugh. It is deep and sultry, and before I know it, I'm laughing too, although there is a blizzard whirling around us and now we have no protection; we might as well be on an iceberg adrift in the Arctic.

A low humming in the distance causes our laughter to taper off.

Aksel snaps his head left.

I reach into my sock, retrieve the avalanche flare gun, and fire it into the air.

"You go," I say. "I'll wait."

Aksel looks at me, a surprised expression on his face. Then he untethers the snowshoes, throws them down, and clicks in. Above us, a glowing orange ember rises in the sky and explodes in a blast of light.

Barreling through the heavy snowfall, Aksel leaps down the drift and glides across the snow, disappearing into whiteness.

After several long minutes, I contemplate the odds that Aksel has left me here to icicle. Then he emerges with his cheeks flushed and his eyes bright. "You look surprised to see me."

"I thought perhaps you'd left me."

His eyebrows lift in astonishment. "*Here?*"

I shrug. "I am partially responsible for destroying your car."

Aksel smiles broadly, motioning at the massive avalanche. "A little snow can't hurt a Defender."

Behind Aksel's back, two fluorescent pearls of light round the bend of the canyon, illuminating the sparkling snow and casting a light on Aksel's silhouette.

Somewhere between relief and euphoria, I step toward the snowplow and sink into the drift.

"Hey, easy," Aksel says. Reaching one hand behind my back, Aksel hooks the other beneath my knees and draws me into his arms.

"I can walk!" I protest, half-hearted.

"Really?" He points at the loose powder and single pair of snowshoes, "How?"

"I don't know . . . I . . . okay, fine," I relent, clasping my arms around his neck.

He secures his strong arms around my waist. Whispering into my ear, his lips send tremors across my skin. "You're sure you'll let me lift you?"

"Yes," I murmur, slightly dizzy.

Gallantly carrying me across the snow doesn't slow Aksel down. I am cognizant of every part of Aksel's body touching mine: his forearms looped beneath my bare legs, his warm, broad chest against the side of my hip.

I'm frozen, yet blood seems to pulse through every vein of my body in hammering thuds, as if my body is on fire.

Inside the plow truck, I warm my hands at the vent. The hot air thaws my limbs; although my toes sting, pain is good. *No frostbite.*

The driver begins plowing uphill. "Smart to get under Eagle

Peak," he compliments Aksel. "You're lucky to have walked away so easily from an avalanche that big."

Aksel catches my eye—*Easily?*

"I would have reached you sooner had I not towed another driver out first." The driver grunts over the rustic country music. "I had to convince him to let me. He seemed more upset I'd found him than pleased I'd offered to help."

"Who?" Aksel asks the driver casually. With the heater blaring, I'm finally warm.

"Some tourist driving with no chains," he scoffs. "I told him he couldn't access the ski resort from Eagle Pass, that most of it was private land. He didn't seem to care . . ."

Aksel glances furtively in my direction. In the cramped cab, our bodies are pressed close together. Aksel's thigh is against mine and his arm draped across the back of my seat; therefore, I feel his body tense, ever so slightly.

"Sure you don't want me to drop you off now?" the plow driver eventually asks Aksel; we've reached a wide turnaround in the road. "It will be hours otherwise."

"Sophia first," Aksel answers, pointing at my bare thighs. "She's frozen."

The driver eyes me reprovingly. "You're not from around here either, are you?"

"No, sir." I smile.

Two Waterford Police cars are parked in my driveway.

"Here." Aksel offers his hand as I hop down from the truck.

Walking up to my house alongside Aksel, I am certain of only one thing—despite everything that's happened between us, I trust Aksel Fredricksen.

On the porch, we stand in strained, intimate silence. It's as though I finally know him, and he knows me, and yet we both know absolutely nothing about each other.

After tonight, will everything return to how it was? Or have we become friends?

His eyes surprise me—Remorse? Confusion? What is going on inside that impenetrable head of his?

It feels as though we are at a precipice. Tonight will either matter, or it won't. So why does it feel like the decision is up to neither of us?

Unsure what to say, I lower my lashes and bite my lip, trying to assemble my scrambled thoughts.

"You should know, Sophia . . ." Aksel's voice is earnest and imploring, and when he says my name I flush from my face to my chest.

He looks frustrated—like he wants to say something he shouldn't. His deep voice clings to my skin. "If things were different; if we'd met a year ago, or even six months ago, and I—"

The door opens. A bright light floods down on us.

I am swarmed. My mother reaches me first. "Sophia!" Hugging me, she ushers me into the house. "We've been so worried about—"

"Who are you?" my father demands, staring directly at Aksel like a hound.

Aksel doesn't flinch. In fact, he doesn't seem scared or intimidated. His calm, controlled demeanor reappears instantly.

"Aksel Fredricksen," he answers, shaking my father's hand.

"Dad," I say, attempting to defuse any escalation, and watching

Aksel out of the corner of my eye. "I went for a run up Eagle Pass near Charlotte's house, but it started to blizzard . . ."

While I talk, Aksel ducks out. I am surprised how disappointed his departure makes me feel; it's like I fell asleep in the Seychelles and woke up in Yakutsk.

My mother brushes damp hair off my face. "We're relieved you're home safely."

I point at the officers. *Police?* We never call police. But the officers seem unconcerned—as if this happens often.

"We assumed you were with your friends, waiting out the blizzard on Main Street," my mother explains—speaking the way we do in front of strangers. "Then an hour ago, Charlotte's mother called, saying you hadn't been seen since school, so she called the police."

As my father walks the officers out, my mother asks, "You must be hungry, sweetheart. Can I make you *soupe à l'oignon? Chocolat chaud?*"

I shake my head. I need to be alone, to unclog my head. "No, thanks."

My mother wraps her cardigan around my shoulders and touches a hand to my cheek. "Do you need help getting out of your wet things? Or I could draw you a hot bath?"

Her gentleness unnerves me. The point of choosing Waterford was so they wouldn't have to worry. So I would be safe.

"Mom," I begin, "I'm so sorry—"

"Sophia, stop." Her voice is haunted, as if she's known what I planned to say and has been dreading it. "Please, don't apologize," she whispers.

"But I should have at least left a note and—"

"I don't care. You're home. You're safe. That's what matters."

I know what she isn't saying, won't say. We don't talk about it.

I wiggle my aching toes. "Actually, a bath sounds perfect."

After undressing and tossing my chilled clothes into the hamper, I duck into the bathroom and turn on the faucet in the porcelain claw-foot tub. I place Aksel's sweater on top of the heat vent to dry.

Naked, I stand in front of my floor-length bathroom mirror and stare at my body. I look the same as I did this morning. My blond hair is long, sun-streaked, and tangled; my clear eyes are wide-set and blue; my face pink and flushed, with a spattering of freckles across the bridge of my nose; my limbs lean and toned.

But tonight, I feel different. Better. Stronger. Alive.

Shivering, I sit on the edge of the tub and wait for it to fill.

My father says functioning in bitter cold is an essential survival skill.

I've always been good at it. Aksel is better.

Aksel. His name sends little tingles across my clavicle and down my body.

Folding my arms over my chest, I slip into the porcelain tub, gasping at the heat, which burns my cold skin.

Looking across the bathroom at Aksel's sweater, I can't stop hearing his words in my head. What did he mean "if things were different"? Did he mean if I were different? If I weren't so afraid? If I didn't have so many things to hide?

I don't know why Aksel was in Berlin, or what it means for me in Waterford.

I only know I am conflicted in a way I have never experienced. After everything that happened tonight, after everything Aksel told me, I am more drawn to him than ever.

Staring at his sweater, I feel a hesitant excitement in my chest. Maybe I'm not ready to leave Waterford after all.

CHAPTER 19

Charlotte corners me outside class. "It's time you get a phone—"

"I'll ask my father again but—"

"You better spill!" she demands as the bell rings.

Throughout the morning, I try to stop watching every doorway out of the corner of my eye, wondering when Aksel will appear.

In English, there are a dozen ways to say "nervous"—anxious, apprehensive, excited. Anticipating seeing Aksel again, I feel each one.

How will I act? How *should* I act? Has anything changed between us? Or was it all an interim facade, a primitive survivalist response that temporarily bonded us?

However, Aksel is not at school.

I double-check my clothes: skinny denim jeans, sneakers, a Ralph Lauren sweater, and a scarf. I probably should have brushed my hair, but other than that I don't look that different. So why is everyone staring?

I sit down in the cafeteria beside Emma and unscrew the lid of my thermos.

"Come on," Emma groans. "Share."

I slide over the thermos of tomato bisque. "Sure."

"You were buried in an avalanche with Aksel Fredricksen!" Charlotte hisses, slipping into a nonexistent spot between me and Emma. She'd been taking a test during French; we haven't spoken until now. "How did *that* happen?" she demands.

I stare at her. "It was an accident!"

"I knew it!" Charlotte exclaims. "Something's been going on between—"

"Has not!"

"So, you were *accidentally* in Aksel's car, *accidentally* parked on the side of the road, and an avalanche *accidentally* landed on top of you?" Charlotte makes quotation marks with her fingers when she says the word "accidentally."

"Charlotte, avalanches don't *accidentally*"—I imitate her quotation marks—"happen."

"Actually," Emma interjects, "*accidentally* is exactly how avalanches happen."

Charlotte grins at me. "So you were *intentionally* in Aksel's car, parked—"

"How do you even know all this?" I ask her.

"Lydia told me," she answers dismissively.

"How does Lydia know?"

"Liam."

"How does Liam know?"

"Henry."

"And Henry knows because—"

"Aksel used Henry's truck to dig out his Defender this morning. Sounds like it was buried pretty deep. How did you survive? Did you have to cuddle naked—"

"Charlotte!" Emma scolds her, laughing.

"Look," I say, "I only ran up Eagle Pass because *you* said it was picturesque—"

"You *spontaneously* ran up the road where I *told* you only Aksel lives?" Charlotte asks victoriously.

Blushing, I hear my father's voice in my head—*Nothing is a coincidence*.

I tear off a piece of roll. "Why does it even matter? I didn't plan it."

"Right. You always run up dangerous, narrow canyons in blizzards?"

"No, I map out the most likely avalanche route and run there."

"Sophia, you spent the night with Aksel *in his car*."

"We weren't in the back seat!" I protest, flustered.

"It's not that, Sophia," Charlotte says dramatically, looking around the cafeteria. There seem to be two hundred sets of eyes on our table. "It's Aksel."

The bell rings. We gather our trash, put it into the bin, and leave the cafeteria together.

"What do you mean?"

"He didn't grow up here," Emma explains. "He spent winters here ski racing, and his family vacationed here often, but he attended some prep school back east. He was always super-focused and driven—"

"Athletic. Hot. Mysterious," adds Charlotte. "*That's* never changed."

"We wondered why he didn't move out here sooner . . . but after he transferred to Waterford permanently, well, besides Henry and a few others, he's mostly cut everyone off. It's just, well . . . he's been *different* . . . ever since . . ."

. . . *Different* . . . the emphatic way she says it causes the hairs on my arms to stand on end.

We've reached Krenshaw's class. The tardy bell rings.

"Since what?" I ask.

Charlotte switches her physics book from her left arm to her right.

Emma smooths her forefinger over her thumb. "It was all over the news. It was tragic . . . Henry's parents knew them best because he and Aksel raced together. But even my mom sobbed for days . . ."

"What happened?" I persist impatiently.

Charlotte purses her lips. In spite of the rowdy hall, it is eerily somber in the pocket of air between us. "His parents died, Sophia, two years ago in a plane crash."

"Are you staying?" Mason asks me several days later, on the way to gym.

I freeze in place. "Staying?"

"In town?" he says slowly. "It's a holiday?" He crinkles his forehead. "Sophia, you know about Thanksgiving, don't you?"

I break out laughing. "I *am* American, Mason!"

"Nah, you're Parisian." He grins.

"That's *not* a nationality!" I respond as he darts into the locker room.

Throughout the week, my feelings about Aksel have only intensified—intrigue and trust now precede suspicion.

I don't know if my instincts about Aksel are correct, or what he was like before, or why he moved here after his parents' plane crash. I know so little about him; *the avalanche* remains a complicated tangle of emotions.

And Berlin has thrown a wrench in the turmoil.

However, Berlin *is* a coincidence, so it shouldn't necessarily affect—

"Ms. Hepworth?"

Blinking, I look around the Art History classroom. The shades are drawn over the windows. The room is dark. "Yes, ma'am?" I say to Mrs. Bernhardt.

"Can you please tell us about this?"

I squint at the building on the screen. The image is out of focus, but I would recognize it anywhere.

Immediately, my throat constricts. I have no time to prevent it. *Hot moist air. The adhan echoing in my ears. Running through the souk. Dirty hair. Dirty uniform.*

I clutch the desk. I have to block it out.

"Sophia?"

My nails dig into my palms.

I have to do this, or I have to run.

Mrs. Bernhardt gives me an encouraging nod.

"Hagia Sophia," I exhale.

I wipe my hands on my jeans. "It was a Byzantine Christian church before it became an Ottoman mosque. You can see the gleaming minarets from both sides of the Bosphorus; it's cavernous inside . . . stunning . . . every tile is hand-glazed . . ."

I'm trying so hard to block it out, I am dizzy. A thin layer of sweat coats my skin.

Emma is braiding her hair, prepping for swim practice after school. She stops with the three sections pulled apart, dangling beneath her ear, watching me keenly.

Mrs. Bernhardt's eyebrows rise. "You've been there, Sophia?"

Clenching my hands, I nod.

Emma's large eyes are like saucers, glued to me. *Who has cold sweats in Art History?*

"Can you tell us more?" Mrs. Bernhardt asks me.

I unfist my hands. "We lived in Sultanahmet, nearby. Hagia Sophia means 'Holy Wisdom' in Greek, because it was also a Greek Orthodox cathedral."

"Like your name, Sophia." Mrs. Bernhardt beams. "It must have been a special place for you to visit."

My cheeks burn. I pinch the edge of my seat between my fingertips. It is everything I can do to stay seated and not bolt.

I nod.

To my relief, she begins asking Abigail Montgomery about Gothic gargoyles.

Emma catches my arm after class. Her voice is maternally fierce. "What's wrong? Are you okay?"

I look down at my trembling hands. I twist the cap off my water bottle. "Fine," I say.

"Sophia, you're not fine, you're white as a ghost—"

"It was hot in there." I swallow the water, avoiding eye contact with Emma.

After so long, the places from my past all blend together, like a watercolor in a puddle—murky layers of incongruent memories.

Everything about my past scares me.

Every place has a story.

I need to find out why Aksel was in Berlin.

CHAPTER 20

My parents encourage me to sleep in, but by seven I am dressed and in the kitchen.

"No running today," my mother says, eyeing my sneakers. She is pulling baking ingredients from the cupboard and tapping her foot to Nina Simone.

I push aside the curtain—another blizzard.

"The point," she laughs, "is to relax."

Relax? The woman talking looks like my mother, and is dressed like my mother, but she sounds nothing like my mother.

For Thanksgiving dinner, we order Indian food from the one ethnic place in town and eat two apple pies I help my mother bake. In the evening, we watch American football on my father's laptop. I learn all sorts of rules about a game that makes little sense. Why do they wear so much padding? Rugby players don't wear pads.

Friday, we decorate the living room with white ceramic stars, boxwood wreaths with red velvet bows, and a Swedish angel chime I haven't seen since I was eleven. However, after two days of *hygge*, I'm eager to get out.

When Emma honks outside, I step into my parents' study to say goodbye.

"Be safe," my father says, looking up from his book. "No avalanches."

My mother is standing at the bookshelf, admiring her antique encyclopedia collection—faded binding, gold lettering, and purchased at an auction in England.

"Have fun, darling," she says over her shoulder.

"See you at midnight," I respond—I adopted Charlotte's curfew weeks ago, and my parents didn't object.

As I turn on my heel to leave, my father holds up his forefinger. He reaches into the drawer of his desk and removes a shiny black box with a white ribbon tied around it.

Passing me the box, he motions for me to open it. I unravel the ribbon and lift the lid.

Stunned, I stare at it. "I can have one?"

My father lifts out the cell phone, drops the box into the trash, and hands it to me. "After a long and thought-provoking discussion—"

"Fourteen seconds," interrupts my mother, smiling.

"We decided it's time you become a typical American teenager."

Although it is only five o'clock, the twilight sky is a velvety blue scattered with an endless sea of crystals.

It's something I like about Waterford—seeing the stars *Botswana bright.*

Plump mounds of snow barricade the sidewalks. Around us, the shops are decorated with pine boughs and ribbons; lights strung from the lampposts form an awning of twinkling lights above us.

Beside the entrance to the Creamery, a man wearing an oversize fur parka, its hood drawn low over his face, watches us.

I've become accustomed to this—Charlotte is possibly the only 178-centimeter Dominican-Korean American girl in Waterford. She's stunning. *Everyone* stares.

Inside, we partition ourselves into snug booths. I sit across from Charlotte, who sits down between Mason and Henry.

"You made it." Mason grins at me.

"Happy Thanksgiving," I say.

"No, no. Thanksgiving finished, so now you say Merry Christmas."

"*Joyeux Noël*," I laugh.

Tate strolls over, nudging everyone aside to make room for himself in the booth.

Zipping down my Moncler puffer jacket, I reach into my pocket to pull out my phone.

A *typical American teenager.*

I turn it around in my hand, wistful. Tate peers over at my lap. "What is that?"

"My new phone," I say proudly.

Tate snatches my phone from my hands. He guffaws so loudly he nearly chokes. "This is not a phone." He inspects it. "This is an antique."

The phone is fifteen centimeters tall, and nearly three centimeters thick. *From 2002*, my father said, ancient. But it can text, and it can make and take calls, and most importantly, it has no GPS. Only a satellite transponder, which is activated by a distinctive SOS power-on-power-off system my father installs on all our phones.

I move to snatch it back, but Tate is swifter; he passes the phone behind him to Oliver who passes it to Emma, who passes it to others, who each take a turn examining it.

Mason holds me hostage, keeping it firmly in his hands. "You have to *press* buttons?" he mutters, squinting to read the dim screen. "And scroll with an arrow? *Each* time?"

"It's sophisticated," I divulge. "In Shanghai and Tehran, journalists utilize old school tradecraft to protect their sources. An electronic trail is transparent. My parents . . ." I falter at Mason's confused expression, ". . . read about it online . . ."

Laughing, I slide my phone out from Mason's fingers and return it to my pocket.

When Charlotte prances away to collect her waffle cone from the counter, Tate puts his arm around my shoulder. "I was hoping you would be here tonight," he says.

Emma once said memories of kissing Ryan Rice in ninth grade give her the "heebie-jeebies." This is what I feel when Tate puts his arm around me—the heebie-jeebies.

Across the table, Henry glances discreetly at me before typing into his phone.

Tate's fingertips touch my knee. "Want to hang out later?" he asks me. Behind his leering eyes I sense an arrogance. "You're coming to the movie, aren't you?" He is attractive, and well built from basketball, but his playful, predatory smile unnerves me.

He drums his forefinger on my kneecap, the muscles in my thigh tense.

I swirl out of the booth so quickly I bump into Charlotte.

"What's wrong?" She stares at me, puzzled.

Tate raises both his arms in surrender. "I scared Sophia," he snickers.

Charlotte's puzzled frown breaks into a stern look. "You didn't tell her about last summer when you were attacked by a bobcat—"

"Cougar." Tate rolls up his sleeve, showcasing his forearm. "I still have the scar."

"Kitten, whatever." Charlotte's mouth curves upward. She tosses her glossy hair over her shoulder. "Because Sophia has a habit of running into bigger game."

Once everyone finishes their ice cream, we migrate to the doors—it takes time in such a herd.

I stay close to Charlotte and Mason, but Tate slinks his arm around my waist. "Sophia, you're coming with me."

"I'm riding with Emma," I counter.

Tate nods to Emma and Oliver, entangled in a flirtatious, embracing argument. "You don't want to ride with those two." Tate's hand moves from my waist to the top of my butt.

"Where's Charlotte?" I shrug away from Tate.

"Here!" Charlotte waltzes toward me.

"Aren't we riding together?" I ask her.

"We're going to the same theater," Charlotte says airily. Waving me ahead, she glides her hand through Mason's arm. "We'll meet you there in five minutes."

"You heard her," Tate laughs. "Come on. I'm parked around the block. We'll beat her there."

Reluctantly, I trudge forward with Tate.

Outside, Main Street is bustling, thick with the smell of winter: roasted almonds and cinnamon and fresh snow.

Tate chatters ceaselessly, "I've been playing basketball as long as I can remember . . ."

Passing Charlotte's dad's ski shop and Waterford Bakery we walk down Main Street. However, as we turn onto Second Avenue, my hex sense flips on like a switch.

Twenty meters farther down is a man standing alone, with the bottom of his left shoe propped against the wall—*him*.

Same height. Same fur trim on his parka. His elbow bent at the same awkward angle. It's the same man who watched us enter the Creamery an hour ago.

A sedan turns onto Broadway; its headlights illuminate the man briefly. He's casually using his phone; bowing his head, his hood conceals his face.

Something in his stance discomforts me.

Tate continues talking. "I'll get a scholarship . . . my dad played at Montana too . . . that is if I don't fail German . . ."

As we draw nearer, the man in the parka steps away from the wall, alert, like he's been waiting. Anticipating. Preparing.

A stiffness seizes my limbs. I am not afraid. Not in Waterford. I've incorrectly evaluated threats since I arrived. I *am* safe here.

Parked on Broadway, beyond the intersection, I see a red truck. Rusty, with a broken taillight. Though there are plenty of beat-up trucks in Waterford, fear tingles my nerves.

I recall the night at Fish Market a few weeks ago—*why* didn't I scan its plate?

"Sophia?"

I blink up at Tate. "Yes?"

"I can teach you to drive if you want," he suggests. "You should never do that move in a vehicle with a high center of gravity."

"What move?" I ask, perplexed.

"Your spin-charade at the dance? That was dangerous."

"That was an escape-and-evade maneuver, Tate. We were evading you."

He nudges my arm flirtatiously. "I'm not that easy to avoid."

"Evade," I say softly. I'm preoccupied with watching the man, who is still a distance away.

Tate snakes his arm around my shoulders again. For the first time all night, I let him. I even put my arm around his waist—insurance.

As we near the man, he remains on the far side of the street, still staring at his phone, still not flinching. My tension dissipates. My body begins to decompress.

But then Tate drops his arm from my shoulder.

Fumbling around, he groans. "I left my keys." He pats his pockets. "Wait here, I'll be right back."

Seconds later, he's jogging around the corner back to Main Street.

I am alone.

At once, my eyes snap to the man. He lifts his eyes slightly. As if he's been observing us all along. He watches Tate disappear from view, then he looks at me, then quickly looks down at his phone.

He fiddles with his headphones. Then he holds his phone casually to his ear.

In the distance, I hear everyone laughing and shouting—Mason's laugh is so loud it echoes. My friends are a block away. Thirteen seconds, if I sprint.

Ahead, the man starts walking along Second Avenue toward Main Street, toward me.

Abruptly I turn on my heel.

I divert toward Broadway, intending to loop back to the Creamery. I walk faster, eager to put distance between us.

A crunch of salt on the sidewalk—a thick grinding sound of soles scraping along concrete—causes me to glance back.

The hooded man has crossed the street and is stepping onto the sidewalk behind me. His footsteps beat rhythmically in time to mine, quickening as they get closer.

My pulse thumps in my chest. He is so close I can hear the cadence of his ragged breath—ten meters. Five.

I'm not afraid. I shouldn't pull out my Ladybug.

Compromising, I unlatch my silver watch and wriggle it off.

The ragged breathing nears.

I'm almost to Main Street. I walk faster.

His gait loosens. His stride lengthens.

Heavy boots hit the pavement.

I position the clasp in place atop my second knuckle, listening.

Every walk has a signature. This one *is* familiar.

Behind me, a smooth engine approaches, braking fast. A door opens. Footsteps hasten.

Adrenaline pumps through my veins, coursing like lava.

I have to confront him. *Them.*

At once, I reach into my waistband and spin around.

The man in the fur-trimmed parka jerks to a stop.

Someone is standing between us.

CHAPTER 21

"Back off."

The man in the parka steps toward me.

Aksel puts his hand on my hip, sweeping me completely behind him.

"I said, back off," Aksel snarls.

The man goes still—too still—like he is contemplating how to react. Then, he pushes off his hood.

He has brown curly hair and hazel eyes; I don't recognize him. At all.

I drop my fingertips from my waist.

He stares at us wide-eyed—startled. Dumbfounded. Shoving his phone into his pocket, he tugs the headphones out of his ears.

"Ex-excuse me," he stutters, pointing ahead. "I'm on my way to Alpine Market."

My ears buzz. Nine words that should sound like basic Montana English . . . except something about his velvety voice . . . the way he pronounced his *r* in a guttural way . . .

"M*arket*," I whisper, imitating his accent.

Aksel looks at me sharply.

"Excuse me." The man offers another polite nod—a request to pass.

Reluctantly, Aksel steps aside, keeping me squarely behind him.

As the man passes, I smell it.

Cologne. Cigarettes. Not just any cigarettes—*Ziganov* cigarettes.

Adrenaline converts to panic.

The man disappears into Alpine Market. Aksel's hand glides up from my hip, where he holds my forearm gently yet firmly, as if he's trying to get my attention.

"Sophia, do you know him?" Aksel searches my face.

Behind him, a Range Rover idles on the side of the road. I realize my fingers are tangled in Aksel's sleeve. Instinct tells me not to let go.

I shake my head, swallowing the fear, calming myself. "I don't . . . I thought . . . for a second . . . but it . . . wasn't . . ."

Why does he always have to see me this way?

Aksel swivels his head toward the voices and laughter coming from the Creamery.

"Hey, there you are!" Tate jogs toward us. "I found my keys. They'd fallen behind the booth, and we had to remove the cushion . . ."

Slowing to a stop, Tate notices Aksel.

"What's going on?" He looks between me and Aksel.

I let go of Aksel's jacket. "Nothing, I—"

"Were you meeting Fredricksen here?" Tate asks me accusingly.

"No, I—"

"You're coming with me, remember?" Tate takes his keys out of his pocket. He presses the fob. An Explorer, parked a few spots down, lights up and beeps.

Another car turns onto Broadway—Emma.

Crammed inside her Jeep: Oliver, Abigail, and Cole watching us like spectators.

With disjointed movements, I fumble with the clasp on my watch. It takes two attempts to latch it back on.

I can't do this. I can't stay here. I am barely keeping rationality ahead of paranoia.

"Can you take me home?" I ask Aksel.

"Sure." Aksel steps toward the Range Rover and opens the passenger door.

"I can drive you home," Tate interjects angrily, stepping between me and the door.

"I don't mind," Aksel says coolly.

Although the same height, Aksel has about thirty pounds of muscle on Tate and looks like he could squish him between two fingers. Right now, he looks like he wants to.

I notice it now—it's not only Aksel's build that's intimidating; it's *him*. Fearless and confident, Aksel isn't scared of anything, or anyone.

Certainly not Tate McCormick.

For that matter, neither am I. "I'll see you later," I say to Tate.

"Seriously, Sophia?" Tate says belligerently. "You're ditching—"

"Let it go, man," Aksel orders.

Ignoring the accusations and caustic remarks, I get into the Range Rover.

We drive in silence. At the end of my driveway, Aksel shifts into park.

A car drives past. We watch the headlights dissolve into the night.

"Thank you," I say, composing myself. "I didn't mean to overreact—"

"You didn't," Aksel interrupts curtly.

"My nerves got the best of me—"

"He was walking behind you," Aksel says, cutting me off, "close—really close—with his phone out, awkwardly ahead of his body, like he was filming you."

Filming me? A sharp ping hits my gut.

"Some guys are creeps." I shrug it off. "Thank you for the ride."

I put my hand on the door handle, but Aksel reaches across my body and puts his hand on mine. "Sophia, that's not all." His fingers meet my wrist beneath my jacket. I am acutely aware of how close his forearm is to my shoulder, of how near his beating heart is to mine.

Sitting back, Aksel drags a hand through his hair. He seems uncomfortable. "It's not the first time I've seen him near you."

Tentatively, I let go of the door handle. "Sorry?"

He drapes his hand on the back of my seat, facing me. "You were jogging alone when you came upon that grizzly, right?"

I nod. *The grizzly?* That was weeks ago.

"When I heard the grizzly, I scanned the forest. First, I spotted a guy, farther back on the trail. He was stopped—motionless. When the grizzly roared a second time, he took off and that's when I saw you a few meters ahead."

"It's a trail," I point out. "People jog there all the time."

"Not people from Waterford," Aksel says, exasperated.

I remember what the plow driver said. *Tourist.*

"*You* were there," I say.

"Target shooting," he explains. "I expected the other runner to show. I assumed you were together, and he'd gotten spooked and would come back to check on you. But when I lifted my scope, he was sprinting in the opposite direction—"

"There was a grizzly! I tried to run too, remember?"

He eyes me warily. "My scope has a x400 magnification. I saw him clearly, Sophia. Same profile. Same build. It was the same guy tonight. And I'm guessing it's the same guy you thought was following you at Fish Market," he adds darkly.

"Waterford is small," I say, trying to placate him, not wanting to assemble these pieces. "It's just a coincidence."

"Coincidence," Aksel says under his breath. "Right."

I know I should be concerned, but the longer I sit here with Aksel, the further I can—*must*—push the man with hazel eyes and curly hair from my mind.

Aksel has no proof I am being followed.

Neither do I. All I have is instinct. And fear. That's what it was tonight—fear I would be found. Followed.

My throat constricts as I try to block it all out. The smells. The voice. *His* voice.

I *am* safe here. Because *not* being safe here has an outcome I can't consider.

"Sophia, you should tell your parents, or even the police."

"I'm not telling them."

Aksel jerks his thumb toward town. "He's trailed you twice, and those are only the times you know about—"

"You don't get it!" I say adamantly. "If he *were* following me, I wouldn't still be in Waterford!"

Saying it aloud catches me by surprise.

Aksel tilts his head against the window. His angular face is impassive, unreadable.

I sense the friction building between us.

"How did you even know he would be there tonight?" I peer over at him from beneath my lashes.

"I didn't," answers Aksel diffidently. "I knew *you* would be."

"*How?*"

"Henry texted me." Aksel shifts in his seat. "And I thought, sure, yeah, why not . . . But then this happened tonight, and I don't know, Sophia . . ."

Beneath his stoic expression, I struggle to maintain eye contact. My heart beats vigorously in my chest.

"Why are you so determined to not . . . hang out—"

"Sophia." His voice is calm, but his eyes are fierce. "I *do* want to hang out with you—"

"So why do you keep acting like we have nothing in common? Like you can't decide whether you want to be friends or . . ." My voice catches in my throat.

"Because, Sophia . . ." He seems torn. Rattled. Flustered. The defined line from his cheekbone to his jaw sets into place; his eyebrows are drawn tight, frustrated. Like he doesn't understand why *I* don't understand. But I *don't* understand. *What* is restraining him?

"What if we have too much in common?" he asks quietly.

I stare into his eyes, a piercing green that seems to smolder. "Don't most people consider that a good thing?" I prompt.

"Do you?"

"Yes." I pause. "No." I shake my head, "I don't know."

Buzz. I look down at my phone. Charlotte, wondering where I am.

"I have to go," I say, biting my lip. "Thanks for the ride."

I get out and start walking briskly toward the house, circled by a tempest of emotion. A stiff pain ripples across my chest. It's clear. Aksel recognizes I have a past. And he doesn't want any part in it.

I have almost reached the porch when I hear Aksel jog up behind me.

"Sophia, wait."

His strong fingers wrap gently around mine.

Rotating to face him, my insides flutter—I grip the edge of my sleeve.

Staring at Aksel, I am sure of almost nothing. I have no idea how to interpret my feelings for him. And I have no idea how he feels about me.

I only know that being in Aksel's presence is exhilarating and thrilling and transcends all the complicated emotions I've felt since I arrived in Waterford.

Is this what it's like to *like* someone?

His fingertips linger on my skin, sending pulses of heat up my arm. It feels like there is so much, yet so little, distance between us.

"What if I'm wrong?" Aksel asks.

"You *are* wrong. He was just some guy—"

"I meant wrong about thinking we shouldn't be . . . together."

When Aksel says *together*, my heart fumbles a beat. Or two. Or ten.

My chest tightens as I search his gaze.

"Sophia, maybe this can never work"—his eyes lock with mine—"but *maybe* it can. Maybe it's worth trying. Because the truth is, I haven't stopped thinking about you since that day in the forest. Since Berlin, if I'm honest; I had no reason to think I would ever see you again, yet I still remembered *you*," he declares.

Aksel shifts his posture. "And now you're here, and I meet you, and I question everything—" He stops, catching his words.

Indecipherable thoughts clutter my head.

He steps closer to me. Tingles rise up my chest and spread across my collarbone.

"I want to see you, Sophia, hang out with you, date you, whatever you want to call it. And if we get a few weeks, or a few months, fine. I only know I don't want to spend one more day trying so hard to *not* see you."

A *few weeks*. A *few months*. Does Aksel assume I'll leave Waterford?

Is *that* what is holding him back?

I am too stunned to speak.

"And I suppose I don't want to wait for circumstances to change to make it easier, or better, or safer," he finishes brazenly.

My circumstances.

I grip the sleeve of my jacket so tightly I start to lose circulation in my fingers.

I push my tongue to the back of my teeth to stop my lips from quivering. Heat flushes through my body.

"So don't wait."

A glimmer of a smile crosses his full lips. "You want to go out with me then?"

I check my Skagen watch. "Now?"

Aksel grins. "Unless you have a seven o'clock curfew?"

"No." I blush. "Considering I ditched my friends, I don't have plans. And I don't want to be home yet. So, sure, I'll come."

He slides his hand down to my palm and interlocks his fingers with mine. "Hungry?"

CHAPTER 22

With icicles dripping from the rooftop eaves, the homes in Waterford resemble gingerbread cottages.

We drive north to Silver Canyon. Beneath the velvety black sky, the forest thickens—grand houses are interspersed among old mining cabins until eventually they disappear—and Aksel veers into the entrance of Waterford Ski Resort.

He winds around the back of the resort to a gravel lot. Ahead is a diminutive cottage with stained glass windows glowing amber. Smoke swirls up from the chimney. Twinkling lights line the pathway to the arched front door. A Tyrolean painted sign across the second-story balcony reads: *Alpenhof.*

"It's so . . ." *Not-American*, I think. "Unexpected," I say.

"It was one of the first homes built on the mountain," Aksel tells me, catching my eyes surreptitiously sweeping the perimeter as we enter the restaurant.

We are seated at a table near a stone fireplace. A candle in the center sends flickering shadows dancing across the white linen.

Noticing those around us wearing Gorsuch après-ski gear, I glance sidelong at Aksel. "Are we old enough to be here?"

Aksel laughs under his breath. "Don't order wine. This isn't France."

After the waiter tells us the specials in very gastronomical terms, Aksel asks, "Did you understand what he said?"

I grin. "I heard fondue."

"Melted cheese? I'm in."

Aksel puts aside the menu. "So what's the strangest food you've ever eaten?"

"Pop-Tarts," I say, wrinkling my nose.

Aksel laughs. "Pop-Tarts are *not* strange."

"Strange is relative!" I proclaim. "Fine. What's the strangest food *you've* ever eaten?"

"Blood pudding." Aksel shudders. "My grandmother makes it for Christmas."

"Blood pudding is delicious!"

"Okay, what's the most obscure-to-a-Montanan food *you've* ever eaten?" he asks.

I click my tongue. "Chicken feet? Pig ears? Snake? We would have these competitions, daring each other to eat things we'd never seen before. My father always won until one day in Laos he told me if I ate a grasshopper I would win *forever.* So, I ate it."

Aksel nearly spits out his water. "*Alive?*"

"I don't like *dead* grasshoppers," I explain.

Aksel pushes his lips together and swallows.

As the waiter pours our water, I motion to the framed black-and-white ski photography on the walls. "Is this what you do when you skip school?"

Aksel averts his eyes. "I don't skip school. I have permission, like other seniors."

"What do you do with your free time?"

His leg shakes incessantly beneath the table. Does he ever

stop moving? "I'm taking different college courses," he answers reticently.

Usually, I can tell if people are lying. Aksel seems to be both truthful yet omitting—reflecting my own style of deceit.

"Which courses?"

"Advanced Physics. Engineering. Arabic." Aksel pauses. "Are you interrogating me?"

I smile demurely. "If I was interrogating you, you'd be sweating."

"I am."

I laugh. "Doesn't look like it. What exactly do you intend to do? Attend the Naval Academy?"

Aksel looks discomfited. "I haven't been admitted," he answers. "Not yet."

I open my mouth, surprised that I guessed right.

"I've wanted to go to the Naval Academy since I was a kid," he continues. "I can study nuclear physics, swim competitively for four years; graduate as an officer."

"Your future seems all planned out."

His brow is tight. "Not quite."

Our fondue arrives. I unfold my napkin and lay it on my lap. "I could help you—with the languages," I offer.

In the firelight, Aksel's vivid eyes shine bright. "You speak *Arabic*?"

I skewer a bread cube and swirl it through the cheese. "*Bittab*," I say. "That means 'of course' in Levantine Arabic. In Egyptian Arabic it's '*tab'an*.' Many countries develop their own dialect. Tunisian is my favorite. It's singsongy with a lilt at the end . . ."

Aksel shakes his head, smiling. Beneath the table my foot bumps his. Why does being around Aksel make my skin feel like it is perpetually on fire?

"How many languages do you speak?" he asks.

I drink some water. "Not as many as my father."

"How many is that?"

"Like a native? A few. But if you include basic fluency, I have a few more."

"There's a spectrum?"

"Sure. Many languages and dialects are similar; you can speak one and understand another. For example, after I learned Danish, Scandinavian languages derived from Old Norse took only a few weeks to master. Same with Slavic and Germanic languages. Though we didn't spend a lot of time in East Asia, I loved Taipei so I tried really hard with Mandarin when we were there. And Africa . . ."

I inhale, catching my breath. "Africa is the epicenter of linguistic diversity. Thousands of languages and dialects coexist: merging together and breaking apart and constantly evolving. It's impossible to learn even a fraction of the commonly spoken languages. I learned Swahili in school in Nairobi, but thrived learning less widely spoken dialects, though I never became fluent in any of them . . ."

Aksel's eyes gleam in the dancing firelight, "A number, Sophia?"

I stop chattering. I hold up all five fingers on one hand, and all five on the other. Then I close my fists and reopen my right hand with four fingers. "Although if you include proficiency, there are dozens. However, my father says I can only count native fluency . . ."

Aksel whistles. "I'm impressed."

Fiddling with my napkin, I look down. "You shouldn't be."

"You're ashamed," Aksel says. Then he shakes his head and leans toward me. "How can you possibly be ashamed of anything you just told me?"

"I want to be normal," I explain. "Like everyone else here. But my normal is driving in armored vehicles at high speed while watching out for IEDs . . ." I eat a cheese-soaked apple off my fork. "Staying at a St. Regis one night—visiting refugee camps with my father and sleeping on cots the next."

Aksel looks pensive. "You *want* to be like every person in Waterford?"

"Of course! What American teenager do you know who speaks fourteen languages?"

"Why do you say it like it's a bad thing?"

"It's weird! Emma can't conjugate a verb in French, and she's taken it since seventh grade!"

"How does Emma's lack of French proficiency make *you* weird?"

"It . . . does!" I proclaim.

"Don't you get it, Sophia?" Aksel says, becoming agitated. "You can have what your friends have—"

"No, I can't—"

"Yes, you can," Aksel says emphatically. "But no one can simply *have* what you have."

"And they shouldn't—"

"Not your past, Sophia!" Aksel's eyes blaze. "I'm talking about the way you challenge yourself—the way you challenge me. Yet, you remain oblivious to how remarkable, how resilient, you are. You can be anyone you want, Sophia . . . but no one can be you."

As we stare at each other, I have the distinct impression that we—our lives—are welding irreversibly together.

For the first time my past doesn't feel like it's smothering me, but buoying me.

Later, after devouring several pots of fondue, we retrieve our coats from the maître d'.

"The Kirov Ballet!" I pull a flyer off the noticeboard tacked behind the coat closet door. "It's coming *here*?" I utter, astounded. "I saw them in Oslo when I was seven. The prima ballerina signed her slippers for me. I still have them someplace. Or had them. I always loved the ballet—watching, rehearsing, performing. I eventually had to quit because we moved too frequently, and now . . ."

I pin the flyer back onto the board, laughing, "I should have taken line dancing."

As we reach the Range Rover several minutes later, I turn to Aksel, "So what do you want to do now?"

He grins, "Are you up for a walk?"

We drive back out of Silver Canyon to the fork by Charlotte's house. Here Aksel turns left into Eagle Pass. Five kilometers up he points at a high rock wall. "We climbed that," he reminds me, almost smugly.

Against the rock wall is a huge snowdrift. Only the far side of the road is open. I clutch my seat belt, hoping we don't tumble into the ravine.

"Yikes," I murmur, looking back through the rear window.

Farther up Eagle Pass—past several limestone walls with gates concealing long driveways—Aksel turns through an iron gate and onto a stone driveway, leading to an enormous estate covered in cedar shingles and stone, surrounded by towering pines.

I raise my eyebrows at Aksel who evasively says, "It's way too big."

"Not exactly the Wuthering Heights I expected," I murmur. "More like the Winter Palace."

Aksel laughs.

We park beneath a portico on the side of the house, ascend a flight of stairs, and enter through a side door. We walk by a wood-paneled library, down a long hall with polished floors, and emerge in a magnificent room with high-beamed ceilings, a river rock fireplace, and windows along the far wall, facing sheer rock cliffs.

"You live here by yourself?"

"Technically, yeah, though my family visits often. Here, gear room is this way."

After Aksel outfits me with a pair of snowshoes, we exit through the mudroom door, cross the meadow beyond the deck, and enter the woods. Above us, the sky is an inky blue. The moon peeks out from behind a barren oak tree, like a polished freshwater pearl.

A brisk twenty-minute hike later—snowshoeing in deep powder is *not* a "walk"—we reach a clearing. In the center of the clearing, from a rocky ravine fifteen meters high, a waterfall crashes into a small lake whose incandescent surface glistens in fractured moonlight.

Unclipping his snowshoes, Aksel points to a rocky plateau jutting out from the western shore. "In the summer, this is the best swimming hole. The lake is warmer because of the hot springs, and you can see all of Waterford from that rock."

Sitting down near the lake's edge, I unclip my snowshoes.

Above us the stars stretch out in a canopy of diamonds. A soft wind ripples the lake.

"You chose a pretty great place to move," I say.

Aksel sits beside me, stretching out his long legs. "Waterford's my favorite place in the world."

"Hmmm, I'd choose Portillo in summer, Kitzbühel in winter."

He flashes me an audacious smile. "You must be a good skier."

"I haven't skied for a long time."

"Sophia." Aksel chuckles softly, and when he says my name, heat shoots up my spine. "You're sixteen, aren't you? How long can it be?"

"Two seasons," I answer.

"A lifetime," he says, which is ironic because it is true. A lifetime has passed since then.

I wring my fingers. *Not now. Please don't happen now.*

"Last time I skied," I blurt out, "we were in Gstaad. I begged my dad to race. He won so I demanded a rematch, but as I was persuading him, he got a call to return to Pakistan—"

Aksel's hand twitches. Momentarily, I stop talking, but he says nothing, so I continue.

"I was devastated to leave early, so driving through Geneva, we parked near the Rhône Bridge to play my favorite game: I would lead us to our favorite place using landmark navigation. My father would follow behind, never interfering, until eventually I reached Patisserie Claudette. My mother would be waiting there with the car, and we'd all eat *pains au chocolat* . . ." I trail off.

Among the barren tree branches, wind whistles softly. Aksel watches me quietly.

"You didn't want to return to Pakistan?" he asks.

"It wasn't that," I smile. "I loved Karachi. The intense atmosphere—the volatile politics, the walled complexes—it all intrigued me. I loved my friends. I loved the seamstress who embroidered me my own *shalwar kameezes* . . . But I was sad to return to Pakistan because it meant my father would disappear often. He was always busy on assignments . . ."

Silence lingers in the air between us.

Intuition warns me to be cautious, hesitant, especially after earlier tonight.

However, the fear has receded.

A more dominant part of me craves how my heart races in Aksel's presence. Perhaps if I stop thinking so much about being afraid, I won't be. I *can* live a normal life without assuming everyone around me is a threat.

"You don't like talking too much about your past, do you?" Aksel asks cautiously. We are dancing around an issue neither of us wants to confront.

I gather a chunk of snow from the ground and squeeze it in my mitten.

"I was seven when I recognized it the first time. We'd been living in Tehran almost a year when I arrived home one afternoon to find our house packed: the rugs, the art, gone. We left that night in a troop transport. After that, I never knew when it would happen, but I always knew it would. I could try to have a normal life, and yet I could still wake up and have to board a train to Turkmenistan or a plane to Yemen." I drop the snow from my mitten back to the ground: "Like that."

My hair tumbles loose from behind my ear. Aksel reaches his

right arm across his body and tucks the stray lock back. Tingles spread down my ear to my neck, collecting at my throat in a wave of heat.

"What about you?" I ask, trying to maintain my composure.

Aksel smiles tentatively. "What do you want to know?"

"Why were you born in Germany?"

"My dad's German—he met my mom at Harvard during medical school. They were visiting relatives when I was born."

Germany. Berlin. The Bubble. It must all be related—but how?

"When did you first come to Waterford?"

Aksel gestures back toward the house. "I spent my childhood here. My parents were both doctors, but my dad was always committing to speaking assignments, humanitarian missions . . . My mom went with him when she could, but mostly, she loved the mountains, the privacy. She grew up with a summer home here. On this property actually, though my parents rebuilt it."

"So, you moved here to get away?"

"Yeah, I guess. It's fun here. Swimming and running in the high altitude. Shooting." Aksel shakes snow off his boot. "Waterford adults think teenagers *should* target practice in the woods." He smiles coyly.

"Aksel, why were you in Berlin?" It comes out suddenly.

With his sleeves pushed up above his wrists, I see the muscles in his forearm go taut. His smile fades. He gathers a chunk of snow and throws it into the lake like a baseball.

A stream of clouds roll in, shrouding the moon. When they clear, Aksel pushes his palms against the ground, reclining with his legs straight out in front of him. His chiseled profile is silhouetted in the moonlight.

"I was in Germany over spring break when I got a request to meet an official at the American Embassy." He glares ahead at the lake. "They said they had information about my parents' plane crash . . . *to be shared in person* . . ."

Although less than a meter away, Aksel feels distant, almost robotic. I pay attention to every syllable that crosses his full lips.

"The embassy seemed normal enough until they escorted me to a secure floor. It was weird being inside the Bubble, you know? This woman asked me a few questions, told me what she said they knew, and that was it." He shrugs.

Restlessly, his fingers spread out over his knees, then he balls his hands into fists and extends his fingers out again, his knuckles cracking.

"Did you learn more about the plane crash?" I ask, wondering if he's told me all he will.

Aksel smiles, but it is a sad smile and doesn't reach his eyes.

"My parents' plane didn't crash, Sophia." He brings his knees up to his chest and stares out at the lake. "It was shot down."

CHAPTER 23

Planes don't just get shot down. That happens in my world—not his.

Several seconds later, I still haven't let out a breath.

"Aksel, I'm so sorry," I breathe out, but a sideways glance tells me he doesn't want my sympathy.

"Yeah, I know," he apologizes. "One day I'll learn to say thank you when people say that." He stretches his hands out again. I notice a small scar across his left knuckles.

The intimacy of our shared history is overwhelming—we are seated feet apart, and yet I have never felt closer to someone, or more vulnerable, in my life.

Tucking my hands inside the lining of my jacket, I stand and walk to the edge of the luminescent lake. "You must swim here often," I comment.

Aksel sits forward, propping his hands on his knees. "Sometimes. The hot springs keep the lake from freezing over. It's not warm, but it's not too cold either."

I take off my mittens and toss them on the rock. "Do you want to race?"

His eyes gleam. "You're joking."

"If you'll get in, I'll race you." I peer at him challengingly. "Unless you're scared."

Aksel stands and points to the lake, apparently checking which lake I am referencing. "You will get in *there*?"

I tug at the laces on my snow boots. "Sure."

Suddenly, his hand is on mine. His palm sends fiery sparks across my skin. I pause, pulling the lace out of its knot. My heart thumps in my chest.

"The lake may not be freezing, but it's November," Aksel cautions, "and we don't have any towels."

"As long as there's no avalanche, we should be good, right?"

His eyes linger on mine. Briefly they land on my lips. How long would it take for his mouth to reach mine?

"The only thing we're missing is the northern lights," I say.

"Let me guess, the last time you swam in a mountain lake in *winter*"—he exaggerates the word, letting go of my hand—"was in a Norwegian village above the Arctic circle?" He shrugs out of his jacket.

"Iceland, actually."

"Close enough."

"Not really. It's a thousand nautical miles from Reykjavik to the western fjords."

"You've sailed that route?"

"Oh no, it's dangerous."

Aksel stops with one boot in his hand and the other on his foot. He is bent over, tugging the laces free. He stares at me, incredulous. "*You* think a boat ride between Iceland and Norway, the *two safest countries* on earth, is dangerous?"

"Not a boat ride. Sailing," I clarify. "The North Sea doesn't have piracy problems like the Black Sea or the Gulf of Guinea, but the conditions—strong winds and icebergs and rough currents—are dangerous."

"Very," he says, smiling.

"It's true. Fact-check me. The North Sea is as unpredictable as Cape Horn."

He sets his boots on the ground. "So you would never sail to Norway?"

"Never say never." I shrug.

"Not about you, Sophia," Aksel says, and when he looks at me, my breath catches in my throat. He lifts his sweater over his head.

Blushing, I look away. With my boots off, I unzip my puffer, slip my sweatshirt over my head, and slide out of my pants. I've begun wearing a camisole and seamless shorts beneath my clothing for warmth. I'll swim in these—it isn't as though I am swimming naked.

The lake is temperate, and small at less than two hundred meters across; Aksel's house is only a half kilometer back through the woods.

Hypothermia risk is low.

"Depth?" I query.

"Twenty feet," he answers.

I dive. Before I hit the surface, I see Aksel follow.

It's not freezing, but it's not exactly Reykjadalur. Turning toward me Aksel shakes his wet hair off his face, grinning. "You're indomitable," he remarks.

"I'm not in here alone," I point out, treading water.

His mouth curves up ruefully. "Peer pressure."

Even in the dark, I can see the taut muscles etched across his neck and shoulders.

Stretching his arm backward, Aksel places his hand on the rock. I do the same, settling my fingers into a cleft to keep steady.

Only a few centimeters of serrated rock separate our fingers. Why did it bother me so much when Tate put his fingers on my knee, while now, I wish Aksel's were closer?

"It's one hundred seventy yards to the far side of the lake. The farthest point is that clump of evergreens," Aksel says, pointing across the smooth, dark surface. "Whoever touches that large boulder in the water wins. You say 'go.' "

I nod. "All right. Three. Two. Go."

I kick off from the rock. Ignoring Aksel's position—and speed—I focus on getting into my own rhythm. Every few breaths I check to make sure I am headed toward the boulder. In my peripheral vision, I can see Aksel ahead, gliding smoothly across the surface.

By the time I reach it, Aksel is treading water, waiting. I brush my hair off my face.

"That probably wasn't fair," he apologizes.

"You're right," I agree. "We'll have to race back," I say. "Except this time, underwater. Whoever goes farthest with one breath wins."

Aksel scrutinizes me. "Okay, Sophia, but we don't have to race—"

"Three," I interrupt, taking a breath. Because I do have to race. I have to prove to myself that I am no longer afraid. Not of the men who attacked our boat off Djibouti, or of who killed our guides in Kenya, or of whoever Aksel thought was following me tonight.

"Two."

I take another breath.

I am not afraid. Not anymore. Not in Waterford.

"Go."

I plunge back into the lake. Kicking my legs and pushing aside water, I propel forward. After thirty seconds, I want air. After forty-five seconds, I need it. At sixty seconds, I wonder if I'll lose consciousness. Ninety seconds. One hundred and thirty seconds. I need to emerge. It's been too long since I last practiced. One hundred and eighty seconds. My lungs flare.

I break the surface. Curious how far ahead Aksel is, I whirl around, scanning the water. The lake is a glass sheet.

Panic rises in my throat. I look across the tranquil lake back at the clump of evergreens, then ahead toward the rocks where I see his clothes.

Four meters behind me, the water stirs.

As soon as he surfaces, I sense something is wrong.

"SOPHI—" Halfway through yelling my name, he sees me. With quick, deft strokes he swims to me. "Where were you?"

"Underwater—"

"Yeah, but . . ." Aksel glances at the evergreens and back to me. He ducks his head into the water and emerges half a meter from me. He is so close I can see droplets of water on his carved shoulders. "I've been out over a minute. I didn't see you come up for air."

Adamantly, I shake my head. "I did not cheat!"

Aksel's mouth tilts upward, like he wants to smile but can't. "I wasn't worried about you *cheating* . . ." The word lingers in the air.

We stare at each other in uneasy silence. The fervor in his eyes doesn't subside. He runs a hand through his wet hair, pushing it off his face. We both tread water; at some point our legs brush by each other.

"You're not exactly who I thought you were," Aksel finally says.

"Who exactly did you think I was?"

Aksel looks at me in a way that feels like he is looking through me, not at me, before saying, "Come on, this way."

Unsure if he has complimented or criticized me, I roll onto my side and swim after him. Back near the flat rocks, a bubbling current of hot water drifts into the lake. We swim through a crevice between two rocks and into the pocket of hot springs. The warmth is instantaneous. I was wrong: this part of the lake *is* like Reykjadalur.

Above us the night sky is clear—a sea of gemstones sparkling against indigo silk. Silhouetted against the sky, the mountain hovers above us like a jagged triangle cutting into the night.

Aksel watches me pensively; behind his smile, his eyes are simmering.

"What is it?" I ask, sensing that tension in the air between us like a thick fog.

"When I saw you in Berlin," Aksel says abruptly. He pauses, as if giving me an opportunity to stop him. I hold his gaze steady.

"You were pale," he sighs. "Your eyes were hollow; you looked more ghost than person, except . . ." He leans against a rock, staring into the sky.

I swallow, but keep my eyes on his. "Except what?"

"Except you were the one being haunted," he says softly.

Aksel leans toward me. His eyes glint in the steam swirling around us. "Sophia, I didn't think I would ever see you again and yet I still remembered you, and it wasn't because you were beautiful—I mean, you were, you *are* beautiful," he adds, and a blush rises up his neck—"but it was the way you walked, with those men on either side of you holding your elbows, like they could touch you but not actually touch you. Like you possessed some ethereal power to prevent them from hurting you."

Shouting . . . warm blood . . . running . . . engines.

Sparks of light flash behind my eyelids; I'm concentrating so hard to prevent it.

My body is hot, but my face is cold. I dunk my head into the near-scalding water. I stay under until a large hand grips my left forearm.

"Hey," Aksel says sharply, pulling me out of the water. "Careful." His eyes flash with concern.

I can see every wet eyelash, every water droplet on his skin. Steam rises up from the hot springs and swirls in mist around us.

Something about Aksel ignites every nerve in my body.

He exhales slowly. "I'm sorry, I shouldn't have brought it up."

"It's not that." I wipe the condensation off my face.

Aksel's chest heaves with each breath; his body is broad and sculpted and I truly have no idea how he is only a senior in high school. An American high school.

Yet, he saw me in Berlin. It has to be a coincidence. And maybe, if I tell myself it is only a coincidence enough times, I'll start to believe it.

I climb out of the hot springs and sit on a burnished rock at the edge. I tug my knees up to my chest. "Aksel, what happened . . . before . . . I can't . . ."

He hoists himself up onto the rock beside me. Tentatively, he wraps his arm around my back. Nestled in the crook of his shoulder my skin is hot from the water, cold from the night air, and warm beside Aksel.

"You don't have to," he says firmly.

My palm is open, resting on my thigh. He takes my hand and weaves his fingers into mine. He presses the top of my hand with his thumb.

Deep inside me, something triggers.

Whether I want to admit it or not, I know that Berlin is only the beginning. Our lives are irrevocably connected, and I just don't know how deeply.

Above us, a tiny clump of clouds sweeps past, temporarily veiling the moon.

I feel something for the first time in more than eighteen months.

Safe.

Back on the flat rock, I dress quickly and turn to see Aksel slipping on his coat. He strides over to me, shaking out his hair. Looking down at me, he takes off his coat and places it around me. I shiver when he zips it, his hands dangerously close to my chest.

For a moment, we stare at each other in silence. His brooding, deep-set eyes search my face. Is he looking for permission? He has it. He *has* had it. For, like, weeks.

"I should get you home," he says, dropping his gaze. "Let's hope the grizzlies are hibernating," he adds with a wry smile, "because I don't have a weapon."

I pat the waistband of my pants. "I do."

Aksel's mouth twitches. "You should at least carry bear spray when you're running. Your knife might make her angrier—even if you're accurate."

"I am not defending myself with a can of aerosol," I respond. "Besides, Charlotte says bear spray doesn't work."

"People often use it incorrectly. You have to wait until the grizzly is less than thirty feet away before spraying."

I stare at him, confounded. "While a grizzly is charging me, I'm supposed to stand still and casually calculate the distance between us?"

"Technically, you should play dead. If you can't, bear spray works."

"How many times have you been charged?"

Aksel smirks. "Once too many."

I shake my head, laughing. I have lived in a lot of dangerous places, but none of them involved fighting off a charging grizzly with a can of spicy hairspray.

Standing to clip into our snowshoes, Aksel reaches down to help me from the boulder. I place my hand in his, but as I stand, my snowshoe catches an edge. I stumble forward into Aksel, clinging to his sleeve and landing with a soft *thump* against his chest.

I smell his clean skin, feel his warm torso against mine.

His arm is braced firmly around my waist to keep me from falling. He stares down at me, and my cheeks go blisteringly hot. I feel light-headed. Snow and starlight envelop me in a bright wave.

I've forgotten how to breathe, how to talk.

Aksel contracts his arm around my lower back. My breath quickens. I'm torn between embarrassment and a thrilling desire to be closer to him.

Reaching my other hand forward, I place my palm against Aksel's chest. I feel his heartbeat—steady, not charging like mine.

Aksel gently nudges the wet hair back from my face. Gliding

his hand down, he cradles the back of my neck; his thumbs graze the skin below my ear, like matches lighting my skin in flames.

Our eyes lock. Our faces are centimeters apart. Our lips, millimeters. His forearm tightens against me, drawing me into him. His palm settling into the concave of my lower back. I want him to kiss me—I want him to kiss me so badly I feel like I might explode.

Aksel's lips press against mine. His fingertips trace my cheek, my jawline, before returning to the nape of my neck. My fingers weave into his. His lips are against mine, and mine are against his.

Then Aksel pulls away. His eyes catch mine, and there is a flash of intriguing vulnerability.

We stare at each other in protracted silence. Emotions filter through me—as if the hesitation between us has finally been obliterated.

Then our lips are meeting again and every nerve in my body is electrified.

In the cold winter air, I discover the one word in English that adequately describes what it's like to be near Aksel Fredricksen—consuming.

CHAPTER 24

"How was your night?" my father calls to me from down the hall.

Thirty seconds ago, I'd been standing on my porch with Aksel. Now, I call out to my father. "Good," I answer.

"Sophia, come in here."

Grudgingly, I step away from the banister and walk to the den.

My father is seated at his pine desk, which is cluttered with papers. His voice is calm, but his eyes have gray lines beneath them.

Shoving aside a box of envelopes, I sit down in a cozy leather chair in the corner.

I don't want to discuss Aksel with my parents. Not yet. Apparently, the freedom I've had in Waterford is going to take some getting used to—for all of us.

My father must see my wet hair, my chilled face—

"What's that?" I point over his shoulder.

"Analysis," he answers.

On the far wall, a new whiteboard is tacked up. Six whiteboards, actually, assembled in a grid pattern to form one large wall of writing space. "Thinking space," he calls it.

Taped in the center of one whiteboard is a map. Cobwebbing across the map are pushpins and sticky notes with names drawn on them, all connecting to one another with different-colored strings. Some strings dangle loose, unassigned.

This is my father—forgoing hard drives for twine and pushpins. *A computer can store everything I might possibly need, but then I can't see it. I can't solve it.*

My eyes roam over the whiteboard to the rest of the den. The books are stacked haphazardly in the bookcases. Several boxes are shoved into the corner. A tangle of electronic devices litter the floor beside his desk.

What problem is he solving now?

He's looking again at my hair. He's going to ask me about tonight—about Aksel.

I gesture around the usually tidy space. "I haven't seen this much paperwork since Prague."

"I'm consulting on a report for the United Nations Humanitarian Council on the effect of the migrant crisis on the island economies of the Aegean Sea," he answers easily.

"That's *all* you're doing?"

He hands me a paper from one of the files. "I am consulting, Sophia," he says, walking over to the wall of whiteboards, "analyzing the acquisition probability of special atomic demolition munitions—ADMs. That's what they're after now."

For years, I've understood that his work is much more layered and nuanced and complex than an average diplomat's.

But now that it's over—shouldn't it *be* over?

"Who?" I ask, scanning the economic graph.

"Everyone. Anyone," he says. "There are more terrorist cells now than ever, and each wants to get their hands on one."

"And what exactly is a *special atomic demolition munition*?" I ask.

"In slang? It's a backpack nuke."

"Those exist?"

"Sure."

"But they can't get one," I say, "right?"

"America kept track of her nuclear weapons at the end of the Cold War. Others didn't."

"You mean Russia."

He surveys one of the whiteboards. "The development of ADMs changed everything. Small nukes that could be transported easily and carried across borders? I couldn't think of anything more dangerous. Until the Russians succeeded in creating the first micronukes. Smaller than a fire extinguisher, light enough to carry in a handbag."

"Is it scientifically possible to create a weapon that small?"

"Absolutely."

I motion to the wall. "And you believe they exist?"

"I know they did exist, Sophia. But they were dismantled. That's the important part."

"How do you know?"

He exhales. *And that, Sophia, I will not answer.*

"So, what are you doing now?" I prompt.

"Wondering," he says slowly, stepping back over to his desk, "that's all."

Handing the economic graph back to my father, I suppress the urge to tell him that I was afraid earlier, that my blood ran cold when the man walked up behind me. The nervous adrenaline I felt in the street seeps into my bones—both distant and raw. It feels like days, not hours, since the Creamery.

"Darling, is there something you want to discuss?"

I imagine the conversation: *I was afraid when I saw a hooded figure in the street walking toward me . . . It was nobody . . . Just some guy.*

Then he would say: *It's over. You have to believe that.*

And I'd say: *I do.*

And I'd be lying.

What will happen if I tell him that although the man appeared to be from Waterford—wearing a Carhartt parka and work boots and strolling confidently into Alpine Market—by the way he pronounced his *r*s he sounded as though his first language wasn't English, but . . . Chechen?

"Sophia?" he asks.

"I'm going to bed," I say, backing out of the den.

Suddenly, I am so scared I'm trembling. Because I realize what I am truly afraid of, and it's not that man.

It's leaving Waterford.

CHAPTER 25

My phone beeps. It's another text from Charlotte, her seventeenth since Saturday. *This is why you have a phone—call me!*

Instead, *she* calls *me*, demanding, "Did Aksel drive you *home*? Tate says—"

Downstairs, the doorbell rings. "Charlotte, I have to go. I'll see you—"

"Is Aksel picking—"

"See you soon!" I hang up, hurry to the front door, and swing it open.

It's been fifty-six hours since he dropped me off Friday evening, and I've been thinking about this moment for each one.

Aksel is dressed in jeans and a collared shirt under a canvas jacket; his hands are tucked casually in his pockets. His face is windburned, and his green eyes flicker gold in the morning sunlight. Stepping forward, he brushes his lips swiftly against my cheek.

"You look beautiful," he says. I've heard this phrase hundreds of times from my parents; it's entirely different coming from Aksel.

He glances into the foyer and living room; he doesn't look curious, rather relieved.

Twisting a piece of hair in my fingertips, I try not to smile too widely. "Let me, um, grab something."

Inside, I retrieve Aksel's clean sweater from my drawer. On my way back outside, I duck into the den.

"See you after school?" I say to my father. He's focused, reading at his desk. Behind him, I scan the whiteboards for a clue, an indication my father is keeping something from me. I see nothing. It is a typical thinking wall—sticky notes, paper, twine, and tape.

"Sophia?"

I halt.

"You remember how to use it?" He looks up from his papers. He points to my hip where my phone is zipped inside the pocket of my Moncler puffer.

I laugh, "I *am* a teenager."

"I meant use it." His voice is quiet. Why is he reminding me of this? As if I could forget. By default, it blocks all GPS tracking, but it can also do the reverse—enable GPS tracking with a specific SOS protocol.

He gives me a hard look.

"I know." I pat my pocket, grinning.

A minute later, Aksel laughs when I give him his clothes. "I forgot," he says, which frustrates me—I should have kept them.

Outside, I notice a familiar vehicle—sparkling in the daylight.

"It's back!" I exclaim.

Aksel holds the door to the Defender open. "Dropped off early this morning."

Its olive-green exterior has been waxed. No visible dents. The interior smells like oiled leather.

"I *am* sorry," I say honestly.

He laces his fingers into mine. "Don't be." He grins. "I'm not."

Inside the school several minutes later, we head to my locker in the north hall, where I unload my backpack. "See you in Krenshaw's?" he asks.

"You're not staying?" I ask, surprised.

"I only have to turn in a physics assignment."

"If you don't have to be at school, then why . . ."

Aksel hooks his finger around my coat sleeve and tugs. My chest bumps into his, and I giggle. "I wanted to see you," he says simply.

Blushing, I lace my fingers through his, stand on my tiptoes, and sling my arms around his neck.

"See you in"—Aksel checks his watch—"four hours and three minutes?"

"Don't be late," I warn, smiling.

"I wouldn't dare," he says. I shove him gently in the direction of the stairs. With an easy grin, he releases his hands from mine and bounds up the steps.

"So you've been sneaking around with Fredricksen this whole time?"

The words snap me into reality. Tate slams his locker shut and walks over, staring me down with a malevolent sneer plastered across his face.

I adjust my books. "I was not *sneaking*—"

"You played me!" Tate doesn't seem upset, he seems infuriated.

My face flushes. "*Played* you?"

Tate seethes, "Don't pretend you weren't leading me—"

"Hey, man," Henry interrupts, "I don't think she meant—"

"Shut up, Henry. You saw her all over me, before she ditched me to hook up with Fredricksen—"

"I did not!" I fire back. "You need to get your facts straight, *frauenfeindlicher Vollidiot*."

My words echo in the stark hall. After so many weeks trying to blend in, it's like I've exposed my identity. Everyone looks at me.

Tate's eye twitches. "What did you call me?" he asks furiously.

My cheeks redden with fury. "Pay attention in German, and you'll learn."

Tate steps toward me. "You think you're so cool because—"

"It's not a big deal, Tate." Mason steps between me and Tate, trying to placate him.

"Did you think we wouldn't find out, Sophia? That *you* could play *us*? We always find out the girls who—"

"*Who* what?" an icy voice says from over my shoulder.

Tate takes a step back.

Charlotte is standing beside me, hand on her hip, glaring at Tate. Henry purses his lips together, holding in a laugh.

Charlotte glances over at me. "Everything okay here?"

"Certainly. *Du bist ein Chauvinistenschwein*, right, Tate?" I smile. "It means 'We're good' in German."

Tate turns on his heel and stalks off.

"It's a good thing he's failing German," I utter to Charlotte and Henry.

Henry looks over at me, grinning. "Why?"

"Because it doesn't mean 'we're good.' "

If word travels fast in most small towns, it travels at lightning speed in Waterford.

Tate is convinced I *played* him—and by lunchtime the story is that I *hooked up* with Tate outside the Creamery, then *hooked up* with Aksel hours later. So not only does word travel fast, but it has left the truth in a different galaxy.

As I fiddle with my cucumber and tomato sandwich, Charlotte stands and slings her bag over her shoulder. "Come on."

Inside the Art History classroom, Emma sits on top of a desk and unwraps her sandwich. "Sophia, maybe you should apologize to Tate and this will—"

"That's a terrible idea, Emma!" Charlotte says, aghast.

Emma narrows her eyes at Charlotte. The freckles on her cheeks seem to change colors with her moods. "Perhaps *you* should apologize. *You* pushed her at Tate—"

"She was having fun!" Charlotte counters. "She kept smiling at him!"

"You wanted Sophia to ride with Tate so *you* could ride with Mason!" Emma retorts. "He's my brother, Charlotte! You could have anyone! You flirting with Mason is weird—"

"Oh please," Charlotte says, a faint redness glowing in her face. "I was not! And I didn't know Tate would overreact!"

"It's Tate!" Emma declares. "You dated him! Of course you knew he would—"

"It doesn't matter what Tate or anyone else says," I interrupt. "I wasn't planning to tell everyone I'd gone out with Aksel!"

A thick silence drapes over the Art History classroom. Emma and Charlotte exchange glances. It's like they've morphed from enemy combatants into allies again.

Charlotte tugs at a string on her sweater. "You weren't going to tell *us*?"

"I didn't think you would understand," I explain.

"Understand what? Liking someone? Do you listen to anything we say, like—ever?"

I rub my cheeks with my palms. Wringing my hands, I pace back and forth. I breathe in through my nose and stare at them.

"I didn't think you would understand what it was like to want to be with someone every moment, while at the same time be terrified of the moment it might disappear"—I snap my fingers—"instantly."

"Are you *oblivious*?" Charlotte tosses her apple core across the room. It lands with a *thump* in the trash bin. "Aksel Fredricksen hasn't taken a girl out in this entire town. If he's taking you out, Sophia, I guarantee he's not going to—*poof*!—disappear anytime soon."

"I didn't mean him." I twist my finger through my necklace. "I meant me."

CHAPTER 26

Front door is unlocked, Aksel texts me.

After I stay late completing a French assignment with Charlotte, I run up Eagle Pass to Aksel's house. However, Aksel is nowhere in sight: he's not in the library, kitchen, or great room. I notice nothing out of the ordinary except a coffee mug in the sink—Aksel doesn't drink coffee.

Quickly, I descend the staircase to the ground floor. Beyond the gear room is a misty opaque surface—a swimming pool. A very grand swimming pool, framed by a high cedar-planked ceiling and plate glass windows overlooking the steep mountain summit.

Aksel is underwater at the far end. Sidestepping a heap of underwater diving equipment, I sit cross-legged on the pool deck and pull off my Dale of Norway headband.

"Thought I heard an intruder," Aksel says, surfacing. He swims over. When he reaches me, he wraps his large hands around my ankles and stands up in the water, nearly pulling me in. I laugh, pushing back at his shoulders.

He shifts to place his arms on either side of me, elbows locked, holding himself upright. Heat spreads like wildfire across my chest until it constricts my airways, like I can't breathe.

His hand is wet yet warm when he strokes my cheek. He

outlines my lips with his thumb. He bends forward to kiss me, then stops, eyebrows knitting together.

He touches my chin with his forefinger, tilting my neck back.

"You *do* have a scar," he says bluntly, tracing the delicate skin with his forefinger.

"It's old," I say quickly, my ears pink.

"I never noticed . . . ," he murmurs.

The scar is the length of my pinkie, a millimeter wide, and directly in the crease where my head meets my neck. "It was a car accident. A piece of glass." I shrug. "It's not a big deal."

I draw my feet up and fold them into my chest.

He opens his mouth, then shuts it.

"You had a visitor?" I ask, trying to change the subject.

Aksel places his palms flat on the edge and hops out of the pool. "How'd you know?"

"The coffee mug in the sink."

He stares at me, amused, half smiling. However, his smile fades as he looks darkly across the water. "He shouldn't have come." He grimaces.

"Who?"

"Martin," Aksel sighs. "My grandfather. Guardian now."

After a moment's hesitation I say, "Why didn't he stay? Did he want something?"

Aksel looks over his shoulder. I follow his gaze. On the cedar pool deck is an envelope with a letter halfway out. I stretch my arm back to retrieve it. On the top of the page is a blue embossed letterhead. I only have to read the first paragraph.

"You've been admitted," I say faintly.

Aksel nods.

"Congratulations," I force out. "So, you're going?" I try to stifle the unexplained panic rising in my voice.

Aksel leans back, resting his weight on his elbows. His expression is contemplative.

"I've dreamed of becoming a SEAL since I was twelve—getting helo-ed into some Siberian inlet, sneaking underwater to some fortress, ambushing bad guys . . ." His voice is tinged with sincerity and regret.

I glance at the letter, trying to decipher his guarded response. "And your grandfather—Martin—came here to persuade you to *not* attend the Naval Academy?"

Aksel shifts his hands, scowling. "He insists I should attend an Ivy League school like the rest of my family."

A lingering suspicion that he is hiding something leaks into my thoughts. "And . . . that's a bad option?"

Aksel's jaw clenches. He looks disgusted. "He says the military is no place for 'someone like me.'"

"Has he *seen* you shoot?" I laugh. "Aksel, the only people who shoot better than you are combat snipers."

Aksel draws his hands through his wet hair and then shakes it out. "He doesn't mean someone with my marksmanship." Aksel looks down at his hands, averting his eyes from mine. His neck is a blistering shade of red. "He means someone . . . privileged."

I whistle under my breath. "If my mother meets Martin, she might punch him in the nose."

While Aksel's presence still unnerves me, my presence seems to conflict him. Aksel's eyes dart between me and the far side of the pool.

"I suppose it's my own fault for confiding in him about my

parents' deaths." Aksel shrugs. "It was already hard enough for him, losing his daughter. But my dad flew into the mountains and performed surgery on those who otherwise would have died. He believed in it, you know? Using medicine to save the world. He would never have done anything to get himself, or my mom, killed."

When Aksel looks back at me, as if he's said too much, the turquoise of the pool reflects in his eyes so they appear a vivid blue. He stands and grabs my backpack off the floor. Throwing a sweatshirt over his head, the corner of his lip tilts upward in an exasperated, restless smile. "Let's get some food," he says, pulling me onto my feet.

On the staircase, I turn around to face him. It is dark without any natural light. Confined. With Aksel standing on the step below me, we are the same height. Our eyes lock. My heart bangs against my rib cage.

I know it now, more than ever. Aksel intimidates me. Not in an alarming way, but because when I'm around him I feel so much less in control of my thoughts, my instincts.

The connection between us is visceral.

His hands entwine my waist, resting on the hollow of my lower back.

Gently, he pushes me against the wall.

I slide my arms loose and crawl my fingers up his chest until they reach his neck. I tangle my fingers into his hair, and before I know it, our lips are meeting, quickly and urgently.

An intense heat races throughout my body. Blood pulses in my ears. I want nothing more than to be close to him. To feel his skin against mine.

We kiss until he leans away.

My breathing is so heavy, he must be able to hear it. He smells faintly of salt and sweat; his skin is still damp. With our bodies pressed tight together, I can feel each finger of his hand against the small of my back, holding me close to him, firmly, but not tightly. Securely.

His voice is calm, but concern and worry are etched into every syllable. "Sophia . . . I think . . ."

"Maybe you still shouldn't be getting involved with me?"

He chuckles softly. "Maybe I shouldn't be thinking."

I push back against his stony chest, and saunter up the stairs. "So don't."

In the kitchen, Aksel opens the fridge, takes out a copper pot, sets it on the stove, and turns on the flame. "Henry's mom dropped off dinner." He grins. "My mom left her with a spare key, and she refused to give it back."

I take a loaf of bread from a paper bag and slice two pieces using a serrated knife from the block on the counter.

Aksel notices the knife in my hand: my wrist tucked against the blade, my fingers clasped around the shaft. Immediately, I loosen my grip and spin the knife around to face the ground. "What do you eat when she doesn't drop off food?"

"I have a cook," he answers nonchalantly, ladling some soup into a bowl.

I raise an eyebrow. "And Krenshaw thinks *I'm* spoiled?"

While I eat the creamy, peppery potato soup, Aksel runs down the hall for a quick shower. When he reemerges, clean and dressed in a wool sweater and jeans, the skin on my neck warms.

Eventually, we leave the kitchen and wander into the cozy great room. With snow falling outside and a fire crackling in the hearth, the last thing I want to do is homework.

I empty the contents of my backpack onto the sofa. My calculus text lands with a *thud*. "I despise Krenshaw," I groan.

Laughing, Aksel takes my calculus textbook and opens to our assignment. "You definitely have that in common with every other student at Waterford."

I peer over Aksel's shoulder as he pencils out the equation, his damp hair loose on his forehead, his mouth tight in concentration.

Even in Kabul, eating MREs and using flashlights, my father tutored me relentlessly. But here with Aksel, the numbers blur. "I don't want to do schoolwork," I say, and drop onto the sofa.

Aksel taps his pencil against his wrist. "We can go skiing? Fresh powder today."

I scrunch my nose. "There's fresh powder every day."

He looks amused. "What about shooting?" he suggests.

"I'm not firing your rifle."

"That's fine. I want you to teach me to shoot a handgun."

"You're an excellent shot!"

Aksel shakes his head. "I can hit a soda can from four hundred yards, no scope, no problem—eight hundred yards on a clear day with a scope, but that's long-barrel shooting. With a handgun, I can't hit a stationary target at ten yards. It's so unpredictable—it aims wherever it wants."

I fold my legs on the couch. My knees bump against his thigh. "It's not the gun that's unpredictable," I say. "It's you."

He lifts his eyebrow audaciously. "Me?"

"Technically, it's because of the shake."

The side of his mouth curves upward. "The *what?*"

"You know, 'the shake' . . ."

He tilts his head, as if trying not to laugh.

I push his biceps. "Go get your SIG, sniper, I'll show you."

Aksel hops over the back of the sofa and disappears around the corner. He descends to the ground floor and, a few minutes later, reemerges with a SIG.

"How many guns do you keep?" I ask.

"Only my hunting rifle and this. I got rid of the rest after my dad died." Aksel locks the slide back and passes it to me.

"First," I say, "disassembly." I take the SIG apart and point to the pistol components in my lap. "Magazine. Chamber. Slide. Barrel."

Aksel whistles. "You do that fast."

"It's always easier with your eyes open."

Aksel watches me with a disconcerted expression. My skin tingles.

I point to the grip. "A pistol is always a compromise of accuracy, power, and concealment. You can have one, but you compromise the other two—you can't have all three. Understand?"

Aksel nods. I begin reassembling the SIG.

"Concealment is problematic for me because I don't wear baggy clothes. And I don't like too much power—I want accuracy. With a pistol, it's important how the gun fits in your palm. The FN 5-7 has a nice grip; it gives me the most accurate shot. I prefer it over a SIG, but my dad prefers an HK45."

"And your mom?" he quips.

"Beretta Tomcat in a thigh holster, but I've only seen her use it once." I take his SIG in my hand.

"When you hold it . . ." I lift Aksel's hand off my knee, keeping it steady in the air. My fingers graze the top of his. He smells so good—like pine and leather and sandalwood—I have to concentrate on what I'm trying to explain.

". . . insert the magazine, load a bullet into the chamber, then tap, rack, and roll as usual. Now, you'll want to hold it taut but loose, like you're cradling a small bird, a swallow: don't crush it but don't let it get away. When you're ready to shoot, aim like you would with a rifle, except control the shake."

I put my hand out, palm down. "See it shaking? That's the natural resting point of a hand—moving. With a Remington, the tremors in your hand are compensated for by the rifle lodged here . . ." I place my hand on his chest, my palm flat against his pecs. He smiles.

I force my voice not to quiver. ". . . distributing the shake throughout your muscular and skeletal systems, neutralizing it." I draw my fingertips across his chest and down his arm to his fingertips.

Under Aksel's intense stare, my breathing is heavy. His presence makes every nerve in my body feel like it's been scorched.

"When you're shooting a pistol," I continue, "all the shaking in your fingers is concentrated into the trigger pull. If you want an accurate shot, you have to train yourself not to shake." I hold my palm out again. Aksel frowns, putting his hand next to mine. His fingers twitch, nearly invisibly, but enough to affect aim at twenty meters.

"Don't clench your fingers. Relax your muscles," I advise.

"You're making me nervous," he mutters under his breath.

I move my hand closer to his. Our hands drift in the air side by side, like spaceships hovering above earth.

"If you control the shake, you control your aim."

"That simple, huh?"

"So simple an eight-year-old can do it."

"Don't tell me—"

"Can't help it." I grin. "My father likes guns. Very Montana of him."

Aksel laughs, dropping his hand.

Gathering the disassembled parts of the pistol together, I return them to Aksel. "I learned to control the shake by reassembling a pistol in less than twenty seconds."

Aksel seems to refrain from rolling his eyes. Nevertheless, in twenty-nine seconds, he has the pistol reassembled and passes it back to me.

"Nine seconds too slow." I eject the mag, check the chamber, clip the mag back in, and hand it back. While he practices—twenty-seven seconds, twenty-four seconds, twenty-three—I stare out at the wilderness beyond the massive plate glass windows.

In the distance, pine trees at the edge of the clearing tremble in the breeze; their peculiar cone shapes and deep green hues intersect a sky thick with snow clouds. In the west, a patch of sunlight threatens to break through.

I look back at Aksel. His collar is slightly askew, and his neatly trimmed hair is mussed, giving him a ruggedly beautiful look. Aksel makes me feel secure. I trust him in a way I've never trusted anyone—in a way that transcends everything my parents have trained me to believe.

"Aksel, why *did* you think you shouldn't become involved with me?" I ask sedately. It's been weeks since the Creamery, and I've been unable to get his words out of my head.

"Twenty!" He pushes the safety on proudly, placing the SIG on the table behind the sofa.

He looks at me like I have morphed into some complex equation he needs to solve; he drags a hand through his tousled hair.

"I don't know, Sophia," Aksel eventually says. "I should be concentrating on other things, I suppose." He weaves his fingers into mine. "Except when I'm not with you, I think about being with you. And when I'm with you, I *only* think about you. And I get that maybe you don't want to discuss places you lived, or people you knew, or why you can disassemble and reassemble a pistol faster than I can load my rifle . . . But if anything feels right, Sophia?" He traces the inside of my palm with his thumb. "This does."

Aksel kisses my neck. Linking my hands behind his neck, I close my eyes.

"And maybe we're wrong for each other." His lips brush my jaw, sending warm currents tearing through me. "Maybe, Sophia, this is a really bad idea, maybe it can't last . . ."

Aksel's hands slide across my neck, slipping down my back. Goose bumps rise up my spine. His lips are inches from mine; flames of heat surge across my throat.

I feel his pulse, flush against my chest. Our lips hover.

"I'll go with you," I whisper.

Confused, Aksel props his head up on one elbow and touches my lips with his thumb. "Where?"

I nudge his thigh with my knee. "Skiing."

Afternoon sunlight breaks open the clouds and pours into the house through the windows. In the brilliant sunlight, Aksel's green eyes are nearly translucent.

"Finally." He casts me a wide smile. "It's my turn to teach you something. Skiing is always a compromise of three things: speed, style, and slope . . ." He pulls me in, wraps his strong arms around my waist, and kisses me.

But I can't get his words out of my head, that *we* might be a bad idea.

That *I* might be a bad idea.

I sit upright and look at him. "Aksel, are you scared of me?" I ask quietly.

Aksel watches me like he can read every thought that circulates inside my head. Maybe now is the moment he'll decide I have too much history. That my past is too strange—that I am too strange.

But I also feel like there's a live wire connecting us, and severing it would detonate an explosion.

Aksel locks his arms behind my back and draws me toward him. His words come out smooth, breathless almost. "Sophia, you scare the hell out of me."

CHAPTER 27

Saturday arrives blustery and cold. Aksel texts me at seven: *Wake up, weather's perfect.*

The floorboards creak as I walk to the bathroom. After combing my tangled hair, I pull on ski leggings and a Fair Isle sweater.

Passing by the living room on my way to the kitchen, I see my father asleep on the velvet wingback chair beside the piano.

In his fist is a tiny note. I pluck it from between his fingers. On the paper are words scribbled in Cyrillic letters. One near the bottom is circled. Even in sloppy Russian, I can read my father's slanted handwriting: *Nemcova.*

I go into the den. The map has moved to the bottom right whiteboard on the grid. On it dozens of strings create a web of words; my father constructed it using his own encryption technique. It isn't undecipherable, but it slows someone down to translate a sentence of mixed-up Hmong-Arabic-Swahili-Portuguese-Latvian-Icelandic.

Nemcova is written as an acronym in the bottom left corner of the top centerboard. One end of a string is attached to the name. The other end is hooked around a pushpin jabbed into the center of Helsinki, Finland.

"*Godmorgen*, Sophia."

I turn, startled. Discreetly, I tug on the hem of my sweater and slide the note into the waistband of my pants.

"Any clues?" I ask, motioning to the board. The fire is burnt embers, and the room smells faintly of peppermint. My mother's teacup teeters on the corner of the mantel.

My father tidies his cluttered desk, stacking papers, files, and three open laptops.

"To what?" he asks.

"To how Farhad found us in Tunis—how he got into the safe house?"

"None, Sophia."

My mother enters the den from the kitchen. "Good morning, darling." Although she is dressed in pleated slacks and a cardigan, she looks disheveled; wearing no lipstick, she looks as though she hasn't slept in three days. Two days with no sleep she can fake. But on day three? The shadows around her eyes darken. The pallor of her skin alters.

By the drawn looks on their faces, I know they've been up all night. And I assume they know I can tell, so why are they pretending otherwise?

"Why are you working?" I demand.

The teakettle whistles from the kitchen. My mother switches off her desk lamp and kisses me on the forehead. "Old paperwork, Sophia."

My father nods at my clothing. "Going somewhere?"

The teakettle is still whistling from the kitchen, and my mother leaves the room.

"Skiing, with Aksel," I answer.

His face reveals his surprise. "How nice." He taps the desk with his fingertips. "I suppose I should be worried about you spending so much time with Aksel," he says, "but it's part of being an American teenager I suppose, dating American boys."

I twist my hair around my fingers. "You're okay with it?"

A contemplative expression appears on his face. Behind him through the window, wind rustles the branches of the barren oak tree in the back garden. A clump of snow plummets to the ground.

When he finally meets my nervous stare, his steel-gray eyes are moist and vulnerable. "My dear Sophia," he whispers, "I'm just happy to see you smiling again."

In addition to a Gruyère soufflé, my mother makes cardamom waffles with apple streusel topping and hot cocoa with freshly whipped cream.

"She's fattening you up in case you get buried in an avalanche," my father says with a wink.

"False," my mother objects. "I'm making waffles because I haven't eaten Bisquick in a decade."

After breakfast, my father disappears and doesn't reemerge until Aksel knocks a half hour later. Rushing to beat my parents to the foyer, I fling open the door.

"Hi." He grins. Aksel is wearing a ski jacket and snow boots. His eyes are bright in the morning sun, and the little azure flecks in the green sparkle.

My father shakes Aksel's hand. "I'm Kent Hepworth."

My mother steps forward. She has applied lipstick and put on an ironed blouse—she no longer looks tired.

"I'm Mary Hepworth," she says in her soft, melodic voice. "We must thank you again for bringing Sophia home safely a few weeks ago."

Aksel shakes her hand too. "Sure, Mrs. Hepworth." He says this easily, but I sense a wariness in him and wonder if it has anything to do with the fact that my mother is watching him in a peculiar, inquisitive, slightly unnerving way.

Now I know why Charlotte detests introducing her boyfriends to her parents.

"Okay, well, we need to leave." I tug Aksel's hand and promise my parents we won't enter the backcountry.

It isn't until we reach the Defender that I see them—shiny, white, waxed pristinely. Propped against the bumper is a pair of new Stöckli powder skis.

My father must have kept them hidden in the garage this whole time. Perhaps, I think with a rush of affection toward my father, he knows me better than I know myself.

When I look over at the house, the door is closed. But through the front window I see a shadow—my father is standing in the back of the living room near the piano, watching us.

Thank you, I mouth. He tips his head forward and disappears into the den.

CHAPTER 28

"Nervous?" Aksel asks.

Above us, the sky is a thick layer of white cloud pierced by knifepoints of blue. A deft wind sends snowflakes swirling around us.

I click into my gleaming new boots and laugh. "Skiing doesn't scare me."

"What does scare you?"

I point across the road. "Them."

Tourists, wearing expensive one-piece ski suits, have prematurely clicked into their skis and are attempting to walk across the pavement. Their helmets are on backward, and their goggles are on upside down.

Aksel snickers. "Steer clear."

At the base of Waterford Resort, we ski into line to access the upper runs.

The lift creaks around the track, and I sit down on the hard seat. As we swing upward, I want to reach out and touch the spiky treetops. I want to stand at the peak of the mountain. Challenge it. Conquer it.

We ski off the lift and pause on the flat plateau at the head of the run. To our left, an intermediate trail descends gradually.

Directly ahead, the steep mountain narrows into a chute descending through trees.

I angle my skis toward the top of the chute. "Here?" I shout to Aksel.

I don't hear his response. Instead, I am blinded by assaulting snow flurries.

Laughter explodes behind me. A figure in all black—from helmet to boots—has hockey-stopped beside me.

"Took you long enough!" Blond hair curling out from the bottom of his helmet indicates who sprayed the snow—Mason.

"Sophia is finally skiing, and she chooses a double black as her first run?" another familiar voice shouts.

Grinning, I look over at a skier in a pink helmet and fur-trimmed ski outfit—Charlotte. "Skis look good on you!" She whistles. "Sure you can keep up?"

"I didn't know Parisian girls could ski!" Mason taunts.

"I'M NOT PARISIAN!" I proclaim, laughing.

I look at Aksel, who is bent forward, on his poles, watching me, smirking. Henry and a girl named Sarah are beside him, laughing.

I flick my pole at Aksel's chest. "I'll see *you* at the bottom."

"Is that a challenge?" Even while wearing a helmet and fluorescent goggles, Aksel is betrayed by his smile as the best-looking boy on the mountain.

I laugh. "Last one to the bottom buys lunch."

Digging my poles into the packed snow, I angle my skis downhill, drop off the flat plateau, and descend into the narrow chute.

Behind me Emma shouts, "We're not allowed to race!"

"A rule you only follow because you never win!" Mason shouts back.

Waterford may not produce the fastest skiers on the circuit, but it definitely produces the most fearless. Charlotte does a 360 off a mogul even my father wouldn't try—and lands it. From the chute, I ski over into the light, fresh powder, hidden among tight clumps of pine trees.

In seconds, it returns—the rhythm, the icy thrill.

"On your left!" hollers Emma as she skis past me, bypassing a tree with low-hanging branches. I catch up to Charlotte as she catapults off another jump.

I only lose my balance once, while in thigh-deep powder at full clip.

Back on packed snow, I carve down the steep terrain. I push my shins into my boots, curl over my knees, and tuck my arms close to my hips. Accelerating faster and faster, I fly down the steep mountainside.

I soar, and for the first time in over eighteen months, I am free.

CHAPTER 29

Driving home in the late afternoon, I am warm, glowing from skiing all weekend. Aksel squeezes my hand and turns to me with a smile that makes me flush.

I start to say, "I'm so glad," but stop.

Two unmarked black vehicles are reversing out of my driveway onto Edgewood Lane.

My body stiffens. My heart starts pounding.

"Sophia?" Aksel's sharp voice feels distant.

Sudden tension locks my body into place.

The vehicles pass us with windows so dark we can't see through them.

Aksel slows to a stop. "Who was that?" His even tone fails to mask his stony expression.

"No one. I'll see you tomorrow, okay?" I say hastily.

"Sophia." He clutches my hand. "What's going on?"

"Promise you'll pick me up for school?" I say placidly. "I had fun this weekend."

Aksel's face betrays his unwillingness to let me go, but I must go inside, and he must leave. Inside is my past and Aksel is my future and the two can never meet. Not now. Not today. They have to remain apart.

"Sophia—"

I unbuckle my seat belt, push open the door, and sprint to the house.

I race over the threshold. "Dad? Mom?"

They are standing in the living room speaking softly to each other.

"Who are they?" My words slice through the quiet room.

"Acquaintances," my father answers.

"What were they doing here?"

"Sophia, it's nothing—"

"Nothing does not look like that!" I shout.

My father has always told me—*Shouting undermines credibility, Sophia.* I breathe through my nose. "What were they doing here?" I ask with a seething calm.

My father's nose twitches, like the bulls in Pamplona before the running starts. "Do you remember a few years back, we were visiting the Musée d'Orsay? You asked if we could go to St. Petersburg to see the Hermitage and—"

"You said no because you had a dangerous job there before I was born, and afterward, returning to St. Petersburg became impossible."

"It wasn't just a dangerous job, Sophia. It changed everything."

"Okay, fine, so that was in St. Petersburg twenty years ago—"

"Nineteen years ago," he exhales, "I was assigned to St. Petersburg to become acquainted with the SVR—the Russian Foreign Intelligence Service. I found someone to talk to, who eventually defected with more weapons intelligence than we could have ever hoped to acquire—"

"Why are you telling me this?"

"Because I recently contacted Andrews to express my concern that St. Petersburg might have been compromised."

"So that was Andrews?" I motion in the direction the cars left.

"Andrews is in the Ukraine—those were some colleagues."

"So, you're *not* doing analysis?" I say accusingly.

"Everything I do is analysis, Sophia. I'm a regional specialist."

"You're a case officer," I say bitingly. "Stop pretending."

"Sophia, I'm not CIA—"

"Kent," my mother snaps.

My father has always instructed me using vague terms, never disclosing specific details, and never revealing more than necessary.

This method has never bothered me before. Why does it bother me so much now?

"I know there's more." I concentrate on my father. "I deserve to an explanation!"

"I understand you might feel that way, honey, but my priority is to keep you safe—"

"Safe? You think I'm safe in Waterford? Someone was following me!"

Immediately, I regret the words. It is like the room is deprived of oxygen.

"Why do you say that?" asks my father in an edged tone, standing.

I shouldn't have said it. It takes all my composure to remain calm, because if my father thinks I'm worried, he'll worry, and he can't worry about me. Not now.

My palms are clammy. "I thought someone, I mean, he wasn't, but it felt as if someone was following me a while ago. Aksel thought the same thing—"

"Aksel was there?" he interjects.

"It was nothing," I say quickly. "The guy was wearing a hood, so I couldn't see his face, and he was walking straight at me, like he was aiming for me, except I was imagining it. I do that still, sometimes." My eyes study the rug. "I imagine I see him walking toward me."

Clasping his hands behind his back, my father begins to pace. Does he struggle talking about this as much as I do?

I glance at my mother. She is standing rigid beside the sofa, watching us.

It occurs to me how much freedom I've had in Waterford. They would never let me live this way if they weren't sure that it's over.

Collecting my thoughts, I look at my father calmly. "He was just a guy in Waterford, not paying attention, who almost bumped into me."

My father stops pacing. "You've seen no one suspicious since?"

"No."

He nods to my hip, to my phone. "You'll call me if you do?"

"Yes."

"Then, Sophia, stop worrying. My concern that there might be some loose ends to tie up doesn't affect our lives here. This case is only chatter over a wire. Specific words popping up among terror cells we haven't heard in a long time. Anyone with knowledge about the St. Petersburg job is secure."

Secure. I have a prickly sensation on the back of my neck that "secure" means dead—and that "loose ends to tie up" means kill.

He continues, "We know terror groups are discussing certain weapons, but it's nothing more than their own speculation and aspirations. Nothing new."

"ADMs?"

He closes his mouth scrupulously.

I stare brazenly at him, pushing harder. "If Andrews told you to retire, shouldn't you follow orders and pass these *loose ends* on to someone else?"

"Sophia, you must understand that I'll continually be approached for information or asked to analyze data. I've been around a long time. Bureaucracy, I guarantee, I'll never escape," he says wryly.

My father sits down beside my mother on the sofa. He looks tired.

"This fight against extremism is a war against an enemy that is both everywhere and nowhere. Occasionally, if new threats emerge associated with old enemies, old jobs, I'll work. But none of that affects our lives here. We told you this when we moved here. Now you have to trust us."

Trust. It's such a complicated word. How can I trust them when they neither lie nor tell the complete truth?

"Nemcova," I say abruptly, pleased my father looks surprised. "Who is she?"

"Ola Nemcova is an old colleague," my mother answers calmly, rising to her feet. She presses out the pleats in her slacks. "Are you hungry, sweetheart? I made baguettes and vichyssoise."

"I'm not hungry."

"What about Aksel? Have you both eaten?"

"He left."

My mother points over my shoulder. "He's outside."

I whirl around.

"You never heard him drive away, did you?" she reprimands me.

Anger flares inside me. Isn't that why we moved here? So I wouldn't have to pay attention to every sound, every noise?

I run back outside. Aksel unfolds his hands and closes the distance between us in several strides.

"What are you still doing here?" My body pulses.

He scans my face. "I had to know you were okay."

"I'm fine," I snap. "Why wouldn't I be?"

His expression hardens as he tucks his hands into his pockets.

I stare at Aksel's guarded face, searching for answers: *Why did he stay?*

He lifts his eyes from mine. They refocus on my parents. Standing in the window. Watching us.

"I'll leave, okay?" With a swift kiss on my cheek, Aksel gets into the Defender.

Ignoring my parents' eyes drilling into the back of my head, I duck around the hood, open the passenger door, and get in.

"Drive," I order.

Moments later, steep cliffs enclose us in a granite cocoon. As we near the bend around Eagle Peak, Aksel brakes and steers over to a landing on the shoulder. He stops with the wheels a meter from the ravine edge and shifts the car into park.

"What's going on, Sophia?" he demands.

I wanted to drive—not talk. Talking means confronting it, and I don't want to confront it. I am trembling again. A cold sweat has broken out on my forehead. I loop my thumbs into the wrist straps on my sweater.

Aksel knows I have a past—does he know more than he's letting on?

"Why did you really stay?" I plead.

Affronted, he glares at me. "Because I was worried, Sophia!"

"Why?" I prompt. "I was just going home!"

Aksel drags his hands over his forehead. Then he walks around to my side and opens my door. Behind him is the steep summit of Eagle Peak. In the starlight I see the sharp edges of the rocks we climbed. It's hard to believe there was a time when I barely knew Aksel, when he only knew me as that girl from Berlin.

He drapes his arm on the door. His jaw is clenched tight, as though he's trying to conceal emotions.

"Look, I don't know what happened before you came to Waterford and I don't need to—I respect your privacy, your past—but that also means I don't know whether you're going to be staying or leaving . . ." He trails off.

Leaving. Is that what this is about?

"And what about you?" I say hotly, exposing my own fears. "Am I supposed to believe your training, your classes, your target practice is simply for the Academy?"

"I intend to be prepared," Aksel says dismissively. "That's all."

"Fine. I intend to stay in Waterford," I retort.

Aksel's mouth tightens. "That's what worries me. You're not necessarily making the decisions."

"Things are different here," I say emphatically.

"Are they?"

"Yes! So you shouldn't worry about me, Aksel."

Aksel stares at me audaciously. "Well, I do. A lot."

"So, stop!"

"You'd rather I *not* care?" Aksel appears incredulous; his eyebrows furrow over his wide, emerald eyes. "Sophia, do you realize that every night when I go to bed, I wonder if I'm going to wake up in the morning and find out you're gone?"

I bite my lip, pushing aside the voice in my head echoing Aksel's concerns.

I'm safe here. Safe.

"That won't happen." My voice is barely audible. "Not anymore. Not here."

Aksel's shoulders flex beneath his sweater; he is still holding fiercely onto my hand, as if I'll dissolve into air if he lets go.

"You're right," he finally says, "it probably won't. But that doesn't mean I don't worry about it. I care about you, Sophia. A lot. Too much, possibly."

We have never discussed it—this inexplicable communication between us, this ability to understand so much about each other in so little time—but it's here, right now, like an electric current between us.

There is more to this. More to Aksel. More to *us*.

We are combustible.

Eventually, Aksel's hand settles on my knee. His touch sends a voltage down my leg and up my spine.

I twist my fingers through his. "I get it, Aksel. My life hasn't been normal. I'm *not* normal—"

He pushes his lips firmly against mine. "You don't want normal," he says in a sultry murmur, "and neither do I."

An hour later, I am back in my living room.

I sit down at the piano, determined to suffocate the questions billowing inside me.

I recall the memories: tulle and chiffon gathered around my feet, my mother worrying I would get stage fright, a bodice so tight around my waist I could hardly breathe, but a dress I insisted on wearing because of the way the lustrous fabric shimmered on the stage.

The french doors swing open. My father comes in and sits beside me on the bench. "We need to talk."

Ignoring him, I trace each polished key.

"I began tracking the Chechen Nationalist Front when you were twelve," he says in a steady voice.

I play one note. Two. *Don't talk about this.*

"Within a few years, CNF had evolved from naive Chechens posting stupid extremist stuff online and mixing Molotov cocktails in their kitchens to executing poorly coordinated attacks. They'd grown, and I had to pay attention."

Tulle and chiffon . . . Tulle and chiffon . . . If I concentrate on that evening, that memory, I don't have to think about the others.

"I'd been tracking their leadership for months. CNF was quickly becoming an effective terrorist network. I had foiled an attack in Albania when I left a man for dead, who, it turns out, wasn't." My father closes his eyes. "That man was Izam Bekami."

Instantly, I stop gliding my fingers along the keys.

"Darling, whoever you thought was following you, whoever you think you may have seen . . ." My father's voice is so low I can barely hear him. "It wasn't Bekami."

Eighteen months later, his name still sends chills across my fingertips.

Izam Bekami.

Bekami.

I lay my hands in my lap. My throat swells shut. Fear shrouds my vision.

I partition my life into two spheres: before Bekami, and after.

My father continues, "Please trust me, Sophia. Live your life here in Waterford. Izam Bekami remains imprisoned in North Africa. Every other member of that Chechen cell from Istanbul is dead. Farhad was the last one, and you *saw* me kill him in Tunis."

I turn to my father. My fingers seal to my palm.

"Dad, I know. I never once thought it was"—I struggle to say Bekami's name aloud—"him."

My father drums middle C with his crooked forefinger. He takes my hand and squeezes it reassuringly. Standing, he heads back to the den.

He pauses at the door. "It's over, Sophia. You have to believe me."

It's over.

CHAPTER 30

"How romantic!" Charlotte swirls a piece of hair around her finger and sighs.

I unload my lunch bag onto the table and look at Charlotte. "Romantic?"

Earlier this morning as we pulled up to Waterford High, Aksel had turned to me, saying, "I suppose I kind of like you, Sophia."

"Kind of?" I repeated, threading my hand into his.

Grinning, Aksel had opened the glove compartment, retrieved a thick envelope, and handed it to me.

Confused, I tore the seal and reached inside. Two glossy slips of paper met my fingertips, embossed with cursive script: *The Kirov Ballet*.

". . . he must really like you," Charlotte continues matter-of-factly, "because ballet is boring."

"Degas didn't think so," Emma comments, half listening. Her art history book is open, spread flat on the lunch table; she is murmuring at a flash card of Manet's *Olympia*.

"Weren't *you* a ballerina?" I ask Charlotte.

She groans. "I told you that? I usually keep it secret."

"No. It's *obvious*: you point your toes even while relaxing, and your posture . . ."

She tosses a bread crumb at me, laughing. "You are so weird."

Dipping her roast beef sandwich into a steaming container of au jus sauce, Emma asks, "So what are you going to wear?"

"A dress."

"Which dress?"

Beside us, a soda drops to the ground, splashing droplets onto *Olympia*.

"Any dress." I pass Emma a napkin.

"When do you want to go shopping?" Charlotte asks. "We'll go into the city—"

"No, it's okay. We don't have to go shopping."

"Sophia, you have to look *phenomenal*." Charlotte runs a finger through a curl of glossy hair.

I screw the lid onto my thermos. "I'll try."

"Good. Pick you up at four?" Charlotte glances at her watch.

"Can't. I have practice," Emma murmurs, flipping over another flash card.

"No, really. I'll just choose one."

"From where?" Charlotte presses impatiently.

"My closet."

"Sophia, the ticket says you have to *dress up*."

"I have some"—I pause—"dresses to choose from."

Charlotte contorts her face, looking over at Emma desperately. "I'm sure they're nice, but Sophia . . ."

I rub the pendant on my necklace between my thumb and index finger. It's a faceted white onyx stone; years of rubbing it between my fingers have buffed the edges smooth. "Do you guys want to come over and see if anything works?"

Emma snaps her book shut. In unison, they proclaim, "YES!"

A timid knock announces their arrival. Although I hear Charlotte and Emma introducing themselves politely to my mother, I am occupied upstairs, extricating myself from a bundled mass of silk, velvet, tulle, and plastic wrapping.

When I reach the landing, Emma and Charlotte are huddled together in the foyer, observing the rest of the house. My mother beams effervescently at them.

"Hi," I call down, "the dresses are up here."

With polite nods to my mother—did Emma just curtsy?—they ascend the staircase, and I lead them into my room.

"Oh—"

"My—"

"Gosh—"

"I know, there's a lot to sift through," I apologize, "but we should be able to find something—"

"ARE YOU KIDDING ME?!" Charlotte shrieks. She pulls an eau de Nil dress out of a bag and examines the sinamay fascinator clipped to it. "Peacock feathers?" she screeches.

"I'm definitely not wearing feathers." I point to a heap of dresses in the corner. "Or fur."

Charlotte whirls her head around like it isn't connected to her body.

Emma seems to be in a trance. "These aren't dresses, Sophia," she says in awe, "these are gowns."

"*Gowns*," echoes Charlotte.

"Why do you have so many?" Emma admires a soft champagne-pink gown with a twisted neckline.

"When we had a ball or a gala or some diplomatic function my mother would order us gowns from Paris—"

"Paris!?" Charlotte yelps.

Glittering lights . . . Fluted champagne glasses . . . Violin music . . .

"Once," I say, holding up a sequined sapphire gown, "the UN rented out a wing of Versailles for their annual gala, so my mother ordered these. We went to L'Atelier Blanc de Frédéric Mennetrier in the 2nd arrondissement to have our hair done . . ."

I don't include that although I was only twelve, my mother instructed me to say I was sixteen and attending St. Anton Boarding School in Austria. It didn't occur to me then how much harder it should have been to lie.

". . . After the gala, she shipped them to our storage unit in Maryland. I never saw any of them again." I spread my arms out. "Until now."

Charlotte lifts an aquamarine silk gown from the footboard. "You would never find this for prom here. They don't even *sell* stuff like this in Waterford."

"Why don't you guys try them on?" I suggest.

"No, we have to see how they fit you."

"They're bespoke, Emma. They all fit me. You try them on. You can wear your favorite to prom in the spring,"

Charlotte looks astonished. "But, Sophia, they must have cost a fortune."

"Seriously. Please? It will be way more entertaining watching *you*"—I hold up a taffeta blush gown with white feathers sewn across the bodice and a faux swan perched on the shoulder—"wear this."

"I don't need convincing." Squealing, Charlotte pulls out her phone from her back pocket, a speaker from her purse, and turns on blaring music.

Charlotte insists on trying on every dress accompanied by coordinating headwear: diamanté bands, fur hats, feathered fascinators, even a hat with a tiny teacup in the center I wore to a garden wedding in Surrey when I was thirteen.

"Which one are you going to wear?" Emma shouts above the music; she is zipping into an oxblood crepe de chine silk gown. "You haven't even changed."

"That one." I point to a muddy-brown gown lying in a heap in the corner.

Emma scrunches her face in the mirror. "Is burgundy my color?"

"Certainly!" My mother is standing in the doorway holding a silver tray. "Do you remember when you wore it, Sophia? Was it to the symphony in Vienna? Was that when you—"

"Mom," I interrupt, "can you help me find the red gown? The one with the, uh"—I point to my shoulders—"funky straps?"

"Sure, honey." She sets down the silver tray holding three steaming mugs of hot chocolate and a plate of *pfeffernüsse*. She finds the red gown and hands it to me, winking. "Let me know if you need anything else."

"Oh, Charlotte!" Emma gasps, stepping out of the oxblood silk gown.

Swaying from side to side, Charlotte is standing in front of the full-length mirror wearing an iridescent gown that gathers in pleats and darts at her waist and swishes voluminously over her feet; two twisted braids of fabric cross over each other and wrap over her shoulders. "I've found it," she says wistfully.

"Heck yeah, you have," says Emma.

I laugh at her Montana slang. *Heck yeah?*

Charlotte swirls around *en pointe*. "Can you imagine me going to prom in this? Henry will die!"

"You're stunning," I remark.

Emma asks at the same time, "You're going with Henry?"

"Well, he hasn't asked me yet, it's months away, but I'm sure he will soon."

And the way Charlotte says this, looking away from Emma, I am certain it isn't Henry who she wants to ask her, but Mason. By telling Emma, Charlotte probably hopes word will get to Mason, and he will feel jealous and ask her instead.

Maybe I am starting to understand Waterford.

As Emma zips into a scarlet gown with a full petticoat and a string of chiffon roses up the shoulder, Charlotte twirls around the room, jumps onto my window seat, and leaps off. "I can dance in this!" she squeals.

"Those were my mother's specifications, 'Must be able to run while wearing.' "

I toss a pair of satin Prada heels at Charlotte, who clasps them in her fingers, openmouthed. "Do you have anything less than four inches? I'm five ten!"

I open the armoire and retrieve a box. "Try these." I reach across a pile of lavender tulle to pass her a pair of cream suede heels with a thin ankle strap.

Charlotte giddily buckles into them. "YOU AND I ARE THE EXACT SAME SIZE!" Charlotte falls onto her back, spread-eagled onto my bed; the pointed suede toes poke the air. "How can I thank you?" she sighs.

"Don't worry about it," I answer, embarrassed.

Charlotte rolls forward, struggling to sit upright with the

voluminous fabric swirling around her thighs. "Seriously, this is so nice of you. Can I, like, buy you a Waterford key chain with your name—"

"Sophia!" Emma gasps.

How could I have been so careless?

Emma is immobilized, holding a diamanté headpiece in one hand and my FN 5-7 in the other.

We were at the presidential palace in Jakarta, staring across the vast tropical grounds, draped amber at sunset, when my father handed me my first 5-7. *With privilege comes responsibility, Sophia,* he said as we watched the gilded sun sink into the sea.

Calmly, I walk over to Emma and gently ease the pistol out of her trembling hands.

"My dad has hunting rifles locked away in the basement, but I wasn't . . . expecting . . ."

Charlotte turns off the speaker. "Are you okay, Sophia?"

They often ask questions about my life before Waterford, usually with dreamy, wistful looks in their eyes. Occasionally they look at me as they are now—like I am fragile, mysterious. Dangerous.

Can they be my friends if I can't trust them with the truth? If they can't trust me?

"It's not loaded." I show them the empty chamber. "For so many years, living in certain locations, it was normal. Diplomats, any foreigner, really, from a wealthy country, can become a target; it's both simple economics and complicated geopolitics."

Charlotte looks stricken. "Sophia, what do you mean a *target?*"

"Depended on the year and place, really . . ." With one preparatory breath, I tell them about Katu, Peter, and Samuel. It's easier now, having told Aksel. My panic doesn't center on the memory; it centers on concern for Charlotte and Emma.

How do I explain my life?

As I finish, I place the gun on top of my armoire. "Things are different now. Here, I have to break those habits."

Charlotte and Emma glance at each other. I can't tell whether they are going to run, cry, or—

"I know whose side I want to be on in a fight." Emma whistles under her breath.

"Sophia . . ." Charlotte opens her mouth, then shuts it.

"You can ask questions," I say, "it's okay."

"Are you in the witness protection program?"

I wrinkle my nose. "What?"

"Like when people testify against the mafia, the FBI creates new identities for them and—"

"No," I laugh, "I *am* Sophia."

"You don't have to tell us anything else, but you can if you want," Charlotte says, reaching over to squeeze my hand. "And I'll never tell a soul. Cross my heart, hope to die, stick a needle in my eye."

Stick a needle in my eye? I laugh, "*You*, Charlotte, are weird."

Giggling, she turns the music back on, and things return to normal. Mostly.

Eventually I'm alone in my room.

I take down my FN 5-7 from the armoire, eject the mag, and unload the bullets. I count, then shove them back in, and replace the 5-7 beneath my pillow.

I sit down on my bed. Pulling my knees up to my chest, I rest my chin on my kneecaps. How is it that only a month ago I was scared of staying in Waterford? Afraid of staying and never belonging? Afraid I would never be like my friends? Afraid I could never have friends?

My mother knocks twice before pushing open the door. "Here." She hands me her teacup and bends down to retrieve the ransacked silver tray.

"Emma and Charlotte are quite nice, Sophia. I see why you like spending time with them." Her eyes are moist. Subtle wrinkles crease like butterflies in the corners of her eyes; she is more beautiful than ever.

Affectionately, she pats my knee and makes to leave the room. At the doorway, she pauses. "Did you choose one, darling?"

A row of garment bags now hang neatly in the armoire after Charlotte and Emma helped put them away.

However, I point to the far side of the room.

On the tufted chair in the corner, beside the little Russian doll, Katarina, is the same dull dress that has been there all night.

My mother narrows her eyes, walks toward it, and lifts it from the cushion.

She removes the plastic, revealing a gown with a high V-neck, beaded straps, and a fitted waist that cascades into an enormously full skirt that swirls when I move.

Without the plastic covering, the gown's color is neither muddy nor dull, but rather a rich, shimmering, iridescent chocolate brown.

Recognition washes over my mother's face. "You're certain, honey?"

I smile. "Heck yeah."

CHAPTER 31

Standing in my evening gown, with curled hair falling over my shoulders and feet bare on the wood floor, I know what to do.

My life here in Waterford is weaving together like a Belgian tapestry.

I grab hold of the tulle and chiffon fabric and squeeze into my familiar spot between the bench and the piano keys.

The small brass lamp is turned on, illuminating the sheet music that my mother must have taped back together. With my toes, I trace each pedal. Stretching my fingers, I see the conductor saunter forward in his white tie and tails.

My fingers grace the keys.

My thumb presses first. The sound echoes. My hands quiver. My pointer finger touches next. The note rings in my ears.

Closing my eyes, I stroke the shiny porcelain keys. Occasionally I glance at the paper, but I don't need it. The music pours out of me like I am a storm cloud and it is rain.

Soon, my fingers are racing toward the finish line, each trying to get there faster than the next. Despite their race, they work in unison—in exquisite harmony—welcoming me back.

It isn't until I finish the prelude that I hear feet shuffling behind me. I swivel to face them.

My mother is holding a dishcloth in one hand and a glass pitcher in the other. My father stands in his bathrobe, motionless.

I smile. And then we all start to laugh.

I have to maneuver my legs from beneath the layers of tulle to stand, but it feels right to be wearing this fluffy chocolate chiffon gown. After all, it was what I wore the last time I played, on that drizzly spring day in Vienna.

"You have your phone?" My father nods to the satin minaudière in my right hand.

I kiss his cheek. "See you at midnight," I promise.

"You're beautiful," Aksel says as I gather my skirt in my hands to sit down in the Range Rover. I trace a seam of my gown and bite my lip to stop blushing.

Once Aksel has started the ignition and reverses onto the street, he takes my hand, letting go only to shift gears.

Dusk, transitioning swiftly into night, escorts us down the canyon to the city. Aksel looks handsome in his tuxedo, the muscles in his shoulders sculpted beneath his coat, his angular profile defined against the setting, rose-gold winter sun.

From the street, I can see the interior of the theater, freshly renovated to resemble its original 1916 appearance: heavy velvet draping around the doors, crystal chandeliers, and gold leaf banisters. With everyone dressed in Edwardian clothes—a few women look like they raided *Downton Abbey*'s costume department—we fit right in. Aksel in a tuxedo, me in my dress. Charlotte was right: this is romantic.

Inside, the seats are a plush crimson velvet. We sit in the fifth row, directly above the conductor. After a few minutes, the sconces dim; curtains ripple across the stage; the orchestra starts.

By the time the ballet finishes, I feel transported. I forgot how magical it is—the music, the intricate movements, the athletic fragility of the dancers. It has been so long since I danced myself, and yet, I still feel it within me.

The sconces flicker, casting a sultry glow over the theater. Beside me, Aksel's jaw is clenched, like his mind is elsewhere.

For the first time in weeks, the impression reappears, lacerating the intimacy of the moment—Aksel is still hiding something.

"Aksel, what is it?"

He observes me carefully. "Before I picked you up my grandfather called. We had a . . . disagreement."

He says this all very methodically, as if he's been rehearsing the words in his mind during the entire ballet.

"About the Academy?"

Aksel drags a hand through his neatly combed hair. "More about what the Academy might represent."

Aksel glances around before resettling his vivid eyes on mine. "In Berlin, when I was told about my parents' deaths—that their plane didn't randomly fall out of the sky and burst into flames over the Gulf of Oman—I was told I might be able to do something about it eventually, if I chose to."

Neither of us has mentioned Berlin since we swam at the lake. Bracing myself against any triggers, I cement my eyes to his.

"My grandfather has always tried to deter me from applying to the Academy; it used to be a joke between us, that I was in a 'phase.'"

Aksel grimaces, shifting in his seat. "But now it's different. He's been *warning* me against entering the military ever since"—he pauses; his forearm goes taut beside mine—"ever since he found out their plane was shot down by an American Special Operations Unit."

"Sp-special Forces," I sputter, "don't assassinate American citizens. Even if it *were* true it would be deeply classified and . . ." I stop, realizing that its classification is precisely why Aksel would have been brought to Berlin. To the Bubble.

Our life is fracturing. I feel it in the air between us.

Beneath his tuxedo, Aksel's entire body stiffens.

"He is speculating," I declare. "He can't access classified material—"

"He can, Sophia." Aksel exhales. "He *has* access. My grandfather doesn't live in Waterford, because he lives in DC. He's a US senator."

Swallowing, I keep my voice steady, trying to process what this might mean.

"So what are you going to do? Can I help?"

Aksel angles his body toward mine. Withdrawing his hand, he rests it on the back of my chair. He stares at me beseechingly.

"If you could choose, Sophia, between a life that's predictable, and safe, and possibly happy," he begins, his arm falling from the top of my seat to my lower back, his fingers grazing my waist, "and a life that you know almost nothing about, but that you can't simply walk away from . . . which would you choose?"

I purse my lips, pondering his cryptic question. "It depends on which choice gives me what I want more than anything."

"What if I'm not sure which option gets me what I want?"

The theater is emptying. Soon, we are the last two people seated in our row. Aksel's hand adheres around mine, like he is holding on to me, on to us.

"What do you want more than anything?" I implore.

Aksel tucks a strand of hair behind my ear. Tingles ignite down my neck. My heart thuds beneath my corset.

"That's the only thing I know for sure," Aksel says. "I want you."

CHAPTER 32

"*And I* want a cheeseburger. One of those big Montana cheeseburgers."

We've been waiting too long at an elegant restaurant, and I'm starving—rather I am American-starving, which is another way of saying *I want to eat.*

Aksel laughs, relieved. "Me too."

Seizing my hand, Aksel leads us outside. I barely have time to button my coat before we are back in his Range Rover.

Minutes later, Aksel steers onto a dark road, approaches a giant silver bus sparkling under a string of lights, and parks between a rickety SUV on our left and a gleaming F-150 on our right.

Draping his arm over my shoulder, Aksel whispers in my ear, "You, Sophia, are about to eat the best cheeseburger in Montana." With me cradled in the crook of his arm, we cross the icy pavement to the metal steps leading into the snug diner.

At first, I'm concerned I'll look ridiculous wearing my chiffon evening gown, but inside two beefy men in tuxedos dig into a platter of fries at the counter.

Once we are seated, Aksel loosens the collar of his shirt and takes off his tie. I order a cheeseburger, french fries, and onion rings.

"Save room for milkshakes," Aksel remarks, ordering two.

When the waitress brings out our cheeseburgers, I stare, confounded, at my plate. "How am I supposed to eat this?"

"Like this." Aksel takes his enormous cheeseburger in both hands, brings it to his mouth, and eats half of it in one bite.

"Not okay." I burst out laughing. "Definitely not okay wearing corseted couture. I need a knife and a fork." The waitress must overhear—she passes me a set on her way to another table.

"So why is this cheeseburger the best?" I say, cutting off a piece, which keeps falling apart. Forgoing the fork, I lean over my plate and use my hands, moaning, "My mother will kill me."

"Bacon," Aksel answers. "Good cheeseburgers always have bacon."

The waitress sets down two milkshakes in the middle of the table, each with whipped cream piled above the rim. Pulling a shake toward me, I put my lips around the straw and suck. None comes out. "It's too thick," I mutter.

"No, no, no," Aksel says. Reaching across the table, he takes a fry from the platter, scoops it into his chocolate shake, then eats it.

I throw my head back, laughing. "Americans are so bizarre."

"I'm not sure what to make of that comment," he responds, "coming from the girl who kills grasshoppers with her teeth."

Holding my hands far away from my dress, I scoop a salty fry into my shake and then shove it into my mouth.

Within ten minutes, my fingers are adequately covered in grease, salt, and cream. "Excuse me," I giggle, standing to go wash my hands. Aksel politely stands.

The diner is crowded, especially in the narrow aisle separating the rowdy booths from the long counter.

Beyond the booth, near the single bathroom, is a second

entrance. As I reach the bathroom door, a man steps inside the diner, a few feet away from me.

He is wearing glasses and a baseball cap. Dark tufts of hair curl up from under his hat. I can't see his eyes; they are focused on a phone in his hand. But I sense him watching the movement of my dress.

My hex sense hits like a jolt of electricity.

The effect is instant—my hands clench, my limbs stiffen.

My eyes snap to his boots. *Same size.*

His skin. *Same shade.*

Same man.

I check my surroundings—an elderly man is standing at the counter to my right: pulling the soda fountain nozzles while joking with the men in tuxedos.

The waitress walks up to the man with the curly hair. "I'll get you seated. Which do you prefer, booth or counter?"

"Neither," he answers in a smooth voice. Lifting his head, his eyes meet mine. "I actually won't be staying."

A bolt of fear fires down my spine.

My throat tightens. Hazy memories wash over me: *voices inside a van . . . hot sweaty skin on mine . . . fingers at my throat . . .*

The door to the bathroom clicks open. I spin around and hurl myself inside. I shove the latch, locking it into place. I slump back against the door, panting.

My chest thuds. I shut my eyes. I can still feel it—the taste of dried blood on my cut lips, the scratchy cloth against my eyelids, the burning on my wrists.

I stare ahead into the mirror. My face has lost all color; my pale eyes are wide; my hands are trembling.

I am Sophia again—the Sophia before Waterford.

Inside the tiny stall, my vision blurs. I sit down on the toilet seat lid and press my hands together until the tips of my fingers turn purple.

Memories assault me—*my mother's tears on my forehead . . . the taste of metal, and sweat, and blood . . .*

No!

I won't let this happen. My life is different now.

I no longer need to be afraid.

I am with Aksel. In Waterford.

No one is following me.

I turn on the faucet.

It's a coincidence.

Cold water trickles out in sporadic bursts into the metal sink before turning into a steady stream. I rinse my fingers, scrubbing vigorously beneath my fingernail tips, scouring until my fingers are raw and red.

Bang! Bang! Bang! "Sophia, are you okay?" Aksel's voice is low. Urgent. He knocks again.

I flip the lock, open the door, and collapse into Aksel's broad chest.

He wraps both his arms around my waist, drawing me into him so quickly he nearly lifts me off the ground.

I scan the restaurant over his shoulder.

"You're okay?" he says—not quite a question.

"Fine." My voice trembles. My whole body trembles.

Aksel takes my cold, damp hands in his. I see in his eyes that fierce desire to protect me.

"You saw him?" I murmur.

"He walked right past me," Aksel snarls.

Keeping me behind him, Aksel surveys the restaurant. I slide my fingers around Aksel's upper arm.

My head is spinning. My senses are exploding inside my skull.

. . . *It's impossible* . . .

Aksel's eyes are dark and accusatory, sweeping over every patron.

But the man is no longer in the diner.

Aksel's grip tightens. "We're leaving."

Outside, we hurry toward the Range Rover. The rickety SUV has been replaced by a sleek sports car, but the F-150 is still parked on the passenger side.

Standing between this truck and Aksel's Range Rover is the man in the baseball hat.

He is leaning casually against the truck, smoking a Ziganov cigarette, with his arms folded, his head tilted to the side, watching us. Waiting.

Aksel steps forward, shielding me. His face is livid.

"Excuse me," Aksel says with cold politeness. He nods toward the passenger's side of the Range Rover, a half meter from the man. "You're blocking our way."

The man looks between the door and me. "Am I?"

His voice. His eyes. His buffed and polished fingernails.

Aksel's breath comes out in a thin silver vapor. "You can move, or I can move you, but either way, in five seconds, she's going to get into the car and we're going to leave." Standing beside me like a Spartan warrior, Aksel's eyes blaze.

Abruptly, the man takes a step toward Aksel, like a tiny squirrel provoking a chained dog. Glinting in the man's hand is the shining, polished edge of a blade.

"Get out of my way, boy," the man says.

I slide my hand toward my clutch, my Ladybug.

Aksel steps closer to the man. He towers over him menacingly. "Five."

Aksel's knuckles are white; his right hand is clenched so tightly I worry he'll break his own fingers; his left hand inches toward his side—his SIG. "Four."

The man watches Aksel, still not moving.

"Three," Aksel growls. His eyes are daggers. His body reminds me of the grizzly, about to charge.

I take a breath, preparing my motion.

The man's face breaks into an impish grin.

Sneering, he mutters to me in a raspy, repulsive voice, "A scar for a scar."

Then he ducks around the truck and disappears.

Seconds of stunned silence follow his departure.

Aksel unlocks the door, ushers me in, and walks brusquely to his side. It isn't until Aksel is seated beside me and reversing onto the street that he grimly asks, "What did he say?"

As the shock recedes, fading to a dull hum in my ear, I realize why Aksel asks me this.

The man hadn't threatened me in English.

He threatened me in Chechen.

CHAPTER 33

"Aksel, take me home."

"*Home?*" he says, like I've suggested the moon. "I'm not taking you home."

Between staring at me and checking the rearview mirror, I'm not sure how Aksel can watch the road. I reach into my satin minaudière and fumble for my phone. I call my father. One. Two. Four. Seven times. No answer. I call my mother. Nothing. I clutch my phone—what use is this anyway?

"I need to go home, Aksel," I insist. "I have to talk to my parents."

"Damn it, Sophia! That guy will know exactly where you live—"

"He doesn't . . . he can't . . ."

. . . *A scar for a scar* . . .

He does.

Aksel clenches the steering wheel. "I'm not taking you home," he grits through his teeth.

"You're going a hundred and ten. That truck can't go over eighty—"

"Which truck?" says Aksel.

"His red one. He's been driving it for months. Rusty Dodge.

Mid-eighties. I don't know American cars well . . ." I chatter to keep my mind occupied. "But we're ahead of him—this is the fastest route to Waterford, right?"

Aksel grimaces. At the ramp crossing Highway 81, Aksel acquiesces. He turns east. Soon we turn onto Edgewood Lane. The tires crunch over the salted pavement as we pull into my driveway.

Outside, Aksel draws his SIG with his left hand. With his right, he seizes my hand in a ferociously protective grip. Side by side we rush up to the house. The living room is dark. I push open the glass french doors into the den. The six whiteboards have been taken down. A few embers burn in the fireplace, but the Prussian sword . . . the Dala horses . . . everything else remains.

My heels click as I run to the kitchen. *No note.*

Aksel walks around the perimeter; he checks the back door, side door.

"Sophia, we shouldn't stay here." He doesn't sound afraid, but exasperated, like it's the obvious conclusion and why am I not agreeing? But it is all thundering through me. I don't know how much longer I can hold it back.

Breathe . . . Hold . . . Count backward from a thousand by thirteens in Dutch . . .

"Sophia?"

This isn't happening. I bite my lip to stop it quivering.

"We really should go," he says.

Attempting to regain my composure, I nod in agreement.

In seconds, we are rolling through Waterford's quiet, dark streets and up into Eagle Pass.

Inside Aksel's house, I can't see straight. My head is fuzzy. I feel delirious.

Moonlight streaks through the wall of windows facing the deck. The night sky is so clear I can see across the meadow to the steep granite mountains, backlit by the moon.

Aksel lights some kindling, then disappears. By the time he returns from the ground floor, a fire roars in the hearth. He has his bolt-action Remington rifle in his hand. Unholstering his SIG from his belt, he puts it on the table. "For you."

I shake my head. *No.*

I can't shoot. Won't shoot. Because shooting means accepting this is actually happening.

Things are different here.

"I turned on the security system," Aksel states. "The entire property is fenced—the alarm is synched with my phone. We'll stay here until you reach your parents."

Your parents. He doesn't say it accusingly, but almost irritably—as if he sees them as the problem, not the solution.

His movements are methodical. Calm. Trained.

Aksel was right. I should have told my father everything—told him I was scared, told him I still wake up sweating, thinking it isn't over. I could have prevented this. Now I've put Aksel in danger. I've put everyone around me in danger. Because if he's been watching me, has he been watching Emma and Charlotte too? I feel violated. Guilty.

Aksel watches me from his perch, standing beside the window like a sentinel between me and the world beyond the glass.

Except for the fiery glow, the room is dark.

"Aksel . . . ," I exhale, "I need to tell you something." My voice strengthens with each word. "And I understand if you don't want to see me anymore or—"

"What are you talking about?" Aksel sounds perplexed. Exasperated. Angry. "Nothing you say could make me *not* want to spend every moment with you—"

"It's not that simple—"

"Sure, it is!" In several long strides, he crosses the room. He sets the rifle onto the table and stops in front of me. He reaches toward me, firmly resting his palms on the back of my neck, interlocking his fingers above my collar.

Concern, devotion, anger, and confusion are etched across his face in a twisted map of emotion. "Sophia, I care about you more than I care about anyone. It doesn't matter what you tell me or what happens from now on, because nothing can change how I feel about you. I will fight for you—"

"Don't say that." I shake my head.

On the verge of hyperventilating, I pull away from Aksel's determined face and walk toward the fireplace. Staring into the embers, I push my tongue against my front teeth to stop my tears.

"Sophia," he pleads, "nothing you say will change how I feel about you."

Let the memories come, my mother says.

Aksel hasn't moved; his body remains tense, watching me. Like I really do scare him.

"Aksel, I need to tell you why I was in Berlin."

CHAPTER 34

I sit down on the couch—my dress spreads out over the seat, draping onto the carpet. I avert my eyes from the shimmering brown fabric.

Aksel looks unsure of where to be. He compromises by propping his Remington on the side of the sofa and sitting beside me, not touching, but close.

"We arrived in Istanbul two years ago," I start. My heart thumps like a drum inside the depths of my body. "One afternoon, as I was leaving school, I couldn't find my driver. He was a kind man who spoke no English, so we spoke in Turkish. He was from outside Ankara, and had come to Istanbul for a job. He was so impressed that I could understand him. *Sinekkuşu*, he called me—'hummingbird' in Turkish—because he said my limbs never stopped moving. He said he had a granddaughter my age . . .

"Our apartment was only a few blocks from Lycée Français Saint Benoît, my international school in Istanbul; I figured he'd forgotten so it would be faster for me to walk home than to wait.

"I wasn't supposed to walk alone, but I knew the way and I loved Istanbul. A few blocks south of school, I turned onto a side road to avoid the congested route we usually drove. Two women wearing expensive Chanel kaftans stepped in front of me. *Excuse me?* one asked me in Turkish. *Do you live here?* I nodded. *I can't find this café, and I'm late. Can you help me?* I answered, *Sure.* She smiled gratefully, stepping closer to me. *I think it's this way.* As she pointed ahead into an alley, I felt movement behind me. Instantly, I knew. I turned in time to see the second woman corner me. Her hand shot out like a viper from the folds of her pleated dress, snatching my wrist in a viselike grip. The first woman threw her shawl over my head, muffling my screams as they dragged me into the alley."

Aksel's body stiffens beside me.

"It took only seconds to thrust me into a sleek van—only seconds for my life to change forever.

"I don't recall much about what happened immediately afterward . . . the men in the van blindfolded me . . . shoved me to the floor. They were rough . . . aggressive . . . I remember the way their hands smelled. Like garlic and vinegar.

"Eventually, they stopped beating me. I woke in a dark room. Although I was blindfolded, the cloth was loose enough that if I tilted my head backward, I could see out the tiny slit beneath the fabric. The room had mold on the walls, a tin basin in the corner, a broken tile floor, and one grimy window. Through it I could see the red rooftop of a taller building . . . I could hear traffic, bartering from the souk, the adhan five times a day . . . I was still in Istanbul . . ."

Aksel's fists are wound tightly in his lap. He whispers hoarsely, "Sophia . . . you don't have to . . ."

I do.

"I tried to scrape the coagulated blood off my skin. I was tied to a copper pipe jutting out from between the floorboards; I slept on the chipped tile floor, shivering despite the heat, terrified of when someone would open the door . . .

"The next day, a man entered my room. He walked with a limp, like his leg had been broken and never fixed properly. He had asthma and wheezed; I heard him breathing from down the hall. He yelled at me in French. He was irate. He said the French government didn't recognize me as a French national and la Direction Générale de la Sécurité Extérieure—France's intelligence arm—refused to pay a ransom for my return.

"Farhad was his name. He wanted to know why the Lycée listed me as a French citizen. It took him days to realize that my American parents used foreign passports for cover. Once Farhad learned I wasn't French, that he was unlikely to get a ransom, everything changed. He decided he'd get the next highest amount of money if he trafficked me.

"I was scared. I knew I would be sold to a terror group, or a wealthy buyer. My parents would never find me. But then . . . another man arrived. His hair was tied back in a ponytail. He wore a gaudy opal ring on his forefinger. He smelled like Yves Saint Laurent cologne and spoke French with a Parisian accent, but he rolled his *r*s in the top of his throat, so I knew it wasn't his first language.

"Bekami untied me from the pipe in the floorboard and took off my blindfold. He asked about me and my family. Where had I lived? Where was I born? When I didn't answer, he touched my cheek and rubbed his hand against my neck . . . That was worse than when he hit me. And he did . . . often . . . he made me bleed. He came every day, threatening me. He'd slink his slimy hand along the back of my neck and swivel my face toward him, speaking with his hot, smoky breath a millimeter from my mouth . . ."

Aksel makes a sudden twitching movement. His green eyes stare into the fireplace—reflections of flames erupt in his irises. I can't look at him or I'll stop. I focus on the pattern of the oriental carpet beneath our feet.

"When Bekami left, he'd order the others not to touch me, not to sell me, no matter what price was offered. Bekami would say reverently, *Cash does not compare to what she can offer us . . .*

"It sounded like they were holding me hostage as revenge . . . or blackmail. Farhad and the others tormented me. They'd sit around me eating, feeding me nothing. They'd touch my face. They'd joke in broken French about hurting me. In Chechen, they graphically described what they would do to me once Bekami let them . . .

"In the late afternoon heat, they'd smoke and discuss their plans: blowing up the Köln Cathedral, bombing the Chunnel, burning down the Rijksmuseum. They were envious of the notoriety of other terrorist groups, but mostly, they were obsessed with a singular weapon they simply did not have.

"Farhad was eager to get rid of me. He'd concluded my father must be a foreign spy—a *fantôme* maybe—or even CIA; he worried a military team might come for me and they'd all be killed. I hoped he was right.

"Later, Bekami returned, desperate this time. *Your father is Kent Hepworth, isn't he?!* he shouted in English, shoving a photograph of my father in front of my face. I shook my head, denying it in French, *I don't know that man!*

"Farhad was belligerent; he didn't want me in the apartment when he could ransom me for ten thousand euros. *We need the money*, he'd plead. Bekami kept explaining I was worth much more than ten thousand euros.

"Farhad wanted to torture me until I gave Bekami answers, but Bekami refused. So Farhad pulled out a rusty knife and put it next to my throat. I'll never forget the sound of his voice, like coarse salt on a shiny stone: *Tell us who your father is or I send him your head.* I spat in his face. So, Farhad sliced my neck."

I touch the scar directly beneath my chin.

"A car accident?" Aksel remarks in a low voice.

I grip the chocolate chiffon gown drowning my legs and take a deep breath.

"Farhad had loosened his grip on the knife, so I grabbed it; he lunged for me and I swung the knife, cutting him from his forehead to the bottom of his cheek.

"I ran past Bekami and the others, through a kitchen and into a hall. I ran down the nearest staircase, circling until I reached a pair of turquoise doors on the ground floor.

"Outside, the sun hit me in a blinding flash of light. My head pounded in the bright sunshine. Blood trickled down my neck and onto my clothes. My legs were weak. I wanted to stop. To collapse. But I ran.

"A scooter revved up behind me—Bekami. But I was more agile on foot. I darted into one alley, then skidded into another, narrower alley. Behind me, Bekami couldn't turn the scooter fast enough; he had to loop one hundred and eighty degrees before turning after me.

"The alley intersected a souk. I entered it through a spice stall. Inside I stole a scarf from a vendor and wrapped it around my head to cover my hair. My navy school blazer was soaked in my blood, so I slipped it off and grabbed another scarf, covering my shoulders and holding the ends together in my fists.

"Bekami drove up behind me, plowing people aside on his

scooter. My only choice was to run faster. I emerged from the souk on a café-lined street; I saw the dry cleaners that serviced my uniform. I knew where I was—five hundred meters from a diplomatic mission.

"Although the embassies are in Ankara, hundreds of kilometers away, the consulates are in Istanbul. And many of these are even bigger, and more heavily guarded. The Slovak Consulate was closest. I knew this because my father's friend Jozef worked there. Only a month before, we'd met him nearby for lunch . . .

"People at the cafés stared as I ran past. I was wearing my oxford school shoes; my shirt and skirt were ripped and filthy; my matted hair flew like a dirty broom behind me. I was fast. But Bekami was faster.

"Glancing over my shoulder, I saw him drop the scooter and sprint after me. He shoved an old woman to the pavement; her groceries rolled into the gutter.

"I reached Sultana Park, situated between me and the consulate. It's small—surrounded by a wrought-iron fence, with openings on each corner. I had already passed the southeast corner, so I jumped onto a bench and hurdled the railing. I cut through the wooded park and exited at the northwest entrance. Bekami chased me like an attacking dog. I could hear him panting.

"I ran along the building's east gate, knowing the guards wouldn't be able to see me until I was practically in front of them. Bekami was closing in on me, his footsteps like a dark rhythmic drumbeat welcoming me to hell.

"Rounding the corner, I screamed I was a citizen—*Som Slovák! Open the gate! I'm being attacked!* I cried. I shed my scarves as I reached the boxwood hedge.

"No alarm sounded. I couldn't tell if the soldiers heard me. I was about to run headfirst into a wall of iron posts . . . Two meters away they glanced at each other . . . as if they weren't sure whether to believe me . . . *Som z Bratislavy!* I shrieked. *I'm from Bratislava!* The gate slid open. I ran through. It snapped shut behind me.

"I passed the first soldier and collapsed against the second. The stunned soldier placed me behind him. Panting, I turned—Bekami stood on the other side of the gate, heaving. His eyes were wild. His hair had come loose from its knot. His hands were coiled around the bars like he intended to break them.

"The soldier raised his rifle. In Turkish, he ordered Bekami to back away from the gate. The second soldier kept me tight behind him, barricading himself between me and Bekami. The gatehouse radioed Turkish police—*orange alert*—potential terror attack.

"Bekami still clung to the iron posts. *I will find you,* he sneered at me in Turkish, *and my knife will cut deeper. You will never escape me,* fahişe.

"I stepped out from behind the soldier. *Not before I tell my father everything I heard,* I said to Bekami in Chechen. *Your names, your families, the villages you come from. The attacks you are planning and how you'll do it. You are right about only one thing—my father* is *dangerous, so now it is you who should be afraid. My father will find you, every one of you, and he will kill you.*

"I'll never forget Bekami's look of astonished rage. He never considered I spoke Chechen—why would he? I can't imagine what went through his mind—he knew what they had carelessly discussed in front of me.

"From the gatehouse, I ran straight to Jozef's office. He went pale when he saw me. He called in a military medic who didn't ask questions, just stitched me up. Jozef kept me sequestered in his office until my father arrived.

"We left Istanbul under heavy security that night. We met my mother at the airport and traveled straight to Head Office of Counter Intelligence Europe, Berlin."

Aksel's eyes flash at me, horrified. He draws his hands over his mouth.

"It was in Berlin that my father told me who had betrayed us. Who had betrayed me."

Aksel stares at me intensely.

"It was that nice old man from outside Ankara, my driver. He must have also been surprised . . . when the 'hummingbird' got away."

After a heavy pause, I continue, "He was the first."

"The first what?" Aksel asks uncertainly.

"The first one my father found."

CHAPTER 35

"Inside the Bubble, I told my debriefer every detail of my kidnappers I remembered: eye color, hair length, accent, favorite brand of cigarette, every scar, piece of jewelry, conversation . . .

"Bekami said my father had foiled an attack in Albania—I assumed Bekami wanted revenge. Based in Istanbul, Bekami and Farhad's cell was affiliated with a larger separatist organization—the Chechen Nationalist Front, CNF for short.

"CNF claimed to want the peaceful establishment of an independent Chechnya, but the plans I overheard indicated warfare. Farhad's job was to develop a transnational network capable of executing attacks; Bekami's job was to acquire the weapons.

"Though I told the man inside the Bubble everything I remembered, I understood little—why did they think *I* could help them get their weapons?

"After three days of debriefing, we left Berlin. For eighteen months, we stayed off the grid. On the move. But no matter how covertly we lived, Bekami's men were always one step behind, or occasionally one step ahead.

"We'd been at our safe house in Tunis for seven days when my parents left me alone for the first time in months. Minutes later, the door creaked open. Someone stepped inside the flat. I hid behind the fridge.

"I heard those uneven footsteps, his jagged, wheezing breath. I watched his lace-up boots cross the tile floor, each footstep one cadence off because of his limp.

"Then, right before he entered the kitchen—two *pops!* He slumped to the ground, dead. He was the last of the kidnappers my father captured or killed—Ilyas Farhad. Across his face, from his brow to his chin, was the scar I had given him.

"The following day, we left North Africa and flew to America. My parents told me they could retire now because it is over. *Over.* My kidnappers are dead. Bekami is imprisoned in Libya. CNF fell apart after my father decimated their leadership . . .

"Bekami *can't* be in Waterford. Farhad's Chechen cell *isn't* in Waterford. I shouldn't still be afraid . . ."

My voice dries up. Aksel's face has been growing more vehement as I speak. I can hardly bear to see the way he is watching me—like I am contaminated by it all. By Farhad. By Bekami.

"I'm sorry," I say. "It's my—"

"Stop that!" Aksel stands. "Stop apologizing! This is not your fault! Do you understand? Your kidnapping—what they did to you? None of it is *your* fault!"

"Except it is!" My dress cascades to the floor in glistening waves as I stand. "*I* left school—*I* disobeyed orders! *I* put my parents through hell. *I* will always be afraid! Traumatized. Tainted. It's who I am—"

"No, it is not who you are!" Aksel roars. He takes me by the shoulders, swiveling me to face him. "You're not defined by what others did to you, Sophia!"

He bends his head down until our foreheads meet. Gently, he holds the back of my neck with his hands, his thumbs resting on the skin behind my ear.

"Those men, Sophia?" He pauses. "Bekami? Farhad? The others? They took twenty months out of your life. Don't give them the satisfaction of taking another second. You can't control a lot of what has happened to you, but you can control that. And it doesn't matter what Bekami wanted from you, because you are strong, Sophia, the strongest person I have ever met, and no one . . ."

Aksel touches his finger to my chin. I look up at him. Firelight sparks in his eyes. "No one can defeat you unless you give up."

Aksel strokes my hair. His voice is both fierce and calm. "Farhad is dead. Bekami is in prison. Your father certainly won't let anyone near you, Sophia, and I swear I'll die before I let someone hurt you."

"Don't say that," I whisper, squeezing my eyes closed, remembering the man with the curly hair and hazel eyes. "Are you forgetting what just happened?"

"I'm saying it *because* of what just happened," he declares. "You are *not* alone, Sophia."

"You can't . . ." I don't finish my sentence.

Eighteen months of tears pour out of me in a torrent of memories I can no longer dam.

Aksel's arms lock behind my back. We sink to the floor in an entwined heap of limbs and chiffon.

My tears wash over Aksel, soaking his shirt, seeping into his skin, and connecting my past with his future.

After a time, the only sounds are the crackling of the fire and Aksel's steady breathing as I burrow myself into his chest.

Warm and safe, I neither know, nor care, how much time passes. All I know is that I would trade every day of my life without Aksel for just one more day with him.

CHAPTER 36

Aksel shakes my shoulder. Rubbing my eyes, I look around. The room is dark. The fire is out. He is sitting beside me, his back against the sofa. I am curled next to his warm body, my arm draped across his torso.

Suddenly, Aksel springs to his feet.

"What?" I sit up, alert in an instant.

Aksel's eyes find mine. "Not sure."

I glance at the large windows overlooking the snowy meadow. Lanterns hang from the cedar shingles, lighting the deck in a soft luminescent glow.

"I'm going to check outside." Aksel is still wearing the crisp white shirt and black suspenders of his tuxedo. He takes his parka from the back of the couch and heads toward the front door.

"Sophia," he says, turning around.

Something isn't right.

Aksel's body goes rigid. Solid as stone.

I hear it in the distance. A crash. The grating sound of metal smashing metal.

Aksel looks down at his phone, vibrating in his hand, alerting him. "The gate has been breached," he utters.

A siren goes off inside the house.

Instantaneously, Aksel runs toward me. He picks up his rifle and seals it in his left hand. He pushes his SIG into my right hand.

Standing, I shake my head. This *isn't* happening.

Nonetheless, the SIG molds into my palm, comfortable and familiar.

I exhale. This *is* happening.

"It takes twelve seconds to reach the house," he murmurs, looking defiantly out the back windows, steeling himself.

He is right.

CHAPTER 37

The lights inside the house go out with a snap.

I grab my satin clutch, retrieve my Ladybug, and slip it down the top of my shimmering bodice.

Aksel pulls me to the library.

From the dark room we can see into the night. The night-vision video on Aksel's phone shows movement surrounding the estate—green figures encircling the house, blocking our exits. I step over to the window.

Two shadows move below us, descending to the lower deck near the mudroom door. Silently, I unlock the window and push it open. It is an angled window, and the hinge halts at six inches.

But we don't need six inches. One will do.

I motion to Aksel. He walks over, threads on the silencer, and thumbs off the safety.

We glance at each other, luminous eyes meeting in the moonlight.

He kisses me hard, and I know, with this one, simple kiss, that Aksel *is* different. Dangerous.

Not to me. To them.

We are in this together.

He fires twice.

Two down.

Running low, we dart back into the great room.

A sound from the foyer causes both of us to turn our aim.

I catch Aksel's eye and pivot, going back-to-back with him.

Facing the windows in the great room, I halt—for one everlasting second, I watch four figures, silhouetted in the moonlight against the snowy meadow, approach the deck.

One of them throws a grenade. It arcs toward us—

"Aksel, get down!"

Crash!

The floor-to-ceiling glass windows shatter. The trim erupts in bright flames, splintering shards of wood across the room.

We throw ourselves to the floor. Aksel turns midair, landing on top of me, shielding my body.

Boom! There is a deafening gunshot to my left, another shot to my right.

A sharp piece of glass strikes my leg like shrapnel. I push my hand to the wound.

Through the shattered glass and flames engulfing the woodwork, I see shadowy figures, blurry and smudged in the smoke, moving in.

Aksel props his rifle against his shoulder. He slides the barrel around the sofa. Angling the weapon, he fires twice.

Both bullets hit a man's chest. His knees buckle and he drops. Aksel moves the rifle 15 degrees and hits a second man in the thigh. Aksel curses below his breath, adjusts his angle, and pulls the trigger again. This time he punctures the man's neck. A geyser of blood sprays across the foyer.

Four down.

Together, we crawl across the glass-strewn floor. It smells like aluminum and burning cedar. A shot whistles past my ear. A bullet lodges into the pillar behind the fireplace, narrowly missing Aksel.

We take cover behind an antique marble-top dresser.

My dress is slick with blood.

Aksel hovers over me, firing his rifle.

A man cries out in pain.

I swipe Aksel's loose tie from his neck and knot it around my thigh.

Shadows move among the billowing smoke, surrounding us.

One figure is getting bigger. Closer.

Aksel switches his rifle to his right hand and reloads.

I lean around Aksel and shoot.

Five down,

Suddenly, the mudroom door opens—*Bang!*

Direct gunfire bombards us. Behind me, an oil painting drops to the floor, breaking the frame; the flat-screen TV mounted above the fireplace crashes onto the flagstone hearth.

Pop! Pop! Pop!

Covering our heads, we dart from the room.

We are back where we started, in the entrance to the library. A blast hits the woodwork millimeters from Aksel's shoulder.

Above us, an antler chandelier plummets.

Behind us, books tumble off the shelves in a cascading wave as gunfire ricochets around the room.

Another grenade rolls in. It explodes as we dive from the library.

"Stun grenades," I murmur, rolling onto my stomach. Between my thigh and the explosion, I've lost my SIG.

Scanning the rubble, I get to my feet.

Aksel fires back from behind the wood pillar in the hall.

Another blast hits the front door, blocking our exit.

"To the kitchen!" Aksel yells.

Aksel covers us with his Remington as we maneuver through the great room and into the kitchen.

Because of the house's elevation, the kitchen windows are two stories high—inaccessible from the deck.

A man wearing a black mask turns the corner. Aksel takes him out point-blank.

Aksel plows through the kitchen, tossing aside barstools. He slides the doors shut, jamming the lock into place.

Footsteps beat down the hall to the other entrance. Aksel races to seal it off too.

There is no way in. Or out. The locked doors will give us only seconds.

Aksel glances around the room. Rather than looking scared, he seems invigorated.

His eyes catch mine. "We've got this," he says, half smiling. Because we don't have this. We are outnumbered, outgunned, and cornered.

But I see in his eyes the confident, soothing calm I saw when we were trapped in the avalanche. He is unequivocally fearless, assertive, and willing to do anything to save us.

Boom! In a flash of bright light, the doors burst open. The force of the explosion thrusts me across the room. I land hard on my bleeding leg. A man charges forward through the smoke.

Aksel shouts at me, his words muffled in the echo of the blast.

The man lunges for Aksel's neck. Aksel spins hard around, hitting the butt of his rifle into the man's face with a bone-crunching sound.

A second man comes at Aksel from behind. Aksel wrestles him to the ground and connects his knuckles to the man's jaw. He shouts at me again, "Get out of here, Sophia! Now!"

But all I see is . . . him.

The man with the curly hair and hazel eyes is walking toward me, smirking.

I scramble backward on my injured leg.

He swipes for me. I skid around the counter, my dress catching beneath my feet. He snatches the chiffon fabric of my skirt, ripping half of it from the bodice.

I reach behind my back. My hand slides across the counter.

If I can somehow . . .

My fingers find the hilt. My palm finds the blade. When he reaches for me a second time, I swing the kitchen knife forward, aiming it straight into his stomach. He turns, so I lance his hip instead.

His forearm cuts down hard onto my right elbow, sending the blade clattering to the floor.

The man flips me around and pushes my face brutishly against the countertop.

"Sophia!" Aksel roars.

Yelling to the others, the man holds my arms behind my back and wraps a cable tie around my wrists.

Impervious to the gunfire around us, Aksel shoots at a man coming from his left, dodging bullets and backing toward me.

The man with the hazel eyes—the Chechen—tightens the cables, attempting to clip them together. I thrash, trying to wrestle my wrists away from him.

Another man, wearing a bulletproof vest, enters the kitchen from the great room and raises a semiautomatic, trying to get a bead at Aksel's back—

"NO!" I scream.

I throw my head backward with as much force as I can. *Crack!* The Chechen lets go of me, pulling both his hands up to his fractured chin. Instantly, I sweep his legs from under him, reach into my bodice, lock the blade into place, and fling my Ladybug across the room.

The Ladybug pierces the man's suprasternal notch, right above his bulletproof vest. The semiautomatic drops from his hands as he tries to stop blood spurting from his neck.

Standing, I rip more pleated tulle fabric from the bodice so I can move. The wound in my thigh is still leaking blood, but adrenaline numbs the pain.

A man springs forward, swinging his knife at me.

Aksel vaults over the table, takes the man's right forearm, and twists him around. The man spins, attempting to swing his knife backward. Aksel hits him brutally on the side of the head, and the man drops to the ground with a *thump*.

The men regroup. Aksel has his rifle again, taking aim. He shoots at the men fanning out around us—*Pop! Pop! Pop!*

I look down. Aksel's backcountry pack is open on the floor, its contents rolling out onto the rug. I reach forward, snatch the aerosol can, and snap off the top. When the man nearest me raises his gun, I spray him in the face.

He shrieks as the bear spray burns his eyes. Rather than drop his weapon, he blindly pulls the trigger, screaming and shooting wildly.

A bullet grazes my left shoulder, singeing my skin. I cry out.

Aksel shouts my name.

With a look of frenzy devouring his hazel eyes, the Chechen lunges at me.

Out of the corner of my eye, I see another figure barreling toward me like a cannon. Suddenly, a blazing orange flame shoots from Aksel's hand, engulfing the room in a blinding, incandescent light.

Aksel swings his rifle onto his back, hooks his arm around my waist, and hurls us into the windows.

CHAPTER 38

With an earsplitting crash, we catapult through the glass. Even with a meter of snow packed onto the lower deck, we land hard.

Above us, the avalanche flare fades to an orange shimmer.

Instantly, bullets burrow like torpedoes into the snow millimeters from Aksel's head. Although I feel dazed, it's Aksel who bears the brunt of the fall; his forearm is shredded, as he used it to break the glass.

Standing, I tug Aksel's hand. "Come on," I urge.

However, between my tattered gown, bare feet, and injured thigh, I also struggle to move.

Leaning on each other, we hurtle down the steps, plowing through the snow in the direction of the forest.

I hear shouting far behind, Aksel's steady breathing beside me, then the whine of motors.

More of them.

We veer left, away from the sound. Aksel swings his rifle from his back, glancing between the house and the forest. We are surrounded.

The snowmobiles reach the forest edge. One of the snowmobiles breaks off and drives at us. The driver unslings an assault rifle.

Aksel steps in front of me and raises his bolt-action, taking aim—

"No!" I shout, knocking aside Aksel's rifle barrel.

Before the snowmobile comes to a complete stop, my father launches from it, firing.

He surges past us, evading the muffled cracks of gunfire. He returns fire at the house—smooth, efficient, effective.

Another snowmobile circles us. In seconds, my father is back on his snowmobile, pulling me up behind him. Aksel leaps aboard the second snowmobile and we steer into the forest.

I curl up behind my father as he swerves every thirty meters, careening through the pine trees, taking air over a ledge. I keep my head low to avoid branches. Bitter wind tears at my cheeks.

Snowmobiling down Eagle Pass, we eject from the forest near the top of Charlotte's driveway. A large black Suburban idles in front of us. The snowmobiles come to a halt and we jump off.

"Careful," Aksel says in a low voice. He is at my side, holding his hand to my bleeding thigh as we clamber into the Suburban along with the others.

Within seconds, we are speeding through the dark streets.

Steadying my breath, I turn to my father.

"*Them*," I say. Terror stains the simple word. "Dad, it was them." My voice catches between a whisper and a scream.

How? Why? I want answers so badly I feel incendiary.

The vehicle has been fixed with two bench seats facing each other, so although I'm in the back row, I'm facing my father. He is dressed in a blue button-up shirt and a sport coat, like he's just come from dinner.

Aksel's mangled forearm is being bandaged by a young African American man who, unlike my father, is dressed in combat gear—all black, with a bulletproof vest, two Smith & Wesson revolvers holstered cross-draw at his waist, and an HK in his belt.

Watching my father, Aksel appears to be forcing calm. Breathing in through his nose and holding his lips tight, he doesn't acknowledge the disinfectant being poured onto his wounds.

Prying my eyes from Aksel's injuries, I turn to my father. "Dad," I force the words from my parched lips. "How?" My left shoulder aches. I cradle it with my right to alleviate the throbbing.

Moving aside a remnant of tulle, my father winces at the laceration in my thigh. "It's deep, but clean," he utters. "Should heal fast."

He knots a rubber tourniquet above the wound.

Warm blood trickles from my left temple and drips onto my cheek. I wipe it off with the back of my hand. The medical kit is on the floor; I snatch a loose butterfly strip and pass it to my father. He adheres it in place on my temple.

When my father finally meets my gaze, his steel-gray eyes appear heavy and worn. His skin is pale, but what startles me most is the return of that hollow, calculated stare. With its reappearance, I feel a torrent of dread.

I glance sideways at Aksel. He knew I was being followed. He tried to convince me. Warn me. I knew too. And I denied it.

Aksel's eyes shift from my father to the man plucking shrapnel out of his arm, to me; he doesn't look hurt, he looks enraged.

"Who is he?" I ask again. "I kept seeing him . . . I told myself . . . believed . . . it was a coincidence . . . I should have trusted my instincts . . . this is my fault . . ."

My father interjects, shaking his head, "No, Sophia. It's mine."

My whole left side is bruised from the fall; I can feel scratches on my face from the snowmobile ride and a stinging pain where the bullet grazed my left arm. But these wounds hurt less than the look on my father's face—he's not surprised?

Aksel makes a deep growling sound in his throat. The man pops Aksel's shoulder back into place with a grinding, snapping sound. Aksel doesn't flinch.

My father applies pressure to the wound in my thigh. He pricks my skin with a needle of lidocaine.

"You knew?" I whisper.

He doesn't have to speak to answer my question.

"I believed you!" I exclaim. "You told me I was safe here! I believed you from the night we left Tunisia!"

"You were safe here, Sophia!" With a pair of sturdy tweezers, he removes the glass shard lodged in my flesh. He begins stitching.

"How is this safe?" I ask through gritted teeth.

"Because at first, he only wanted to observe you," my father says, ripping open a bandage with his teeth and holding it to my leg.

"You call that observation?!" I shout.

"He's been watching you for months. He was sent to confirm, then return, and reconfirm. They were only tracking your movements, so we let them. Monitoring him while he followed you gave us essential intelligence into how CNF has rebuilt."

My voice is barely audible. "You *let* him follow me?"

Beside me, Aksel glowers at my father with barely concealed rage.

"Since he was imprisoned in Libya, Bekami has grown CNF into a transnational organization of multilingual, technologically sophisticated terrorists with access to untraceable funds and an endless supply of recruits—"

"So, you used me to draw them out—"

"We did it to protect you!"

The driver turns onto Highway 81. I slide harder into Aksel. With my body pressed against his, I want to cry, to stop this.

"How is this protecting me?!"

"I killed every man who hurt you," my father declares, "except Bekami. And I would have killed him too had he not landed in a Libyan prison—"

"But Bekami is in prison, so how . . ." I trail off.

My father says nothing.

"He *is* still in prison, right?" I persist, a cold sweat dampening the back of my neck.

My father tosses the bloody cloth onto the floor, avoiding eye contact.

"Bekami escaped from prison eighteen days ago. We have no idea where he is."

CHAPTER 39

I always imagined that if I ever heard those words, *Bekami escaped from prison*, fear would cripple me. Instead, fury roars through me.

"Go back there!" I order. "Find the Chechen who's been following me and interrogate him until he tells you where Bekami is!"

"We will, Sophia. A team went in behind us. But those men tonight know nothing. They are an action team; they follow instructions from encrypted text messages—"

"He has to know where Bekami is!"

"He doesn't! That man who followed you is a Chechen American, a pawn; he's an extension of Bekami's international terror branch of CNF. He doesn't even know Bekami. We have only one purpose now, and that is—"

"We?" I interrupt. "You mean you and Andrews?"

"Do you want the truth?"

"I deserve the truth!"

My father holds my gaze. "You know my work is attached to—"

"Kent," the man tending to Aksel's arm interjects.

"Todd, she deserves to know—"

"Know what?" I demand.

"Not too much," Todd says coolly, reaching into the emergency kit.

My father starts addressing the graze wound in my arm, applying a disinfectant gel.

"I work for a counterterrorist team at the Department of Defense." His eyes flash to my neck. "Operations Network YX is its official name, but we go by our acronym: ON-YX."

Almost of its own accord, my finger moves to my neck. Hanging at the base of my collarbone, embedded in the gold pendant, is a small crystal—a white onyx stone I've worn every day since my parents first gave it to me ten years ago.

Never take it off, Sophia. Wear it always, Sophia. Promise, Sophia.

I rip it off my neck. The clasp breaks. Clenching the delicate chain in my fist, I want to destroy it.

This is why they let me live freely in Waterford. This is why . . .

"You knew." The words tumble out of me in gasps. "You knew where I was in Istanbul," I stammer. "Y-You knew where I was, and you didn't rescue me?"

My father's face is pallid. "We tried . . . there was interference on your tracer." He points to my necklace.

"I don't believe you!"

My father is so pale he is gray. "When we came for you, Sophia, the room was empty. It was a trap. A part of me died that day, Sophia. That was the only moment I thought we had lost you forever."

I fight back the memories threatening to surface—the rough cloth fibers binding me to the copper pipe. The smell of smoke and yenibahar and black tea and Yves Saint Laurent cologne. His slimy skin. His voice I can never forget.

Aksel grimaces under his breath. Todd is using medical tape to cover the abrasions on the side of his face.

"Why didn't you keep searching?" I ask, wincing at the sight of Aksel's lesions.

"We lost a man in that raid, Sophia. Andrews risked everything to convince HQ to let us go after you. But they wouldn't risk more men on bad intelligence."

"So why didn't you ignore Andrews?"

"Andrews was trying to help, but we had no idea where you were—your mother was tracking a new lead when Jozef called saying you had escaped."

My head is foggy. I feel faint. I've tried for so long to block it that it physically hurts to remember.

"Wait, Mom is . . . *actually* involved with ON-YX too? Not just covering you?"

Something about this thought—that she's not on *my* side—unravels me.

"Your mother is our best operator," my father mutters. "Her cover is airtight. We were both pulled from CIA to start ON-YX years ago; we operate the way CIA originally operated. We can do this because we don't exist. You, Sophia, don't exist."

"I don't *exist?*"

"Not until Istanbul."

Trying to comprehend this logic, I shake my head. "And what about Nemcova? What does she have to do with Bekami?"

My father wraps my wound with gauze. "Everything, unfortunately."

Beside me, Aksel twitches.

"You got another one here," Todd tells Aksel.

"Another what?" Aksel says combatively, looking over at him.

Todd retrieves a pair of tweezers. "Another bullet, Rambo."

I slide my hand into Aksel's; he squeezes it tight.

"If you're who they want"—I turn back to my father—"why don't they go after you? Why are they so determined to get revenge through me?"

My father sighs. "CNF thinks *you* can help them get what they need."

Aksel winds his free arm protectively around my waist.

"Still?" I say, both infuriated and bewildered. "Why?"

My mind spins. I've been used as part of my parents' diplomatic covers my entire life. My parents chose their operations over me. They are no different than Bekami—using me to accomplish their missions.

The truth cuts into my skin like Farhad's blade—Istanbul was because of my father. He chose his job—his obligations—over keeping me safe.

I will always be in danger because through me, terrorists like Bekami can retaliate against my father. Blackmail him into doing, or giving them, something.

I hit the window button with my right finger, rolling it down. Frigid air sweeps through the car.

I catch my father's eye and throw my necklace out as far as I can.

My father finishes bandaging my arm and wipes his hands off on his pants.

Aksel straightens up. His arm behind my back flexes hard as granite. His fingertips press down on my hip, as if he's holding me in place.

Ahead, I see lights on the ground.

Tarmac.

We've been in the car twenty-three minutes when the Suburban brakes beside a C-2 at the edge of an empty runway.

CHAPTER 40

Panic rises within me like a fast-approaching tide.

An airman ducks beneath the doorframe of the plane, stepping onto the platform at the top of the retractable stairway. Another airman in a flight suit at the bottom of the stairway bellows, "Two minutes!"

My father reaches the bottom step and turns back, beckoning me forward.

I stand motionless beside the Suburban, whispering, "No."

"Sophia." Aksel steps in front of me. His eyes sweep my face. "You're leav—"

"No, I'm not," I say, shaking my head. I look over Aksel's shoulder at my father, standing at the base of the stairway.

"We've got to get in the air, Sophia, come on!" my father bellows.

Fear that has nothing to do with Bekami overwhelms me. "I'm not leaving you," I gasp. "I'm not going." I link my fingers determinedly with Aksel's.

An airman steps up to me and puts a hand on my elbow, easing me forward.

"Hey," Aksel snaps, pushing the airman's arm off my elbow. His eyes are hostile. "Do not touch her."

My father runs back toward us.

The airman puts his hand back on my elbow. "She has to come."

"No, I don't!" I wrestle my arm free.

"We have to go," my father says, reaching us. "Flight plan's initiated—"

"I don't care!" I shout. My vision is blurry. Clutching Aksel's hand, I stumble backward, away from my father, from the plane. "I'm not leaving!"

Tears roll down my cheeks. I feel the blood drain from my face, from every part of my body.

"We'll come back soon," my father reassures me.

"No, we won't!" I shout. "We never come back!"

Aksel's eyes flash between my father and me.

Can we escape? I can grab my father's gun, take a double-shot at the left fuel tank. Aksel can get into the SUV, spin and reverse, enabling me to climb easily into the passenger seat—

"Now," my father says firmly. "We go now!"

"I'm not going with you—"

"—or they will be able to track us."

"They have been tracking us! Almost two years they've been tracking us, and you haven't stopped it!"

"Ninety seconds!" another airman shouts from the bottom of the staircase.

"Stop being obstinate and get on the damn plane, Sophia! You know protocol!" My father is hurting. I see it in his eyes—that same glassy, tormented expression he wore when he walked into Jozef's office; when he saw me for the first time in eleven days—beaten, filthy, and covered in blood.

Now I am standing, beaten, again.

The jet revs high. The airman shouts again. "Seventy-five seconds!"

Out of the corner of my eye I notice movement. I look up to see my mother emerge in the doorframe atop the stairway. She is dressed in jodhpurs, boots, and a dark green button-up blouse, her hair pulled off her face in a barrette.

Ordering the airman to stand aside, she leaps down the steps two at a time.

"Sophia, honey, come on. Aksel will be fine," she cries desperately.

But a glacial crevasse separates me from my parents and there is no way I am crossing it. My body trembles. "I'm not going with you."

My mother's face lights up in vibrant blue flashes as the jet's navigation lights blink above us. "Todd will take Aksel back, make sure he's safe."

"And what about Sophia?" Aksel snarls. "Who's going to make sure she's safe?"

My father studies Aksel as if seeing him for the first time.

Aksel is taller than my father, muscular, with broad shoulders, and large hands, tightly fisted around mine. He resembles a battle-hardened soldier rather than a high school senior. He glares brazenly back at my father.

"We do," my father answers icily.

"Like you did before?" Aksel asks vehemently, stepping toward my father. "Like you did tonight?"

"We have to get in the air," my mother says, stepping between my father and Aksel. "We have to get in the air before they can track us—that's how we stay safe."

"But you're not safe!" Aksel interjects furiously. "Sophia hasn't been safe, and you can't protect her!"

"And you can?" my mother snaps. "You don't understand."

"Sixty seconds!" the airman yells.

"I understand she should stay!" Aksel responds angrily. He turns to me, "Stay." Then to my father: "Let her stay."

My mother takes my free hand. A fissure splits my heart—Aksel on one side of the crack, and my parents on the other.

"If we don't leave now, Sophia won't be safe," my father says to Aksel. "It's simple, how we operate, and one day you'll understand."

"Is that what you told my father?" Aksel asks.

My gaze snaps to my father in time to see a shadow pass over his face, a quick pocket of surprise. "I never knew your father, Aksel," he says coolly.

"And yet you just happen to move here."

"Precisely," my father says.

"You're lying," Aksel sneers.

"And you're about to get Sophia killed. Let her go. Or we are going to be forced into a fight we might not win."

Aksel glares at my father. Untrusting. Undoubtedly assessing him the way he assesses everyone.

I sense his conclusion—my father is a threat, not to Aksel, but to me.

"I'm staying with you," I say ardently to Aksel.

But suddenly Aksel's grip around me releases, like he has unbuckled the harness that has prevented me from falling to earth. He takes my waist in both hands and turns me in front of him.

"What are you doing?" I cry.

Aksel tilts his head forward until our foreheads touch, holding the back of my head with his hands. His vibrant green eyes lock with mine, as if memorizing them.

"Promise me, Sophia," Aksel says, his fervent voice piercing my skin, "no matter what happens, no matter what you hear—you'll remember I meant everything I said. I have loved every minute I've spent with you, and I *will* see you again," he says fiercely.

"Stop it." I shake my head. "Don't—don't say that." My words come out in choking gasps.

"Promise me!" he yells above the roar of the jet engine.

"I'm not leaving!" I whisper frantically. Pushing at his chest, I try to force him back. This is our chance. We have to go. *We have to try.*

But pushing against his chest is like pushing against a stone wall.

"You have to go, Sophia!" he says urgently.

Cradling my face in his hands, Aksel presses his lips hard against mine.

Then he pries my hands from his neck, unlocking my fingers.

I whip my head side to side. "I'm not—"

"Sophia, now!" my father roars.

"You'll come back," Aksel whispers in his deep, familiar voice. In a single motion, he thrusts me into my father's arms.

"NO!" I reach for Aksel, but he is staggering backward, as if he can barely walk. Todd clamps his hand onto Aksel's forearm like a handcuff. Aksel doesn't resist.

The engines reach capacity, muffling my screams.

I try to break my father's tight grasp, but he lifts me off the ground, throws me over his shoulder, and bounds up the stairway.

"I'm not going with you!" I pound both of my fists into my

father's back. I pull at his ear as if I can rip it off his head. "Put me down!"

But no matter how loudly I scream, no matter how furiously I hit him, no matter how badly I want him to stop—he keeps going.

My father hurls us through the doorway, the staircase rolls away, and the door closes on Waterford.

CHAPTER 41

For nine hours, I fight to quell the maelstrom brewing in my stomach. Now, I feel it in my throat. I suck in long breaths of stale air to force the sickness down. My eyes are raw and puffy, but still I squeeze them shut to block out everything around me.

". . . Sophia . . . ," my father says.

It is his fault—all of it. For becoming involved in ON-YX. For lying. For taking me away from Aksel. *Aksel.*

"Sophia." My father touches my shoulder. Lifting my head, I notice the plane is still. The rumbling jet engines have stopped.

Across the tarmac of the Berlin Airport Private Terminal, a small red Peugeot waits for us, its vibrant color murky beneath the hard sleet.

After driving a short distance through Berlin's wet streets—kebab shops with neon signs tucked into nineteenth-century *Altbau* buildings, bike paths converging at every corner, women strolling by wearing fur coats and kitschy sneakers—we reach the Brandenburg Gate and turn left onto Ebertstraße.

We drive alongside the Tiergarten until we slow ahead of another gate—this one metal and three meters tall. Behind it stands a four-story stone building with elaborately carved moldings around the windows.

A female marine with freckles and a brunette bun waves us through the gate. We descend into a parking garage beneath the American Embassy in Berlin.

Two more marines greet us underground. They are accustomed to visitors: intelligence officers, foreign dignitaries, congresspeople.

"Right this way," says a marine with dark brown hair and black eyes that crinkle around the edges, like if he wasn't in uniform, he'd be smiling. He watches me with concern, recognizing immediately we are not like the others—*I* am not like the others.

The marine uses a badge to open the embassy door. Inside, he escorts us past security, scanners, and metal detectors, and behind a bulletproof-glass-wall barricade. We walk up three flights of stairs, turn left down a long hall, and take an immediate right into a room with computers, screens, maps, and two dozen people.

We walk through this room to the far wall. Behind a vault door is a spacious white room where a few people quietly work on headsets. The marine takes us to a door in the center of this room—a room within the room.

It is a windowless, dome-shaped structure, constructed of beveled, reeded glass. Although light filters through the glass, the blurry shapes inside are unidentifiable.

My mother has a hand on my shoulder. Her fingernails dig into my shoulder blade; whether for her sake or mine, I can't tell.

A barrel-chested man greets us at the door to the Bubble. "Come in," he says.

CHAPTER 42

While the man debriefs my parents, I sit between them in one of four aluminum chairs surrounding a table. I want to turn everything off. Make it stop. Return to Waterford. To Aksel.

The domed walls of the Bubble are closing in around me—I place my head between my knees to stop the movement of the room. I am wearing an oversize air force jumpsuit I was given on the plane. Now, I grip the stiff khaki fabric bunching at my ankles.

". . . We have some questions for your daughter . . ."

I burrow my head deeper against my thighs, wishing for something to hold on to, pleading for some way to escape the pain of knowing I will never see Aksel again.

". . . Sophia?"

I lift my head; my long, matted hair falls like a curtain between me and my parents.

". . . It shouldn't take long," says the man. He is wearing a gray polyester suit. Baggy. Ill-fitted. American.

"Please"—he stands and motions behind us—"if you'll step inside, we'll continue."

Collectively we turn. To the left is a tall glass box, with metal wires running at intersecting angles through the glass. Attached to the outside is a small, glowing screen.

"She has no reason to go in there." My father's deep voice startles me.

I notice my father's right leg has inched in front of my chair, like I'm back in one of our old photographs, always partially obstructed from view, fully protected.

But we are inside the Bubble—a fortress within a fortress—there is no safer place. So why do my parents look worried? Are they concerned with what I might say?

"It's routine," the man explains. "Only a few questions."

"She's barely sixteen! Who ordered this?" my father asks.

"Headquarters. Your daughter might have useful information—"

"You mean she is suspected of—"

"No. I've simply been asked to debrief—"

"This is absurd," says my mother, rising to stand beside my father. "Sophia is not going in there."

"It's for her own protection," the man answers.

"In an interrogation cube?!" my father interjects, eyes blazing.

"The Chechen Nationalist Front knew you were in Waterford within hours of your arrival, and since she was with them for eleven days—"

"You're not suggesting—"

"Nobody is accusing her of anything."

"We won't force her in there, and neither will you."

While they argue, I walk over to the glass box. On the front, below the screen, is an orange button. I press it. The door slides open.

Their heads snap my way. I step into the box. My mother moves for me, but the door slides shut, separating us. Her palm lands on the glass.

You don't have to do this. I see her lips move, but I hear nothing.

CHAPTER 43

"Do you recognize this person?" The man stands on the opposite side of the glass, holding a photograph—fuzzy and gritty around the edges, taken at a distance and zoomed in close. I don't need a high-resolution color image to recognize the Chechen who followed me, the man with the hazel eyes who attacked me in Waterford sixteen hours ago.

I see my reflection in the glass. My blond hair blurs into the khaki uniform. I glance at my parents. They are standing on either side of the man like sentries—arms folded, faces expressionless.

"Ms. Hepworth, have you seen this man before?" His voice is clear inside the cube's speaker system.

My parents' impassive faces offer no clue of how they want me to answer. I look away from them and nod.

"Verbal answers," the man says sharply.

"Yes," I say. My voice is raspy. After so much crying, it hurts to talk.

"Where?" he asks.

"In Waterford." I swallow. "Where your drone took that picture."

He glances to my right, at the screen attached to the front of the glass box.

"How many times have you seen him?" he asks, not taking his eyes off the screen.

"Three."

"How long were you aware you were being followed?"

"I wasn't aware—"

"You saw him three times. With your history, I presume you thought that odd?"

"With her *history*?" my father interrupts. His face remains expressionless, but his voice has dropped an octave.

The man pivots to my father. "Kent, you neutralized an entire terrorist cell based on a fourteen-year-old girl's recollection of conversations that occurred during a violent kidnapping, in a language she hadn't heard since she was seven. Her *history* is better than most of our recruits."

Turning his back on my father, the man shifts his weight to his left hip and points to the figure in the photograph. "Ms. Hepworth, why was he in Waterford?"

"Objection," my mother says coolly. "Speculation."

The man sighs. "Why do you think he was in Waterford, Ms. Hepworth?"

"Ask him." I nod at the photograph.

"I'm asking you."

I remember once, a very long time ago, we attended a horse race in Dubai. My parents stood silently, motionless, awaiting the end of the race in anticipation. This is how they stand now. Riveted.

"Why was he in Waterford?" the man asks.

"To kill me, I guess."

"Who ordered him, Ms. Hepworth?"

"I wouldn't know, sir."

The man holds up a second photograph, also poor quality; but this time it is a different man's profile, zoomed in until his face covers two-thirds of the photograph.

My throat seizes.

"When was the last time you spoke with Ilyas Farhad?"

I swallow. "In Istanbul, twenty months ago."

"But you've had contact with him since Istanbul, correct?"

"Are you serious?"

"Did you Snapchat, text, tweet, email, darknet, use a chatroom, or communicate with Farhad in any way after Istanbul?"

"Do you see that scar across his face?" I point at the photograph. "*I* did that."

The man inspects the photograph, then looks back at me. "Notwithstanding, you saw Farhad in Tunis before his death, correct?"

"When he broke into our safe house with a locked and loaded Makarov? Yeah, I saw him."

"And what did Farhad say to you?"

"Nothing. He was dead."

His eyes switch rapidly between the screen and me. "Was he dead the entire time he was inside the flat?"

"No."

"Then he had time to speak with you, yes?"

"He entered the flat, came into the kitchen, and my father shot him in the back of his head. So, yeah, he was alive inside the flat"—I pause—"but only for twenty-five seconds."

The man stares down at me like Krenshaw did when I told him I took a test at the embassy in Tunis.

My father watches the man carefully—assessing his threat potential, calculating whether he is an enemy or not.

"How did Farhad get into the flat?" he asks.

"He broke in," I say.

"How? Through a door, or a window?"

"The door. He used a key."

My mother's mouth twitches. I must have said the wrong thing.

"A key?" The man puts down the paper. He looks pleased. Like he's been placing a bet on another racehorse, and his horse just crossed first. "Using a key isn't breaking in."

"He wasn't supposed to be there. That's breaking in."

"It was a poorly equipped and infrequently used safe house on the outskirts of Tunis. No one except your parents and HQ knew you were there, and you're saying Farhad, uninvited, happened to have a key to let himself in?"

I flush. He thinks I'm lying? "I heard the lock turn," I say firmly.

"And you're certain he used a key?" He watches the screen, eyes rapt.

"Yes. He would have had no way to open that door without one."

There is a pause. A slight wrinkle in my father's forehead.

The man studies the screen, then looks at me. "Unless you let him in."

"I did not!" I object angrily. *He thinks I let in Farhad?*

The man steps toward the cube. My father mirrors his movement. It doesn't matter if we are inside the most concealed, defended position in Europe; if this man tries to hurt me, my father will kill him.

"Farhad arrived at the safe house while your parents were out. Since Farhad had no key, and only one person was in the safe house at the time of his arrival, there is only one person who could have let him in. You."

"Do you know what Farhad did to me?" I counter.

"When was your last contact with Izam Bekami?"

My mother paces behind the man. My father seems to be holding his breath.

"Outside the Slovak Consulate on Sümbül Sokagi, Istanbul. I saw him outside the gates. Bekami spat at one of the soldiers as he watched me run inside."

"A Slovak soldier said Bekami spoke to you in English and you responded in a language that wasn't Slovak, Arabic, Turkish, Russian, French, or English. Which language did you use?"

I shake my head. "I didn't."

"You didn't speak to him?"

I've told no one except Aksel and my parents about what happened at the gate. I definitely didn't tell my debriefer here in Berlin that I told Bekami I would send my father after him—told Bekami I understood everything he and his cell members had said. Now, Bekami knows *my father* succeeded in destroying his network. Bekami has come after us for revenge. This is *my* fault.

"No," I lie, "I didn't."

With his eyes on the monitor, the man's posture shifts. He raises his eyebrows. "You're being deceptive."

Now I realize why my parents tried to stop me. This cube must be a sophisticated polygraph—measuring my heart rate, body temperature, perspiration, eye movement—I shouldn't have stepped inside here.

"Did Bekami say anything to you?" the man asks.

I watch my father. He appears calm, motionless, standing beside my mother, except he isn't. He is breathing slowly, his eyes boring down hard on me—he wants me to drop my heart rate, confuse the technology.

I inhale for three seconds. Hold.

I exhale slowly. "He said, 'I *will* find you,'" I answer, "'and next time my knife will cut deeper.'"

"Did he say anything else?"

"He called me *fahişe*." I clench my fists, remembering. "'Whore,' in Turkish."

"And what did you say back?" He glances between my father and the monitor.

"Nothing." I shake my head, lowering my heart rate again.

He stares at the monitor, longer this time. Then he says, "Clever, Ms. Hepworth, but if I don't get an accurate read, we start over."

After another moment, the man holds up Farhad's picture. "Farhad was a young, charismatic, educated man. It's not unreasonable that after eleven days together you developed sympathies for him—"

"Sympathies?" I spit the word.

"—and agreed to assist the Chechen Nationalist Front with acquiring weapons. Our intelligence indicates you were Farhad's agent—"

"Your intelligence is wrong!" I shout. I got my heart rate down; now I need to maintain it.

"While in prison, Bekami told a Libyan national that Sinekkuşu—the code name for his agent—was helping CNF acquire a weapon more valuable than any on the market. I assure you, this intelligence is accurate."

"And you actually believe it?"

"Farhad sent a text message an hour before his death that he was heading out to meet Sinekkuşu—you."

"Farhad came to the safe house to kill me!"

"Did he say anything to you?"

"Yeah, he said, 'Hi, Sophia, I'm here to kill you,'" I say sarcastically.

The man's eyes flit between me and the screen. "You say Farhad was sent to kill you. We think he was sent to get information from you."

"I have no information, *sir*."

"David," he says easily. "My name is David."

I smile. "Now, who's being deceptive?"

He observes me carefully. Am I an enemy—or not? He taps the photograph against his hand. "How did you communicate with Bekami once you arrived in"—he glances down at his notes—"Waterford?"

"I didn't."

"Ms. Hepworth, Izam Bekami is running a skilled terror operation. Either CNF employs an advanced intelligence network or they have someone on the inside."

An informant on the inside.

So, this is why I am inside the cube? They think it's me? Claustrophobia creeps in. Now I feel boxed in, trapped. An interrogation cube must not only monitor my heart rate, but have other, more sinister capabilities . . .

David is still talking. ". . . You are suspected of disclosing intelligence to Ilyas Farhad and Izam Bekami and assisting the CNF terror organization—"

"You think I have Stockholm syndrome?"

"—in the acquisition of weapons—"

"Because Farhad entered *your* safe house with a key?" I ask incredulously.

"You lived in Chechnya, Ms. Hepworth, correct?"

"We visited."

"You're documented to have attended a local school and associated with local children. You learned the language, correct?"

"I was only there seven weeks," I say.

"Nevertheless, you learned Chechen. You developed sympathies for radical Chechen nationalists."

"I don't sympathize with terrorists," I say tartly.

David steps backward, reaches across the table, and switches out the picture of Bekami for the Chechen with hazel eyes who followed me in Waterford. "Why didn't you tell your parents this man, Ramzan Dimayev, was following you?"

"He was just a man in a street. I'd been told not to worry, so I didn't."

"Or is it because you were meeting him clandestinely to discuss intelligence you'd stolen from your parents?"

"Excuse me?" I say softly.

"He was your new CNF contact after Farhad was killed, wasn't he?"

"Never!"

"During your kidnapping, you developed feelings for Farhad. Afterward, you agreed to help CNF. Bekami sent Farhad to be your contact in Tunis, but your father killed Farhad and you moved to Montana. From prison, Bekami ordered a CNF member—a Chechen American—to be your new contact."

David walks toward the cube until his nose is a millimeter from the glass. "You planned to deliver Bekami something, information, didn't you?"

My fingernails dig into my palm. "You don't have clearance to read it, do you?"

He stares me down. "What did you agree to give Bekami?"

"You haven't read it," I continue, "have you?"

I uncoil my fists and slam my open palm against the glass. "Because if you had read my previous debriefing, *David*? If you knew anything about what happened in Istanbul? You would know that if I saw Izam Bekami, I would not help him. Ever." My words come out crystallized. "I would kill him."

For several seconds the Bubble is silent.

Then, David presses the orange button beside the glass door, releasing me.

CHAPTER 44

It was *never* over.

We—traveling as Henrik, Karolina, and Helle Marcussen from Denmark—enter an art nouveau structure with a marble exterior and a slate pitched roof—the Hotel am Steinplatz.

After riding an elevator to the presidential suite, we enter a wood-paneled closet. My father pushes his index finger against the corner panel—it swings forward, revealing a steel door with an embedded screen. My mother scans her retina. The door opens to a staircase, leading to another suite, an annex.

Here my mother checks the closets: weapons, changes of clothes, stacks of canned food, and piles of electronic equipment. My father double-checks the air vents.

"Is Aksel safe?" I finally ask, desperate to hear *anything*.

"I'm going to a pharmacy." My mother slips into a black trench from one of the closets. "No toothpaste," she says placidly, like this is *normal*.

"Why aren't you answering me?" I demand. "I need to know he's okay!"

My mother drops lipstick and a knife into her purse and leaves.

I walk to the triple-paned bulletproof windows overlooking Berlin. Eleven stories below, people are shopping at the Christmas market and eating roast duck and apple dumplings in cozy, candlelit restaurants. In the fresh rain, the streets are glossy; headlights shimmer in the water sloshing against the curb.

But all the way up here in this black-site suite, I try to keep from screaming.

My old life is back.

"These old Soviet safe houses will survive the apocalypse." My father smiles warily.

At dawn, we left the hotel for Berlin Central Station, switched trains in Munich, and rode until we disembarked at a village on the outskirts of Budapest. After walking a mile in the cold sunlight, we reached an isolated hunting cabin in the woods beyond the city.

Now, my mother passes me a stack of folded clothes, adding, "There's plenty of hot water." I can't believe I never realized she is part of this too—or that my presence enabled their cover. My mother is a veneer. Do I know her at all?

Showered, I dress in black jeans, boots, and a cashmere wool sweater. I braid my hair the way Emma does, leaving a long section loose at the end.

The cabin is sparsely decorated—an old wood table with several mismatched chairs and a slouchy sofa, burgundy with gold threads fraying on the edges. My father sits at the table, his briefcase open in front of him.

"It's time you get this back," he says, holding the barrel of my FN 5-7. "But first"—his gray eyes meet mine—"you need practice."

Putting my gun in his waist holster, he stands and hands me a backpack.

"Why can't I talk to Aksel? I need to know he's safe, that he . . ."

My father stands beside the grimy window overlooking the cloudy sky, his eyes hollow. "If I could have let you stay, I would have. But we were this close"—he places his forefinger millimeters from his thumb—"to losing cover. We depart before anyone knows our destination. That's how we stay safe. We don't compromise this. Ever."

"It's all for operational integrity," I say bitterly.

"Operational integrity." A shadow of sadness passes over him. "Exactly."

"Did he make it back safely?"

"Sophia, you need to forget about Aksel—"

"Forget?! I want to return to Waterford and explain what happened so—"

"You can't, Sophia."

"What are you not telling me?"

"All I'm asking you to do right now is forget Aksel and concentrate. You have only one job, Sophia, and that is to survive."

We enter the dense woods behind the house, jogging twelve hundred meters to a clearing.

While I run, I adjust the strap on my shoulder; the backpack is heavy, like it contains a thousand rounds of ammunition.

I have so many questions: Why did we go to Waterford? Why did we leave? Why did Aksel ask: *Is that what you told my father?*

My father stops in the western corner of the clearing, which is shrouded in thick foliage and concealed from the sky by a canopy of frost-laced branches.

Holding my 5-7 in his left hand, he unwraps a wool scarf from around his neck and holds the fabric out to me.

I shake my head, casting my eyes to the snow-covered ground beneath my feet.

"Please?" he prompts. I see the hurt in his eyes. I've seen that look many times—it is a look that says: *I'm sorry for all this, but not sorry enough to quit.*

Relenting, I take his scarf, cover my eyes, and secure it at the crown of my head. When I reach my hand out, my father places the Belgian gun in my palm. Against my skin, it is hard. Cold. Powerful.

I wrap my fingers around the grip, relaxing as my fingers settle into the contours, modified on my fourteenth birthday to fit my slim hand.

Locking back the slide, I remove the magazine and clear the chamber. I drop the bullets into his hands: one . . . two . . . twenty . . .

Next, I pull down on the lock and release the slide forward. It too drops into my father's hands. I remove the spring and take off the barrel. In less than seven seconds, I have the pistol field-stripped.

"Assemble," he says. Feeling for each component with my fingers, I reassemble everything I took apart, insert the magazine, and in another few seconds I am finished.

I hold the loaded pistol in my right hand. My heart pumps in my chest. With my left hand, I reach around the back of my head, untie the scarf, and push it against my father's chest.

He loops the scarf around his neck and points to a cluster of trees a short distance away. "We'll start at twenty meters and increase from there."

Slowly, I lift the FN 5-7 and prepare my body for the jolt.

Standing with my feet shoulder-width apart and my fingers wrapped around the pistol grip, adrenaline courses through me. My pistol has always given me the ability to defend myself, to protect myself.

But shooting like this is something I haven't done since Africa.

Snow falls in a light dusting, but in these dense woods, little reaches the ground.

I hold the grip securely, resting my right hand on my left.

"The black knot on that tree." My father points to the trunk of a spindly pine in the center of the cluster.

I miss the first two shots. Both bullets burrow into a mound of slushy earth behind the tree. Behind me, I hear my father shift his feet.

Keeping my gaze steady on the knot, I aim again—*Taut but loose*.

I try not to remember the last time I said these words. With Aksel. *To* Aksel.

Anguish tears through me so viscerally I wince. I suck cold air through my nose, hoping to quell the onslaught of memories I don't want to endure.

In for three . . . Hold for three . . .

Slowly, I exhale, and empty the mag.

My father motions for me to follow him to the pine tree. The black center of the knot is decimated, ravaged by a clump of shiny copper bullets.

"Decent," my father says. "Now move fifteen and hit the same target."

Clipping in a magazine and racking another bullet, I walk fifteen paces west, aim, and fire.

While I shoot, my father asks me to recite the answers to the same questions he's asked since I was five.

Rhythmically, I fire back answers as I unload the magazine.

"When I tell you to hide, what do you do?"

I shoot a pine tree. "I hide."

"When I tell you to shoot?"

I hit the same target, a dead tree, from several more angles. "I shoot."

"And when I tell you to run, what do you do?"

I check the bullets in my mag. Three left. One in the chamber.

I don't know why he insists on this.

I fire all four bullets before answering. "I run."

After hiking farther in, my father breaks. Eager to have the backpack's ammunition weight off me, I drop it to the ground.

"*Cuidado, mi amor,*" he cautions, unzipping the bag. He unloads the contents: sausage, cheese, canned herring, and rye bread.

"That's what I've been carrying?" I scowl.

Chuckling, he takes out two thermoses. He hands me a vintage thermos made of cracked taupe plastic. The bitter hot chocolate is still warm.

I look over at his nonsteaming thermos.

"Tokaji gets better with age," he says in Hungarian.

How can he make me laugh when I remain so angry with him? Rebuking myself for giving him this satisfaction, I finish eating in silence.

"Let's wrap up at forty meters," he says, returning everything to the backpack. "Black pine over there with the sloped trunk."

I spot the tree, stand, lift the gun, and pause.

"You haven't answered my questions," I say. "Is Aksel safe?"

"Yes. Shoot two."

I shoot the tree forty meters away with two rounds. I drop my gun to my side.

"How long did you know that we'd be leaving Waterford?"

"Move ten left. Shoot two."

I walk ten paces left and fire both shots. "How long?" I insist.

"The entire time, Sophia." He hands me another magazine. "Ten left, shoot two."

I pop another magazine into the chamber. After two shots I glare at him. "Why did we move to Waterford?"

"Sixty meters northwest. The tree with one root and two trunks. Shoot four."

I grimace, but shoot.

He shoots a tree adjacent to my target. Then he drops his gun at his side. "Sophia, we needed you *back*."

He walks to the tree to inspect our targets. I raise my gun in his direction and fire. I hit a branch above him. It breaks. Clumps of snow drop on him.

"Back?" I say.

Half smiling, he brushes the snow off his clothes. "Bekami was released weeks before we were informed. I assume that's why you were interrogated. Bekami must have someone on the inside. ON-YX needs to find out who it is."

"One of your people is working for Bekami?"

"There's always someone—"

"—willing to betray you for a price," I finish his sentence.

His smile fades. "With untraceable funds, Bekami has turned

Farhad's tiny cell of Chechen thugs into an effective team of terrorists, capable of transnational movement, and striking at will. He hasn't forgotten I obliterated his first team."

He picks up two pine cones from the ground. "But the problem is we can't stay ahead of them."

He holds the two pine cones in his right hand. "You have two remaining?"

I nod.

He throws both pine cones high into the air. They arc on different parabolas. I shoot the first, pulverizing it as it reaches the apex of its flight. The second I hit on its way down. Splinters of pine spray to the ground like brown snowflakes.

With both of our guns at our sides, we face each other. "Why did you lie and pretend it was over?"

"Sophia, after your kidnapping, it felt like we lost you." His silver eyes glimmer. He looks younger out here in the snow and cold. In the elements. In *his* element.

"Everything you had learned, everything you could do . . . disappeared. For eighteen months, you were a shadow of your former self. So, we put our hope in Waterford, in small town American life. We hoped that if we let you believe it was over . . . you'd come back."

Dusk is falling so we jog again.

"Take the lead," my father says. *You're never safe unless you can see in the dark*, he's always said to me. He is sixty, and his eyesight remains sharper than mine.

From the direction of the fading light, a clearing emerges, trees pockmarked with bullets; moments later, we reach the old wood cabin on the edge of the meadow.

I stop my father at the door.

"You deceived me," I say. "The whole time we lived in Waterford, you wanted to lie fallow until you were called back into the field; meanwhile you hoped I'd get over it—"

"That's not the only reason, Sophia—"

"Well, your plan worked, because I am over it! And now I want to return to Waterford, but I can't. Because instead of going after Bekami and figuring out who is leaking information, you tricked me. While Bekami hunted you, you told me to go to dances and go skiing with my friends, *friends*, Dad, actual friends. And do you know what is worse than not experiencing any of that 'small town American life' you wanted me to experience? Having it all taken away."

We stare at each other in heavy silence. No words are strong enough to articulate how angry I am with him.

Eventually, he opens the door. Reluctantly, I follow him inside. My fists grip the sleeves of my parka. My mother has lit a fire in the coal stove. She's set the table with mismatched blue-and-white dishes and rust-colored Bakelite flatware. Two flames flicker out of carved pewter candlesticks depicting Hungarian folk children.

In front of the stove, my father takes my gun, wipes down the barrel, clips in a fresh mag from his briefcase, and hands it back to me.

"It's yours," he says.

Running my finger along the edge of the cold plastic, I set it down beside the Hungarian candlesticks. "Keep it."

CHAPTER 45

"Onward," my mother says a few days later as we finish eating palacsintas at the train station in Budapest.

South through the Balkans. East to Lebanon. We travel light. My essentials—a Prada coin purse, a mesh bag of underwear, a toothbrush—barely fill my petite leather duffel.

From Beirut, we fly to Azerbaijan, then Turkmenistan, south to Qatar, and eventually back west to Egypt. We use only cash. Phones, computers, and electronics are turned off and sealed inside a Kevlar container my father keeps in his canvas carryall.

I am lying on a mattress at the Al Shalaam Hotel in Cairo, watching a melodramatic Egyptian soap opera when my father turns off the television. "We need to travel west," he says carefully.

"Exactly *where* west?" I prop myself up on one elbow.

My mother tucks her notebook into her Celine handbag and clasps it shut. "Andrews is in Tunis. Our car arrives in ten minutes."

A breeze sweeps down from the Mediterranean, whistling through the rows of jasmine trees shading Tunis's broad boulevards. Mint-green Vespas weave into narrow streets concealing quaint boutiques and leafy courtyards. After years of unrest, an undercurrent of optimism flows through the ancient city.

In the medina, we check into Dar Ben-Salah, a former French palace converted into a hotel. Bedroom walls peel paint and the floors are a chipped mosaic tile, but it has access to the main highway and reliable Wi-Fi.

"You've been here before?" I ask my father.

"Years ago." He points outside. "Safest place to stay in Tunis."

"Clear sight lines and numerous exits," I remark, scanning the horizon.

"*Precisely*," he says in Arabic.

I shut the drapes to block the heat and noise. I sit down on the bed; I don't want to see the spires of the mosques rising above the foliage, the red-tile roofs of the ancient city, the colorful woven textiles covering the souks.

While my mother runs surveillance, my father places a few photographs in my hand.

With trembling fingers, I flip through the stack: Lycée Français Saint Benoît, the corner two blocks south where the women ambushed me, an iron staircase, turquoise doors, plaster walls, a copper pipe protruding from a hole in the floor . . .

I snatch a bottle of water from the nightstand and drink so fast it trickles down my chin and soaks my collar.

"I want you to see where this happened, so it doesn't haunt you any longer." He points at a photograph; his finger lands on a broken piece of tile. "These walls are made of stone and plaster. They do not control you, Sophia, and *he* cannot control you. No matter where he is."

"You promised they would never return." I swallow. "But they did. *He* did."

My father takes a match from the bedside table and strikes it on the iron bedstead.

I watch the photographs wrinkle black and gold around the edges. I watch until finally, they are nothing at all.

"I'm sorry, Sophia," he says with tears in his eyes. "I am so sorry I didn't kill him."

I have never seen my father cry. Not once. Not even when he found me in Jozef's office. Wet eyes, red faced, yes. But never tears. Until now.

If he can track the most elusive terrorists in the world, why couldn't my father find me in Istanbul? Why didn't he search every building, every house, every apartment? If he killed all of Bekami's men, why didn't he kill Bekami too?

By late afternoon, the hot room has begun to smell of spices from the downstairs kitchen; the fan in the corner spins the heat and saffron into a suffocating aroma. My mother comes and goes. She seems agitated. Worried. She says little.

On the balcony, I sink against the railing. Outside, the cacophony hits me at once: cars honking, voices, blaring sunlight, the mixed smell of jasmine and exhaust.

Ahead, I see Place de la Victoire—a large freestanding gate, resembling a miniature Arc de Triomphe. In the late afternoon sun, men fill the plaza surrounding it, sitting on benches casually sipping mint tea and chatting.

Using the rail to hold myself up I rehearse the number series: *14-36-53 . . . 55-65-96*. I count prime numbers in Mandarin. I envision my favorite café on Beirut's corniche. I recall the latitudes of South American capitals. I try everything *not* to think about Aksel, but he enters my mind like a tempest.

I see his furious eyes looking down at me on the tarmac as he realized I was leaving. Did he think I had lied to him? Betrayed him? If only I could call him . . . I won't tell him details . . . I just need to hear his voice . . .

I step back inside. My father is doing one-handed push-ups on the Moroccan carpet.

I have two options. I can cross the room and retrieve my phone before he stops me. Or, I can use the hotel telephone, which is closer. I walk across the carpet and lift the receiver from the cradle.

It is an old 1990s model. Most of the buttons are worn away. I dial carefully. One beep. A second. I anticipate his voice. *Sophia?* he'll say. *Come back, I miss you.*

Instead, I hear: *This number is out of service*—I slam the receiver into the cradle and whirl around.

"Where is he?" I shout.

My father continues his push-ups. "Safe."

"Why can't I talk to him?"

He does two more push-ups, then springs his legs forward and stands.

My father pulls out his phone, swipes, then hands it to me. On the screen is a room with a river rock fireplace and polished wood floors, scattered with glass and debris.

"Aksel's house was wired with a video alarm system," my father explains. "He turned it on when you returned from the ballet."

Stunned, I watch Aksel enter the frame. His hair messy and soaked in sweat, his jaw tight, his face expressing devastation, sadness, rage . . . it must be after the tarmac.

Resting both of his arms on the back of the sofa, he looks unsteady. Suited figures move behind him, cleaning.

Grimacing, Aksel places his hand on the side of his stomach. Wincing, he lifts his shirt and inspects the bandage wrapped around his wounded ribs.

Abruptly, Aksel bends over, snatches up a piece of glass, and hurls it against the wall. He takes a chair with two missing legs and launches it across the room. It shatters against the fireplace.

The icy wind from the broken windows whips past him. He turns toward the hall, his emerald eyes burning in anger. Glass crushes beneath his boots. Swiftly, he yanks down a black duffel from the top shelf of the hall closet, walks back to the demolished great room, and hesitates. After a quick look around the house, he exits the frame. Then the image goes pitch black.

I can't pry my eyes from the screen. My hand clenches the phone. Immediately, all the fury simmering inside me since we left Waterford boils over.

"Where is he?" I shriek. "We have to go back—"

"Aksel's fine—"

"Where'd he go?" I can't see my father through the tears streaming from my eyes.

"Any person close to you, like any person close to us, is a potential target. He left for his grandfather's home in DC. He's safe there, Sophia. Don't contact him."

"You can't stop me from calling him!"

"Sophia, he fought Bekami's men alongside you. If he wasn't exposed before, he certainly is now. Every time you contact him, you risk putting him in danger."

"So I don't get to see him ever again?"

My father doesn't answer. I throw the phone at him. He steals it from the air before it hits him in the face.

CHAPTER 46

While my father leaves to meet Andrews in the souk, my mother reconnoiters the hotel. I'm alone in the room, and the heat is smothering. I step over the ashy photographs and make for the door.

Outside our hotel, the heavy air melts into my skin. I walk west along Avenue Habib Bourguiba, wading through throngs of Tunisians doing their evening shopping and savoring the shade of the street's lush trees.

Ahead I see it: fuchsia fabric draped elaborately over a breezeway.

Trailing a man carrying a crate of figs on his shoulder, I enter the souk.

I don't feel lost. The noise, the smells, the congestion of people—despite the apparent chaos, all bazaars have a rhythm, a harmony to the dark intersecting streets and labyrinthine alleyways.

Cloaked by long rows of carpets, I wrap a silk scarf loosely over my light hair.

After several minutes, I spy my father beside an antique stall. I nearly miss him because he is wearing a floral button-up shirt, a straw hat, and a neon fanny pack—quite the British tourist. He speaks to a man I've never seen—Andrews.

Andrews is taller than my father, with fair skin and straight black hair parted neatly to the side. Despite the heat, he is wearing a suit and smoking a cigar. Beside Andrews is a prim woman wearing a linen dress and carrying a straw handbag. She looks like she'd rather be anywhere other than a crowded bazaar. A paisley scarf is knotted haphazardly over her gray hair.

As the woman buys a sparkling silver ashtray, my father nods to Andrews and then slips away.

I follow my father through two more congested alleyways before pushing between the crowd to step up alongside him, adjusting to his pace.

His hex sense must alert, because he instantly looks down at me.

Lifting the scarf off my face, I glance up at him.

I can't help the satisfaction that ripples through me at his look of surprise. He doesn't break his gait. "Your mother?"

"Running the perimeter. She doesn't know I left."

"You're not a little girl anymore, Sophia."

"Exactly, so you should tell me what is going on. What did Andrews say? Does he know where Bekami is?"

"*Have you eaten?*" he asks in Swedish—my favorite language.

"*Not recently,*" I answer in French, his least favorite. He smiles.

I follow him through a stall, around a corner, and past a charcoal stove with a hot fire raging inside. I am that fire—flaming, bursting, roaring. Trapped.

In an alley, my father discards his floral shirt into a trash bin, his straw hat and pack into another bin. At the next passageway, he unsnaps the hem of his pants from the buttons at his knees. He is left wearing a black T-shirt and slim black cargo pants; he no longer resembles an oblivious tourist.

After a few minutes of silent maneuvering, we reach a hillside restaurant overlooking the medina.

He must be waiting for something, or someone. It's the only time he stops to eat.

Speaking in Scandinavian-accented Arabic, he says to the waiter, "Bring us whatever your chef is cooking."

A few minutes later, the amiable waiter brings two yellow bottles of Boga to the table, pops the lids, and returns to the kitchen.

Lowering his voice, my father asks, "What did you tell Aksel about Bekami? About Istanbul?" He speaks in code. Norwegian vowels. Dutch verbs. Swahili descriptions.

I say nothing.

"Sophia, I'm trying to find out why you were interrogated, and I can't do that if you don't tell me—"

"Everything," I interrupt him. "I told Aksel everything, okay? About Bekami and what happened in Istanbul and what I told Bekami when I escaped. How I was stupid enough to let Bekami know I'd overheard everything. But I'm not *leaking* information."

My father pushes his lips together a moment, then exhales loudly. "You were brave to defy Bekami, Sophia, It's my turn to be brave and tell you about St. Petersburg."

"I don't care about St. Peters—"

"You will."

It used to fascinate me when he spoke about his experiences, the enemies he had defeated. However, now that I've experienced that life, I never want to hear about any of it again.

"Years ago, ON-YX assigned me to recruit an agent within the Foreign Affairs Directorate of Russia's espionage arm, SVR." His eyes look away from mine. "Anton Katranov was a perfect fit."

I spread my napkin across my lap. My father hasn't shaved since we left Waterford. He has an ever-thickening mass of silver-blond stubble across the bottom of his face. I stare at this while he speaks.

"The head of the Foreign Affairs Directorate, Sergei Abramovich, was one of the most feared men in Russia. Anton Katranov was Abramovich's second in command, and Abramovich trusted Katranov completely. They had a special bond.

"Once recruited, Katranov became our highest-ranking asset in Russia. His intelligence was invaluable: missile capabilities, submarine routes, terrorist leads in the Caucasus . . ."

My father speaks slowly, choosing his words carefully. Whether this means he is lying or telling the truth, I have no idea. The waiter delivers a plate of merguez—a spicy mutton-based sausage—and my father slices off a chunk.

"But most importantly, Abramovich had orchestrated Russia's most secret tactical nuclear operation since the Cold War."

"Micro-nukes," I intercede, remembering what he told me in Waterford.

"*Kosheleks*," he says in Russian. "That's what Abramovich called them, Kosheleks."

"Purses?" I translate. "They were that small?"

"Like cans of whipped cream," he says dryly.

"Katranov told you about those weapons?"

"He agreed to pass us intelligence about them and anything else Abramovich directed. So yes, Katranov told us all about Abramovich's top-secret program to develop micro-nuclear weapons."

He takes a sip of Boga and bares his teeth. "I love this stuff."

I take a sip of the flat soda. "Me too."

Smiling, he continues, "But Abramovich was also an arms

dealer. He allied with terrorist states for profit. Because of men like him, terrorists don't need science, or infrastructure, or materials to create weapons. They only need enough money, or leverage, to buy from the right dealer. You see why weapons like those—easy to move, nearly impossible to trace—should never exist? Not on our side and certainly not in the hands of someone like Abramovich."

I nod. "So what happened to—"

My father silences me with a twitch of his nose. From behind me I can hear footsteps. Then the waiter leans over my shoulder and delivers a plate of fresh figs and dates.

Once he's left, my father stabs a fig with his fork. "SVR knew someone inside its Foreign Affairs Directorate had turned. We suspected they were close to identifying Katranov. So, to protect himself, and simultaneously take down Abramovich, Katranov framed Abramovich."

"You mean betrayed?"

My father grimaces. "Abramovich was a tyrant, a ruthless, Machiavellian oligarch. Our only way to get close to him was to turn one of his own. Katranov did the right—"

"If Katranov was a traitor, how could you trust him?"

"At some point operators have to make a call. Can we trust an asset or can we not? On Katranov, I was right. I arrived in St. Petersburg to exfiltrate Katranov the same night SVR raided the Foreign Affairs Directorate—and Abramovich's office as well as his home."

Sensing his hesitation, I prod him along. "And then?"

He sighs. "We got Katranov and his family out of St. Petersburg. SVR located the documents. Abramovich was captured, convicted of treason, and taken to prison at Lefortovo in Moscow. A few years later, Abramovich died 'of heart failure.' "

"And you found the weapons?"

"We destroyed the Kosheleks that had thus far been developed and dismantled the program."

I swirl a date through the fennel yogurt, wondering what St. Petersburg has to do with Bekami. "So, if you exfiltrated Katranov, where is he now?"

My father glances at his watch, scoops the last of the merguez into his mouth, puts ten euros on the table, and stands. "Time to go," he says. He lifts his bottle of Boga and drains the last of the soda in one gulp. "We have a rendezvous."

Ten minutes later, my mother meets us beneath the arch in the Ville de Nouvelle. She has our duffels. Earlier the square was crowded with men sipping mint tea. Now, it is deserted.

We walk four hundred meters through the tangled, tree-lined streets until we reach the south edge of the medina. My mother hails a rickety cab. She speaks in rapid Arabic to the driver.

"*Aren't we supposed to be off the grid?*" I ask in Finnish—the most obscure language to come to mind.

"*Not anymore,*" she answers. "*Andrews ordered us back on.*"

We pull into the Tunis Airport.

I turn to my father. "*Where are we going? What's happened?*"

Before the taxi comes to a complete stop, my father opens the door and we glide onto the pavement. He doesn't answer me.

He is occupied with his phone. I look over his arm. Having downloaded the SUISSEAIR app, he purchases three airline tickets for Flight 2334.

I scan the nearest monitor.

Flight 2334 is already boarding.

CHAPTER 47

My mother matches her stride to mine. My father stays close on my right. In the first few weeks after my kidnapping, they circled like this, hovering like a president's security detail. However, I am no longer certain whether they are protecting me or imprisoning me.

In the security line, we—François, Lizette, and Adeleine Dubois—smile demurely at one another and speak French in hushed voices. Four hours later, we land in Geneva. Before leaving the terminal, my mother steps into a duty-free store.

A shuttle drives us to the long-term parking lot at the periphery of the airport. My father leads us down two rows and over one. He pushes his phone against the key lock of an Audi hatchback.

As my father drives, my mother hands me her purchase—a slate-gray Longchamp nylon backpack. It is folded into a tiny two-inch square with a leather snap.

"You don't need to put anything in it now," she says as I tuck the square away.

We drive a short distance and, at midnight, check into a bed-and-breakfast.

Early the next morning, I shower and change into my black pants, boots, and a clean sweater.

In the center of Geneva, the narrow streets are empty. Cradled between the mountains, the city is calm and sleepy. Most Genevese go to their country homes for the weekend; the remaining citizens stroll leisurely to church or Sunday brunch.

We drive on Rue des Moulins over the Place de l'Île with the windows cracked.

On the south side of the Rhône River, my father stops adjacent to the Cathédrale Saint-Pierre. Farther down the road is the Geneva branch of the Swiss National Bank, with an eleven-story stone facade with no windows above the sixth floor.

My father opens my door.

There is only one wardrobe in Geneva in December—an expensive ankle-length coat. My mother has one ready. Putting it on, I step onto the sidewalk and face my father.

His steel-gray eyes, the color of washed-out rain, meet mine. "We're good?"

I peer down the road. They've been flanking me like security for hours; now they want me to proceed alone?

"We're good," I murmur softly.

Stepping away from the curb onto the cobblestone sidewalk, I walk south along Rue Guillaume-Farel, in the direction of the bank. Behind the thick, bulletproof-glass windows, the gleaming lobby is awash in a fluorescent light to deter theft—should anyone dare to approach the burly, armed security team pacing the marble floor.

Inhaling long, steady breaths, I near the entrance to the bank—a pair of tall antique wood doors with matching brass handles—and keep walking.

Within a few strides, I have passed the building. A few meters farther down, I casually cross the street.

I walk several blocks, past rows of tidy buildings with painted blue doors and shutters, until I reach an old building with a brass doorframe lodged into stone.

Through the window is a beveled-glass case of pastries. In front of it, chairs are tucked in to tables covered in lace tablecloths.

Gently, I push the door open, ushering in the familiar smell—chocolate and almond cream and fresh yeast dough.

Patisserie Claudette is quiet except for the hushed conversation of two elegant Swiss women wearing their ankle-length coats and pearl earrings.

I wait for the women to collect their pastries from the white-haired *boulangère*, Claudette, then I step up to the counter—an intricate etched-glass dome conceals rows of fruit tarts, pear galettes, and petits fours with lavender frosting.

Immediately, Claudette looks over my shoulder. I turn. The only other person inside is an old man reading a paper while drinking a cup of coffee.

She watches me apprehensively. I run my hand along the supple velvet trim on my wool coat, unsure what to say. However, Claudette steps out from behind the counter, walks to the glass door, and flips around the sign—*Closed*.

"*Suivez-moi*," she says reluctantly. So, I follow her.

Behind the counter, past the ovens, around the thick slab of marble on which she rolls out dough, Claudette leads me through the building and down a steep spiral staircase into the basement.

I follow her to the far side of the room where she opens a door to a closet and motions for me to step inside.

Protruding from the back wall of the closet is a shiny brass knob. The wall around the knob isn't wood like the rest of the basement, but metal—titanium alloy—like the outside of a jet.

I look at Claudette expectantly, but she only sighs and leaves. I listen to her feet pass through the kitchen and into the front of the shop. Then, silence.

I stare back at the vault. I run my forefinger along the cool, gray metal.

A ring of numbers circle the knob. I trace the grooved numbers with my fingertips.

Cramped in an old closet, in the basement of this charming *boulangerie*, I realize I've known the combination to open this vault my whole life.

It takes only one pass to unlock it.

The vault creaks open. On the floor, wedged between the sides, are several metal boxes. After I match the right lock with the right code, the first box unlatches.

I scan the contents: stacks of files and envelopes, an abecedarian list of names, sealed documents.

Some files are in Cyrillic, some in German, Farsi, Hebrew . . . most are in English.

I open the next box. It's the same. Frustrated, I unsnap the Longchamp backpack and shake it open. I dump the contents from the first two boxes in.

I open the third, larger box and blink.

I pick up a brick of euros, calculating quickly . . . 500,000 euros—I scan the other half—and 450,000 American dollars.

I gather enough cash out of the third box to fill the bag and leave the rest. I snap the lids shut, twist the locks, open the vault door, and step back into the closet.

Upstairs, the boulangerie is bustling. I walk to the door, with my backpack tight around my shoulders.

"*Mademoiselle, attendez!*"

I turn on my heel. Claudette motions me forward sternly.

She pushes a white carton into my hands. "*You forgot your order,*" she reprimands.

Inside the carton, set on ivory doilies, are three warm pains au chocolat.

CHAPTER 48

I half expect to be stopped, apprehended, arrested, but ten minutes later, we are at the train station.

"Why did you send me in alone?" I ask my mother. "You could have done that."

Her azure eyes stare reluctantly into mine. "Claudette's orders were to lead *you* to the vault."

"But why alone?"

"Don't you see, Sophia? You aren't alone. You have a network, our network, so that if something were to ever happen to both of us—"

"Nothing is going to happen to you," I snap, irritated.

"—you have contacts. You will be looked after," she finishes.

My father takes a clean stack of euros and buys three tickets at the kiosk.

"Why Vienna?" I inquire, staring over his shoulder.

"We're tracking where Bekami gets his money. We find out who funds his network? We find him."

"And this person is in Vienna?"

"Nearby. In Odessa. There was a money transfer there last night. It's our best lead."

At 11:38, we give the boarding agent our tickets and file down the train to the last remaining enclosed compartment.

Separating us from the aisle, two Plexiglass doors enclose the row seats.

Once the train departs, my father unwraps his cashmere scarf and tosses it aside in a heap.

My mother takes the Longchamp backpack from me and removes the contents, dispersing the items from the safe between her bag and my father's duffel. Standing up, she tucks all our bags onto the metal luggage rack above our heads.

We eat the pains au chocolat. All afternoon and into the evening, I try to sleep, but it comes in restless chunks; every time I fall asleep, I wake up thinking I am back in Waterford and the pain hits all over again.

Why do I have to go along with this? Why do I have to stay with them? I watch the front of the train twist around snow-covered mountain peaks. The intercom announces we have passed into Austria. We speed by signs marking the road to Hallstatt, an old village with timber houses, chocolate shops, and a church whose reflection shines in the lake beneath it.

When I first arrived in Waterford, it reminded me so much of these alpine towns. Now the alpine towns are near again, and Waterford is across the world.

"I want to go back," I say. The intercom has announced dinner. We are all awake. "I'll tell a story—we had to unexpectedly visit your dying aunt—and unless our house is gone, I'll stay there. After you find Bekami you can come back too."

"You can't go back," my mother rebukes me. "Not yet."

"'Not yet' as in it's a possibility? Or 'not yet' as in never?"

A woman wearing a maroon uniform and jaunty hat opens our compartment doors, pulls down the collapsible table, and delivers three entrées of beef bourguignonne, three bottles of San Pellegrino, and a bowl of demi-baguettes.

"Did Aksel ever tell you about his parents' plane crash, Sophia?" My father tears off a piece of baguette and dips it into the rich wine sauce. My mother sits quietly, writing into a notepad, ignoring the food for now.

I stare coldly at my father. "Is this when you tell me about knowing Aksel's father?"

"I didn't know his father."

"Then why did Aksel ask you about him on the tarmac?"

Remembering when I left Waterford is like being asphyxiated—Aksel's arm tight on my waist, his lips pushed hard against mine, his words muffled by the engines, *No matter what happens . . . I have loved every minute I've spent with you . . .*

"What did he tell you about his parents' plane crash?" my father asks again, deflecting my question. In the fading daylight crackling through the windows of the speeding train, my father's face passes between being shadowed and lit.

I take a long sip of San Pellegrino.

"Sophia?" he prods.

"He said their plane was shot down," I confess. "Which you *obviously* know."

The train rocks as we ascend through the mountains. I wait for the movement to stabilize before I spoon some beef bourguignonne onto a piece of baguette.

"Aksel's father, Dr. Fredricksen, visited Pakistan frequently on humanitarian missions. While there, he was contacted by Intelligence to pass on information he gained while high up in the Hindu Kush. His information led to a raid on a village harboring a terrorist mastermind. Two weeks after that raid, Dr. Fredricksen's plane was shot down over the Gulf of Oman on its way back to Dubai."

"How do you know this?" I ask. I see the tension in his face. His new silver beard may disguise his bone structure, his skin tone, his identity, but it doesn't conceal his emotions. Not to me, at least.

"Because it's my job to find out everything I can about Aksel. To learn everything about his family, his parents, his past."

I nearly spill my drink. "Because I was hanging out with him? Because we spent time together?!"

He looks exasperated. His fingers are turning red, gripping his mug. "In Berlin, Aksel was told his parents' plane hadn't crashed. He was told the truth—his father had been a hero in the fight against terrorism; Pakistani Intelligence, infiltrated by terrorist sympathizers, shot down his plane in retaliation. After Aksel was told this, someone told him differently, that it wasn't Pakistani Intelligence who shot down his parents' plane, but a rogue American Special Operations Unit—"

"It was his grandfather," I interrupt. "He doesn't want Aksel to join the military. I think he is worried that Aksel will end up dead like his parents . . ." I trail off.

"Sophia." His voice is like a deep bass drum, echoing my beating heart. "Aksel's grandfather, Senator Martin Kennecott? He told Aksel it was ON-YX. He told Aksel it was me."

CHAPTER 49

Standing, I knock the bowl of bourguignonne to the carpet. The thick stew seeps beneath my father's seat.

"It's not . . . It's not true . . ." Except it could be; if there is one unequivocal fact I know about my father, it is that he is capable of anything.

I am on the verge of exploding—I can't stand to look at my father one more second.

If Aksel believes Martin, he will never want to see me again.

"Sophia, calm down," my mother scolds me. "We did not shoot down that plane!"

I glare at her, unwilling to believe anything either of them says.

"We contact dozens of agents like Dr. Fredricksen all over the world to help us gather intelligence," she says brusquely. "HUMINT—human intelligence—is what we do! We're not technicians; we deal with on-the-ground intelligence from real people."

"So, maybe he wasn't even working with ON-YX. Maybe it was another intelligence arm . . . CIA . . . MI6 . . . FVEY . . . maybe it was friendly fire . . ." I am desperate for an alternative explanation.

"Dr. Fredricksen was working for ON-YX, Sophia," my mother

says firmly. She takes her cardigan from the seat and buttons herself into it. "A year before Dr. Fredricksen was killed, an ON-YX operator met him at a café in Lahore and asked him to relay intelligence, told him he would save many lives if he did, and warned him of the risks he was accepting if he agreed."

"How do you know this?" I whisper.

My mother breathes in deeply. "Because *I* was that operator."

I sway. I have to sit. I have to stand. I have to keep moving. My mother keeps talking.

"When Pakistani Intelligence found out we had killed one of their own based on Dr. Fredricksen's intelligence, they shot down his plane. Retaliation. Revenge. We don't know. What matters is someone killed *my* agent," my mother says fiercely.

Processing this information is like pushing gravel through a sieve. Is this another fabrication to conceal the truth?

Whether they shot down that plane or not, my parents *are* responsible.

"Why did we move to Waterford?" I ask.

"Andrews thought it would be a good fit," my father recites, "mountains, fresh air, skiing—"

"Stop lying!" I shout. "I know there's more! We could've gone anywhere, since it was never truly over. Why Waterford?"

For so long, I've always accepted their deviations from the truth, their lies of omission, because I felt that by accepting them, I was playing along too. I never felt betrayed, but, rather, that I was somehow part of the secret, because I kept it.

Knowing they've deliberately deceived me is like being knocked unconscious. "There is no retirement in our field, Sophia. There aren't enough of us. A terrorist needs only an ideology and an afternoon to train. We need a decade. We can't afford to let our operators phase out. In Waterford, we were as close to retirement as we'll ever be."

"And?" I prompt, sensing his hesitation.

"Our enemies—terrorists, arms dealers, dictators—multiply each day. We can barely find enough special units, let alone covert operators. But occasionally, someone emerges who is a perfect fit for the way we function: discreet, capable, motivated, and easily taken off the grid . . ."

How did it take so long for me to realize it? To connect it? To see the truth?

He continues, speaking faster now: "We didn't know when we arrived. It was weeks before we learned his name."

I am starting to hyperventilate. I don't want to hear it.

My entire life I have been trained to trust my instinct, and from the day we arrived in Waterford, my instinct warned me.

Nothing is a coincidence.

"Recruitment?" I choke out. "The phase of retirement you entered was recruitment?"

"Yes, Sophia."

"We moved to Waterford for you to recruit Aksel?"

My mother swallows. "Not quite. We were running Rec-S, recruitment surveillance, on Aksel, it's not the same—"

Fury erupts like a volcano within me. "You had video footage of Aksel's house! Of us!"

"Only after he turned on the video security system, Sophia. We didn't turn it on, although we should have, and we didn't access it until we had to!"

"So, I should thank you?!"

"We didn't want to invade your privacy, Sophia, but we had to protect you. It wasn't an easy position—"

"You've been underwater for four minutes, trapped in razor wire, and you figured out how to survive! But you didn't know what to do when Andrews told you to spy on my boyfriend?! On me?!"

"We wanted you to have a life in Waterford, make friends, go to school, have fun—"

"And you gave me this life by spying on us?!"

"You make it sound like we were peeking through his windows with binoculars! That's not what it is! Rec-S takes years; it's what makes ON-YX operators unique. We observe personality, reaction time, threat perception, aggression control, survival instinct, emotional intelligence. These traits can't be assessed in a three-month training camp. Some recruits are watched for years before they're even *approached* by ON-YX."

"But ON-YX has already approached Aksel," I say. "Right?"

"He's a once-in-a-generation candidate, Sophia. We don't turn down Andrews's orders. It's how we recruit. There is one difference between highly trained operators and cold-blooded killers and that is knowing when to take the shot. You can't assess this in an application process, or at a training facility. You can only discern this quality through years of observation—"

"So, if we'd stayed in Waterford, you would have been monitoring Aksel *until he graduated*?!"

"We only wanted what was best for you, Sophia," my mother says. "We left the field as soon as your father killed Farhad in Tunis. We didn't know who our Rec-S assignment was—it could have taken us a year to receive it—but you ran up Eagle Pass in the middle of a blizzard and Aksel brought you home, and"—my mother pauses—"well, he looks like his father. I contacted HQ to get status on our Rec-S assignment, and that's when Andrews sent us Aksel's file."

"All those coincidences weren't coincidences. Moving to Waterford wasn't a coincidence at all."

"The only coincidence is you fell in love with our recruit, and that's not good for any of us, least of all him."

I have to find Aksel. Tell him this before he learns it for himself, before he thinks that I knew, or was involved, or complicit . . .

Outside, I see the train is descending through the Alps.

Abruptly, I yank my leather bag down from the luggage rack. The contents spill onto the seat—a sweater, a copy of *Palace Walk* I picked up in Cairo, Vichy face wash.

"Sophia," my mother says sharply. She looks out through the glass door to the aisle. Apparently, no one is nearby because she turns back toward me, but she doesn't leave her position guarding the door.

I tear open the Longchamp backpack—it is lighter than my leather duffel—and start shoving everything I need inside.

"Sophia, stop it," my mother says harshly.

I grasp for anything within reach: my Swedish and South African passports, my FN 5-7, extra ammunition, a dark lipstick, three bricks of euros and three bricks of American dollars from my mother's handbag.

"I'm leaving. I'm going back to Waterford—"

"Sophia, you can't."

"Yes, I can!" Every part of me wants to detonate. I shove in an extra euro brick because the backpack isn't yet full. "All you tell me is what I can and can't do, and I'm finished listening to you.

Your rules have never protected me. I'm safer without you, and I don't care anymore what you say or what you're trying to teach me because I don't want to be anything like you!"

I slip on my wool coat and fasten the buttons.

"I was kidnapped because of you. I left Waterford because of you. Aksel's parents are dead because of you! Bekami thinks by capturing me, he can blackmail you into providing him weapons, and I won't be a part of this anymore! I don't want to be a part of anything you're involved in!"

I sling the bag over my shoulder. Their reaction isn't what I expect. Simultaneously, my parents reach their hands forward, grasping mine. The quick, synchronized movement stuns me.

On my skin, I feel my mother's delicate fingertips, and below my palm, the chapped, sturdy skin of my father's thumb.

My mother's back faces the glass now. I am like a child, cradled between them. But the way they are looking at me . . . It is as if they are becoming extremely ill, extremely fast. My mother's face is ashen.

My father is sweating. "There's more you need to know. About Katranov and St. Petersburg—"

"I don't care about Katranov or St. Petersburg or any other mission!" I yank back my hand, but my mother keeps me in place, her fingers like a strand of pearls strangling my wrist.

"I care about Aksel! And it doesn't matter what you tell me unless you explain why you're determined to destroy my life!" I struggle to free myself of her tight fingers.

My mother speaks first. "After we got him out of St. Petersburg, Anton Katranov was killed, Sophia. I should have protected him. I should have saved them all, but I didn't. I couldn't."

"Let me go!" I say through clenched teeth. "I'm leaving!"

"Sophia, you can't." My mother lifts her azure eyes to my father. "You're in danger—it's why we're always here to protect you."

"I don't want to be protected!"

Almost imperceptibly my father nods to my mother.

She swallows. "We have to explain . . ." Her face glistens beneath a film of sweat. Her eyes are blue oceans of sadness.

My father squeezes my hand.

Finally, as if it takes all the breath in her chest to push out the words, my mother speaks clearly to me. "Sophia." She closes her eyes. "Honey . . . you're not our daughter."

CHAPTER 50

I remember when I dropped into the water in the Indian Ocean and had to count to a hundred before breaking the surface. It was as though all the oxygen had left my lungs, and I would never get it back. I feel that way now—as if I'll never breathe again.

"Y-y-you're lying," I stutter. Losing my balance, I thrust my arm upright and grab hold of the luggage rack.

I heard her wrong. My mother resembles me—wide-set eyes, a similar pale blue color to mine, and freckles across the bridge of her nose. We both have a tall, slender build—people comment on how lucky I am to have her long legs and elegant stride. We have different noses and my lips are fuller, but I look like both of them. *I do.*

My father starts to speak. "This is difficult—"

I flee to the bathroom and vomit into the toilet. My hair gets caught in it, and tears run down my face. Before I know it, I am choking and sobbing.

Leaning against the wall, I close my eyes. My backpack slides off my shoulder and onto my wrist. I drop it to the floor, slumping down after it.

I fold myself into the tightest shape I can manage; I can't stop shaking.

After a few minutes, I manage to stand. I swish clean water

around in my mouth and spit it into the sink. I rinse my soiled hair in the faucet and push it back from my face. Holding myself upright at the counter, I use both hands to steady myself. I stare in the mirror.

How can I ever face them again? Has my entire life been a lie?

I lunge for the toilet and it starts all over again.

After I've cleaned myself off a second time, there is a rap on the door. My father steps inside the cramped bathroom. His eyes are moist.

"We know you need time," he says. "We never knew how to tell you, or when."

"Or *if*," I say bitingly.

His large hand crosses in front of my face. Through my tangled wet hair, I watch him place a sealed, faded folder from the safe on the counter. It's labeled in Cyrillic.

"When you're ready, read this. It will help you understand."

I glare at him. "Who are my parents?"

His gray eyes don't leave mine. His skin is pallid.

"Where are they?" I demand.

He turns to leave the bathroom and stops with his hand resting on the doorknob. "We love you, Sophia. With every fiber of our beings, we love you. Unconditionally."

His words light a fire in my veins, scorching my skin.

I throw the folder at him, screaming, "You've lied to me my whole life!"

My father's eyes are wet and pained. How can *he* be hurting right now? *He* chose to keep this information from me. *He*'s the one who lied.

He glances at my backpack on the floor, then his eyes resettle on mine. "Just read it." His voice is unusually raspy, like his throat has been grated by sandpaper.

He closes the door behind him.

I don't read it.

Time passes. I stand, numb.

Soon, the intercom announces that the train is approaching Hütteldorf, a few kilometers southwest of Vienna. Beyond the small window, the countryside has transformed into rows of Bavarian half-timbered buildings adjacent to modern complexes of concrete.

I glance at my watch—22:00.

My decision isn't a decision at all; it is a reaction. An expulsion.

I stuff the folder into my backpack and turn on the tap. I flush the toilet again, hoping the noise will give me time.

I lift the escape hatch on the bathroom window. Hesitating, I wait for a sound—no siren blares. Cold air and snow whip me. With my backpack slung securely over my shoulders, I wriggle through the window and land on the grated platform at the back of the train.

Years ago my father instructed me how to fall while skiing, sky-diving, horseback riding. It's all the same—curl, and land rolling.

Standing on the platform, I throw the Longchamp backpack as far out to the side as I can, then I leap from the back of the train.

CHAPTER 51

Landing in a rolling mess on the earth, I wince at the impact. Eleven days after the attack at Aksel's, my wounds aren't yet healed. Nonetheless a quick glance to my thigh assures me—no blood.

I make it to my feet, strap on my backpack, and dart down the embankment. Scanning the stars, I head east, toward the dim lights of town.

Before I have time to fully process what I've done, I cross the dark, manicured grounds of a park surrounding an old castle—the sign reads *Schloss Wolfersberg.*

I run along a lamplit street, ducking into an alley every time headlights near me.

I don't exactly pass for a jogger—I am carrying a backpack and wearing black boots over my leggings. The last thing I want is for a police officer to stop me.

Betrayal. Devastation. Dozens of languages and I can't think of a strong enough word to express what I feel.

I reach a row of mustard-yellow painted buildings and enter a marble-laid plaza with a fountain in the center and a cathedral towering over it—Hütteldorf is a typical Austrian town.

I walk beside a stone wall. All sense of clarity has been stripped from me. My stomach churns, my hands quiver uncontrollably.

Several restaurants and cafés surrounding the plaza are still open. I enter a café with iron chairs and tables set outside, shielded from the snow by a dark green striped awning. I sit down near one of the heat lamps and order hot cider.

I set my backpack on the chair beside me and pull out the folder.

Do I even want to read it?

Reaching inside, I retrieve two sheets of paper stapled together, carbon copies, yellowed at the edges. An envelope is stapled to both. I detach the envelope and set it on the table.

The top page is a report regarding strategic weapons intelligence—names, departments, drop zones, scientific data, and other details that mean little to me.

On the second page, in black ink, typewritten on a manual typewriter, is a transcript—an excerpt from a debriefing.

This isn't uncommon. Since any computer can potentially be hacked, and since extremely sensitive information is still stored on paper, a typewriter is simply the fastest way to safely document sensitive information.

But that isn't the interesting part. The interesting part is my mother's name, printed near the top of the page.

Embassy of the United States
Stockholm, Sweden

TS84-CLEARANCE
Operation **NEMCOVA**

TO: B. Alden Andrews, Deputy Director

FR: Case Officer Mary Hepworth (ON-YX)

RE: Transcription of ORAL DEBRIEFING (partial)
Strategic Intent of Operation NEMCOVA-Exfiltration of Anton Katranov

Agent: Anton Katranov—Officer, Foreign Intelligence Directorate, SVR, RUSSIAN FEDERATION
Use: Sub-director under command of Sergei Abramovich
Director-general, Department K, Foreign Affairs
Directorate—SVR
Intelligence: Tactical Nuclear Weapons Intelligence

". . . Katranov was at a government summit in St. Petersburg when we learned he had been exposed. We had to exfiltrate immediately.

Kent collected Katranov from the summit. I collected Mrs. Katranov and the children from their apartment and we fled separately, reconvening at the Neva river marina.

However, our 'A' route, Tallinn, was blocked by Russian security checkpoints, so we proceeded to our 'B' route through Helsinki. Awaiting orders, we stopped at a safe house in Kotka . . .

The green light never came.

We improvised an alternate route, through Stockholm.

It was during this delay that we first learned . . . The former ballet dancer had somehow concealed it . . . at the safe house we learned . . . not only was Mrs. Katranov near full-term pregnant, but the stress of the escape had induced preterm labor.

We procured the services of a discreet Kotka-based midwife . . . the child was born . . .

Four days later, Kent went to gather supplies for our journey to Stockholm. I was surveilling the pier when I overheard a fisherman telling two Finnish border guards his boat had been hijacked by 'Cheka.' He said two Russians had held him at knifepoint and forced him to bring them to Kotka.

. . . I knew . . .

I sprinted back through the woods . . . {indecipherable} . . . But I was too late . . . I halted at the door . . .

Facedown on the floor, arms outstretched, was the body of Anton Katranov. Behind him were the lifeless bodies of his two boys. And behind them, blocking the entrance to the back bedrooms, lay the crumpled body of Mrs. Katranov.

She moaned. I ran to her. I applied my hands to her bleeding abdomen. I scanned the room for medical supplies.

But I knew what we had, and what we did not. Time.

Mrs. Katranov was bleeding out . . . {indecipherable} . . . gurgling blood . . . she clutched my wrist. "The baby," she rasped.

Instantly, I leaped over her into the hall and raced to the back bedroom.

Inside a single dresser drawer, on the floor beside the bed, was the delicate body of the Katranovs' four-day-old baby.

In the middle of this massacre . . . she was alive . . . asleep.

I brought the swaddled newborn to Mrs. Katranov. She was losing too much blood; her face was pale; her eyelids fluttered. She pressed her lips to the baby's forehead. Her eyes clasped desperately onto mine—*harmaakarhu silmät*—'mama grizzly eyes,' they say in Finland . . .

She pleaded with me to take her . . . that *he* must never know . . . that was the only way . . . she would live . . .

As she spoke the door opened behind me. The Cheka had returned. I placed the baby on Mrs. Katranov's chest.

. . . I killed both cheka at close range.

When I looked back at Mrs. Katranov she was dead and the newborn was suckling on her lifeless breast. I kissed Mrs. Katranov on the forehead, tucked the newborn inside my coat, and fled . . ."

Trembling, I snatch up the envelope and slide my fingers along the seal, ripping it open.

I pull out an old color photograph. It is the angled profile of a blond woman with a straight nose and wide-set eyes. Her neck is bent forward, her lips soft, meeting the downy fuzz atop an infant's head.

I turn the picture over. Inscribed on the back of the photograph in my mother's neat cursive is a name alongside my own:

Katarina.

CHAPTER 52

Katarina.

I push the tears off my face with my palms. I blink until I can see. I reread the dossier until the last few paragraphs when my vision blurs so badly I have to stop.

Conflicting emotions pummel me from all sides.

My family was murdered, and I lived. *I lived.* My brothers—I had *brothers*—died, and I lived.

Furiously, I wipe my eyes with the back of my sleeve.

Katarina pleaded with my mother to take me, and never tell me.

Yet a faded memory surfaces. When Consular Petrenko gave the porcelain doll to me, I wasn't sure what to name her. My mother suggested the name of a ballerina she once knew. *A very brave woman,* she said. She suggested I name my doll *Katarina.*

I bite my lip to fight more tears.

It takes several minutes to calm my breath.

My hair is in my face, so I braid it and tie the end with an elastic. I rub my hands to keep warm.

The waiter is nearby, glancing in my direction and smoothing out his apron. I drink my now cold cider, leave a twenty-euro note under the glass because I forgot my coin purse, and exit the café.

The dossier explained who my birth parents are, but now I have more questions.

Across the plaza, beside the church, is an internet café with a painted sign on the window—*Open until Midnight.*

Inside, the café is crowded with teenagers. An Austrian boy—tight dark jeans, white sneakers, and a black sweater—stands in the corner by the cash register. He catches my eye and motions to an empty slot.

The building is two hundred years old, but the computers are brand-new.

My fingers are clammy and stiff, still trembling—I mistype the name twice.

First, I do a basic search for Anton Katranov. Nothing. I log on to a Russian server. Still nothing. In fact, there is no reference to Anton Katranov anywhere. Next, I type in my birth mother's name, Katarina Katranov. There is one link to a twenty-five-year-old article in a Bolshoi Ballet Company review. Other than that, there is nothing.

Next, I type in Sergei Abramovich. *Tyrant. Oligarch. One of the most feared men in Russia. Directed Russia's most secret tactical weapons operation . . .*

Austrian Wikipedia has a brief entry on Abramovich: a former Foreign Affairs Director of Russian Intelligence who died of heart failure, ten years ago. Many assumed he would become the next head of the Russian Foreign Intelligence Service. Nothing about defecting. Nothing about Lefortovo Prison.

There is a single grainy picture of him—a shock of dark hair, thick eyebrows, and an aquiline nose.

I click on every citation attached to his profile. I log in to the

British Wikipedia page, the German and American ones. The pages are identical. Nothing more than this basic description exists.

I pull out the folder and scan my mother's dossier.

. . . *had somehow concealed it* . . .

No one within SVR knew about me.

SVR killed my birth parents, killed my brothers, and would have killed me too if they had known I existed, had known I was sleeping in a drawer in the back bedroom.

Katarina asked my parents to take me—and never tell me—so I would be safe. If I didn't know my identity, I was less likely to be found. Less likely to be killed.

Suddenly, my hex sense flicks on like a switch.

I glance at the door. A man of medium build, wearing a Munich Football jacket, watches me through the glass.

CHAPTER 53

I shut down the computer, yank the cord out from the wall, and scoop my bag onto my shoulder. I push my way to the Austrian boy at the cash register.

"*Is there another exit?*" I ask in German. Nodding toward the front door, I attempt to look annoyed. "*That guy won't leave me alone.*"

The boy looks out the window where the man in the football jacket is still watching me. "*Kranker Typ.*" The Austrian boy smirks, insulting the man—*Creep.*

He leads me through a dank office and into a utility room. He unlocks a creaky door that opens into an alley behind the buildings.

"*Danke.*" I smile.

"*Where are you going?*" he calls out after me. But I don't look back. I run through the alley, my boots gripping the ice, until I reach the main cobblestone road circling back to the plaza. Here I turn onto a narrow road off the grassy knoll in the center of town.

I pass a busy nightclub—*Spass Nacht*, the sign flashes in neon lights. A short line of people linger outside, awaiting ID checks from the burly bouncer in the doorway.

Veering left, I walk briskly in the direction of the train station.

Suddenly, the man in the Munich Football jacket steps out of the shadows.

Halting, I scan my surroundings. Idling at the end of the street, close enough to block my exit, but not close enough to reach me, is a dark Mercedes sedan. I can't risk it. Munich Jacket is rapidly closing in. His heavy boots scrape the sidewalk.

Impulsively, I pivot. Turning around, I slip off my coat and tie the sleeves at my waist. As I near Spass Nacht, I take my sweater off and shove it into my backpack. I apply a coat of dark lipstick and muss my braid. I rummage through the zippered pouch of passports and pull out the first one I touch.

Concentrating on the bouncer's eyes, I bypass a group of girls wearing sparkly earrings and approach the entrance. The scraping footsteps behind me falter—he won't confront me here, not with all these people. Wearing only a tight white tank top and leggings, I place my hand casually on my hip and stare down the bouncer. After a few seconds, he looks in my direction. Offering an approving smile, he holds out his hand. "*Ausweis?*"

I show him my passport: *Elsa Lündt, 19, Sweden.*

He scans the passport and pulls the rope aside. As I step behind the curtain, I look over my shoulder—no sign of Munich Jacket.

I bump into a girl with long dark hair as she leaves the club, shouting into her phone.

"*Achtung!*" she snaps, brushing me aside.

Inside, techno music blares through the speakers. Cobalt and fuchsia beams of light flash overhead. It is hot. Dark. The whole building vibrates.

From behind a pillar, I watch the entrance. The bouncer pulls aside the curtain, tucks something discreetly into his pocket, and motions two bulky guys forward. I step back—

"*Hey!*" a voice says. I've bumped into an older boy who slinks his arm around my waist. "*What's your name?*" he asks amiably, staring down at me.

"*Elsa,*" I murmur, watching the two men over his shoulder. I allow the boy to draw nearer. He's unintentionally offered me a position of temporary camouflage.

I assess my options—where are my exits? Small European clubs in small European towns don't follow strict modern building codes—there are no "safety" exits. And if these men *are* with Munich Jacket, then where is he? Guarding the back doors? I spot the *Toilet* sign, but it will be in the basement, likely without a window—it's not worth trapping myself to find out.

As I watch the men, I find myself answering the boy's questions: "*. . . nineteen . . . from Göteborg . . . studying piano performance at the University of Vienna . . .*"

The two men divide—the more heavyset one steps aside, hovering near the entrance; the bald one moves into the crowd.

Wiggling out from the boy's arm, I smile and say, "*I have to go.*"

Feeling his hand drop from my waist, I slip between two people dancing together and move for the back doors.

It's easy to navigate through a crowd—focus on the overall movement of the people, evaluating when someone will be moving right or left, forming "tunnels and bridges," as my father calls them.

I've almost reached the exit when I duck beneath a dancer's arm and emerge face-to-face with the bald man.

I hop aside before he grabs me. I spin on my heel and dive back into the crowd.

Keeping my head low, I make for the front entrance, hoping the heavyset man has moved elsewhere. I glance over my shoulder—the bald man is having difficulty maneuvering; he's using his elbows to plow through the mass of dancing bodies.

I scan the room. The heavyset man is now angling toward the curtains, effectively cutting me off. I whirl around.

There has to be another way out.

Ahead of me, I spot my exit—*it's easier going up than down.*

I pivot left and shimmy among the swirling, dancing bodies until I reach the stairs.

I twirl around the balustrade and run up the steps. Two floors of dancing. Three. On the fourth floor, I'm met by a steel door. I pull on the blue handle and push it open; it swings into the wall behind it—*thud!*

Closing the door behind me, I run to the edge of the roof and peer over. Below, people wait to be permitted into the club.

Down the street is a row of parked cars, including an idling Mercedes.

A bitter wind sweeps across the rooftop. I hastily put my sweater and coat back on as I run to the other side and look down. A man is pacing the alley, guarding the back exit.

Thud! The door to the fire escape opens.

Instinctively, I swing my legs in front of me and slide over the edge—two inches of window ledge is all that keeps me from falling four stories.

Holding my breath, I tighten my fingers in the grooves of the brick. The mortar is aged and cracked, creating crags to sink my fingers into. Nonetheless, I strain every muscle in my body to stay steady.

Above me, footsteps pound across the roof. A smoky voice rasps out in accented German, "*She's not up here!*"

Another man answers, "*I saw her run upstairs!*"

"*Are you certain it was her?*"

I cling to the brick. The sinews in my fingertips burn with exertion. I push my soles onto the window ledge, anchoring my weight.

I hear muttering—a phone call perhaps—then the smoky voice says, ". . . *recheck the other floors* . . ."

Their footsteps retreat. The door shuts.

I stay put. What if it's a trap? Are they waiting in the stairwell? Or on the third-floor landing? Others are guarding both ground floor exits . . .

I tilt my chin, examining the street below me. It's my best option.

I take three long breaths and start my descent, feeling carefully for deep grooves in the mortar. With each movement, I fight to keep my balance. My arms shake. My fingertips scrape raw; the tender skin bleeds as I negotiate the brick wall.

Halfway down, I reach a wide window ledge. I turn carefully, backing against the wall of the building, and leap. I land on the lower roof of the adjacent building. I cross to the far side and jump over a narrow alley to another rooftop. I spot an iron fire-escape ladder. I scale it down to the last rung. It ends three meters above the walk.

I let go, landing nimbly on the sidewalk.

Easy, right?

In the distance, I hear the soft throbbing of the techno beat. I walk farther down the block, cut through an alley, turn the corner, and halt.

In front of me, leering appreciatively, as if he's been expecting me, is the bald man.

I reverse, but two other men approach me from behind. They've stepped out of a dark alley to my left, and they're not alone.

Between them is a girl with long, dark hair, and silver hoops in her ears. The girl who snapped *Achtung!* at me as she left the club.

Now, she stares at me, wide-eyed. Petrified.

Blood is coagulating around a cut in her eyebrow. Her bottom lip is swollen.

The man in the Munich Football jacket stands at her left, pushing an HK into her temple; the heavyset man twists her arms behind her back.

My FN 5-7 is in my backpack. *Stupid move, Sophia.* I can't get to it, but my knife is in my boot. I reach down—

"*Move and I kill her,*" Munich Jacket says to me in German.

The heavyset man punches the girl in the stomach. She lurches forward, gasping. He pulls back to hit her again—

"*Don't!*" I shout, holding up my hands.

"*Hilfe,*" the girl whimpers. *Help.*

Munich Jacket looks at the bald man prowling behind me. "*Tell him we have her,*" he orders. Then, to me, he calmly says, "*We don't want a scene.*"

To my left is the dark alley; to my right is a row of dilapidated buildings. I have an exit. I can get out.

Click. Munich Jacket loads a bullet into the HK's chamber. The girl struggles against his grip; her eyes flit between me and the men holding her. I know what it feels like—to have unfamiliar hands smothering you, holding you, touching you, terrifying you.

"*Come with us and she lives,*" Munich Jacket says. "I'm tired of chasing you."

I glance down the alley. If I can reach my knife, I'm certain I can make it—

"*Choose now.*" Munich Jacket reaches forward, coils his hand around the girl's throat, and squeezes. She moans, grasping desperately at his hands. Her fingernails claw his shirt. Her face goes red—

"*Stop it!*" I shout, looking between the girl and the alley.

He squeezes harder. The girl's eyes bulge—

"*I'll come!*" I gasp, focusing on Munich Jacket. "*Let her go and I'll come with you!*"

Munich Jacket smiles malevolently. "*I have your word?*"

"*Yes,*" I answer.

Munich Jacket drops his hand and mutters something to the heavyset man, who releases the girl's arms and shoves her so hard into the dark alley she stumbles to her knees.

Catching herself with the palms of her hands, the stunned girl flashes her eyes between me and Munich Jacket.

"*Run!*" I shout at her in German. "*Get help!*"

A meaty hand shoves me off-balance. Yanking my braid, he roughly pulls me back.

I watch the girl disappear into the shadows, then I elbow the man behind me in the gut and knock my head back into his jaw.

As I reach the handle of my knife, a Mercedes careens around the corner. Its tires skid into the curb before jerking to a stop. The door swings open. The heavyset man snatches my knife away and tosses it into the gutter.

Munich Jacket tightens his arms around my torso and pushes

me toward the Mercedes. Arching my back, I lift my feet and kick against the doorframe with the soles of my boots.

"*You broke your promise, Sophia,*" he snarls into my ear.

Gasping and kicking, I claw at the arms encircling me. I bite the finger nearest me, drawing blood. I scream as loud as I can. But even if someone hears—even if the girl gets help—it won't be in time.

Their combined weight overpowers me. Together they push me into the Mercedes, and Munich Jacket clambers in behind.

Inside, I scramble for the opposite door. Munich Jacket snatches my wrist and wrenches me back. He throws me facedown onto the seat. He pries my fingers from the door latch and binds my hands together with a cable zip tie. I wince at the pinching pain in my wrists. The Mercedes accelerates away.

The driver doesn't stop for lights. Doesn't stop for pedestrians or cyclists. The bald man in the front seat tells him where to turn.

Munich Jacket's knees jam into my quads, pinning me down. He zip-ties my ankles.

"Get off me!" I snap.

Abruptly, Munich Jacket's palm collides with the skin above my eyebrow and everything goes momentarily black. Stars flash behind my eyelids. I feel dizzy.

"*Who sent you?*" I ask Munich Jacket. Blood trickles down from my temple, seeping into my eye. I blink it out.

We ascend a curving road. Steep embankments rise up on either side and merge into a dense wooded forest.

I kick at the door as hard as I can. Furiously, I try to wriggle out of the tie. They aren't going to do this again. Not to me. Not now. Not ever.

"I know what you're planning to do, but my father will stop you," I say in German. *"Do you know what happened to the men who kidnapped me last time?"*

The bald man in the passenger seat looks back at me like he wants to know.

"First, he broke their fingers. Then he peeled off their skin. Then—"

The car erupts in shouting. The driver pounds his fist on the dashboard. *"Keep that girl quiet!"* he orders Munich Jacket in heavily accented German.

I know that accent. I recognize that guttural *r* in the throat . . .

Munich Jacket hits me again. He pushes down hard on my back, smothering the air from my lungs.

Frustration defeats the rational, self-preserving side of me that says, "stay quiet." *"Who sent you?"* I ask Munich Jacket in Chechen.

Munich Jacket puts his dirty lips against my ear. His damp breath is like slime on my skin. "Girls like you shouldn't ask so many questions," he says in broken English.

"You should meet Charlotte," I mutter. Facedown, with my cheek smashed against the seat belt attachment—the metal gouges my jaw.

"Stop talking!" he sneers in my face. Drops of spit burst out of his mouth.

He lifts his arm, but as he makes to strike me a third time, I duck. With my hands tied together forming a solid mass, I hit his exposed neck with my knuckles.

He gasps for air. Recovering, he lunges toward me, using his entire weight to push.

My skull hits the window. I slump, going limp. Blood pools on the leather seat beneath my forehead. I inhale and hold, slowing my heart rate.

Momentarily, the car is quiet.

"Did you kill her?" the driver gasps. "Tell me you didn't kill her!"

Play dead. Don't run. Don't fight back.

Munich Jacket frenetically puts his finger on my wrist, nowhere near my pulse.

"If you killed her, he will kill us!" shouts the driver, panicked.

"Stupid *fahişe* hurt me!" Munich Jacket yells. "He said she was dangerous but—"

I keep still, motionless, inert.

"She's a little girl!" the driver hisses. "How dangerous can she be?"

I curl my knees into my chest, pivot to the left, and rocket my legs out from my body. My boot heels collide with the back of the driver's head.

The Mercedes swerves violently. The tires skid across ice. I grasp the door handle with both hands.

The driver palms the wheel to the left to prevent us careening off the road, but the wheels lock.

In a thundering collision, the car plows through a guardrail, tumbles off the autobahn, and crashes at the bottom of an icy embankment.

CHAPTER 54

. . . *Screeching* . . . *Stars* . . . *Throbbing* . . .

The Mercedes is sideways.

The bald man in the passenger seat is definitely dead.

The driver is slumped against the wheel, possibly dead.

Beside me, Munich Jacket is starting to stir.

I take a piece of fractured glass and saw at the zip tie around my wrists, grinding the edge against the tiny grooves in the plastic until it snaps in half. With both hands free, I squirm out through the shattered sunroof window. I land on the ground with a *thump.*

"*Fahişe!*"

Spinning around, I see Munich Jacket watching me. He unbuckles his seat belt and drops onto his shoulder. Recovering, he reaches for the sunroof and exits clumsily through it. Making it to his feet, he lurches toward me.

I can't move fast enough. With my ankles still bound, I crawl backward like a crippled spider.

Frantically, I stretch my fingers across the snow for a weapon—another piece of glass, metal, a pipe . . .

Munich Jacket reaches me in seconds. He punches my throat with his fist. I gasp for air. He puts his left knee on my thigh and pushes down hard on my chest. My elbows collapse under his weight.

Straddling me, he puts his left hand on my neck and lifts his right to strike me again—

Abruptly, his whole body is jerked violently backward.

I blink. Munich Jacket is dangling eight inches off the ground, his toes scraping for earth. He is being held aloft by a figure who, in the misty gray light of dawn, is no more than a silhouette.

"You think you can hurt my daughter?" my father growls viciously under his breath. Wearing neither a coat nor a hat, holding the man in the air by his collar, he looks like a Siberian tiger.

Munich Jacket spits in his face.

Unflinching, my father bends Munich Jacket's forefinger so far in the wrong direction the bone snaps in two.

"Where are you meeting him?" my father snarls menacingly.

Munich Jacket howls.

My father breaks a second finger, sideways. "Every time you don't answer, I'll break a limb. Where. Are. You. Meeting. Him?"

When Munich Jacket still doesn't answer, my father takes his wrist and bends it until it snaps and hangs limply against his forearm.

Munich Jacket falls to the ground, hunching over, clutching his wrist, and wailing.

My father unholsters his Heckler & Koch pistol and shoots Munich Jacket in the thigh. "Where?"

Hysterically, Munich Jacket starts to blubber words in Chechen. "*He told me to drive east until I get more instructions. He told me I would be . . . rewarded . . .*"

"Where?" my father asks. He fires another round into his leg.

"I don't know," the man whimpers.

With a swift swipe of his HK, my father breaks Munich Jacket's skull.

My father reaches forward to pull me up, but a spray of red ink bursts from his skin, splattering us both.

Several cars shriek in our direction, firing at us.

He claps a hand to his bleeding neck and yells, "Cover!"

We dive to the ground beside the overturned Mercedes.

Bullets dent the hood of the car.

My legs are still tied together. My father holds a handkerchief up to his wound to stem the bleeding. "Here"—he motions to his boot. I remove his Kabar knife and cut the zip tie binding my ankles with a single swipe.

Bullets ricochet off the undercarriage, pinging against metal.

Inside the Mercedes, the driver is alive, coming to; until a bullet enters through the front windshield and plunges into his cheek.

Under a barrage of gunfire, I reach through the shattered window and fumble around the interior to reach my backpack.

Twenty meters away, the first car stops. Then a second, and a third.

I touch the smooth nylon fabric of my Longchamp bag. I wind my finger around the leather strap and pull. It doesn't budge. I stretch my arm farther, cutting my shoulder on the window frame's jagged glass.

Through the broken windshield I see men exiting three black Mercedes sedans—men wearing black jackets and black knit caps, and with black scarves concealing their faces.

I tug harder—*nothing.*

"We have to get into the woods," my father says to me in a low voice, ". . . reach a clearing for exfil."

I tug again as hard as I can. The strap breaks free. I swing my backpack toward me and reach my hand inside. My fingers meet solid polymer.

"You take north flank, I'll cover south. Reconverge in forty-five meters," he commands.

I nod, pulling out my FN 5-7 pistol.

"In three."

I release the safety.

"Two."

I rack the slide.

"One."

CHAPTER 55

My father launches from our cover, shooting.

Five men duck behind their cars. Two others fall to the ground.

More men emerge—several have AK-47s and one has an MP5.

Following, I stay beside my father as we back toward the woods, firing.

At the tree line, under a staccato gunfire barrage, we pivot forward and run.

Weaving between thickets of trees, we zigzag downhill, advancing. We can outmaneuver them. We can outpace them.

However, our boots imprint the snow—they won't have to be experts to track us.

I'm forced to let off round after round over my shoulder. A shot passes so close to my ear it singes my skin.

Covering my head, I yell to my father, "Out!"

On the run, he lobs a mag over to me.

Hurdling a tree root, I catch it with one hand, push out the empty, and punch in the new one.

We dart downhill, gaining distance.

Chechen orders are called out behind us. Then every nearby tree explodes in bits of shrapnel, bark, and branches. Machine-gun fire whistles overhead—

I dive behind an enormous evergreen trunk.

Muffled by the snow, footsteps shuffle in the distance. Are they moving at us? Around us? Away from us? I steal a glance around the trunk. A spray of bullets lodge into bark centimeters from my face.

Ducking back, I look over at my father. He's taken cover meters away.

His skin is turning an eerie gray. His neck is red. His jacket below the collar is crimson.

Applying pressure to his neck wound, he winks at me. "Ready, tiger?"

I mouth back, "Ready."

Crouching, he unloads his empty mag and shoves in a new one. Holding my FN 5-7, I check my own mag. One round left.

"I'll be right behind you," he continues.

"What do you mean—"

"Go!"

Simultaneously we lunge from our cover, firing.

I leap over a tree stump and maneuver the steep incline, navigating gnarly branches and pushing aside foliage. He'll be right behind me, covering for us both, like he's always done, protecting me.

Glancing over my shoulder, I watch him approach the wall of Chechens, firing with both hands.

Two men go down. A third.

My father continues advancing farther away from me, toward the enemy, until—

A bullet sinks into my father's left pectoral. Another in his right. A third bullet ravages his ear.

"Dad!" I shriek.

His knees buckle.

Behind him, a Chechen rises out of a bush with an AK-47.

"NO!" I shout.

Using my last bullet, I aim my FN 5-7, and drop the Chechen.

Out of nowhere, I am tackled.

I tumble downhill, rolling over and over until the momentum stops.

Shots whistle high above my head, but I don't shield myself.

I dash up the steep incline, curvetting over rocks and logs toward my father. By the time I reach him, he's taken cover inside a hollow.

I push my fingers into his chest wound. "You're fine . . ." I cup my palm over his ear to keep it from falling off. "It's clean . . ."

His face is gaunt; his eyes blink rapidly; a ghostly pallor has overtaken his skin.

Shielded inside the hollow, I peer uphill. The men flank us—moving toward us while spreading out, forming a circle, like a pride of lions stalking prey.

He shifts his legs, attempting to stand, pushing his hand against the massive stump.

I drop my spent FN 5-7. Wedging my arm behind his back, I prop my father's body against mine. I'm unable to support his weight; we sink to the frozen earth.

As they close in, circling us, I hear the Chechens: murmurs, heavy footfalls, the clicking sound of guns being reloaded. But the only frightening sound is my father convulsing, choking on his own blood.

"Dad, you have to stand!" Clinging to him, I tug at his coat. "I can't carry you!"

Gently, his palm meets my cheek. "Bearings?" His voice is weak.

I squint at the sky. Moonlight is fading into dawn. "North at my six. We can make it—"

"Yes," he chokes gutturally, "you can."

A thick hand grabs my shoulder, yelling at me to stand, attempting to haul me backward.

Snatching my father's HK, I shoot the man's kneecap.

He howls, releasing me. Wriggling away from his writhing body, I refocus on my father. I need to shield him—protect him.

His eyelids flutter. "Sophia . . ."

This time, I am torn from his chest—my fingers ripped from his coat.

Reaching for him, I shriek, "Dad!"

Thick arms lock around my chest, dragging me gruffly back. I am being pried away, but the tears are coming so fast I can't see anything.

Move! I want to say. *Get up! You're supposed to be fighting them! We're supposed to be doing this together! We always shoot together!*

I am wrestled uphill, farther and farther away from him—

Suddenly, a perfect, hard *pop!* splits open the earth.

The man dragging me slumps to the ground, a dark wound centered on his forehead. Startled I look back.

My father lowers his spare Smith & Wesson revolver. It falls from his fingertips, empty, its shiny handle glinting in the dawn.

Sprinting back beneath assaulting gunfire, I reach him in seconds. My father's steel-gray eyes settle on mine. "The AK," he rasps.

I look at the still-writhing man nearby. An AK is strapped across his back.

I lunge for the man, wrap my hands over his neck, and tug on the rifle strap.

He tries throwing me off. I unhook the knife from his belt and sink it into his chest.

He stops moving.

I loop the rifle strap over the man's head. It catches on his ear. I free it and return to my father, skidding to my knees beside him. I give him the AK and a spare magazine.

Sitting upright, my father loads the magazine into the AK and racks back the slide.

Around us, the Chechen wall breaks through the trees, converging upon us.

"Go south at double pace"—his words are labored gasps—"until you reach the road—"

I shake my head furiously. "I'm not leav—"

Pop-pop-pop!

My father stands. A bullet hits his chest. Another bullet in his thigh.

I scream—an anguished primitive sound.

But he's impervious. Made of iron.

Propping his back against the stump, he unleashes a procession of precision AK gunfire.

"Sophia!" he shouts. "Run!"

Wrenching forward, I run.

CHAPTER 56

Stay south. Head downhill.

I'll reach the road. From there I can find a way to contact my mother.

I have to tell her . . . *Stop it! He'll survive.*

Settling into a rhythm, I focus on keeping my pace.

At first, I hear footsteps behind me. Then, silence.

A branch cuts my cheek. My sleeve snags on a bush. In the distance, beyond the tops of the trees, a bright winter sun is rising above the mountain, gold slashing aside the gray.

I emerge from the dim forest at the edge of a clearing. I'm standing on a pebbled shoreline, looking out over a smooth, glossy surface that spreads eight hundred meters ahead, and fifteen hundred meters in either direction.

Covered in a thin sheet of ice, the alpine lake glistens amber in the rising sunlight. Across the lake, shaded from the sun, the forest continues. I nudge my toe against the ice.

A chunk breaks off the edge in a pocket of bubbles.

Behind me, heavy footfalls gather like cavalry. I haven't run fast enough. Now I have no cover.

Thirty meters to my left, two men burst from the forest. Spotting me, they run faster, their weapons slung over their backs.

I put my foot on the thin ice. It splinters beneath my weight.

Forty meters to my right, three more men tumble out of the forest. They run down the bank in my direction. Twenty-five meters. Twenty. Two of them drop their Kalashnikovs to run faster. One bends over, panting.

Somewhere in the periphery of my subconscious, I understand what I've been unwilling to accept since I was fourteen. These men don't intend to kill me; they need me alive, and this makes me more afraid than I ever knew possible.

I take another step onto the lake. The ice sheet stays. No splintering. No bubbles. I slide farther onto the precarious surface. How long will it hold?

The fastest one is nearing me. Ten meters. Five.

Run. His voice is in my head. Over and over again until I can't stop hearing it. *Run!*

The ice is so thin, I can see the pebbles below it. I begin to run.

Keeping my feet light, I head toward the dark shoreline. Behind me, someone steps onto the lake. Beneath his boots, the ice starts to fragment. A fissure moves toward me and I sprint.

Halfway across the lake—*Crack!*

I turn to look—he sinks into the lake so quickly I barely see him. Behind him, another man has also run onto the lake, but the ice splinters beneath him too. Like a train crashing into a mountain, the ice ruptures in a deafening roar.

I force myself to keep running, deftly, delicately, across the fracturing surface.

Two more men creep cautiously onto the lake, trying to skirt the veining ice. I hear a yelp. I turn to see the ice dissolve beneath them too. Their bodies plunge into the frigid water.

In the distance, one has decided to run around the lake. *Good.* He'll never catch me.

I reach the opposite side of the lake still in the shadow of darkness. I increase my pace, run up the bank and into the woods.

I'll stay inside the tree coverage until I reach the road. Then I'll find a way to contact my mother.

However, as I crest the wooded slope leading out of the forest, I halt.

Terror cuts open my bloodstream.

He steps toward me, smiling. His hair is neatly tied in a ponytail.

I stumble backward into a wall of men.

It is like they've been tracking me from above, corralling me like a lamb to the slaughter. Before I can retreat, two men grab my wrists. I kick, trying to writhe out of their arms, but they tug me toward a car, parked on the empty road.

"*Hilfe!*" I scream in German. "*Help!*"

A greasy cloth is shoved into my mouth and tied around the back of my head. I start to choke. It nearly suffocates me.

The trunk is opened. They push me inside.

Before the trunk slams shut and a scarf is knotted over my eyes, I see him again, staring down at me, watching me, an arrogant smirk across his silky face.

I know his face well. I have seen it every night for the past six hundred and thirty-two days.

Bekami.

CHAPTER 57

Inside a small jet, I am lashed to a seat. For three hours and twenty-two minutes, hardly a word is spoken.

Wild, uncontainable pain steeps inside me as I try *not* to think about my father. The sounds of the AK gunfire. Him shooting at the Chechens to save me.

I squeeze my eyes shut and begin counting to infinity.

When the jet lands, someone reknots my blindfold, knocking the back of my head when he's finished. Momentarily, everything goes fuzzy. But my mind clears as clammy hands linger on my neck and a voice says, "*You thought your father had eliminated me. You were wrong. Instead, I eliminated him.*"

He shoves me down the aisle, drags me across the jet stairway, and throws me into another car trunk.

Drawing a map inside my head, I calculate a radius: depending on airspeed, we could be as far south as Tripoli, as far east as Odessa, as far north as Stockholm, and as far west as Dublin . . . I could basically be anywhere.

Paying attention to the noises outside, I try to hear voices, to identify a language. I listen for a stray siren, something to indicate where we are. Vespas? Church bells? Sports cars? Rickety vans? Buses? Dogs? Even silence tells me something.

The road is straight, paved. Noise increases steadily until it becomes a dull, incessant hum.

I pull my knees up against my chest and press my back into the corner so I won't roll. I should sleep after being awake for so long, but every time I close my eyes I see my father's face . . . pale white skin . . . blood drowning his words . . .

With the cloth in my mouth, my tears suffocate me. I have to figure out how *not* to think about my father.

The car turns sharply, and I roll against the wheel well. Wincing, I readjust myself.

Something jabs my left hip.

I try to roll away from it, but it follows me. It is a hard box with rounded edges. Maneuvering to my side, I still feel it; it stays lodged into my hip, poking me from within my coat pocket. I stretch my tied hands across my back.

After several attempts, my fingers fasten around the small rectangular box. I gasp.

Instantly, I know what it is and who put it there. I resist the onslaught of more tears at considering how my father managed to slip it into my pocket.

Fervently, I attempt to power on my phone. Nothing.

Again, I try. Nothing. The battery is dead. It's useless.

But then I hear my father's voice inside my head. *You know how to use it?*

I smile, despite the tears. *Yes, Dad, I know.*

I wedge my feet into opposite corners of the trunk, position my back into the side, and use the muscles in my thighs to bear down so I won't roll.

A car horn breaks my concentration. Ignoring the possibility that we might stop soon, I refocus.

Accessing the power button with my left thumb, I press down and begin counting from zero. The timing must be accurate. At ten, I release. At sixteen, I press again. Then, at twenty-six, I release. I repeat this pattern twice more.

Three signals at sixteen-second intervals. According to my father, this initiates the linkup with a satellite transmitter, not connected to the power source. *This is not a phone*, Tate McCormick said weeks ago, and he was right. This isn't a phone. It's a lifeline. Maybe.

The car stops. The engine idles. Doors open. Muffled voices surround me. I shove the phone down my boot.

The trunk is unlatched. Arms grip me, tearing me out of the cramped space.

I don't resist; I don't want them to have a reason to search me, or touch me.

Gravel crunches beneath my boots.

Even blindfolded, I know where we are.

I hear the adhan, the purr of a city vibrating in the distance.

A gentle breeze swirls around me; I feel humidity on my skin; I inhale the smell of exhaust, and cardamom, and salty sea air . . .

I am in the one place I never expected to return.

Istanbul.

CHAPTER 58

Blindfolded, disoriented, and with a stiff rope shackling my ankles, it's difficult to maneuver three flights of stairs. It doesn't help that his greasy hand is coiled around my wrist, tightening every time I stumble; the cloth in my mouth makes me gag.

He drags me down an echoing hall. The floors are smooth stone; with no rugs to soften the sound, his footsteps march grimly in time to mine.

Ahead, a door creaks open. We walk farther. Abruptly, bony hands shove me onto a seat. My arms are raised behind me and yanked down over the back of the chair. He tightens the cord binding my wrists, effectively straitjacketing me. Then, his footsteps fade.

The room is silent, except for the ticking of my watch.

One hour passes. Two.

The longer I sit, the less scared I become. Hatred burns away my fear.

My mouth grows parched. My skin is dry, cold. I try rocking the chair back and forth, but it is solid wood, heavier than me, and possibly bolted to the floor; it doesn't budge.

Three hours in, I hear footsteps. They start faintly, but grow louder until the heavy door creaks open and I can hear their conversation.

". . . then you have a way out, to avoid detection?" asks an unfamiliar voice. "I don't want this to—"

"A diversion," a familiar, repulsive voice answers, "Of course."

Their footsteps click past me, continuing several meters until stopping.

"Remove her blindfold." The unfamiliar man is speaking English, but his first language is clearly Russian. "I want to see Sophia Antonovna's face," he adds softly.

Sophia Antonovna?

I don't immediately process that this Russian is talking about me—that Sophia Antonovna's face is *my* face. I don't think of Sophia Antonovna as me, and yet she is me.

I am Sophia Antonovna.

And this man knows.

The dirty cloth is untied from my mouth. I spit it onto my lap. The scarf covering my eyes is yanked off. I blink rapidly, my eyes adjusting to the light.

When the shock of brightness dims, I see two men standing before me. The one farthest away is in the shadow beside an ornate desk, watching me.

But the one near me—eyes full of hatred, bony hands, an unrepentant leer on his face—he chills my bones.

Bekami kneels in front of me and curls his manicured fingers around my thighs. He squeezes; his palm pushing down on the still-tender glass-shard wound from Waterford.

"*Finally . . . you are here, fahişe,*" Bekami whispers.

Biting down on my lip, I fight every urge to scream; I fight every muscle in my body to remain still, to not recoil. I can't be weak. He can't think I'm weak.

"*He wants to see your face.*" Bekami leans forward until his mouth is centimeters from mine. His breath smells of yenibahar and black tea; his skin still emanates an overwhelming aroma of Yves Saint Laurent. "*But I know your face well . . . I could draw you in my sleep.*"

"You don't know me at all," I say viciously.

Bekami slides his hand around the back of my neck and pinches my spine so savagely between his forefinger and thumb I nearly black out.

"I know you're still the spoiled little girl from nowhere," he taunts.

I can see every pore on Bekami's smug, malevolent face, every tiny hair above his sneering lips.

Slowly, I tilt my neck back then ram my head forward. My forehead collides into his face with a hard *crunch*.

Bekami claps a hand to his nose, stumbling backward. Blood gushes from his nostrils, soaking the collar of his shirt.

His face wrinkles in fury. He lunges for me—

"Izam!" the man obscured behind Bekami snaps.

The man has been leaning against a large mahogany desk with a tumbler in his hand, watching. Now he walks toward us.

Disguising his weathered face is a bushy beard and shoulder-length silver hair. He is wearing an Italian navy wool suit with a waistcoat. His leather shoes are shiny and polished. On his left lapel is a pin of the Russian flag. He looks both lustful and impatient, like he wants something now and also has someplace else to be.

Above us is an old crystal chandelier, and when the Russian steps forward into the light, I inhale sharply.

"You look as though you recognize me." His lips part, revealing dazzling white teeth too big for his mouth.

The photograph had been grainy, but that hadn't disguised the drooping left eye, the overprominent brow.

His nose must have been broken many times in Lefortovo because its aquiline shape is mangled; it bulges at the bridge and veers sharply to the left. He is also now missing an earlobe.

But it is, unmistakably, him.

A tremor ascends my throat.

"Abramovich," I breathe out, stunned. "You're Sergei Abramovich."

CHAPTER 59

"Sergei Abramovich is dead." I stammer, "H-He died in Lefortovo."

Yet, the dead man before me runs a pudgy finger along the rim of a crystal tumbler. Tiny particles of condensation sweat from the glass.

He raises the tumbler to me and savors a slow sip of vodka. "I am not a medical miracle, I assure you."

"How are you alive?" I want his blood test. I want dental records. I want to be wrong.

He switches to his native Russian, and with it his voice shifts—throatier and deeper.

"For five years I was tortured, until, finally, they released me. They offered me a new name and a new position, Dmitri Yesnev, assistant to the sub-director of the Russian Foreign Intelligence Service in the Caucasus. They couldn't let a highly skilled officer like me simply retreat into civilian life."

"Why change names?"

"Russia does not admit to torturing the *wrong* man for five years," he laughs. Then abruptly, he stops. "I died when they said I died."

Bekami continues circling the perimeter of the room,

pretending to admire the Ottoman art, the brocade draperies, the ornate eighteenth-century molding. But holding a hand to his bleeding nose, watching me, like a viper ready to strike.

Assessing Abramovich as the more powerful of the two, I focus on him. "What do you want from me?"

"From you?" Abramovich drains the last of his vodka. "Everything."

He puts down his tumbler and walks toward me, taking off his immaculately tailored suit jacket. Though older, he is a strong and fit man. He lifts his hand. It hovers on my cheek. I refuse to flinch, to give him the satisfaction of terrifying me.

"You've become a pretty girl," he says. "Strong, slender, like Katarina."

Katarina—*I look like my mother?* For one moment, I want time to stand still. I want Abramovich to tell me everything he knew about Katarina.

With his thumb, he tilts my chin back. When he touches my scar, he makes a *tsk tsk* sound in his throat. "I told him not to damage you," he says, indicating Bekami. To my surprise, Abramovich sounds almost upset.

"Well?" Bekami lets go of the brocade drapery. He shoves the cloth he's been holding up to his swollen nose into his pocket. "Are you satisfied it's her?"

Abramovich's eyes linger on mine, the way my father's do when he is waiting for me to understand, the way he tells me everything, without telling me anything.

"Most certainly," says Abramovich. "It is her. You did well. Finally."

"Then our deal is done," Bekami says.

Abramovich walks behind his desk. In the center of the wall is a gilded ornate frame encasing a painting of a ship. Abramovich opens the frame, reaches his hand into a concealed, hollow spot in the wall behind it, and removes a dusty, aluminum case.

He pauses, holding the case above the desk, and stares at me. "I've always appreciated irony."

I purse my lips, frustrated I don't understand what he means.

"After my life was destroyed, and the program I'd spent a decade developing was dismantled, I searched for you. Sixteen years I searched for you."

Abramovich grins with his cosmetically restructured mouth. "It was Mr. Bekami who found you the first time. My offer was simple. I would give him what *he* wanted most, if he brought me what *I* wanted most." Abramovich lays the aluminum case flat on the desk.

"You see, before I was imprisoned, my enemies did not entirely dismantle my program. A few Kosheleks remained. So, it's ironic, isn't it? The weapons that once destroyed me . . ." He bends forward and takes an antique key from his breast pocket.

Click.

The case unlocks; the lid opens.

"Those weapons now save me"—he pauses—"because I get you back."

Bile rises in my throat. Bekami never wanted my father. Never cared about revenge. Never intended to use me to "get to him." From the time he kidnapped me in Istanbul, he has only wanted me.

Me. To trade me.

Bekami leans forward over the case, scanning the contents. Then he opens a Louis Vuitton briefcase, sets it on the desk, and cautiously reaches both hands inside.

He lifts out a simple metal canister thirty centimeters tall by eight centimeters wide, surrounded by an interlocking cage—a Koshelek—and places it into the briefcase.

Gloating, he snaps the gold buckles closed and then buttons his coat.

Bekami glides back over to me. He bends forward to stare me in the eye. He traces my collarbone with his fingernail. His nose has blood crusted in the nostrils. "Girls like you need to learn their place," he says in a chilling voice.

"Because boys like you can't keep up?" I smile.

With the back of his hand, he swings the weight of his forearm across my jaw.

Blinking lights go off in my head. All the pain, all the bruises, all those nights on a cold tile floor come flooding back.

"You *dare* insult me?" he fumes.

Except those memories that once haunted me now fuel me. I lift my chin. "Whatever it is you're planning?" I glare at Bekami. "I will stop you. Again. And again—"

He grips my neck, pinching my esophagus, strangling me.

"*Never*!" he declares, dousing my face in a barrage of spit.

"You have what you want." Abramovich steps between us and places his hand on Bekami's chest. "It's time for you to leave, Izam."

With a final squeeze, Bekami lets go of my neck.

I slump forward in my seat, coughing blood onto the marble floor. I listen to Bekami's footsteps fade.

Abramovich takes a silk handkerchief from his breast pocket and shakes it loose.

"Why are you helping him?" I ask. "He'll kill innocent people—"

"Many, possibly." Abramovich presses the embroidered edge to my cheek, wiping away Bekami's spit, my blood, my sweat. "A small price for you."

Refolding the silk handkerchief, Abramovich places it back into his pocket. Blood stains the wool of his jacket. "None of this would have happened if your American parents had surrendered you from the start."

"You mean if your men had found me in Kotka and killed me too?" I retort.

Squirming in my seat, I try to loosen the knot, but it is so tight that my hands become covered in sweat and blood.

"I wasn't entirely truthful earlier," Abramovich says abruptly. He folds his fingers together, then unfolds them, and tucks his hands into his pockets. "The truth is, I died long before they signed my death certificate in Lefortovo."

His eyes gleam as he watches me, captive, immobile, unable to do anything except twist my hands and listen to him.

"Shortly after your father, Anton . . ." He pauses. "You know about him, the traitor?"

I grimace. "Hero. Yes, I know."

He scoffs. "After Anton escaped with your American parents, SVR came for me. We were staying at our dacha when Spetsnaz arrived in the middle of the night. My wife, Elizaveta, ran outside. 'My father is wealthy,' she pleaded with the commander, 'He will pay you to go away, to leave us alone.' "

Abramovich removes a tusk-handled knife from his breast pocket and twists the handle between his thumb and forefinger. "It is Anton's fault she was killed." His voice becomes almost a whisper. "It is Anton's fault they both died."

"Both?" I ask with trepidation. I watch his fingers curl and uncurl around the handle. I can't be sure if he is telling the truth. Is this some elaborate tale to gain my sympathy? My trust? I continue working on the knot.

"Elizaveta wasn't alone." Abramovich goes still. "He followed her outside. He never let her out of his sight . . . Spetsnaz gunned Elizaveta down with my little boy clinging to her chemise. So, you see, Sophia, Spetsnaz may have shot them, but it was your father, *your hero*, who killed them."

"You're lying." I force back tears. He's not going to see me cry. He's not going to make me feel sorry for him—make me feel guilt.

Abramovich puts the blade on my scar and runs the tip down my clavicle. I dare not breathe. "I was being tortured in Lefortovo when she told me you had survived. I can't express to you what I felt. You gave me a reason to *live* again."

Exhaling, Abramovich steps away from me, and returns the knife to his pocket.

I rub the rope up and down the back of the chair, hoping for a nail or a splinter in the wood to catch it. But the back is smooth, varnished mahogany, and the blood-soaked rope slides along it seamlessly.

"Do you know what is harder than seeing your family murdered?" He begins pacing, his head snapping in my direction every other syllable, as if he's rehearsed his words a thousand times and now he has stage fright and can remember none of them. "What is more tormenting than years of torture and starvation?" He steps behind his desk. He puts both his fists on it, straightens his elbows, and angles his body forward. "It was the moment I learned my own brother . . . my own brother . . . did this to me."

I stop wrestling with the knot and blink up at him, unable to grasp the irrationality of this statement. *His brother*?

"You look like Katarina," he says softly, "but you have our mother's eyes. They are neither gray nor green nor blue. Baltic eyes, our mother called them." Abramovich is staring not at my eyes, but through them.

He opens a desk drawer and lifts out a Tokarev pistol. He loops his forefinger into the trigger, dangles it from his hand, and walks back around the front of the desk.

A choking sob rises from the back of my throat. I don't want to believe him, but his words pierce my veins like a syringe of venom, infecting me.

"You're wrong," I say. "Anton died protecting his family! He would have never hurt his brother—"

"You didn't know your father!" Abramovich roars. He pushes the barrel hard into my temple. His eyes are alight, little flames burning in the irises. "He was a traitor to his country, to his family."

He's going to kill me.

"This is all I want," he says. "To see you this once, my only family." He looks exhilarated. "I made myself live to see this moment. To see you. To finally achieve вендетта."

Vendetta.

He thumbs off the safety.

At least he has the courage to look me in the eye.

A gunshot sounds. Followed by another. *Pop! Pop!*

Neither bullet strikes me.

Abramovich crumples back against the mahogany desk, blood pouring from the silk handkerchief in his pocket.

CHAPTER 60

Craning my neck, I stare, shocked.

Standing in the hall, backlit into a silhouette, his towering physique fills the doorframe.

There is a moment of complete silence—then everything goes into overdrive.

Tucking his SIG into a left hip holster, Aksel rushes toward me. With a knife, he saws at the ropes on my hands first. Dropping to his knees, he cuts the rope binding my ankles. He loosens it around my feet before wiping the blood off my cheek.

He scans my features, the green of his eyes growing fierce and bright; his face betrays how bloodied and bruised I must look.

His fingertips skim my jaw, tracing toward the nape of my neck. With my face braced between his hands, he leans forward and kisses me.

I clasp my hands around the back of his head, tangling my fingers into his hair. We kiss again, more desperately this time, and his hands tighten against my back, drawing me into him.

He kisses me hard. Our lips cling; my body trembles in shock. *Aksel is here?*

I'm breathless; our foreheads touch.

"Looks like you've got your aim down," I murmur, nodding at the SIG.

Aksel pulls away from me, smiles, brushes his lips against mine once more, and lifts me from the chair. "Actually, I meant to hit him in the head," he utters under his breath.

The rope had cut off the circulation to my feet, so I stomp, flinching in pain, to get the blood flowing.

"I have to find Bekami," I say to Aksel, who is holding me tight around my waist as I stumble along with him into a cavernous hall.

"We have to get you out of here," Aksel says.

We reach a landing overlooking a courtyard. We are on the third floor of what must be Abramovich's estate—an old Ottoman palace with wood-paneled walls, intricate tile work, and arched moldings.

It is eerily quiet. Men like Abramovich don't live without security—where is his guard?

"How did you even get in here?" I ask Aksel as we descend two flights of a blue-mosaic staircase.

Before Aksel can answer, a *pop-pop-pop* of automatic fire interrupts us. We have found Abramovich's security, or they have found us.

At the bottom of the staircase, we turn into a glass-roofed atrium with a black-and-white parquet floor and lush ferns sitting atop marble pillars.

Aksel pulls me behind a pillar. "I've got her," he shouts to the figure letting off the thick *pop-pop* rhythm.

Todd backs over to us, firing an HK on semiautomatic.

He glances in our direction. "Then it's time to roll."

Through the atrium windows, I count nine guards scattered among the ring of cypress trees outside the palace entrance. All are shooting in the same direction. Ours.

Glass shatters behind us. We cover our heads and dart for the atrium's back door. Aksel moves first, sweeping me aside as a bullet hits the wall beside my head. Todd covers us from the north, backing toward us, firing off rounds.

Two guards attack from the far side of the atrium while four others position around back, attempting to flank us.

Outside, we take cover behind a low garden wall adjacent to the estate. The guards motion to one another, maneuvering around us.

Todd makes eye contact with me and lifts his Smith & Wesson revolver from a hip holster. I nod. He passes it to me.

Although now, I'm not sure how my hand, slippery from my own blood, can hold it. I look out—the guards are ten seconds from outflanking us.

"We have to find Bekami," I say to Todd.

"We have to leave Istanbul," he answers, watching the guards.

"Listen!" I persist. Beneath a sporadic assault of gunfire, the words tumble out of me. "Bekami left with one of Katranov's weapons—a micro-nuke. Bekami was working with Abramovich this whole time, and he—"

"Abramovich?" Todd interrupts.

"Yes, Sergei Abramovich didn't die in Lefortovo, and Bekami traded *me* to him for one of Katranov's weapons, the Kosheleks he defected with—"

"Those weapons were . . . destroyed," Todd says haltingly.

"Not all of them." I wipe my bleeding hands on my pants. "I just saw one."

Shots whiz above us, and the three of us burrow into the earth.

Aksel chambers a bullet, rolls onto his stomach, and fires back.

"My father died because of me!" I shout at Todd beneath the staccato of gunfire. "All those years they were after *me*! Now Bekami has one of those weapons, so we go after *him*!"

Todd stares back at me. He is young, midtwenties, maybe, but his eyes have a familiar, hollow, calculated look—how long has he been living this life too?

I implore Aksel, "Bekami hunted me for almost two years so he could exchange me for one of those weapons. He *will* use it—"

"This is not your job, Sophia!" he responds furiously.

Thick vibrations of gunfire pound in my skull. Todd crouches beside us, reloading.

"But this is my fault!" I put the back of my hand over my mouth, fighting emotion.

"Why?" Aksel stares at me, incredulous.

"Because I survived!" I choke back tears. "If Katranov hadn't betrayed Abramovich he'd still be alive! And . . . Katarina . . . and my brothers . . ."

Aksel's bewildered expression reminds me he has no idea who I'm talking about.

He stares at me resolutely. "Sophia, we're not equipped to go after Bekami!"

"I don't care!" I shout. Shots sink into the garden wall with piercing thumps. The guards are so confident they have adequately outmaneuvered us that they are now stepping out from the cover of cypress trees, advancing. "I'm going to find Bekami, and when I do, I'm going to kill him."

A torrent of gunfire explodes from the bushes to our right. Todd fires back methodically, dropping a guard with a single bullet. "My orders are to retrieve and return you." He fires two more shots. "Safely."

"You killed Abramovich, Aksel. His men will track you down, torture you, kill you—"

Aksel leans forward and kisses me. When he looks at me, his familiar vibrant eyes penetrate my very core. He speaks with a defiant confidence. "So they'll try." He tightens his grip on my hand, intertwining his fingers into mine. "And they'll fail."

Aksel glances left, aims his rifle toward the atrium, and fires off four consecutive rounds—the roof shatters; sheets of glass rain down on the two guards.

Another has come up on our left. Todd swings his rifle fast around, whipping the barrel across the attacking guard's neck. The man collapses to his knees, unconscious. Todd shoots a second approaching guard.

A third leaps over the wall and wraps his arms tight around Aksel's neck. Aksel lurches forward and hurls the man's body over his own. With a *thud*, the man lands on his back. His eyes roll into his head.

Aksel picks up the man's rifle, unclips the magazine, and throws it like a javelin into the cypress trees.

We are no longer being fired at.

"I am doing this," I say, standing.

Aksel wipes his bloody mouth with the back of his hand. "Then I'm coming with you."

Todd watches me with the same impossible-to-read expression as my father. He disassembles his rifle into three parts and slides them into a chest holster under his shirt. He looks at his watch and back to me. "We have fourteen minutes."

CHAPTER 61

In a wooded grove at the edge of the estate, we reach two motorcycles. Aksel and I climb aboard one, and Todd takes the other.

"He was driving a silver Maybach. New. Four-door," I recall, hoping I'm right.

"It left as we were coming in," Aksel says, confirming it.

Todd switches on an earpiece. "We'll see if we can get an eye on him."

Aksel places his hand on mine, squeezes, and revs the engine. Moments later, we are careening down steep, tree-lined streets toward the sea. I tighten my arms around Aksel's stomach and burrow into his back. There remains a dull pain thudding in my forehead and a throbbing in my neck, but Aksel is somehow . . . *here*.

We are in the hills of Üsküdar, rising above the water. Ruthless oligarchs control this south side of the Bosphorus in a violent state of corrupt stability, a facade of prosperity, my father called it. Now I know why Todd and Aksel are eager to get out.

In minutes, we reach the terraced hills leading down to the water and soon skid onto a crowded street, deftly merging into the late-afternoon traffic.

Below us, the Bosphorus laps serenely at a gravel-sand beach. Northwest, four kilometers away, against a backdrop of a sapphire sky pierced by beams of rose light, gleam the minarets of Hagia Sophia.

Aksel levers up and down, switching gears, swerving between cars, staying close behind Todd.

In the middle of a crowded intersection at the entrance to a souk, Todd turns his motorcycle so swiftly he appears to skim the pavement. Without braking, Aksel downshifts and follows Todd's hairpin turn like there is water beneath us, not concrete.

Todd waves us forward. "There is a silver Maybach at Çengelköy Pier."

I point in the direction of the fishing docks.

Todd motions to us. "You stay north, and I'll hit from the east. Do not engage. Understood?"

Aksel nods. Todd looks at me, revving his engine; he doesn't accelerate until I have nodded too.

At the Kuludar roundabout, Todd exits first and we stay on Yalibou Road. Colorful Turkish rugs flash by as vendors close their market stalls. Salty wind from the sea whips my hair, and I push my cheek against Aksel's back.

Minutes later, we reach Çengelköy Pier. Traffic funnels into two lanes. Aksel snakes between cars and parks beside an old Renault.

Five years ago, Çengelköy was a small fishing pier—now, it's one of the busiest ferry terminals in Istanbul.

Engage? We'll be lucky to find him.

I count quickly. Nearly five hundred people are converging in a twenty-meter radius.

Swinging my legs off the bike, I survey our surroundings. Hundreds of cars are packed in line like tinned herring, waiting to drive onto the ferry.

We move discreetly, searching the area for Bekami.

Overhead, an intercom blares in Turkish. Aksel looks at me quizzically.

"Boarding," I translate.

Commuters, scattered around the terminal, begin to congregate at the entrance to the pedestrian ramp. Others step back into their cars to drive onto the ferry.

I spot the Maybach first—a radiant diamond among all the older Turkish cars. I grab Aksel's shirt, pull him behind a Renault van, and point in the direction of the Maybach.

For a moment, nothing happens, then the driver's door opens, and Bekami steps out.

"That's him?" Aksel glowers at Bekami with unreserved rage.

"*Kranker Typ*," I say under my breath. Which causes the corner of Aksel's lip to curve upward, ever so slightly.

Shielded by the Renault, we watch Bekami, Louis Vuitton briefcase in hand, stroll casually to the passenger line, demarcated by swags of rope.

Like a film reel, I see it unfold: Bekami will return to CNF headquarters victorious, having secured a nuclear weapon while thwarting American intelligence operators. In a few months, he'll detonate the Koshelek . . .

The automobile ramp lowers. The pedestrians clump together, waiting for the ferry master to unhook the rope and usher them onto the deck.

But why did Bekami come here? Çengelköy Ferry only shuttles north, to European Istanbul. CNF headquarters are—or were—set up here, in isolated pockets along the south shores of the Black Sea.

Bekami's eyes sweep over the cars. His silver Maybach gleams lonely amid all the rusty Renaults, Fiats, and Peugeots. Why isn't he in it, like the other drivers, waiting to drive up the automobile ramp onto the ferry? And where is Todd?

Bekami steps onto the pedestrian ramp. People follow, obstructing my view.

I have three options: I can board the ferry and follow him, I can wait for Todd, or I can end this now.

I ease my hand into the small of my back. My fingers touch the outline of Todd's Smith & Wesson 686.

I've held this gun before. It's the same make as my father's—*accuracy and power.*

Discreetly, I raise the revolver to the open van window.

Although my whole body trembles, I keep my hands steady. I slide my left hand beneath my right. Cradling the grip of the pistol in my palm, I absorb the cool metal into my skin.

The blood on my wrists and hands has dried into cracked rows along the creases of my skin. My palms flake crimson.

Aksel's voice is concerned. "Sophia, you don't have to do this." His large hand wraps over the top of mine. I know what he isn't saying: *Do not engage.*

"I'll do it," he says.

But he is wrong. I have to engage—*I* have to end this. Here. Now. No one is going to do it for me. Bekami forfeited his life when he took mine, three kilometers from this pier. And again, when he killed my father.

Vendetta.

Bekami is not going to hurt anyone else. Not now. Not ever.

I hold Todd's pistol in my hand—taut but loose.

I force my breathing into a steady rhythm: *inhale . . . hold . . . exhale . . .*

I no longer feel pain. Or anger. Only a heightened alertness. If I want to hit him accurately, I have to control my heartbeat, like my father has been teaching me for years.

With my finger on the trigger, I stare at Bekami. I recall his features: coal-black eyes, manicured hands, the smell of sweat and Yves Saint Laurent cologne. I feel his slithery hands on my neck. I feel the burning of the rope tying me to the copper pipe. His crass voice. His oily lips against my skin . . .

My father is right. He won't haunt me any longer. I am stronger than him, stronger than any of them.

I close my eyes. Open them.

Bekami pulls something small and metal from his pocket. He is holding the briefcase in one hand. Though I've been watching him for ninety seconds, I've been so concentrated on the Louis Vuitton in his right hand, I hadn't noticed the second, smaller briefcase he's been carrying in his left.

A tattered leather briefcase, the same color as his pants.

"No . . . ," I gasp.

Rapidly, I calculate the terminal occupancy: three hundred people now loiter within a hundred-meter radius, some buying last-minute tickets at the kiosk, others jogging toward their cars. Some have begun driving up the ramp. The rope is lowered; the deck is filling with people; the ferry is filling with cars.

. . . A diversion . . .

Of course.

Bekami casually steps out of line. He isn't going to the other side of Istanbul. He isn't going to Europe. And he has no intention of staying on the ferry.

A glance at the sea confirms this. A dark blue cigarette boat circles in the water, halfway between the ferry and an idling, glimmering yacht.

To escape, Bekami only needs a way to occupy the Turkish Coast Guard, who monitor water traffic out of the Bosphorus Strait to the Black Sea. If Bekami can reach the open waters of the Black Sea, he can travel anywhere undetected . . . Bulgaria, Ukraine, Russia, Georgia . . . We'll never find him.

Bekami sets the tattered leather briefcase down, so discreetly he barely bends his knees. He steps in front of it, wedging himself in between a group of chatting Turkish men, and proceeds back down the ramp.

"Todd's here," Aksel breathes.

At the far end of the pier, Todd speeds toward the ferry on his motorbike, weaving between the rows of cars filing up the ramp.

My eyes flash from the tattered leather briefcase to the Maybach to Todd.

"Todd, NO!" I sprint for him. "Todd!" I scream.

"Sophia!" Aksel grips my forearm, yanking me back. But I pull loose and run.

"We have to stop him!" I shout to Aksel.

Bekami must hear my screams. He looks over, expectant almost.

Todd reaches the swags of rope partitioning the line to board the ferry.

Bekami steps off the ramp and down the platform onto the dock. He carries the Louis Vuitton briefcase securely in his left hand; a silver detonator is snug inside his right.

Aksel mutters into a mouthpiece.

The cigarette boat speeds toward the pier.

Todd drops his bike at the edge of the pedestrian ramp and runs onto the ferry.

I look between the Maybach and Bekami, knowing what's coming. Bekami planned this expertly. Timed his diversion perfectly.

Aksel leaps over the metal barrier and races for Bekami. A man inside the cigarette boat raises a submachine gun and aims it at Aksel.

Bekami steps carefully off the pier and onto the boat. Teetering briefly, he sets the fragile briefcase down and turns.

He looks straight at me with a proud, silky smile on his face—a look that says *I won.*

Triumphantly, he thumbs off the cap on the silver detonator.

Without remorse, I raise the Smith & Wesson, take aim at the center of Bekami's forehead, and I pull the trigger.

Twice.

CHAPTER 62

Then everything explodes.

The blast crushes my eardrums.

In an enormous plume of smoke and heat, I am launched through the air.

When I come to, my skin is on fire. Hot pieces of metal gash my forearms like fiery embers; they singe my shirt, engulfing the pavement and every nearby surface.

Choking on the smoke, I roll onto my stomach. The air is so dense I can't see.

I push my palms against the ground. It is hot and littered with shattered glass and debris. "Aksel?" I cough out, stumbling upright. A woman is screaming beside me, clutching her daughter. I reach for them as they disappear through the smoke.

I put my hand on a car to steady myself, but the metal's heat scorches me. Stepping over cinders and shoving aside burnt wreckage, I make my way over to the dock where I last saw Aksel, where I last saw Bekami.

Suddenly, an arm coils around my waist. "We need to get out of here," Aksel warns in my ear.

"I want to see him," I say desperately, turning to look over my shoulder. "I have to see Beka—"

"He's dead, Sophia. You killed him."

A coolness has hit me with Aksel's embrace. I realize Aksel is soaked. His wet, burned clothes, blackened with oil and soot, cling to his body. But my attention immediately diverts to Aksel's left, where he is holding an equally wet, battered figure.

Todd's head rolls forward, limp, onto his chest. I gasp, reaching forward to help hold his weight.

"This way." Aksel nods.

As the smoke thins, the sensations hit at once: sunlight, voices, sirens.

People run in every direction. Already, bodies are being pulled from charred vehicles. By the time we clear the wreckage, several bystanders are pointing at us emerging from the rubble.

Somehow, Aksel manages to carry Todd while running alongside me; he has an arm solidly locked around Todd's knees, with Todd's body draped over his shoulder.

"We need a car, Sophia!" Aksel shouts.

Our motorcycles are somewhere in the rubble, but with Todd's condition, they are useless. We move out, searching for a car not blocked in.

Near the ticket kiosk, I find an old Fiat. I take off my tattered sweater, wrap it around my fist, and punch through the glass. Reaching through the shattered window, I unlock the door and drop into the seat.

I reach under the steering column. "Hand me your knife."

Aksel props Todd against the car and reaches into his boot, handing me his Ontario knife.

I pop open the panel under the steering column and fumble around for the wires. I clamp the green ignition wire between my teeth, peeling off several centimeters of insulation.

A policeman runs toward us. Lifting a baton from his holster, he waves it wildly.

I strip the red battery wire and the brown starter wire and twist the two together. The lights on the dashboard switch on.

I pull out the choke once to give it some gas. I take the brown starter wire in my left hand and the red and green wires in my right. With my left foot, I engage the clutch, hold only the insulation, and then push both wires together.

In my side mirror, I see Aksel bodycheck the approaching policeman, launching him backward into a row of scooters.

The ignition growls. The engine rumbles. I press on the gas, revving to keep it alive.

Aksel shoves Todd into the back seat and clambers in after him, their two muscular bodies propped up by the narrow confines of the back row.

Another policeman draws closer. A third is behind him. "*Durmak!*" he yells. *Halt!*

I shift the car into first gear and whirl the steering wheel hard to the left. I accelerate but the car whines and doesn't move.

"What's wrong?" Aksel asks.

"No steering." I grab Aksel's Ontario off the front seat, jam it into the column's metal keyhole, and twist hard. There is a loud crack as the spring unloads and the wheel breaks free. The policeman is two meters away. I palm the wheel hard to the left and accelerate.

From the rearview mirror, I watch the policeman shout into a radio.

Swerving onto Yalibou Road, I grab a half-empty liter of seltzer water from the floor and toss it to Aksel. My head is unsteady from the explosion. My ears ring. A thin film of ash and soot covers my shredded clothes.

I failed. After everything . . . I failed.

"You couldn't have prevented that explosion, Sophia," Aksel says, as if I had said the words aloud. He grimaces. "Nobody could have."

"You saw?" I ask.

"Todd did. He must have realized it the same time as you; he looked between you and Bekami, grabbed the three women standing nearest to him, and dove off the deck into the water right as the blast hit."

"And the women?" Tears flood my vision, and I wipe my eyes with my sleeve, but then soot gets in my eyes and I have to blink rapidly to flush it out. Blocking the images I just witnessed, I force my breathing to steady, my tears to stop.

Aksel wriggles out of his shirt and tosses it in a heap on the seat. It's a shredded, ashy mess. He shakes his head. "I don't know. I pulled them out of the water first, but went back in for Todd. He was barely conscious when I reached him."

"So, the Koshelek," I finally say. "What do we do about that?"

"*You* do nothing," a gravelly voice mutters from behind me.

"Hey." Aksel turns his attention to Todd. He has his arm around the back of Todd's neck, holding him steady as I careen through the streets.

I glance at Todd. "What will you do?" I turn the car hard right. "Bekami dropped that weapon in the cigarette boat before the blast hit. Whoever was in that boat has it now."

Shivers spread down my limbs. I know I need medical care. Aksel too. Our skin is rosy pink, marked with streaks of black, but our injuries are minor compared to Todd's.

I downshift and exit west on the Kuludar roundabout. "So, what will *you* do?" I ask Todd again.

"We find it." Todd's words are labored. I push down harder on the accelerator. *How?* I want to ask. Because I killed Bekami. And what if that was a major mistake? With Bekami gone, how *is* Todd going to find it?

Aksel's forehead is tight, watching Todd. He's ripped his shirt in sections, poured the seltzer water onto each section, and is using the strips to wrap Todd's temple.

"And if you don't?" I prompt.

Todd's eyes close. He is done answering my questions.

A crackling sound emanates from Todd's ear. Aksel unclips the earpiece and shoves it into his own ear.

"Exfil Danube-Green," he relays to me, confusion etched across his brow. "St. Regis. You know what that means?"

"No," I respond, "but I know the hotel."

Sirens pulse the humid air. Shifting down into second gear, I turn toward Bosphorus Bridge. Ahead of us, cars drive in a steady line across the sparkling cerulean water. Sailboats skim in the distance. As we near the bridge, the sirens increase.

The gates at the head of the bridge roll together. The congested road forces me to slow down. Both gates are closing inward, blocking our access. A policeman stands in front of the gates, stopping traffic—a checkpoint for every vehicle.

I turn the car onto the single pedestrian lane, bypass the stopped cars, veer sharply left, and swerve within centimeters of the policeman's back. I take a hard right and enter the bridge via the two-meter gap between the closing gates, clipping the Fiat's side mirrors. I blare the horn, and people jump out of the way.

Fifteen hundred meters ahead on the north side of the bridge, policemen are constructing a barricade—strips of plywood clumsily nailed together.

I crash through it.

Forty seconds is all it takes to reach Europe. In my rearview mirror, I see two police cars turning around to chase us.

"Slow down, Sophia," Aksel mutters under his breath. He is trying to tourniquet Todd's arm with the other half of his shirt.

Speeding up, I head south onto Çırağan Road, then right onto Kadirgalar. Ahead is a wooded hill with landscaped terraces and iron fences; I steer north onto the private lane, leading into the gardens of the St. Regis Hotel. Above us, the pitched hotel roof looms. The tires trample over the manicured flowers as we barrel toward the service entrance, bashing through the striped guard gate.

We cross over the clay tennis courts and onto a grassy meadow beside the clubhouse. Two opulent hotel guests are retrieving their clubs from a golf cart when we drive up. They dive for cover behind a lemon tree topiary.

I slam on the brakes and shut off the engine. Aksel and I gurney Todd out of the car and onto the soft grass.

From this height, I can see the red tile roofs of the city, the spires of the Blue Mosque, the Byzantine spikes of Hagia Sophia jutting into the cobalt sky.

We are only kilometers from the Slovak Consulate. Our position is too exposed; we are too close to the city center—

From the west, a *woosh-woosh-woosh* of chopper blades torpedoes the air; a rush of wind swirls above us, and our burned clothes flap around our bodies.

A Black Hawk descends.

Behind us, breaking through the gates of the St. Regis, are three armored vans—either Abramovich's men, every policeman in Istanbul, or both. They start shooting aggressively before they are even within range.

A soldier inside the helicopter covers us, firing stun grenades from a shoulder-mounted mortar. The grenades land in bright violet blasts.

A second airman hops out of the chopper and runs toward us. Strafing fire whistles above us, trying to hit the chopper. The airman reaches us, throws two smoke grenades over his shoulder, and yells, "Now!"

Under cover of the smoke grenade, he leads us to the chopper.

Aksel heaves Todd into the helicopter, and two soldiers pull him up onto a stretcher.

When a medic reaches his hand down to pull me inside, I take it. Aksel leaps in behind me. In less than six seconds, we are in the air, above the smoke.

Once we have cleared the airspace over Istanbul, a squadron of fighter jets appear on all four sides of the helicopter—an F-18 escort.

An hour later, we land at a NATO base in Kosovo. We climb down from the helicopter. We don't stop. Don't talk to anyone. We follow our escort to an MN-2 transport.

As we ascend the ramp into the plane, someone rushes up behind me and clutches my shoulders; I whirl around, collapsing against her.

"Mom," I cry.

CHAPTER 63

During takeoff, we sit quietly in a row on the bench seat. I hold my stomach, bracing myself against the queasy feeling that accompanies a rapid ascent. As we reach fifteen thousand feet, the pilot eases the MN-2 straight, tapering off the climb.

Aksel drapes his arm over my shoulder, pulling me into him.

I've forgotten how perfectly his jaw meets the bottom of his cheek, the smooth, light bronze color of his skin, his translucent green eyes, but most importantly, how, tucked into the crook of his shoulder, I feel safe. For the first time since I left Waterford.

Aksel brushes my hair back from my cheek and stares at me. I must look ragged. My bandages need to be redressed; the lidocaine jelly applied to our burns will wear off soon. Aksel has a thick bandage on the side of his neck, and like mine, the tops of his hands and forearms are covered in gauze.

"You okay?" His deep, quiet voice is so full of concern that I stop fighting it. As I curl into Aksel's chest, tears pour out of me in a wave of visceral pain.

When I wake hours later, the sky is a black vault of glittering stars. The airmen onboard are asleep. The MN-2 is a reconfigured Soviet cargo plane used by NATO to transport medical supplies. There is a bank of seats on either side and a running platform down the center.

Aksel's arm is taut around my lower back. My head is on his shoulder. He hands me a box of cranberry juice. "You need to drink," he says kindly. "It's all that's on board."

I drink all the juice, so he hands me another box and I drink that too. Finished, he wraps a wool NATO blanket across my body, and I lay my head back onto his shoulder.

The events of the last forty-eight hours whirl inside me; memories both vivid and blurry, both happening at a distance and convulsing inside my chest.

Trying to concentrate on anything other than the overwhelming abyss of emptiness my father's absence has created—I look at Aksel, biting my bottom lip. "Aksel, how are you here?"

Aksel stares darkly down the interior of the plane before looking back at me. "After you left Waterford, I was so angry. I flew out to see my grandfather, to see if he knew anything. But, as I was leaving Dulles, walking through the terminal in a big crowd of people, someone pushed an earbud into my hand. I didn't see who it was, but I clipped it in anyway and listened to the instructions. Fifteen minutes later, I was boarding a flight to Amsterdam."

I stare at him inquiringly.

"I was sitting down in my seat, and a low voice in my ear grunted, 'You can take that out now.' I turned and"—Aksel smirks—"it was Todd."

Todd. Had my father ordered him? My mother?

"How did *he* find me?"

My mother approaches us. I must appear perplexed because she smiles—a soft smile I haven't seen her wear since I played the Chopin. Close now, my mother says, "For eighteen months, it was feasible, unlikely but feasible, for Bekami and CNF to track us abroad, but Bekami's awareness of our move to Waterford could only be a result of either a very sophisticated intelligence network, or an infiltrator."

"An informant," I say, remembering the questions inside the Bubble.

"Yes. Someone on the inside. David tracked us after we left the embassy, hoping to get his own lead on Bekami, but he lost us between Turkmenistan and Egypt. However, a few days afterward, something unexpected happened." She pauses. "David got your signal."

My signal. By using his SOS protocol, my father managed to save my life even after he was gone. I bite down hard on my lip, but that doesn't stop the tears from swelling.

"As a backup measure"—my mother swallows, maintaining her composure—"your father routed your satellite transmitter to David in Berlin."

"David?" I ask, confused. "Why him?"

"He was close to your father for a very long time."

"He interrogated me!"

"He protected you. David was trying to clear your name, Sophia, not incriminate you. He was our fail-safe should something ever happen to either of us." She looks down, because something *had* happened.

After a pause, Aksel nods at my mother. "We had just landed in Amsterdam when Todd got a message. We walked right back inside and boarded a flight to Istanbul."

Istanbul. I can pick up the pieces after that. My restless mother stands and resumes pacing the center aisle out of earshot.

"It was my mother," I say quietly to Aksel, watching her. "The woman you met in Berlin who told you about your parents, wasn't it?"

"It wasn't your mother, Sophia."

"It had to be," I persist.

"It wasn't," he says firmly, looking down at me. "I told you it was a woman who didn't tell me her name."

The jet rumbles side to side as we pass through turbulence. A few airmen wake and glance around the cabin, but seconds later the cabin settles and they reclose their eyes.

My pulse drums beneath my burned skin. "Aksel, I wasn't sure you'd ever want to see me again . . ." I keep my voice steady. I have to ask; I have to hear his answer even if it tears me open. "Your grandfather told you my parents shot down their plane, didn't he?"

With my fingers wound loosely through his, the side of my body tucked against his chest, and his arm draped across my back, I can feel every muscle in his body go tense.

I have never wanted to be more wrong in my life.

"Yes," he answers quietly.

"And do you believe him?"

"No, Sophia," he says.

Hot tears form in the rims of my eyes. "But it could have been. I know what they've done." I gesture around the old jet. "What *this* is, what happens to people."

"Sophia, stop." He clasps my fingers securely between his. "Your parents didn't *kill* my parents. Whoever did—"

"But my mother convinced your dad to be her agent and so because of her—"

"My dad knew the risk. If he agreed to give information, he did it because he believed in it. He wasn't coerced."

I shake my head. "How can you be certain?"

A faint smile appears on his lips. "I can't be, I guess. But I have to believe that there are good people out there, like my parents, who try to do the right thing."

The plane jerks through a cloud, and I wait for the cabin to stop rocking before I make eye contact with Aksel.

"Aksel, I swear I didn't know you were being recruited or—" I start, but he cuts me off.

"I didn't either." He shrugs. "Not really. I only knew I was asked to attend a secret pre–basic training camp by some Navy guy. While I was there, I was approached about entering a special, clandestine track at the Academy. I didn't know it was . . ." Aksel motions around the plane. "*This* . . ."

For a moment, our eyes linger. He lowers his voice, shrugging reticently. "But maybe that's the point? If candidates like me knew before we agreed, would anyone ever join?"

"So, you couldn't tell me about the training camp?"

"Simple rules. If you tell anyone, you're out."

"How many of you are there?" I ask hesitantly.

"A few dozen, I suppose. They don't tell us."

My mother comes over and sits down again. She has obviously been listening, trying to give us privacy, despite the confined space.

"It's been that way for years, Sophia. We compartmentalize. Counterterrorist teams operate on a 'need-to-know' basis. It's how you've learned much from us, but knew nothing about ON-YX, right? It's how Farhad could get no information from you during your kidnapping. It's why Aksel doesn't know about others in his training camp, why he was told so little about his parents' death, yet just enough."

Aksel shifts his body so we face each other. A streak of black soot runs along his jawline.

"So, what now?" I ask.

"I don't know," he says reluctantly. "Training? Recruitment? Joining up? It all feels too far away to think about."

He doesn't want to admit it, and neither of us wants to confront it, but the future is a thick cloud of rain, hovering.

"And what about us? Now that you know . . ." I trail off. Now that he knows my parents are spies? Killers? Traitors? Liars? That my mother sent his parents to their deaths? That terrorists know my name—chased me across the world to ransom me? That because of me, Chechen terrorists now have a nuclear weapon?

The plane rocks again, and we secure the buckles across our laps. There is so much I want to tell Aksel, so much I need to tell him, but none of it seems important. Not right now.

Words can't heal us. Only time. One breath at a time.

Aksel stares down at me. "I realized something the night I first asked you out. None of this stuff matters. It didn't then, it doesn't now, and it won't in the future. Sophia, you are the best thing that has ever happened to me, and nothing, *nothing*, can change that."

My fingers find the hem of his shirt, and I cling to it. "But I'm entangled in some very bad things."

"We both are, now," he points out.

"And you're okay with that?"

"If accepting *this* means being with you?" He touches his bandaged hand to my cheek. "Then, yeah, I'm more than okay with it."

I stare up at Aksel, half smiling, and trying not to cry, and wondering how in the world this can ever work between us. "You've saved my life, like"—I tick off my fingers—"three times?"

Aksel pushes aside a stray lock of my hair sticking to the gauze on the side of my neck. "Nah." He grins. "You could have taken the grizzly. And you've saved me, so on my ledger we're more than even."

But behind his smiling expression is a somber acceptance.

I bite my lip, fighting back the emotion. I never wanted this life for myself, and I certainly don't want it for Aksel.

"I guess all I want to know right now is: What do you hope happens in your future? Beyond all this?" I wave my hand at the cargo net.

To my surprise, Aksel looks at me emphatically. "Nothing's changed." He bends over me, his lips next to my ear. His voice is a low, coarse hum. "I want to be with you, Sophia."

I stare at the bandages down the side of his neck, worry seeping into my skin. I've been naive, while Aksel has been right. He shouldn't have become involved with me. I felt it that first night in the avalanche, a gut feeling compounded by years of fear. Now, it has morphed into reality and I am as uncertain as ever. No matter what happens, our lives are irrevocably linked and we must confront this unknown territory.

Aksel notices the concern on my face. "Hey," he says soothingly. "All we have to worry about is going back to school and"—the corner of his lip tilts upward—"hanging out."

"Hanging out?" I murmur. It seems such a foreign, intangible concept from thirty thousand feet up in the cargo hold of a NATO jet.

Aksel gazes across the plane. His eyes return to mine, and he runs his thumb down the center of my hand. "I suppose I kind of like you."

I look up at him from beneath my lashes. "Still only kind of?"

Aksel's emerald eyes pierce mine. "Sophia Hepworth, I'm in love with you."

CHAPTER 64

The pilot steps out from the cockpit and walks over to us. He is tall, with high cheekbones and a square jaw. He introduced himself earlier, when we stopped at Northwood in England to refuel and take on more passengers.

A small Latvian flag patch is sewn on his right sleeve, and he is wearing a sidearm in a shoulder holster. He eyes my mother a few seats away. Then Aksel. Then me.

He is clearly unaccustomed to briefing two teenagers and an elegant woman wearing pearl earrings and a cardigan sweater.

"If you look out the window here," he says placidly, "you'll see the lights of Narsaq Kujalleq, the southernmost town in Greenland. Since we're flying at low altitude with a bright moon, you might see some of the largest icebergs in the North Atlantic. Then it's five hours of ocean until we reach base."

He pauses before continuing, "I'll remind you, this is an old Soviet MN-2. It's been retrofitted to drop food and aid, but it's not typically used for cargo like yourselves." He points to the ceiling of the jet, politely adding, "The Soviet cockpits monitored the cargo to prevent theft using visual and audio recording systems . . . and those, uh, systems remain."

He's been listening to everything we've said? I blush,

embarrassed. My mother nods a thank-you, and the pilot returns to the cockpit.

"Whoops," my mother says under her breath once he's left.

I am distracted, thinking about something she said earlier. I look at her now, trying to piece it together. "We took so many precautions, but Bekami always knew where we were. Where I was. He found me in Hütteldorf, Mom. Yet no one could have predicted I'd jump off that train. Not even me . . ."

No one knows where we are going before we take off . . . That's how we stay safe . . . We get in the air before they can track us . . . I only answer to one person . . .

"Aksel—" I start, but something has caught his attention.

"Her," he murmurs. I follow his line of vision to a petite figure moving toward us. He tightens his grip protectively around my hand.

"It was her," he repeats quietly, under his breath.

A woman sits down across from us. "You've had some rest, I hope?"

I stiffen beside Aksel. I glance between him and the woman. *Her?*

"Aksel, you performed exceptionally well—ON-YX excels because of recruits like you. It's quite the opportunity you had, demonstrating your skills under pressure like that."

"Thank you, ma'am," Aksel answers, except there is no gratitude in his voice.

"And Sophia," she says effusively, "you are a brave, resourceful young woman. I drove all the way from London and boarded at Northwood to finally meet you."

I recognize her—she was with Andrews when my father met him at the souk in Tunis; she was buying the silver ashtray.

The petite woman has short-trimmed gray hair and is wearing a Burberry scarf knotted beneath her throat. My mother doesn't seem surprised by the woman's presence. In fact, she seems deferential.

"Forgive me," says my mother, noticing my confounded expression. "Sophia, this is Bev Andrews."

I sputter, "Y-You're Andrews?"

She bows her chin. "I only wish you had introduced yourself in Tunis."

Tunis? She saw me?

Andrews reaches her hand forward, and I shake it.

I glance down at her manicured fingernails. She is refined and polished. Her jacquard suit is tailored and ironed. She is an older, grayer version of my mother.

On her wrist is a delicate silver watch. Skagen. Silver with a stream of gold circling through the links, same model as mine.

Why couldn't my parents track Bekami? How did Abramovich find out I was alive? And why is Andrews still smiling at me?

Aksel watches Andrews warily. *Her,* he said. *It was her.*

"Please allow me to offer my condolences," Andrews continues softly. Her eyes are moist. "Your father was an honorable man who served his country with the highest distinction. He saved countless lives, and we *all* lost so much yesterday."

"Thank you," I say appreciatively, but I am barely listening. Synapses fire inside my skull.

I touch my fingers to my collarbone, feeling the hollow where my necklace once lay.

"I'll need to ask you some questions, Sophia. I'm sorry to do it now, but I think we should do it while these events are fresh. A simple conversation."

"A debriefing?" I ask.

"No interrogation cube this time." Andrews smiles, standing. "Let's go to the front of the plane for some privacy."

I stay seated. "I'm fine here, Ms. Andrews."

My mother frowns at me. Apparently, I'm not supposed to disagree with Andrews. "Soph—"

"Here is fine," Andrews says sympathetically, waving off my mother's interruption. She sits back down and removes an electronic tablet from her purse. "Let's start with Abramovich. Are you sure he was dead?"

"Yes, ma'am." I look at Aksel. His brow is furrowed. His eyes darting from me to Andrews to my mother.

"What did Abramovich tell you?" asks Andrews. "Did he mention anything specific about his past?"

"Not really, ma'am."

"Did he mention any names before you killed him?"

"I didn't kill him," I say.

"You confirmed he was dead; are you suggesting—"

"Sophia didn't kill Abramovich," Aksel interrupts. "I did." He's subtly shifted forward in his seat, positioning his shoulder in front of me—an instinctive, defensive gesture.

Andrews looks him over appraisingly. "Thank you for clarifying, Aksel. And thank you for taking action."

Aksel glowers at Andrews; he didn't tell her for praise, he told her because he doesn't want me implicated.

Andrews proceeds to ask more questions—vague, unspecific, leading questions. But her inquisitive voice sounds distant, fuzzy. It is background noise compared to the orchestral presence of the imperious voice of my father.

Command always knows where we are . . . An informant on the inside . . . There is always someone willing to betray you for a price . . .

A price. Abramovich was a corrupt oligarch, worth hundreds of millions of dollars.

"What did you discuss with Abramovich?" Andrews asks. "What details can you tell me?"

. . . I only answer to one person . . .

Only one person always knew where we were. Only one person knew about the circumstances of Farhad's death in Tunisia. Only one person knew about Aksel's parents. Only one person sent us to Waterford. Only one person knew we were boarding a train in Vienna and could have tracked me when I jumped.

I look down at my own Skagen watch.

Silver, with a string of gold circling through it.

Like a rifle shot, I know *who*. The only thing I don't know is—

"Why?" I blurt out, standing. My mother coils her fingers around my wrist. I shake her off. "Why did you do it?" I nearly shout at Andrews.

"Sophia!" my mother says sharply. Her eyes flash between us.

"You betrayed my father, my mother, all of us!"

"Sophia," my mother hisses.

"You worked for the Russians—Abramovich—and you sold us out every time you had a chance. How did they pay you? Cash? Mansions? Or was power enough that—"

"Sophia, sit down," my mother orders. But Aksel stands behind me. I feel the weight of his presence like my own shield of armor.

After all these years I am no longer afraid. Not of Bekami. Not of Abramovich. And certainly not of Andrews.

"How much?" I shout. "How much am I worth? My life? What did he pay you? What did you want so badly?"

If Andrews is surprised, she masks it nicely. "You've been through a lot, Sophia. You're grieving and sleep-deprived. I'll pardon this outburst, given what you've endured."

"Endured? Yes, I've endured plenty. On account of you." Pointing at Andrews, I look at my mother. "They always knew where we were headed, right? Because she told you where to go!"

I hold up my wrist to my mother. "She told you to give me this, didn't she?" I point at the matching Skagen watch on Andrews's wrist. "She found me in Hütteldorf *after* I jumped from the train, and she told Bekami where to find me in the forest!"

Andrews glares at me. "I do not know what you are suggesting, but you are playing a dangerous game. You are delusional and in shock following your father's death—"

"He's dead because you betrayed him!" I fire back.

"You've been through a lot," she says calmly. "You're unwell. I should have brought a physician on board with me. I'm so sorry I didn't."

Steeling my resolve, I touch the clasp on my watch. "Perhaps I am unwell. But we'll see after specialists examine both our watches."

When Andrews flicks her eyes to her own watch, my instincts are confirmed. I may have, at times, been out of my parents' line of sight, but never far from Andrews's. My necklace allowed my parents to keep track of me; my watch allowed Andrews to keep track of *us*.

"Don't be foolish," Andrews says. "I've helped your parents protect you—"

"Then why didn't you tell my parents that Abramovich was

living in Istanbul? Or that Bekami had escaped prison? You knew about the NEMCOVA mission—about me—and rather than protect us, you cut a deal with Abramovich! Because of you, a Russian has been controlling an entire division of America's intelligence network."

"I have done no such thing—"

"Rather than protect people against terrorists, you found a Russian who supplies them weapons and you brokered a deal! Now Chechen separatists have a nuclear weapon—because of you."

Andrews steps toward me.

Aksel is no longer standing behind me, but beside me—his forearm lodged at my hip, ready to protect me like the safety bar on a roller coaster.

Hearing our raised voices, several Latvian soldiers have lifted their eyes to watch us. But they aren't allowed to interfere. Talk to us. Touch us. We are invisible cargo that just happens to be on the brink of imploding.

"I saved you," Andrews declares. "Repeatedly, I refused to deliver you to Bekami—"

"So you played a game, sending us around the world to see who could catch the other first?"

"I helped you! Bekami wanted to kill you."

"Instead you let him kill my father?"

It's obvious how she's gotten away with this for so long—her eyes, wide with innocent sincerity, her delicate features, her immaculately tailored appearance—it is easy to feel like *she* is innocent, like *she* is the victim. Her well-rehearsed, melancholic, manipulative voice ensures this facade.

I look at my mother. "She's the one, Mom. Don't you get it?"

My mother rises to her feet. She looks both stunned and raging mad.

"Mary, you've known me for twenty-nine years," Andrews says softly. "I would never betray my team, my country. You can't believe accusations from an addled adolescent—"

"Except I *do* believe my daughter," my mother says in cold fury. "Kent and I knew someone had leaked information, but it's worse. You're a double agent. And you have been for a decade. *You* prevented us from rescuing Sophia in Istanbul—"

"Mom, she's been a double agent longer than a decade," I breathe out, feeling dizzy. "Andrews knew about the NEMCOVA mission—she organized Katranov's exfiltration, right? She knew where you were hiding my family at the Kotka safe house . . ."

My mother sways, pale. "No," she whispers. She covers her mouth with both hands and closes her eyes.

Andrews is watching my mother. But I am watching Andrews.

"You told Abramovich where my family was hiding in Finland. And then, when my parents told you I'd been born, that I was alive, you told Abramovich that too."

Andrews turns from my mother to me. Her innocent wide eyes are now venomous.

"You think you have it all figured out, Nancy Drew?" she asks me.

"I know I do," I answer.

"Then I suppose I have no choice but to end this." Her voice is authoritative but casual, as if she's said these words many times before.

"Do it," I say.

Andrews glances around at the airmen. They aren't her people. They stare right back at her. She doesn't move.

"No one will believe you," Andrews spits out. "This is nonsense—you're a deranged, traumatized teenager trying to make sense of your father's tragic death. You need to be evaluated for injuries."

"No one has to believe me," I interrupt, looking toward the cockpit. "But they will believe you."

I point to the ceiling. "We're flying in an old MN-2; it doesn't look much like a Soviet transport anymore, but they didn't disassemble the interior, didn't remove the surveillance equipment . . ." I trail off, trusting Andrews to figure out her own mistake.

Andrews's composed defiance dissolves into disbelief. She has all but admitted being a double agent, and the captain on this old Latvian NATO jet is listening to all of it. But, more significantly, it is being recorded and transmitted to some distant, forgotten, but nonetheless reliable, server.

Andrews's gaze scans the fuselage, looking for an escape. "What now, Sophia?" she asks derisively.

"The pilot will radio ahead. When we land, you will be arrested and tried for treason, terrorism. You'll go to prison," I say softly. "Everything Abramovich gave you will be confiscated. That is if your superiors at the Department of Defense don't reach you first. ON-YX was created to operate outside the rules of engagement, correct?"

Andrews looks to my mother. "Mary, this *accusation* will destroy my family. Think of my children, my husband. They'll lose everything. They'll be humiliated." Her hands shake. "You'll destroy them, their futures, with this lie."

"You're right," says my mother. "They will lose everything because of you."

Andrews loosens the scarf at her throat.

"There's another option," I say abruptly. "If you want it."

My mother and Aksel look over at me.

I nod across the platform, my eyes settling on the jump chute. I wait for Andrews to follow my gaze, to understand.

"You can avoid a trial. Prison. Humiliation," I say softly. "You can choose to be remembered for who you were before you turned. No one has to know you are a traitor."

Fastening a tether around my wrist, I walk over to the jump chute door, pull up a red lever, twist the air lock handle, and tug. The door swings inward. A biting wind whistles into the plane. It sweeps the hair off our faces. I walk back to stand beside Aksel and my mother.

Andrews's face is tight. "How dare you—"

"It's your choice."

Her eyes flit between me, my mother, Aksel, and finally the inky black sky and glimmering stars above the Atlantic. "Mary, please. I would never hurt you or Sophia—"

"She's giving you a choice"—my mother cuts her off with a cold glare—"I'd take it."

"After all we've been through—"

"You can do it, Bev," my mother's voice rings clearly beside me, "or I can do it for you, but either way you are finished destroying my family."

Andrews stares at us, suddenly expressionless. She straightens out her jacquard coat. She strides two meters across the platform to the jump chute. She pauses with her toes at the edge, looking out into the velvety night.

The wind ruffles the plastered hair around Andrew's face.

It happens at once—Andrews reaches her hand inside her jacket and spins around. A double-edged dagger flies at us. Aksel pushes me behind him, backing us into the cargo net. My mother shifts in time for it to sail past her and land in the fuselage wall.

Andrews lunges at me. "I have worked too hard to be—"

Swirling in front of me, my mother grabs Andrews by her lapel, flings her around, and shoves.

Andrews tumbles backward out of the plane, sucked into the sky.

I walk over to the chute. Below I can see the cold sea and a stray iceberg.

I unclip my watch and drop it into the night. It will sink into the Atlantic and plummet to the ocean floor.

I will never be tracked again.

CHAPTER 65

My mother sits at the foot of my hospital bed, watching me.

Her face is puffy and red, but she remains entirely composed. She is wearing her black pearl earrings.

"Your father's body was recovered in Austria," she tells me. "There'll be a service this morning. After decades of not *existing*, the president says your father must be recognized. For his military service and his years at the Central Intelligence Agency before he joined ON-YX, your father has been awarded an anonymous engraved star on the marble wall at Langley."

By midmorning, the sky is white and overcast. I put on a black wool coatdress and a velvet fascinator with a net veil.

It has stopped snowing, and the air around us is still and quiet. Beside my mother and me, those present at Arlington National Cemetery are Aksel, two dozen Navy SEALs in full dress uniform, several men in suits I don't recognize, and the Deputy Secretary of Defense.

During the brief service, I sense someone watching us. I glance up during the Lord's Prayer and see a figure in a trim suit standing still against an oak tree, fifty meters away.

Across the white earth, David nods at me.

Smiling faintly, I nod back.

When I lift my eyes at the end of the prayer, David is gone.

After the benediction, each SEAL steps up to the coffin, removes his Navy SEAL trident, and pounds his pin into the wood with his fist. The sound echoes into the sky.

Once everyone has left the gravesite, my mother and I stand beside each other, staring at the mound of dirt in the middle of a blanket of snow.

I turn to my mother, admiring her beautiful clear blue eyes that wrinkle at the corners when she smiles. My eyes aren't hers, Abramovich told me, and yet when I look into them, I see *me*. I love her so much it hurts.

"Mom, I'm so sorry," I start. "It's my fault he's dead and—"

"Hush, Sophia." She presses her cold hand against my lips. My tears melt into her fingers. "Don't you *ever* utter those words again. Your father died protecting the person he loved most in the world. Do not blame yourself for any of this—"

"How can I not? Look at everything that happened because of me. I was so mad at him for taking me out of Waterford, and I told him I hated him and—" The words can no longer pass the strangled sobs escaping my throat.

Her arms tighten around me in a crushing embrace. Her voice is in my ear. "You must try." Tears stream down her face, soaking my cheek, as she says, "You must know that this is not, and never will be, your burden to bear."

After a few minutes, she lets go of me and readjusts the fur stole over her coat.

"Shirley Piper," she says softly. "That was my name before I joined Intelligence." My mother wipes her eyes. "Shirley. I haven't said that name in thirty years."

"And Dad?" I ask, knowing that for the first time in my life I am getting answers.

My mother smiles, and her whole face lights up. "Charles. His name was Charles MacDonaghue. And let me tell you, Sophia, from the moment Shirley met Chuck in Panama, she was smitten."

She continues gently, looking at me. "I always wanted children. My whole life I hoped to have children. But I chose a career that wasn't exactly made out for that. I told myself it didn't matter. That maybe it wasn't meant to happen for me . . . for us . . ."

She pauses. Swallows. "I was forty-four when you were born, Sophia. You came into our lives in the most unexpected, extraordinary, and tragic of circumstances. I've never questioned the choice we made that night."

"All those years, I never considered we were running because of *me*," I confess.

"Sophia, it doesn't matter—"

"It does," I say. "Because you would have been safer without me. Abramovich said if you had turned me over from the beginning, none of this would have happened and—"

"Sophia, neither your father nor I have regretted, for one second, the life we chose with you. Yes, we've been running for sixteen years, but we would do it all over again if it meant raising you. I'll run, and I'll fight, until I die, Sophia, if it means I can be your mother."

I finally stop wiping the wetness from my cheeks. I can't stop looking at her.

"In your face, Sophia, I see your courageous mother, Katarina.

Her blood runs in you, and I see so much of her in you. But I also see myself in you, Sophia. And I like to think that somehow, in another way, I am a part of you too."

I fight back tears as my mother finishes in a whisper, "You are my daughter, and I love you. I love you with the passion of not one parent, but four. Your mother gave us a gift, you see. And I know it's not fair that they died the way they did, but, Sophia, through you . . . they live."

CHAPTER 66

Our footsteps echo in the spacious hallway—white sneakers meeting tan linoleum. We pass a door with a glass window in the center. I stand on my tiptoes to see through it. Two dozen heads are bent forward, pencils scribbling feverishly across papers.

I catch a glimpse of glossy, chestnut hair, freshly curled, and flowing over a plaid flannel shirt—Charlotte. Beside her is a girl with a thick braid of auburn hair, still wet from morning swim practice—Emma.

I watch them both until a hand tugs mine and a deep voice says, "We should hurry."

We walk down the main corridor, past the floor-to-ceiling windows, and up a flight of stairs until we reach the second floor, fourth classroom west of the staircase.

We pause outside the door. He puts a hand on the knob, lowering his eyes to look at me. His green eyes glint in the fluorescent hall lights. "Ready?" Aksel asks bracingly.

My heart thuds beneath my jacket.

Finally, I know.

I no longer measure my life in two spheres: before Bekami, and after.

I measure my life in two worlds: the world within Waterford, and the world beyond.

For the first time, I know where I belong. Like the equator bisecting two hemispheres, I straddle two worlds. Maybe it can last forever, or maybe one day, I will have to choose. But in this moment, I am content to lie fallow.

I want to be nowhere other than where I am—my family watching over me, my mother looking after me, and Aksel standing beside me.

I am home.

Nodding, I grin. "Ready."

The door creaks as I push it open. The final exam has already started. The only sound is the clicking of calculators and the soft rustling of fabric as bodies turn toward the doorway.

His long hair is gray and coarse and still resembles wool; his dingy tweed jacket hasn't changed since the beginning of December.

Krenshaw looks at us gruffly and barks, "You're late."

ACKNOWLEDGMENTS

Perhaps I should have written Sophia as a ghost, because she's been haunting me forever.

I disagree with the general consensus that teenage girls are ditzy, crazy, annoying, obnoxious, needy, dumb, melodramatic, or manipulative. Sure, their *actions* might occasionally be explained this way, but these are *not* characteristics. The teenage girls *I* know are bold, intelligent, hard-working, empathetic, driven, athletic, courteous, creative, loyal, and disciplined.

There is something beautiful and raw about a teenage girl's experience and visceral emotions. Our feminine passion is a gift, not a curse. It enables us to become brave women.

I'm often asked: What do you hope readers feel when they finish reading your book?

Simply, I hope readers see in Sophia the best in *themselves*: their own resilience, compassion, and self-worth. I hope they feel empowered to magnify their skills and talents, not shirk them.

Thank you to the real women who inspired my fictional female warriors: to my glamorous longtime friend, whose own experience helped shape Sophia's, thank you for inviting me to visit CIA headquarters in Langley, Virginia—you are living the life we always imagined. And to my great-grandmother, Mary Astor, who began making movies as a teenager and, after being threatened by Hollywood's most powerful studio executives that if she didn't *give up her child* she would never work again, proceeded to win an Academy Award.

For the book itself, thank you to Claire Stetzer. I no longer wonder why authors profess their editor's brilliance—it is true. How you managed to navigate the storm of mismatched words I threw at you, I will never know. Somehow you led me, guided me, and cheered me on to a better story. Without you, *Girl from Nowhere* would be adrift somewhere.

Thank you to Cindy Loh, for taking a chance on me and for your brilliant command of the Bloomsbury crew. To each of you at Bloomsbury who influenced this book: thank you.

And thanks to my agent, Webster Stone, for believing a stay-at-home mother of four from suburban Utah with no professional writing experience could become an author.

To my selfless, adventurous mother: thank you for always reading aloud to us, even when I was in kindergarten and we frequently finished after midnight. I forgive you for wearing an oversized Beastie Boys T-shirt when my date picked me up for prom.

To my father: I hope to never be as smart as you. Mostly because I think my brain would explode. While the choice remains slightly befuddling, I am nonetheless appreciative that you considered subscriptions to *National Geographic* and *The Economist* proper birthday gifts.

To my husband: remember when you saw me for the first time from afar—but really it was my identical twin sister? No? I do. And now it's in print. Thank you for discreetly switching my name tag before I knew who *you* were so that we could sit side by side. The moment of truth has come: yes, you inspired Aksel. Mostly, your muscles.

To my sisters and my best friends: I love each one of you. Branden might be my eternal companion, but you are my soulmates. To my identical twin sister, Danielle: I have no idea what it's like to be a "single person" and I don't care to—I thoroughly enjoy being half a person. And we all know you are the better half. Which is why if someone tells me they don't like my book, I'll simply say you wrote it.

To my daughters: you are each more kind, clever, and fearless than I. To quote a wise adolescent, "You can become anyone you want to become, but no one else can be you." Our community needs intelligent, creative, compassionate girls to lead. So make those beds, feed those chickens, read those books, and ride those bikes. Learn to learn. Learn to lead.

Just don't become women too quickly.

You only get one chance to be a teenage girl. Cherish it.